DATE DUE

GAYLORD   PRINTED IN U.S.A.

THE ENCHANTED LAND

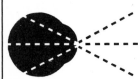

This Large Print Book carries the
Seal of Approval of N.A.V.H.

THE ENCHANTED LAND

JUDE DEVERAUX

THORNDIKE PRESS
A part of Gale, Cengage Learning

Detroit • New York • San Francisco • New Haven, Conn • Waterville, Maine • London

GALE
CENGAGE Learning·

Thorndike Press® Large Print Famous Authors.
The text of this Large Print edition is unabridged.
Other aspects of the book may vary from the original edition.
Set in 16 pt. Plantin.

LIBRARY OF CONGRESS CATALOGING-IN-PUBLICATION DATA

Deveraux, Jude.
  The enchanted land / by Jude Deveraux.
    p. cm. — (Thorndike Press large print famous authors)
  ISBN 978-1-4104-4673-2 (hardcover) — ISBN 1-4104-4673-5 (hardcover)
  1. Large type books. I. Title.
PS3554.E9273E54 2012
813'.54—dc23   2012010512

Published in 2012 by arrangement with Avon, an imprint of
HarperCollins Publishers.

Printed in the United States of America
1 2 3 4 5 6 7 16 15 14 13 12

for CLAUDE —
who gave me
the time to
write

CHAPTER ONE

Morgan stared at the ugly brown dress spread across the bed. She shivered. Remembering again what she must do tonight, she turned slowly and gazed wistfully into the mirror, seeing without interest her pale hair and blue eyes. She tried cocking her head and smiling. But no . . . she wasn't pretty, and she was sure she never would be.

She turned quickly as a knock sounded and her uncle strode in. He was a short, portly man, given to excess at the table. He smiled at her and reached out to touch her chin. She turned her head away.

"What do you want?" she asked coldly.

"Is everything all right? How is your packing coming?"

"Fine." She kept her face averted.

He looked around the room at the closed trunks and, finally, at the brown silk dress on the bed. He touched the silk lightly.

"Why don't you rest before we leave for the ball? You have a few hours yet."

She didn't answer, and he turned and left the room, closing the door behind him quietly.

Morgan removed her dress and replaced it with a plain dressing gown. She lay down but she couldn't sleep. Instead, she found herself going over it all yet again.

The problems had started before she was born. Both her father and her mother had been brought up to the life of wealthy plantation owners in southern Kentucky. But her father had wanted to venture out, to seek the hardships and challenges of the frontier.

After her parents' marriage, the young couple had moved to New Mexico. Morgan was born there. Her mother had nearly died in childbirth. The baby was early, and it was a full eighteen hours before her husband could bring a midwife to his wife. Morgan had heard many times from her mother of the horror and pain she went through all alone. Being a lady, she would not allow any of the ranch hands in the room.

When Morgan was a year old, her mother and she returned to Kentucky. Her mother had refused to bring up her daughter in savage New Mexico. There had been many an argument between her parents and her father had said that if his wife took their child and left him, he never wanted to see either of them again. And that's the way it had been: she had not seen her father in seventeen years.

Her mouth hardened as she realized that he had his revenge now. In death, he was punishing his wife through his daughter.

She tried to keep her mind off the reading of the will, just two weeks ago, that horrible will that had led to her decision about tonight.

She turned her head toward the door when she heard a light knock, smiling at her aunt's voice.

As Lacey entered, Morgan couldn't help but think how well the older woman's name fit her. Lacey was small and frail, as if she might break. She reminded Morgan of a starched and crocheted doily.

"Hello, dear. Are you feeling all right? I imagine you're excited about tonight."

Aunt Lacey was always so sweet. She assumed that, since Morgan was young, she must be excited about going to the ball. And Morgan would have been, too, if the circumstances were different. She gazed at the nondescript brown dress, which she had pushed to one side of the bed, and Lacey's eyes followed hers.

Lacey walked around the bed, touched the silk, and said gently, "Brown isn't really your color, is it, my dear?"

Morgan fought the urge to throw back her head and laugh hysterically. "It's all right, Aunt Lacey. I don't mind. I could have a Paris gown and it wouldn't matter. Nothing could make me pretty, just as Uncle Horace says."

Lacey's eyes were sad. She moved around the room to sit beside Morgan on the bed. She looked at her niece closely. "I know Horace says you're not pretty."

"My mother said so too."

"But I can't help thinking that if you wore brighter clothes and didn't hide your hair . . . you know you have lovely hair." She ran a finger down Morgan's cheek. "And such lovely skin." She paused. "I really feel, dear, that if you smiled more, you would be much more attractive."

Morgan grimaced. Her aunt had often told her that if she looked happier and were a little bit livelier, she would be pretty. Morgan smiled faintly at what her mother would say about her aunt's encouraging Morgan to make herself more "attractive." Attractive indeed — like a flower enticing bees.

Seeing Morgan smile, Lacey patted her

hand. "That's better, dear." She rose to leave, pausing with her hand on the door. "Could I help you dress, or help with your hair?"

"No, thank you, Aunt Lacey. I think I may sleep awhile."

"Good. I'll wake you in an hour."

The door closed, and Morgan was alone again. She lay back and slept. An hour later, Lacey returned to waken her, then went back to her own room to complete her toilette.

Morgan lifted the brown silk dress, stared at it a moment, and tossed it back on the bed. She had to fight the urge to tear it to shreds. Again, she thought of her father. This was all his fault. In all her eighteen years, she had never had to worry about her appearance.

She and her mother had lived alone for fifteen years in Trahern House. *Trahern House.* The very name made her homesick. Trahern House was one hundred seventy-five acres of green, rolling countryside with a duck pond, bridle paths, and woods. Her mother had indulged Morgan's every desire. She longingly recalled her pretty little mare, Cassandra.

Her mother had told her she was plain, but she knew her mother had wanted her to

11

be plain. Her mother had never allowed male visitors at the house. She had told Morgan that men cared only for pretty faces, and that Morgan was better off plain. If she were plain, she could live her life in peace, at Trahern House. And Morgan had never wanted to live anywhere else.

Yet her mother's unexpected, early death two years ago had cast Morgan into her uncle's house. And the will had been a second, terrible blow. Why hadn't her mother told her that her father really owned everything? She knew that Trahern House had belonged to Morgan Trahern, her maternal grandfather, so she assumed her mother had inherited it. What had happened, that the house and lands were given to Grandfather Morgan Trahern's son-in-law rather than to his own daughter?

Morgan looked back at the mirror. Her eyes were cold as she said, aloud, "You may have been my father, Charles Wakefield, but you have not treated me like a daughter. You took away the only thing I had — Trahern House. And you have required an ugly thing of me to secure it." She drew closer to the mirror and her voice was hard, a deep whisper. "But you never knew your daughter. She is strong. I vow here and now that neither you nor any other man," and here her mind touched briefly on her Uncle Horace, "will ever stop me from getting what I want."

She stared at herself for a few seconds and was startled to see her normally blue eyes turn a deep green. What did it matter that she didn't have physical beauty? As her mother had told her many times, she had inner beauty. And that was what mattered. Physical beauty was for silly women who wanted only to catch a man. And the last thing Morgan wanted was a man.

She turned again to the bed and the dress, thinking that tonight, for just this one night, she would like to be pretty. Because tonight, Morgan was going to have to do the very thing she had never wanted to do. She was going to have to catch a man.

She sighed and began to dress, pulling her hair back from her face and slipping into the loose, plain dress.

"You look lovely, my dear," Uncle Horace said as he entered and extended his arm to her.

But Morgan saw the complacency in his eyes, the satisfaction. Of course, he is pleased, she thought. If I were beautiful, in a low-cut, red satin dress, some man would carry me off to New Mexico and he'd lose all the money. But she knew her uncle had no reason to worry about that tonight.

They arrived early. Few others were there yet. Morgan was glad. She would have a chance to appraise the people as they arrived. She must consider them all carefully: she could not afford to make a mistake. Her spine stiffened.

As they entered the glittering ballroom, Horace led Lacey and Morgan over to their host and hostess, Matthew and Caroline Ferguson. Morgan had met the Fergusons several times before.

"Morgan, I'm so glad you are here. You get out much too seldom." Caroline Ferguson smiled.

"Well," said Horace, "our little Morgan much prefers the solitary life, with her books and her walks through the garden."

Morgan shrank as Horace's hand touched her shoulder, but she managed a smile for the Fergusons.

As the little party was walking away, Cynthia Ferguson made her appearance. Cynthia was beautiful, knew it, and made sure everybody noticed it.

"Why, Morgan," she drawled, "you dear thing. I'm so glad you could come to our little party. My, what a . . . charming little dress."

Morgan thought she might strike Cynthia.

Cynthia had on a low-cut gown of mauve watered silk, set off by tiny jet beads around the bodice and hem. Morgan bit her tongue and held her pride. "Thank you, Cynthia. I am glad to be here."

"You just make yourself at home. I know all the boys are going to fill your card and I'll never get another moment to speak with you again all evening."

As Morgan walked away, she heard Cynthia murmur to her mother, "I had no idea silk could look like *that*." Morgan did not hear Mrs. Ferguson's reply.

Horace seated Lacey and Morgan and went to speak to some men friends in a corner of the room. Then Lacey saw some of her friends, and after Morgan assured her she would be all right, Lacey left.

Morgan sat back, enjoying the quiet and the chance to survey the guests. She moved slightly, sitting so that she was in the shadow of a curtained doorway.

As each man entered, she looked him over carefully. It had been strange to learn that an entirely different world existed outside Trahern House, a world which included men. In this new world, Morgan felt awkward and out of place. It was incredible that her personal value could be assessed by such things as clothing, physical beauty, and whether or not she made a good match.

She saw Brian Ferguson enter and considered him for a moment. Tall, slim, handsome, he was about twenty years old. He would probably not want to leave his comfortable home and travel to the wilds of New Mexico. He was an only son and would inherit his father's plantation. She must look for a second or third son, one who would need money, and who would lose little or nothing by moving to New Mexico.

The music started and couples began to dance. Morgan sat in the shadows, wishing she were back at Trahern House and not sitting here, awkward and lonely. Older women began to take the chairs near Morgan. They paid little attention to her, except for occasional glances of pity.

Morgan listened carefully as the women pointed out various people to one another and exchanged gossip about them.

"That Cynthia Ferguson — whatever can her mama be thinking by letting her daughter wear a dress cut so low?" asked a gray-haired woman dressed in black.

"Her mama is thinking very carefully of trying to get that handsome Mr. Seth Colter for her son-in-law," explained another.

Morgan's eyes followed their glances. She

saw him standing not too far from her, and her eyes widened at the sight of him. Seth Colter certainly was good looking, but, somehow, he was not conventionally handsome. For one thing, he was too big. He was probably one or two inches under six feet, but the width of his shoulders and the thickness of his chest made him look terribly powerful. His chest tapered to slim hips and legs, but the muscles in his thighs bulged under snug pants. Morgan blushed and looked away. What in the world was she doing, staring at a man's thighs? She smiled as she thought of what her mother would say!

The women beside her kept talking and she forced her eyes around the room again. She considered every man, most of whom she knew nothing about. She began to listen more attentively to the women. Again, she found they were talking about the man her eyes had so carefully avoided for the last fifteen minutes.

"Well, I don't understand it, either. He has everything. Nora and William Colter have given their lives to that plantation, and everything will be his someday." The lady in black was talking.

"And I don't blame William at all for refusing to give him the money for that place of his. Where is it?"

"New Mexico, I believe the territory is called."

Morgan nearly jumped. She considered what she had heard: Seth Colter needed money and he had a place in New Mexico.

Seth was talking to Cynthia now, and a wave of anger crossed Morgan. He was looking down at Cynthia with a sort of mocking expression, as if he were amused by her.

As Morgan studied Seth's face, she felt eyes on her and looked to see Cynthia staring at her. Seth, following Cynthia's gaze, turned to look at Morgan. He looked at her thoroughly, seeming to look at every part of her. He smiled slightly, but showed no real interest in her.

"Morgan, you dear thing, sitting all alone here in the shadows. No one can even see you. Has anyone asked you to dance yet?" Cynthia obviously wanted to show Seth the difference between her own popular self and this rather plain girl in the ill-fitting dress.

"No," said Morgan timidly, "I haven't danced. But then, we haven't been here very long." She felt she had to save some pride. Why did that man have to keep *staring* at her? Why did she feel so warm under his gaze?

Cynthia's eyes darted from Morgan to Seth. She seemed to enjoy Morgan's obvious embarrassment. "Seth, dearest, why don't you dance with our little Morgan?"

"No —" Morgan began, looking up at the man who seemed to be enjoying her confusion.

"Seth, I promised the next dance to Paul Davis, and if you could just keep Morgan company, I'll come right back to you." Her lashes fluttered, and she gazed up at him with promise in her eyes. Morgan's mouth tightened as she realized that Cynthia thought her thoroughly safe company. She'd be no threat to Cynthia!

Seth Colter looked down at the young woman that Cynthia was pushing at him. Poor Cynthia, he thought, just like my sisters. She thinks that if she flutters her lashes at a man and he dances with her twice, then the next step is an engagement.

Somehow, this Morgan interested him. She kept her eyes lowered, and he looked at the top of her head. He saw hair that was both blond and brown, not evenly mixed, but streaked, with parts very light and parts the color of dry piñon needles. He could tell very little about her body under that horrible brown bag of a dress, but he knew she was small. He doubted she reached five feet.

Seth knew Cynthia considered Morgan no temptation. Certainly the girl knew it too. She wasn't pretty — or was she? He wondered how she would look with her long pale hair loose, cascading across her shoulders and down her back, with no clothes on.

Seth assured Cynthia that he would very much like to dance with Morgan. Doubt crossed Cynthia's face, but only for a moment.

"But would you please introduce us first?" he said.

The introduction completed, Morgan extended her hand and found it totally engulfed by his. His hand was warm, the palm calloused and hard.

"I am pleased to make your acquaintance, Miss Wakefield." His eyes smiled. He showed much more interest in her than he had a few minutes before. He turned to Cynthia. "Please excuse us. A waltz has begun, and I am interested in knowing how Miss Wakefield came by a first name like Morgan." He led Morgan to the dance floor. She could feel the warmth of his body through his coat sleeve.

He took her in his arms and they began to

dance. She was glad now that Aunt Lacey had arranged for her dancing lessons. She wanted to glide, to enjoy herself, but she remembered the job that had to be done.

"Mr. Colter, I heard it mentioned that you have a place in New Mexico."

He paused before answering. What game was she playing? "Yes, I do . . . a small cattle ranch."

How to go on? How do you lead up to asking a total stranger to marry you? "My father lived in New Mexico for a number of years. I was born there." When he didn't reply, she said, "His name was Charles Wakefield."

He tilted his head. "I've heard of your father. A very wealthy man, with a large spread just south of Albuquerque."

She looked straight into his eyes and said it plainly. "Yes, a very wealthy man."

He laughed aloud. He thought he saw her game. He knew her father had died within the year. She probably was an heiress. Since she couldn't flirt with looks, like Cynthia, she was going to dangle her money as bait. It was incredible what a woman would do to get a husband.

Morgan took a deep breath. "I shall be honest, Mr. Colter. I'd like to make a business deal with you. As you say, my father was a very wealthy man. And now he has left that money to me, on a condition.

"In compliance with that condition," she continued, "I'd like to offer you a job. It would be no more than a job," she emphasized. "The job would last one year, you would not have to leave your ranch in New Mexico, and I would pay you twenty-five thousand dollars for your services during that year."

He was about to speak when the music stopped. They both looked up to see Cynthia rapidly making her way toward them. She doesn't waste any time, thought Morgan.

"Miss Wakefield," he said, taking her arm, "your job interests me. Shall we go somewhere where we can talk?"

Much to Cynthia's chagrin, Seth led Morgan away. Of course, he couldn't have seen me coming or he would never have turned his back, thought Cynthia. Yet there was just a seed of doubt.

"Cynthia! What a lovely dress!" someone called. Cynthia turned to accept the compliment and missed seeing Seth lead Morgan into the garden.

Morgan and Seth sat side by side on a stone bench under a copse of trees.

"Now, Miss Wakefield, just what is this job that is so important that you are willing to pay twenty-five thousand dollars for it?" He leaned against a tree, and smiled a half-smile.

Morgan thought quickly. She sensed that if she burst out that the job was to marry her and live with her for one year, he would leave. No, she must explain it all from the beginning and gradually lead up to his part in her life.

She looked at her hands and took a deep breath. "Mr. Colter, this is an unusual story, and before I tell you of the job, I must explain some of its background.

"I have said that I was born in New Mexico. My mother and father lived there, together, for two years, including the year after I was born. My mother hated the heat and the dryness and the lack of comfort. She had been accustomed to much better in her father's house here in Kentucky.

"She left him, took me, and returned to her home. I lived alone with my mother, in the country, until I was sixteen. Then she passed away. For the past two years I have lived with my aunt and uncle here in Louisville." Morgan felt the anger rise in her as she arrived at this point in her story. She rose and stood by the bougainvillea vine at the corner of the bench.

Without looking at him, she continued. "My life was peaceful until six months ago. I had planned to live with my aunt and uncle until such time as my uncle gave his consent for my return to Trahern House, the home of my childhood. I must digress a moment and tell you, Mr. Colter," she met his eyes, "that I do not feel at ease around large numbers of people. My major goal in life has been to live alone at Trahern House. You must understand that."

Seth recalled his home in the mountains of New Mexico, the isolation of it, the peace of it. "I do understand that," he said.

Morgan sensed that he did.

"Please continue, Miss Wakefield. You were saying that everything changed six months ago?"

"Six months ago my father died. He left his money to me, but with a stipulation, which is what puts me here at this exact moment."

"Come now, Miss Wakefield, you do not flatter me. I trust that our friend, Cynthia, would not find being here with me so distasteful."

Morgan stiffened. "I am not at all like Cynthia Ferguson. If I had my wish, I would be at home at Trahern House."

24

"I am sorry. I did not wish to arouse your hostility. I am still waiting for my part in this."

"My father had always wanted my mother to send me to New Mexico, but she refused. So my father decided to see to it that I went to New Mexico after his death." She paused to draw a breath, and looked directly at Seth. "If I am to collect my inheritance, I must marry a man and live with him in New Mexico for one year."

She watched him intently. But in the dim light, she could see no change in his expression.

"I must do this before I am twenty-five years old or else everything goes to my uncle." Her voice changed. "And of course my uncle is planning everything in his power to keep me from marrying. You can see the way I am forced to dress. In two days, he plans to take my aunt and me to Europe for an extended trip. My bags are already packed."

She sat back down on the bench, feeling spent. She did not like having to pour out her troubles to a stranger. She could not look at Seth.

There was a long pause. Morgan began to feel that she had lost.

Finally, he spoke. "Well, then . . . am I to

be the man who fulfills your father's wish?"

Her head came up. "I offer you a business deal, sir. I will pay you twenty-five thousand dollars for the use of your name and for a year's room and board in your house in New Mexico."

He said quietly, "What do you plan to do at the end of the year? How do you plan to dissolve the marriage?"

Once Morgan had heard her Aunt Lacey and some friends gossiping about an elopement that had been annulled. "It will be annulled."

"Annulled?"

She could hear the amusement in his voice and wasn't sure that he understood. "Yes. Annulled — as the elopement of Kevin and Alice Fulton was annulled last spring."

He laughed aloud, actually more of a snort than a laugh. "Oh, I see. I believe that brief marriage was annulled on the grounds of lack of consummation. Are those the grounds you would choose for the annulment?"

Morgan was not sure about the meaning of the word, but she had heard whispers. She wanted no closeness with this or any other man. She wanted to be free to return to Trahern House at the end of the year. "Yes," she answered him, meeting his eyes, "this will be a marriage in name only."

Seth looked at her charming, honest face, bathed in moonlight, and smiled to himself. He thought about the isolation of his house in the New Mexico mountains and the coldness of the winters. He wondered whether, after the two of them had lived together all winter long, they would qualify for an annulment. He hoped not.

CHAPTER TWO

"Morgan, Morgan!" Uncle Horace's voice reached them in the garden.

"I must go in, or he will send every person in the ballroom to find me." She turned to Seth with questioning eyes, reluctant to go without a firm agreement between them.

He understood her hesitancy and said, "I accept your offer. You said you were to leave day after tomorrow?"

"Yes."

"There are arrangements to be made. I will come for you tomorrow, but it may be late in the day." As he took her arm and they returned to the ballroom, Morgan begged him to keep their arrangement a secret. She feared her Uncle Horace would take her away if he knew.

As they returned, Morgan noticed a few faces turned toward them.

Cynthia moved quickly to them. "Why, Seth, you are such a dear to make Morgan feel welcome." Her words were confident, but her eyes betrayed her. She touched Seth's arm and fluttered her lashes at him. "Seth, dear, I believe this is our dance."

Morgan saw the frown crease Seth's broad forehead, and guessed that he did not like Cynthia's possessiveness. She spoke loudly, "There is my Aunt Lacey. If you would escort me to her, I'd like to sit down."

He turned to Cynthia. "If you will excuse us, I will take Miss Wakefield to her aunt."

They left, arm in arm, Cynthia glaring.

As they approached Aunt Lacey and the other women, a hush fell over the women's talk. Morgan seated herself, and Seth said in a low voice. "I will see you tomorrow." His smile held the same mocking quality that she had seen before.

"My dear," asked the lady next to Aunt Lacey, after Seth had gone, "do you know who that is?"

"His name is Seth Colter." She was curious to find out what the women knew.

"Have you heard of the Colter plantation outside Louisville?" At Morgan's silence, she continued. "It is one of the largest and richest in the state, and it is all to be his some day. Yet he is throwing it away to live in some unholy place out west."

Yes, Morgan knew this. She wanted to

know more of this man who would be her husband in another day. She smiled when she thought how this overweight woman in damp, green satin would react to the news: "Do you mean that that dowdy little thing, Lacey's niece, married rich, handsome Seth Colter?" Morgan caught herself before she laughed aloud.

She looked at the Green Lady and said innocently, eyes wide, "But I thought he and Cynthia Ferguson were practically engaged. Surely Cynthia wouldn't go out west to live?"

"No," said another woman, the lady in black whom Morgan had heard earlier. "That's just what Caroline Ferguson would like to think. But that daugher of hers hasn't snared him yet."

"She'd just like everyone to assume they're engaged," echoed the Green Lady.

Morgan saw her Uncle Horace approach then, and she rose, knowing he and Aunt Lacey probably wanted to depart.

The three of them took their leave of Mr. and Mrs. Ferguson, and Morgan searched the crowd to find Seth. She needed some reassurance from him. She saw his broad back far across the room, next to a pretty young woman, and she felt a wave of anger. Then she told herself that was silly.

All the way home in the plush-lined carriage, Morgan thought and planned. She would secretly rearrange her baggage so she'd be ready to leave when Seth came the next night.

With a start she remembered that she had not told him which window was hers. She would leave a light, and hope he would find it.

They arrived home after the short journey. After goodnights, she was at last alone in her room.

She took off the ugly brown dress and tossed it across the settee, unfastened her blond hair, and sighed. On impulse, she removed all her undergarments and looked at her nude body in the mirror. She looked at firm, round breasts, tapering to a small waist and flat stomach and then rounding out again to full hips and thighs. She ran her hand down the smooth skin of her waist, onto her hip. She shivered, shocked by what she was doing. No decent woman ever looked at her own naked body, much less at a mirror reflection.

Quickly, she turned from the mirror and slipped her nightgown over her head. But still, she remembered the image of her body. And she thought maybe she wouldn't be so plain if she left her hair in curls.

Morgan climbed into bed and snuggled deep into the warm covers. Soon she was asleep.

She was up the next morning before the rest of the household. She had always liked the early morning and was at her best then. If she were at Trahern House, she could go to the stable, saddle Cassandra, and ride across the dew-covered fields.

Instead, she quietly went to the kitchen and made her own breakfast. One of the many indulgences her mother had given her was cooking lessons from a French chef. Her mother had been appalled when she had first found her little daughter in the kitchen helping Cook. She and Morgan had argued long over that, but in the end, her mother had given in. A month later, Jean-Paul arrived. He planned to stay six weeks, but had instead become a member of the family and stayed for a little over a year, until he had to return to Marseilles.

She remembered the many happy hours with Jean-Paul in the sunny, spacious kitchen at Trahern House, and she was glad that Jean-Paul had taught her so much about cooking. He had made her churn her own butter when she first started. Soon, she could make delicate preserves and jellies, and learned a light touch with breads and pastries.

"Morgan, dear," came Aunt Lacey's voice, "are you up so early?"

"Come in, Aunt Lacey, and I'll make you some breakfast." Morgan knew this might be their last breakfast together. She would miss Aunt Lacey's gentleness.

Over fluffy omelets, oozing cheese, Morgan and Lacey discussed the ball. Or, rather, Lacey talked and Morgan listened.

After breakfast, each woman went to her own room to continue packing for the next day's journey, the start of their long trip to Europe.

In the privacy of her room, Morgan began arranging things in the luggage. She packed a small trunk and one bag to be carried by hand, for the trip to New Mexico.

She had only the plain, too-large clothing that her uncle had commissioned a seamstress to sew for her. He had had her clothing from Trahern House taken away. The last item she packed was her recipe book.

At seven o'clock that evening, as they were sitting down to dinner, the Wakefields' old servant announced, "A Mr. Colter to see you, sir."

Morgan gasped audibly, and Horace and Lacey's eyes turned on her, but she said nothing.

"Show him into the library, please, Roy. If you ladies will excuse me." He turned one last puzzled glance to Morgan, then left the room.

"Is that the nice Mr. Colter you danced with last night?" At Morgan's silence, Lacey continued, "I thought he was taken with you. I wouldn't doubt but that he is here to ask permission to court you."

"In Europe?"

Lacey looked down at her hands and was silent. She had been at the reading of the will. She knew why Horace was taking them to Europe.

Morgan regretted her comment and walked to Lacey's side and patted her shoulder. "I'm sorry, Aunt Lacey. You're probably right. Maybe he is here to speak to Uncle Horace about courtship."

Lacey smiled and resumed her chattering. Morgan paced the room and watched the clock, hardly aware of Lacey's words.

Forty-five minutes later, the door opened and Horace entered with Seth. Seth had a slight smile on his face, but Horace was grim and his voice cold.

"Get your things and go."

It was Lacey's turn to gasp. "Horace . . ." she protested weakly.

At the sound of his wife's voice, Horace turned. His face lost some of its hatred, and his voice became softer. "It seems that Mr. Colter has come to take our Morgan away." He paused. "They are to be married tonight at Judge Stevenson's."

Morgan's eyes widened. What in the world had Seth done to get Uncle Horace to consent to the marriage?

Lacey hugged the stunned Morgan. "Oh, Morgan! An elopement! How very romantic. What ever will you wear? We must pack. There is so much to do."

Seth stepped forward and took Morgan's arm. "We must hurry, my dear." He led Morgan into the hall. He dropped her arm and his manner changed. He stepped back and looked her up and down with a mocking expression. "If the two articles of clothing I have seen are a correct indication of your wardrobe, leave it all here. I will purchase more suitable clothing for you — at least something that fits."

Morgan was about to forget her good sense and tell him what she thought of his manners, when Horace and Lacey came into the entryway. Morgan turned on her heel and went up the stairs to her room.

She returned in a few minutes with only her small bag. In it were a few pieces of jewelry, her cookbook, her nightgown, and a few toilet articles. She would leave her carefully packed trunk upstairs.

After a tearful farewell to Lacey and a cold goodbye to Horace, she and Seth entered the waiting carriage.

They rode in silence for a few minutes. Then Morgan spoke. "How did you do it?" she asked.

"How did I do what?" He turned toward her.

"What did you do to get Uncle Horace to allow me to leave?"

He smiled. "I just mentioned a few names and asked if he thought it was quite ethical to spirit you away, not allowing you to try to find a husband who could help you to fulfill your father's will."

She waited for him to say more, but he turned his head again and seemed to be occupied with his own thoughts. As they rode in silence, Morgan began to feel uncomfortable. She had never been alone with a man before, at least not with a man so near her own age.

"It just happened so differently than I imagined."

He turned, startled, seeming for the first time to realize her presence. "And how did you imagine it?" His tone was condescending.

She felt like a child about to be reprimanded. "I . . ." she started, "left a light in my window . . ."

His face brightened, showing dancing lights in his eyes. "Did you imagine that I'd come in the middle of the night and steal you away?"

She did not answer, but her tightened mouth gave her away. He laughed loudly, and she wanted to hit him.

He sobered somewhat when he saw the hurt in her eyes. He reached over and placed his hand on hers and said quietly, "Did you really think I'd climb a ladder like a schoolboy?"

The appeal in his eyes made her see the humor. No, she could not imagine this enormous man climbing a ladder in the middle of the night to spirit his bride away. She smiled back at him.

They rode on, again in silence, but there was no more hostility between them. Morgan was no longer nervous.

They had been riding for what seemed hours, each occupied with his own thoughts, when the coach stopped, and Seth said, "Are you sure you don't want to change your mind?"

She shook her head slightly. "Yes, I'm sure."

"Good." His eyes danced. "I guess that means you think you can stand me for a whole year."

He got out of the carriage, helped Morgan out, and led her to the front of a large, pleasant, whitewashed house. Morgan looked around. She knew they had been heading south, toward Lexington, but she wasn't sure where they were now.

Finally a servant answered the door and Morgan preceded Seth into the hallway.

"The judge is waiting for you, Mr. Colter," he said.

"Thanks, Elijah."

The servant led them to a door off the hallway into a cozy drawing room.

A large man came toward them swiftly, hand extended. "Well, well, well! I never thought I'd have the honor of this day — I mean night. It's good to see you are finally going to get married, Seth."

Seth smiled. "May I present Miss Morgan Wakefield."

"I am very glad to meet the lady who has been chosen by this young man. Why, I've known his father for years."

"And his mother, too." A small woman entered the room. "Nora Colter is my dearest friend."

"This is my wife, Sara, and if this man of yours hasn't told you, I am Judge Samuel Stevenson."

Morgan extended her hand, which he shook robustly. "I am very happy to meet you."

"Let's begin, shall we?" said Judge Stevenson.

The service was over so quickly that Morgan hardly realized it had taken place. The silence at the end was awkward. Finally, Judge Stevenson laughed and said, "Go ahead and kiss the bride, Seth."

He turned to Morgan with a winning smile and bent down to kiss her, gently taking hold of her shoulders.

At first she was astonished. Then, just as his lips were very close to hers, she turned her head quickly and his kiss landed on her ear, just above the earlobe. His breath was soft and warm in her ear, his kiss moist, and she felt chills on her arms.

Morgan kept her eyes from Seth's and accepted the congratulations from the Judge and Mrs. Stevenson. In spite of their entreaties to stay, the young couple left immediately after the ceremony. They were soon on their way again in the coach.

Morgan had just snuggled into a corner of the coach when she felt it lurch. She looked up to see Seth's broad shoulders leaning toward the window.

"Well, my little bride, we are here." He stepped out of the coach and turned to help Morgan down the two steps.

She saw before her, shining in the moonlight, an enormous white mansion. What was it the woman had said last night? The Colter plantation was one of the largest and richest in the state.

The house had two stories, with massive, white columns extending the full height. There was a deep veranda with several large oak chairs and rockers scattered about. On either side of the veranda were two large old willows, moving slightly in the night breeze.

On the second story there was a balcony, with a delicate, white-painted railing. She could see one pair of double doors leading onto the balcony and guessed there were others.

Seth carried Morgan's bag and led her into the house and up a massive staircase to the second floor. She followed him silently down the thickly carpeted hallway and into his bedroom.

Seth lit the lamp, and Morgan could see

that the room was very large. All the furniture was walnut: dark, rich, and heavy. The prominent feature of the room was an enormous four-poster bed. Morgan stood staring at it, thinking that it was just the sort of bed that a man like Seth should have.

Seth had come up behind her and stood quietly as Morgan was staring at the bed. "It's just as comfortable as it looks," he whispered.

Morgan jumped and turned toward him, their faces inches apart. He bent toward her. "Come, *mi querida,* and I'll show you what it's like to be a real bride." His voice was low and soft and persuasive. But Morgan, unused to the presence of a man, was frightened by his large body and took a step backwards.

Her face betrayed her fear, and Seth laughed. "Don't be afraid, little rabbit, I won't hurt you. Where is that look of fire I saw you flash at Cynthia Ferguson? Anyone who can give such a look shouldn't be afraid of a mere man."

Morgan smiled.

"That's better. You may take the bed and I'll sleep on the couch. Does that ease your fears?"

Morgan hastily took her bag and went to the adjoining dressing room. She was nervous as she removed her dress and put on the plain, white nightgown. As she took the pins from her hair and brushed the mass into fat, shiny curls that reached her waist, she tried not to think about Seth.

When she returned to the room and self-consciously walked across to the bed, she saw that Seth had turned down the covers. He was already wrapped in a blanket on the couch, his head away from her. He appeared to be sleeping. Somehow she felt a tinge of anger that he could ignore her so completely.

As she blew out the lamp and snuggled under the covers, she heard Seth say sleepily, "Goodnight, *mi querida.*"

Morgan smiled and said, "Goodnight."

The next morning, Morgan was awakened by a knock on the door. "Mr. Seth, are you up yet?"

Morgan sat up just in time to see Seth striding across the room towards her. Morgan's eyes opened very wide in astonishment at the sight of him. He was completely naked. Morgan had not seen many men, even clothed, and had never seen a man without his shirt. She glimpsed a broad, heavy chest covered with thick, curling hair, large arms and shoulders, all tapering to a hard, flat stomach. He climbed into bed with her before she could complete her survey.

"Close your mouth, little one. You don't want Bessie to think a newly wedded couple would spend their wedding night apart, do you?" He moved close to Morgan so that their thighs touched. Louder he said, "Come in, Bessie."

A very large woman entered the room carrying a tray of coffee. As she saw Morgan in the enormous bed sitting beside Seth, she stopped and stared. Seth moved even closer to Morgan and put his arm around her shoulders. "Bessie, I'd like you to meet my wife, Morgan."

It didn't take Bessie long to recover her voice. "I declare, Mr. Seth, you didn't give nobody word that you were bringing a bride. I bet even your mama don't know."

Seth grinned and hugged Morgan closer, idly taking a curl in one hand and rubbing it between his fingers. "No, Mother doesn't know, but then it was a rather hurried marriage. Morgan and I just met the night before last."

"An elopement! Your sisters are just going to love that." Bessie had a twinkle in her eye. "Well, I must mind my manners. It's

43

nice to meet you," she said to the still-silent bride.

Morgan managed to murmur, "Thank you."

Bessie smiled broadly and said, "Well, Mr. Seth, I'll just leave you two. You come down whenever you're ready." The twinkle deepened and she winked at Seth. He returned the wink. Morgan looked down at her hands and blushed.

Bessie put the tray on the bedside table and turned to leave. As she did so, she stopped for a second and looked at the couch with the rumpled quilt and pillow, still dented where Seth's head had been. She frowned for a second, then left, closing the door behind her.

The room seemed too quiet, and Morgan was acutely aware that Seth was making no attempt to leave her side or even to take his arm from around her shoulders. She continued to study her hands.

Seth put his other hand beneath her chin and turned her head. Without a word, he tipped her head back and gently touched his lips to hers. Morgan felt she had never experienced anything so sweet and gentle as his lips.

Seth withdrew his lips and looked down at her. The sunlight filtered through the curtains, capturing the brilliance of her long, golden hair. He decided he'd like very much to find out what lay under that billowing nightgown. He smiled at the thought and Morgan opened her eyes to find him smiling.

"Do you always find me amusing?" she asked in a cold voice. Her body stiffened under his arm.

Seth removed the arm. "Quite often. But I also find it astonishing that you can hide all that hair away in such a tight little knot." He lifted his hand to play with a fat curl.

Morgan's voice was cold. "May I remind you, Mr. Colter, that our arrangement is a business one. The way I arrange my hair is of no concern to you."

Morgan saw his jaw muscles flex as he ground his teeth together. "You are right, madam. Your looks, or lack of them, is of no concern to me." Morgan winced. Why did people *always* have to remind her of her plainness?

"Now if you do not want to be shocked, you had better look the other way."

Morgan did not understand his meaning until he threw back the covers. She turned her head, but could not keep her eyes averted. She looked up to see a broad back with a deeply grooved backbone, leading to roundly curving buttocks and firm thighs. The thighs were covered with golden hair. At the sound of Seth's laughter, she looked up to meet his eyes in the mirror over the dressing table.

"So! My shy little bride is not so shy when my back is turned."

Morgan kept her eyes on his. In what she hoped was a cool voice, she said, "Only curious."

Seth roared. He continued laughing as he began to dress. Morgan carefully kept her eyes averted.

He left, telling Morgan to come down when she was ready, that his family would be anxious to meet her.

As Morgan dressed, she had time to think. She did not like the way things were going. Already she and Seth had had one quarrel, and they had been married just a few hours. If they were to live together for a full year, they must come to terms. They could not go on this way, with stolen kisses and angry words.

His three sisters were waiting at the foot of the stairs.

"Hello. You must be Seth's wife," the tallest one called. "This is Jennifer, the youngest, Eleanor, the middle, and I am Austine, the oldest."

"Austine and Eleanor are engaged!" Jennifer chirped.

"Let's go into the drawing room and get acquainted. Bessie says you two have only known one another for a day and a half!" Austine looked at Morgan questioningly.

"Yes, that's true."

"Love at first sight! I would never have guessed that Seth could be so romantic," Eleanor added.

Jennifer smiled, "We're so glad it was you and not that Cynthia Ferguson."

"Jennifer!" Austine's anger did not seem real. "What Jennifer means is . . ."

"Just what she said," Eleanor supplied. "You're our sister now, and we can tell you what we think."

Austine seemed suddenly to notice Morgan's unfashionable, baggy dress. "Did you bring much luggage?"

Morgan blushed. "No, I . . . Seth wanted me to buy new clothes before we left for New Mexico."

"New Mexico!" Eleanor cried. "I thought he'd stay at home now that he had a wife." She looked close to tears.

"Hush, Elly. Seth and Morgan will decide what they want to do. Now we must have time to think about your clothes. Papa will take us to Louisville, and we can buy lots of fabric."

"And ribbons and lace."

"This is so exciting! Why, Morgan, we'll make you the most fashionable young lady in the entire West."

"Girls! Please allow your mother to meet her new daughter." Morgan looked to the door to see a tall, slim woman with an abundance of thick, dark blond hair coiled around the back of her head. She was so different from her plump, pink-and-white daughters. In fact, there was something about her that reminded Morgan very much of Seth.

"Oh, Mama, Seth told her that she was to get new clothes before they left. They are going to New Mexico." Eleanor said this with a hint of disbelief.

The girls' mother smiled at Morgan, and Morgan felt relieved. Here was someone she could talk to — these chattering girls were difficult to comprehend.

"Morgan, my name is Nora. Let's go to the morning room so that we may talk." She ushered Morgan out of the drawing room, down the large entry hallway, and into a small room decorated in green and white. A large window faced the east, and the sun was streaming in. Nora motioned Morgan to be seated.

"I watched you for a few moments with my daughters. You did not seem to take an active part in their chatter."

Morgan immediately liked this woman. She felt she could be honest. "No, I am not used to talk of clothes and lace and romance."

Nora did not change her expression. She continued looking at Morgan directly. "Why did you marry my son?" Nora hesitated for only seconds and then continued. "I know that one of you slept on the couch last night, and I also know my son. He does not fall in love at first sight." She looked steadily at Morgan.

Morgan decided to tell her the truth.

"I will tell you. My one goal in life is to live in my childhood home, Trahern House. I am a quiet person. I am uncomfortable around many people, and I plan to live alone there.

"Two years ago, my mother died. Since I was not of age, I was sent to live with my aunt and uncle. My parents had separated when I was one year old, and my father still lived in New Mexico."

Nora's brows lifted at the mention of New Mexico.

"A month ago, my uncle told me of my

father's death. I never knew him so I could feel little grief. Two weeks ago his will was read. It was a great shock to me. It seems that everything — the business in Kentucky, the land in Kentucky, the large ranch in New Mexico, and Trahern House — all belonged to him. He left everything to me, but he stated that everything would be mine only if I married and lived with my husband for one year in New Mexico. If I did not fulfill this contract, everything would go to my uncle. As you can see," her hand swept across her dress, "my uncle did everything he could to keep men from noticing me."

Morgan paused and looked carefully at Nora.

"I went to a ball two nights before my uncle planned to take me out of the country. I heard some women mention that your son had a place in New Mexico. I offered him twenty-five thousand dollars if he would marry me and take me to live with him in New Mexico. He accepted."

Nora said simply, "Good."

It was too much for Morgan. She rose from the chair and came to stand before Nora, her eyes blazing. "Good? Good that a father would make his own daughter stoop to buying a man's name, to living with a man she doesn't even know?"

Nora waited an entire minute before answering, and her calm encompassed Morgan. "I meant that I was glad you are sensible. You were faced with an impossible situation, and you decided to fight for what you wanted."

Nora rose now and walked to the sunlit window, looked out for a second, and then turned to face Morgan. "Let me tell you about my son. My son believes all women are like his sisters. Don't misunderstand me. I love my daughters. But, as you can see, they are very young and have little else in their heads but dreams. Their father loves this and indulges them. My son does not see women as people."

Nora returned to her chair. "So, I say 'good' to your story, because my son needs a sensible wife, one he can like as well as love. Seth is a very strong man, and when you two learn to love one another, you will make an excellent couple."

Morgan stared at Nora. Didn't she understand? "Mrs. Colter — Nora — you do not seem to understand. This is a marriage to fulfill a business contract. I do not intend to love your son."

Nora looked at Morgan with what was very close to a smirk, and Morgan realized that she had seen the same expression on

Seth's face. "Do you really believe that you can spend twelve full months alone with a man, and at the end of that time feel nothing for him? Do you really believe that you'll be able to leave easily and return to your solitary life?"

"I loved my aunt dearly, and I lived with her for two years, yet I left her."

Nora then threw back her head and laughed. "How old are you, Morgan?"

Morgan tilted her head up and said, "Eighteen."

"The love a woman has for another woman is very different from her love for a man."

There was an awkward pause, and Nora could see the anger in Morgan's eyes. "I am sorry. This is not happening as I meant it to. I asked you in here mainly to welcome you to the family, and to tell you that, from what I've seen, I like you. You are sensible, and I believe you will be a good wife for Seth."

Morgan opened her mouth to protest, but instead let out a sigh of exasperation.

Nora walked to her, patted her shoulder, and said, "Please allow a mother to believe that her son has found a good partner."

Morgan smiled and they walked to the door together. "About the clothes," Nora said. "There won't be time to get but a few things made, but my daughters would love to send yards of fabric with you."

Morgan knew that Nora was her friend, and she felt good about their talk.

Morgan spent the day with Seth's sisters. It wasn't too difficult to feel at ease with them. Their chatter required little response and no deep thought. Austine and Eleanor talked of their fiancés. Morgan gathered that Austine's beau was an older man and very sensible, but that Eleanor's was quite the opposite. Eleanor's intended was Jackson Brenner, and he was the oldest son of an old, very wealthy family. Austine's fiancé was James Emerson, a widower with a young child.

Just before dinner, Morgan went upstairs to wash, and as she left the room to return downstairs, she heard Seth talking with another man. She paused at the top of the stairs to look at her father-in-law.

She had seen some of Seth's expressions in his mother's face, but looking at William Colter was like seeing Seth in twenty years' time. He was a large man. The two of them seemed to fill the room. The older man still had an abundance of hair. And they had the same indulgent, patronizing looks on their faces as they watched the three sisters.

Seth looked up and saw her first. For a second she wished he had looked at her the same way she had seen some men look at their brides, but she buried the desire.

"Well, well, well, I have another daughter, and such a pretty one, too." William Colter extended his arms.

Morgan took both his hands in hers, and said, "I am indeed your daughter, but you certainly must not be seeing me correctly!" She said this with a smile.

William took her arm through his, patted her hand, and smiled. "All women are pretty to me. Shall we eat? I'm starved."

They all entered the dining room, and sat at a large mahogany table. Morgan was seated between William and Seth, with Nora across from her. Austine and Eleanor sat beside Nora, and Jennifer was beside Seth. It was easy to see that Jennifer, especially, adored Seth.

"Papa," Eleanor started, "Morgan needs some new clothes and we must have them made before they leave. Could you take us to Louisville tomorrow to purchase fabric?"

William turned to Morgan, and for the first time noticed her dress.

"May we, Papa?" Jennifer continued.

"Yes, of course. I need to make some purchases myself."

Nora looked at Morgan, aware of her stress. She knew enough about her new daughter-in-law to know that she would not like a day shopping with the three giggling girls.

"Girls, you forget that Morgan is a new bride. I am sure she'd like to spend the day with her husband."

Morgan sent Nora a grateful look. "Do you ride, Morgan?" Nora asked calmly.

"Yes, but I haven't been on a horse in two years."

"All right then. Seth, you must take your wife on a tour of the Colter plantation."

Seth said, "Why, of course." He took Morgan's hand from where it lay on the tablecloth and raised it to his lips. His eyes were mocking as he said, "I'd love to take my little bride for a day in the country. Is that all right, *mi querida?*"

"Oh, Seth," Jennifer breathed, "you are so romantic!"

Morgan turned to see the entire family watching. Eleanor and Austine had rather dreamy expressions, but Nora and William looked like two fat, contented hens. They were pleased that their son had finally married.

Again, Jennifer was the first to break the silence. "But how will we know what to buy

55

for Morgan? She must go with us."

Morgan calmly said, "As you can see, I know little about clothes. Whatever pleases you will please me."

Nora said, "No. My daughters tend toward flounces and laces. You are too small for those. And also," she seemed to inventory Morgan's face, "their dimpled, round, good looks tend toward pastels. You need clear, bright colors — reds, greens, black, and bright blues." Nora spotted the bored look on her son's face. She laughed. "Yes, dear. I will stop talking of clothes."

"Just make sure all the material is sturdy," Seth added.

The rest of the meal was filled with talk of the plantation.

After the meal, Morgan retired to their room upstairs. The last two days had been exhausting. She entered the room to find Bessie filling a large, white bathtub.

"I knew you'd be too tired to stay up very late, so it's all ready for you."

"Thank you so much, Bessie. You don't know how much I'm going to enjoy this." She reached up to unpin her hair.

"Here, young 'un, you just sit down and let old Bessie help you. I've done this more times 'an you can count, what with three little girls to raise."

As Morgan's hair tumbled from the hard knot at the back of her head, Bessie drew in her breath. "Land sakes, child! Why do you want to keep all that beautiful stuff hidden?" She grabbed an armful of it and piled it on top of Morgan's head. "You should let me fix it up for you, like this," she said, as she pinned it loosely on top of Morgan's head.

Morgan laughed and stood up as Bessie unfastened the tiny buttons on the dress. As she stepped out of it, and then her undergarments, Bessie exclaimed. "Why, I thought you were kind of thick-waisted and that you had no bosom at all. But just look at you."

Morgan felt an urge to cover herself. She had never been nude before anyone except her mother and her nurse, and not since she was a child. She stepped into the tub, leaned back, and closed her eyes. She lay there, dreaming, and did not hear the door close behind Bessie, or open again.

Seth stood for some minutes, looking down at his little wife. The blond hair was piled on her head, a few curls falling down her back and a few clinging to her steam-dampened face. Her skin was flawless, glistening over smooth shoulders, its creamy texture leading to the two round swellings just glimpsed above the cloudy water. One slim arm was on each side of the tub. He was looking at these when he realized her eyes were open.

They looked at one another for a second, and Seth grinned. "My sisters sent me to ask you if you have any preference for a style of clothing. That seems to have a good deal of bearing on what fabric they choose."

Morgan, still holding his eyes, said evenly, "No. I know nothing about it."

Seth turned to go and then looked back, his eyes mischievous. "May I tell them that I prefer the style you have on now? That bathtub is by far the most becoming thing I have seen you wear."

"You!" Morgan glanced around for something to throw.

Seth laughed. "Careful, or I'll see more than just the bathtub." He turned and left the room, chuckling.

She tried to return to her dreaming, but Seth had ruined it for her. She finished bathing, stepped from the tub, and dried. Then she climbed into the big bed. As she drifted off to sleep, she remembered Seth's eyes. Why had his gaze made her feel so warm?

She was asleep when Seth returned to their room. He undressed quietly, and settled onto the couch.

■ ■ ■ ■

"Wake up. I thought you wanted to see the plantation." Seth was shaking her gently.

She stretched and smiled up at him. God! he thought. She looked like a cat, all grace in the early-morning light. As he looked at her, he began to feel his desire for her growing. "Either you get out of that bed, or I'm getting in with you."

She was startled by his tone and her eyes flew open. She rolled across the bed and climbed out the side farthest from him. As she ran toward the dressing room, she heard him mumble something about being a bull in the mornings. She couldn't stifle a giggle as she slipped into the same gown she had worn the day before.

She saw Seth's frown as she stepped back into the bedroom. "If you will remember, it was you who told me to leave my clothes behind. This and my nightgown are my only articles of clothing."

He left the room and returned in a few minutes with a riding habit. "This is Jennifer's. Try it on."

She returned in moments in the light-green whipcord habit. Jennifer was taller than Morgan, and weighed a great deal more. The outfit fit as poorly as the one her uncle had bought for her.

Seth grimaced. "I guess it will have to do."

No one was up yet, even in the stables. Seth handed her a thick slice of bread covered with butter, and saddled the two horses for them. Morgan's mare was gentle, and she was glad, because she did not feel up to fighting a horse.

They rode in silence, both of them enjoying the cool March morning. After they had ridden for an hour, Seth slowed his horse. "This stream is the boundary of the Colter plantation. Let's get down and I'll show you a place where I used to play as a child." He helped Morgan down, seemingly unaware of his hands on her waist.

"Give me your hand and we'll cross over these rocks." His hand was large, warm, and dry. After they had crossed the stream, he continued to hold her hand as they walked across the meadow. "I used to come here a lot. It seemed exciting, because it wasn't on Colter land."

"Didn't your sisters come?"

"They were afraid to get dirty."

"At Trahern House there was a special place for me. It was a big, old, sycamore tree, set in a large open meadow. I trampled all the grasses down and made a large area under the tree, but no one could see me from a distance, because the grasses were above my head." Her eyes shone.

"I think I would have liked your place."

She laughed. "I never had brothers or sisters, so I never had anyone to show it to. Maybe I would have shown it to you." She stopped, putting her hand over her mouth.

"What is it?" He seemed alarmed.

"Well, I just realized that when I was a child, you were a great, grown man already."

He laughed with her. "Yes, I guess I was. I'm fourteen years older than you, after all. I think I forget that you are the same age as my baby sister."

Morgan looked up at him, smiling, and squeezed his hand tighter. "I take that as a compliment."

Seth was overcome with an urge to kiss her, but the moment was lost as she saw a great black and orange butterfly and skipped ahead, pulling Seth with her.

Damn it! Women were for kissing and dressing up like dolls, he thought, not for running around the wood together and talking about your childhood.

He forgot his moment's doubt as he saw the tree. It had at one time stood well away from the creek, but the water had washed the soil away, so that it now stood at the creek's edge. The branches hanging over the stream made a roof above the clear water.

"There it is."

Morgan saw the tree, and before he could say any more, she had dropped his hand and was scrambling down the bank to sit beneath the tree. She looked up at him cheerfully.

He stood looking at her. There was dirt on the enormous skirt, and a smudge on her cheek.

She realized what he was looking at. "I thought you already knew. I'm not a lady, and I never plan to be one. I am much happier here than at Cynthia Ferguson's ball."

He laughed. "I like it better here, too." He climbed down the bank to sit beside her.

She seized the opportunity to clear things up. "Seth, I want to talk to you. Yesterday morning we quarreled about the way I wear my hair, and last night I was angry when I was taking a bath." She paused, but he said nothing. She could feel him looking at her.

"I want to keep our relationship on a friendship level. I don't want us to quarrel. What I mean to say is that I want it clear between us that this is a marriage for convenience, a business arrangement."

"I understand. You do not want to share a bed with me." His eyes were cold. "All right." He looked at the tight hair, the baggy dress. "I believe I can refrain from molesting you. Is that what you are worried about?"

She was hurt by his anger. "Yes, I guess it is."

"Then I give you my word that I will not at any time force my attention on you. Does that satisfy you?"

She sighed. "Yes."

For Seth, the high mood of the day was broken. But for Morgan, it seemed an even brighter day. She was relieved. It seemed there would be no more fights between them.

Seth's gruff voice broke the silence. "Let's go back." He started toward the tethered horses.

"Seth, wait!"

He stopped, an impatient expression on his face.

"Seth —" She put her hand on his forearm. "I didn't mean to make you angry. I was trying to say that I want to be your friend. I don't want to fight. Somehow, I seem to have made everything worse."

His anger left him and he smiled. "You're right, little wife. I do have a quick temper. I apologize for my rudeness." He removed his hat and made a bow.

Morgan laughed. "I forgive you, sir."

"And to show my repentance, I shall ask Cook to prepare a picnic basket tomorrow, and we will go to my cabin — a pretty little place much farther upstream. Does that please you, my lady?"

"Well, good sir, it does, except for one part."

A slight frown replaced Seth's smile. "What part is that?"

Morgan's smile was winning. "That you allow me to prepare the picnic basket."

"You! You can cook?"

"I'll let you judge that tomorrow."

Seth returned Morgan's smile. "It seems I got more than I bargained for. A wife who can cook! I hope Lupita doesn't get jealous."

"Lupita?"

"She's my cook at the ranch in New Mexico."

"Tomorrow I want you to tell me about your ranch. I like being with animals."

They smiled at one another, returned to their horses, and rode back to the big house in a companionable silence.

Just before dinner, Morgan heard the voices of her sisters-in-law.

"Morgan, come look!" Jennifer's plump

face had broken into a very large smile. She pushed Morgan toward a table heaped with fabrics and trimmings. In spite of what Nora had told her daughters, all the fabrics were creams, pink, and pale blues. Nora was examining the things.

"But, girls, I told you to get bright, clear colors. Morgan is too fair to wear these."

The three young women looked dismayed. Eleanor said timidly, "But, Mother, they are such beautiful colors."

Morgan felt the thin silks and satins. They would be totally unsuitable for New Mexico.

"Well, I can see my little sisters have chosen well for a grueling trip to the New Mexico mountains."

Everyone turned to Seth. Jennifer tilted her head toward him. "Just because a lady has to travel to a forsaken land doesn't mean she has to stop being a lady."

"Jennifer's right," Austine added. "When a lady wears silk, then she always remembers she is a lady."

"If a woman is a lady, then she is a lady no matter what she wears, including men's trousers."

"Trousers!" Eleanor's voice reflected disbelief. Deep down, she wasn't sure her own plump legs would fit properly into a pair of men's pants. The idea was appalling.

The joking tone left Seth's voice. "All right, sisters, since you have chosen completely inappropriate clothing for Morgan, then you must keep these fabrics for yourselves and supply her with some more suitable garments from your own wardrobes. She will need the sturdiest fabrics you can obtain."

Morgan could readily see that the idea of several new dresses did not displease the girls.

Austine was the first to speak. "Morgan, let's go upstairs and we'll go through the chifforobe."

As the three sisters ushered Morgan upstairs, she turned a backward glance to Seth. He was looking at the pile of silks and brocade with an air of disgust. No wonder he thinks all women are silly, she thought.

Two hours later, Morgan emerged from the girls' bedrooms, totally exhausted. She had tried on dress after dress. No matter what she tried, it was huge on her. The sisters had wanted to start immediately on taking things in, adjusting them so they fit her snugly. Morgan had considered this for only a second. She knew that Seth gave her those special glances only when she had her hair down and she sensed that she would have an easier time holding him to his promise of the morning if her dresses fit loosely. She made excuses to her sisters-in-law, saying anything she could think of to persuade them not to alter the dresses.

At the dinner table, Austine tried to enlist Seth's help in getting Morgan to change her mind about taking in the dresses. But, much to her chagrin, Seth sided with Morgan.

"I think my little wife is right. Tight dresses with heavy corsets" — the girls' eyes widened; they wondered how their brother knew of ladies' corsets — "are not suitable wear for long hours in the sun, sitting on a jolting wagon seat."

The matter seemed to be settled, and the conversation turned to other matters.

After dinner, the family retired to the drawing room. As they began to occupy themselves, a groom came in to tell Seth and William that Susan was about to foal.

Seth was on his feet in seconds. "No, Pa, this is mine. You stay and enjoy your brandy." He looked at Morgan and hesitated, but only for a second. "Come on."

Her face showed her joy as she took his hand and they went quickly and silently to the barn.

The mare, Susan, was lying down in the sweet-smelling straw, her breath heavy and rapid. As Seth assisted with the already-emerging colt, Morgan held the horse's head and soothed her, speaking quietly and evenly.

The birth was an easy one, but still the tension was great. Morgan knew Seth loved the pretty little mare, and that this colt was to be his. Seth helped the mare clean her colt and, within minutes, the little stallion was trying to stand.

Morgan and Seth stood by and watched, laughing together at the colt's clumsiness. When the colt began to nurse, they decided it was time to leave.

As they stepped out of the warm barn into the cool night air, Morgan shivered. Without thinking, Seth put his arm around her shoulders and drew her to him, so that the sides of their bodies touched. Morgan started to draw away, but something in the casual way Seth had put his arm around her was reassuring.

"You were good with the mare."

"Thank you."

"I think you'll do well in New Mexico. There are many jobs like that one."

"I like being outside. Could we walk a few minutes before we go in?"

Without a word, he led her around the barn and toward a grove of trees. "It's been a long day, hasn't it?"

"Yes."

"How were my sisters this afternoon? Did their chattering bother you?"

Morgan laughed. "Yes. They seemed very upset because clothing is not my passion."

Seth halted and swung Morgan around till she was in his arms. His voice was low. "Tell me something, Morgan. What *is* your all-consuming passion?"

Without hesitation, she answered simply, "Trahern House."

Seth continued smiling at her. "I like your honesty. It's unusual in a woman."

"Unusual in the women you've known, maybe, but I assure you there are things besides men that are important to some of us!"

Seth laughed loudly, his whole body shaking with merriment. Morgan moved from within the circle of his arms and repressed an urge to slap his smirking face. Her mother had been right! It was impossible to carry on an intelligent conversation with a man. They were always so sure that you, a woman, were an inferior being. She turned and ran toward the house, her strides filled with anger.

Before she had reached the house, Seth had her by the arm.

"Now wait a minute, Morgan!" His voice

was stern. "Think about what you said and answer me this question: How many of the unmarried women you have met in the last two years cared about *anything* except getting a husband? And how many mothers with marriageable daughters cared about anything except getting that daughter married?" He paused a few seconds and then continued in a lower voice. "When women change their attitudes toward men, see a man as something besides a prize to be won, then, and only then, will men change their attitudes toward women!"

Morgan looked at the ground. He was right. Most women were like Cynthia Ferguson and Seth's sisters. She looked up at Seth and smiled. "You're right. But *I'm* different!"

A teasing look was in Seth's eyes. His voice was low, almost a whisper as he moved his face very near hers. "I can see you don't care about frivolous things . . . but what about men? I think maybe you haven't had a chance to learn about that." His lips moved to her ear and his breath was soft and warm. "Any time you want to find out about men, let me know. I'd be happy to help you in your . . . explorations."

His huge body made Morgan nervous.

She quickly moved from him and ran for the safety of the house.

CHAPTER THREE

"Morgan." Seth's voice was close to her ear. "Get dressed and let's go. It's nearly sunup." He paused and looked at her drowsy face. "Better yet, don't get dressed. I like you that way."

Morgan opened her eyes and smiled up at him. His voice, his always-teasing manner, and his open, generous smile were becoming very familiar to her. They had been married only four days, and had known one another for only five, but already the sight of him was familiar. She wondered how she could ever have been afraid of men. Seth was reasonable, kind, and considerate. The next year would be a pleasant one if their friendship continued to grow.

"Well?"

"I'm getting up." She went into the adjoining dressing room and quickly put on the large green riding habit that had once been Jennifer's. Her hair was still flowing down

72

her back as she returned to the bedroom and crossed to the mirror. She started brushing it in preparation of pulling it back into its tight little knot at the nape of her neck.

"Don't." Seth's voice startled her as his large hand loosely clasped her wrist. "Leave it down. I like to see it." She opened her mouth to protest, but he placed two warm fingers over her lips. "Don't give me a lecture about how your hair doesn't matter. Just leave it loose. Please."

Morgan didn't want to start the day with an argument, so she dropped her hands and left her hair to curl softly past her waist. As they left the room to tiptoe downstairs to the kitchen, she could still feel Seth's fingers on her lips.

"It's even earlier than I thought, if Cook, that old tiger, isn't up," Seth whispered as they entered the large, still-dark kitchen.

"She was very nice to me when I was in here yesterday afternoon, preparing the picnic basket."

"Nice? Cook nice to a lady? She doesn't think a lady is worth a handful of salt."

"Maybe she doesn't consider me a lady. After all, I was cooking. I don't believe cooking is a ladylike occupation."

"Oh, yes. I had forgotten that my little

73

wife cooks. I don't guess there is a lady in five counties that can cook. Wife!"

Morgan was startled at his exclamation.

"Where's my breakfast?"

Morgan bristled at his tone. "I cook only when I want to. No man commands me to do anything."

Seth groaned and turned his eyes upward. "Oh God! Am I going to be cursed with a year of this? A woman without a sense of humor? If I tell her her hair is pretty, she tells me it is none of my business. If I tell her I need food, she tells me she doesn't take orders. Tell me, Lord, what is this poor man to do?" Seth tilted his head down slightly till he could see Morgan out of one eye. She had her hand over her mouth, trying to hide her smile.

Thus encouraged, Seth returned to his prayer. "What's that? You think the lass needs some persuasion? A what? A kiss? Ah, yes, that could bring her 'round. Thanks, Lord."

Seth bent toward Morgan, who now stood staring at him, eyes wide. "Seth —"

"You heard Him. I have nothing to do with it." He began walking purposefully toward her.

Morgan ran quickly to the other side of the big oak table. "Seth . . . don't." As she went to one side of the table and as he pursued her, they both began to laugh.

"I have orders to kiss the cook — to gentle her into making my breakfast." His smile was infectious.

"I'll make breakfast. I don't need persuasion," Morgan said between peals of laughter.

"Enough of this play, lass." Seth leaped up and bounded across the top of the table toward Morgan. She stopped where she was, stunned by the sight of his massive body leaping with such agility.

Before she had regained her senses, his arms were around her. "Now," he began, still laughing. But as his lips moved towards her, all at once both of them were serious.

"What is this? Sounds like the old bull got loose in my kitchen. What are you two doing in here, sparkin' in my kitchen before the sun's even up?"

Cook's querulous voice broke the spell. Morgan was embarrassed and looked down at the floor, but none of it seemed to have affected Seth.

"Good morning, Cook. We were making noise so you'd get up. We knew that if you got up, you'd bring sunshine with you."

"Go on with you." Cook tried to hide it, but Seth's flattery obviously pleased her.

"Look." Morgan pointed to the floor, at the first, tiny sunbeam. It lay at Cook's feet. "Seth's right, Carolyn. You have brought the sun."

The young couple passed the day riding and exploring Seth's boyhood haunts. It was a day of easy companionship and warm good humor.

By the time they arrived back at the Colter house, Seth and Morgan were good friends.

"Morgan, I had a wonderful time today. Thank you."

She smiled brilliantly. "So did I, Seth."

He moved closer, but she shouted for him to catch her, and ran toward the house.

Nora heard their laughter before she saw them. To her delight, she saw them race past the parlor window, both laughing. She turned to Cynthia Ferguson and said in what she hoped was a smug voice, "It looks as if my son and new daughter had an enjoyable ride."

She put down her teacup and rose to go to the door to greet Seth and Morgan. But before she could get to the door, Austine was there. Nora turned and smiled at Cynthia, who was sitting so calmly with her two admirers, Nora's daughters. The girls were almost fawning over the coldly beautiful Cynthia.

As Nora closed the parlor door behind her, she heard Austine's excited, breathless voice telling Seth and Morgan, "It's Cynthia Ferguson. She's come to pay her respects to you. I don't think she really believes you eloped. She says she just can't imagine the two of you together."

"Hush, Austine." Nora looked carefully at Morgan. Morgan's face was just slightly sunburned, and it made her eyes radiant. And her hair! Nora hadn't imagined Morgan could have so much of it. Her daughter-in-law was very close to being beautiful. She looked as if she had just left her lover's arms. Nora truly hoped this was the case.

Seth also had an unusual glow about him. He was smiling now, not that awful, patronizing leer he had so often, but a smile of real joy.

"I must change. I can't very well greet Cynthia in a riding habit and with my hair like this."

"I'll help you, but we must hurry. Cynthia has already been waiting for half an hour." Austine took Morgan's arm.

"Yes. Morgan should go right in," said Nora.

"But, Nora, at least let me tie my hair back."

"No, dear, I definitely do not think you

should tie your hair back. If Miss Cynthia Ferguson can appear unannounced, then she must be prepared to view her hostess and host" — she glanced up at Seth — "in whatever state she finds them."

She started toward the parlor door with Morgan, but Seth took Nora's arm and whispered to her, "What are you up to?"

Nora looked at her son with widened eyes. "I declare, I have no idea what you mean."

"Morgan, Cynthia has come to see you." Eleanor called, awe in her tone. Wasn't Cynthia Ferguson a renowned beauty? And here she was, making a long drive just to pay her respects to Morgan.

"Hello, Cynthia." Morgan couldn't help but feel somewhat intimidated by Cynthia's presence.

"Why, you dear little thing, what an . . . interesting dress." She languidly extended her hand. Morgan wondered wryly whether she was expected to kiss it. "Sit here by me." Cynthia patted the love seat. Then she turned her eyes to Seth. "Hello, Seth. Your mother tells me you've been out riding. Isn't it a little cool for riding?"

Seth smiled warmly at Cynthia. "There are things to help warm a man." He looked meaningfully at Morgan.

Morgan had to hold her laughter. There

was an awkward silence in the room.

"Your sisters have been telling me of your elopement. I find it difficult to believe that I introduced you two the night of my party. Were you, by chance, pretending? Did you actually know one another before that night?" Her question was addressed to Seth. She seemed unaware of anyone else.

"No, Cynthia." He accepted the cup of tea that Austine handed him. "I guess you'll have to say it was love at first sight. We met that night and I did not see my little wife until the next day when I talked to her uncle. A few hours after that, we were married."

Jennifer could not restrain herself. "I hope I fall in love just like that."

Morgan sat quietly. The way Seth told the story, it did sound romantic. She didn't like to remember the night of Cynthia's ball, when she had asked Seth to marry her. She took in Cynthia's dark beauty, the exquisite gown, the intricate yet soft arrangement of her hair. Maybe Seth would marry her in a year, when they had their annulment.

Nora interrupted the silence. "Seth, you and Morgan seem to have had a good time today. Where did you ride?"

"A little past Johnson's meadow."

Nora walked to the love seat to stand by

Morgan. "Well, I'm glad you had a good time." She ostentatiously removed a leaf from Morgan's hair, studying it for a second before placing it on the table.

Cynthia spoke. "Riding horses around in the woods is not my idea of a good time." She looked at Morgan's dishevelment with open contempt. "It's a little too dirty for me."

Seth and Morgan immediately exchanged looks and then laughed aloud. Just the day before, Seth had mentioned that ladies did not like to get dirty. Morgan had replied that she was not a lady. The exchange of laughter over what was obviously a lovers' joke made for another embarrassing silence.

Nora, reassured that Morgan could handle herself with Cynthia, gathered her daughters and left.

When Nora left, Seth was the first to speak. "Cynthia, may I say that you look lovely, as always."

Cynthia tittered. "Why, Seth, dear, you may say it as often as you like. You know . . . no matter how many times you have said it, I still love to hear it." She turned slightly toward Morgan to make sure she heard every word. "Morgan, has Seth told you what old friends we are?" Her voice had a cutting edge.

Morgan returned the sweet smile with one of her own. She reached over and patted Cynthia's hand. "My dear Cynthia, you shouldn't consider yourself such an *old* friend."

Cynthia's features hardened and her eyes blazed. They both turned at a sound from Seth. He was choking on a cookie. "Excuse me, ladies." He struggled to regain his composure. "Won't you stay for dinner, Cynthia?" There was laughter just beneath his voice. Or was there? Cynthia could not be sure.

"No, I must be going." Cynthia rose, as did Seth and Morgan. Suddenly, Cynthia's face brightened. She purred. "What I really came for was to kiss the groom." She moved very close to Seth and placed a lace-covered hand on his chest. She turned her head toward Morgan. "You don't mind . . . do you, dear?"

Without waiting for an answer, her arms slid up and around Seth's neck in what Morgan knew was a much-practiced gesture. Cynthia pulled Seth's mouth to hers, her body melting to meet his as his arms encircled her. Morgan turned away.

"Well, I must say, Seth, you haven't changed." Cynthia then turned to Morgan, as if startled to find her there. "I really *must* be going. You'll visit me before too long, won't you?" She addressed this to Seth, but then turned slowly to Morgan. "And you must come, too, of course."

Seth moved to Morgan and put his arm around her shoulders. "My wife would love to come visit, on one of our return trips from New Mexico."

"New Mexico! I thought a . . . wife would change your mind about that desolate place."

"No, my little wife is just as anxious to go to New Mexico as I am."

Morgan smiled at Cynthia and extended her hand, very aware of Seth's arm around her. "You must come again. Do you know your way out? But of course you do." Morgan's voice held a trace of venom.

Cynthia turned and left, nearly slamming the door behind her. Morgan stood and stared at the door, seething with rage. How dare Cynthia! She was totally unaware that Seth had drawn back from her and was now grinning broadly.

"Be careful. That door is made of wood and your look just might set it on fire."

She turned on him. "And just what are you grinning about? You certainly enjoyed her visit!" Morgan mimicked holding a teacup, her little finger extended. In a falsetto voice, she said, "Didn't Seth tell you we were *very* old and *very* dear friends?" Morgan's anger mounted. "And then, 'May I kiss the groom?' It looked to me as though she had done *that* several times."

Seth's laughter rang through the room. "Calm down, little one. You'll make me think you are jealous!"

"Jealous!" Her voice grew more calm. "I'm not jealous — I just don't like being insulted. She had no right to insult me."

Seth moved close to her and pulled her to him. "Were you insulted? You noticed that she looked familiar with kissing. Were you that interested?"

"No." She was still very angry. "It looked like she was familiar with kissing *you.*"

"So you were interested."

"No . . . I . . ."

"I told you that any time you were interested in trying out kissing — or anything else for that matter — I'm ready."

"Seth, you promised."

"I promised I wouldn't force you, but I didn't promise I wouldn't try to persuade you."

Her anger was slowly receding. How she had hated seeing him kiss Cynthia!

She tilted her head back, and molded her body to his as he started to kiss her.

"Oh, excuse me." Nora had quietly entered the room, and Morgan quickly moved to free herself from Seth's arms. Seth refused to remove them, holding her tightly to him.

Seth told his mother, "Cynthia's gone. She saw what she came to see, and then she left."

Nora was beaming. She had known that nature would take its course.

Morgan, embarrassed at being found in Seth's arms, brought an elbow sharply into his stomach. He didn't flinch. She turned and glared at him, whispering through clenched teeth, "Let me go."

Seth chuckled and, relenting, released her.

"Dinner will be in an hour. Maybe you two would like to rest before dinner?"

Seth immediately grabbed Morgan's hand and led her across the room. "That's a good idea, Mother." He led her quickly up the stairs to their room. "Now, let's start where we left off." He turned to her, but she moved from him.

"No, Seth, I was angry before." Her voice was pleading. "I want to be friends — no more."

Seth smiled. "All right. I have a long time. I'll wait. Why don't you rest? Bessie could bring you a bath."

"I'd love that." As Seth turned to leave,

Morgan said quietly, "Thank you for understanding, Seth."

Morgan sat in the hot water for a long time. She tried not to think about the day, the long ride with Seth, how she had felt when Cynthia kissed him. Everything was moving too quickly! She lay back in the tub and thought about Trahern House.

Life had been so simple, so quiet and gentle there. She had always done exactly as she pleased. Her days had been filled with riding, cooking, embroidery, and caring for her flowers. She had been very happy. There had been so few people in her life then. She had been left in peace.

She thought about Seth's family. Nora was so kind, and always close to laughter. William was always easy to be with. And the sisters — it was funny how a person always thought of them together. They, too, were always smiling. Everyone seemed to enjoy life so much. Morgan slid deeper into the tub, thinking that if she ever did leave Trahern House, the Colter family would be pleasant to live with. But, of course, she never would leave Trahern House. What had made her think such a thing?

She was just finishing dressing when Seth came to the room to change for dinner. He nodded toward the tub, still full of water. "I should have come up earlier."

Morgan smiled at him as she adjusted the tight knot of hair on her neck. Seth strode towards her, touched the knot, and said, "I like it better the other way. But at least this way you're no temptation."

Morgan swung around to meet his eyes, "Good! Now maybe you'll not embarrass me in front of your family."

After dinner, Seth disappeared to the library, and the rest of the family retired to the large drawing room. William read, smoking a large cigar. The three sisters asked Morgan if she'd like to help embroider Austine's linens for her trousseau.

"Eleanor's wedding dress is a light blue silk and Austine's is a pink satin," Jennifer chattered. "They are going to be married together, this summer. I wish you could stay for the wedding."

"That would be nice, Morgan. You could be our matron of honor. It would be wonderful if you would stay. Do you think you could?" Austine looked at Morgan expectantly, but Morgan sat quietly, unresponding, absorbed in her stitching.

"Morgan." Nora's voice was clear in the silence.

Morgan immediately looked up and re-alized what had happened. "I'm sorry, I guess I was thinking of something else."

Nora turned to her husband. "William, do you know where Seth went?"

"He's in the library, reading those old journals of his." Then, as if taking the hint from his wife, he said, "Why don't you go join him, daughter? I'm sure he'd like to show them to you. When he was a little boy, he used to read those by the hour. And he'd read them to anyone who'd listen, too."

"I promised Austine and Eleanor I'd help with the linens."

"Don't be silly, Morgan. This is your honeymoon. Go spend the evening with your husband." Nora's eyes were dancing. She knew that Morgan could hardly say no to her suggestion.

"If I had just been married, I'd spend every minute with my husband." Jennifer was always the romantic.

Morgan left the room, went down the hall, and quietly opened the door of the library. Seth was sitting in a large leather chair behind a massive, carved walnut desk. He was smoking a large cigar and seemed totally engrossed in an enormous book. Thinking he hadn't heard her come in, she moved noiselessly to his side. His voice startled her.

"Look at this." He pointed to a yellowed page with angular, faded handwriting.

We have waited eight days for the flood waters to recede. The sun is merciless. There are no trees for shade. Ahead of us lies nothing but flat grassland. There is much tension among us because of the Indians we have seen.

"Who wrote it?"

"I don't know. When I was very young, my grandfather bought it from a Frenchman he met in Louisville. This is only the center section of the journal. As far as I can guess, and I've read it several times, this was one of the earliest American parties to try to make it to Santa Fe."

"What happened to them?"

"I don't know that either. But as far as I can gather, before Santa Fe gained independence from Spain, all Americans in Santa Fe were either killed or imprisoned."

Morgan was quiet.

"Morgan, what we have ahead of us is not pleasant. The journey takes about three months, and we go through some rugged country. Sit over here, and I'll read to you."

They moved to a small leather couch

beneath the shuttered window. A small fire burned in the fireplace to their left. Morgan curled up on one end of the couch and listened as Seth read. His deep voice was calming even as he read of the horrors of traveling on the Santa Fe Trail. He read of their joy at seeing the Cimarron Spring, of the lack of water in places, and of flooded rivers in others. Morgan tried to imagine herself experiencing these things, but could not do so. She lazily watched the fire and listened to Seth's deep, resonant voice.

Seth stopped reading to look at his little wife. She was sleeping peacefully, her legs drawn up under the voluminous skirt. She looked about ten years old. Of course, he mused, she really wasn't so very much older than that. He blew out the lamp and moved closer to her. In sleep, she nuzzled against his warm body. He put his arm around her shoulders and drew her even closer. Her head rested on his chest.

An hour later, when Nora came in to say goodnight, that was how she found them. She watched the scene for a couple of minutes, feeling slightly guilty about intruding.

Morgan awoke at the sound of the door closing.

"Well, little girl, are you ready to go to bed?"

Morgan was embarrassed by her position and stood up quickly, hurrying toward their room. She undressed rapidly in the dressing room and was soon in bed.

Seth came up the stairs, after she was in bed, and undressed in the moonlit room. Morgan made herself look away as he removed his clothing. She shivered and then snuggled deeper under the covers. It's only curiosity, she told herself. At last she fell asleep.

The sun was high when Morgan awoke the next morning. She stretched lazily. It had been good to sleep late. The last few days had been very wearing. Just six days ago she had been dressing for Cynthia's ball.

She looked toward the foot of the bed and saw that Seth had gone. Immediately, she jumped out of bed, dressed, pulled her hair back, and ran downstairs to the kitchen.

"Good morning, Cook."

"Morning! I've been up for four hours!"

"I'm just lazy. Where is everyone?"

"Who knows? Them gals are out pickin' flowers, I reckon, and the Missus is in her room. Master and Mr. Seth rode out hours ago. You want some breakfast?"

"I'll get it." She paused. "You say Seth rode out? Do you know where?" She tried to sound nonchalant.

"I knowed you'd want to know. He's got every other girl in the countryside after him, why not his own wife?"

Morgan decided it was best not to talk about Seth anymore, so she finished her breakfast as quickly as possible and left the kitchen.

She met Nora in the front hallway. "Seth is planning to take some good furniture back with him to Santa Fe. He told me this morning that I was to let you pick out what you wanted."

Morgan was very pleased by this, and she and Nora went upstairs to begin their search. The master bedroom was enormous, with oak paneling and oak floors. The bed was even larger than the one in Seth's room, and the headboard was intricately carved.

"I couldn't choose any furniture from these rooms."

"Morgan, you may have anything in this house except William's bed. I want you and Seth to have a good start in New Mexico."

"Nora . . . you know about our arrangement. I will return after one year."

As they left the master bedroom and continued down the hall, Nora said lightly,

"Who knows? You may like New Mexico."

Morgan smiled. "I may like New Mexico, but you don't know how much I need Kentucky . . . and Trahern House."

"A house and a piece of land are no replacement for love."

"How is love involved?"

"I've watched you two, the way you tease and the way you laugh together. Friendship is the very best basis for a good love."

Morgan considered this for a few minutes. "Yes, I think you are right. I believe I will love Seth at the end of a year."

Nora stopped abruptly to turn to stare in triumph at Morgan.

"As a sister loves a brother," Morgan added hastily, feeling she had won the joust.

Seth and William joined Nora and Morgan for lunch. The sisters had been invited to a neighbor's, where they would probably stay till dinnertime.

"Well, did my little wife choose every piece of furniture in the house?"

Morgan did not like his patronizing tone at all. "The only thing I really wanted was the carved bed in the large bedroom at the head of the stairs." She watched both Seth and his father as their eyes widened.

Seth nearly choked as he said, "But it

would take an entire wagon just for that bed. And besides, that bed has always been in this house."

Nora couldn't help laughing. "Morgan's only teasing, Seth." She saw the two men relax. "And you deserve it, too, when you talk to your wife the way you do to Jennifer."

Seth looked sheepish and returned to eating. William asked Morgan if she did find any furniture. Then, hesitantly at first, she talked of her idea about New Mexico, of her certainty that this beautiful furniture would not fit in there.

She gained courage as she saw Seth looking at her with respect. "That's just what I told Mother and the girls when I first came back. I wanted to take some furniture back, but Chippendale does not fit into an adobe house."

"Nora, did you show them the attic?" William addressed his wife.

"I had forgotten all about it. Morgan will love the furniture."

After lunch, Seth returned to the fields with his father, while Nora and Morgan went back to their explorations.

A great deal of the furniture that had been in the Colter home before Nora came was stored in the attic. It had been made in

America, and was much plainer than the Chippendale. Here were things that other people had stored in wagons as they came to the Kentucky wilderness. The prize was a sturdy bride's chest with birds and the year 1784 painted on it, all enclosed in a heart.

There were several sturdy oak tables with chairs to match. This was furniture that had been made with love, and although it was old, it was strong. It had been carried across the country before, and it would stand up to that again.

CHAPTER FOUR

There was one more day before they left. Morgan regretted leaving Seth's family — they had been so kind. She was also afraid of the long trek across the country where she'd be alone with Seth. The day passed in a frenzy of packing and preparation for the trip.

After the noon meal, Jake arrived. He was a short, wiry man. Morgan judged him to be about sixty. Jake and Seth hugged one another in greeting.

"You little polecat! I can see by your size that you haven't been eatin' right. You get any littler, and I won't be able to see you," said the small man as Seth's massive frame nearly smothered him. He grinned up at Seth with a nearly toothless grin.

"Well, Jake, I miss your cookin'. A few pieces of your shoeleather steaks and I'll be near as big as you."

They turned toward the house, their arms

around one another. Then they saw Morgan. Seth seemed embarrassed, and stammered, "Jake, meet Morgan. She's my . . . er . . . wife."

Jake turned startled eyes to Seth, dropped his arm, and began to howl with laughter. Seth stared at his feet. Morgan could not help smiling, infected by Jake's laughter. With tears in his eyes he choked, "I told you, I knew it." Then, sobering, "No offense, ma'am, we jist had us a little bet, and I reckon I won." He offered his hand. "Glad to meet you."

Jake turned out to be a born story-teller. He kept everyone entertained during dinner. After dinner, the women went to the sitting room, and Jake and Seth's father went to the library.

Seth took the opportunity to add a last-minute package to the loaded wagons. He put in a small music box that he intended to be a Christmas present to Morgan. He stood in the moonlight, wondering what would be between them at Christmastime. At last he returned to the house.

Jake had retired, and William and Seth were left alone. The two were close, and they had much to share. By ten o'clock they had drunk a great deal of brandy. They both rose to greet Nora, the girls, and Morgan as they came to say goodnight.

As the women turned to leave, Seth called, "Stay with us a little while, Morgan."

Seth smiled, showing his dimples, and offered her a glass of brandy.

"A toast to my new daughter." William's smile was just as impish as his son's.

The liquid was warming, making Morgan feel very relaxed.

"Seth, my son, I want to congratulate you on your choice of a wife." William's words were just slightly slurred.

Seth moved to the back of Morgan's chair and began to knead the back of her neck with his fingertips, feeling the silky hair and the warmth of her scalp. Seth and William were talking, but she heard nothing, feeling only the warmth of the brandy and the touch of Seth's hand. She leaned back and closed her eyes.

She was startled from her reverie by silence, and opened her eyes to find the men looking at her. Seth smiled. "I think you're tired. Why don't you go to bed?" His eyes were bright with liquor, and somehow Morgan found him very appealing.

She rose, silently, and went toward the door. She heard William mutter under his breath, "I'd never let my new bride go to bed alone." He added, "At least you can kiss her."

Perhaps it was the unaccustomed liquor, but Morgan's heart began to pound. Her hand was on the doorknob before she felt Seth's hand on hers. The warmth of him, the size, and the smell of him made her tremble. He turned the knob and followed her out the door. They were in the empty moonlit hallway.

He touched her arm, and she turned. Very gently, his arm went around her waist while his other hand tipped her head up to face him. The moonlight made his hair silver, and the height and width of him made her seem small and delicate. His lips touched hers very gently, very softly. Morgan swayed against him, unthinking, now only feeling, wanting his warmth to touch her. Her arms went out, encircling his neck and drawing him closer to her. Her head was swimming, and she had no idea whether or not she was breathing.

His lips began to move over hers. Her lips parted as he began to be more demanding. They pulled one another closer and Seth leaned forward until Morgan's back was bent into a bow shape. She heard herself moan as she felt Seth's hips move slightly.

Seth lifted his head and looked at her with startled eyes — and with another expression Morgan did not recognize. Silently, he lifted her in his arms and carried her up the stairs to their bedroom. Morgan put her face into his neck, feeling the soft, warm flesh. He made her feel so safe, so protected. Nothing existed but Seth. She moved her face deeper into his neck, touching with her lips the tender spot where the neck joined the shoulder. She felt Seth's breath quicken as he opened the door to their bedroom.

Closing it with his foot, he again turned to Morgan to kiss her. The kiss was searching, and she clung to him as he carefully laid her on the bed and stretched out beside her. His hand caressed her hair, her shoulder, as it found its way to the buttons on her dress. He kissed her throat, and each area of flesh as it was exposed by the unfastened buttons. She felt Seth's leg across her own.

Seth sat up on an elbow and looked at her in the firelight. His eyes were tender. He slowly unbuttoned his shirt and removed it. The hair on his chest was thick and curly, the skin such a delicate, golden brown. She stretched out a tentative finger and touched his shoulder. God! but he was beautiful. His arms made her think of the muscles on horses.

"Seth . . ." His kisses, his gentleness, made

the idea of stopping him seem cruel.

"Don't talk, my love, just enjoy," he murmured.

"Seth, you have to stop . . . please don't." Her voice was barely a whisper. "Please . . ."

It was several minutes before Seth began to hear her. Her voice was so soft. As the sounds penetrated his senses, he began to feel anger rising in him. He did not know why. Abruptly, he dropped her onto the bed.

His jaw was clenched. "No, madam, I will not force you. I will not have a woman who says no to me." He stood up and grabbed his shirt, angrily thrusting his arms into it. "There is a name for women like you — women who kiss a man like you kissed me in the hall, who allow a man to get worked up and then refuse him." His eyes were very angry. "You've said no to me several times, but this will be the last time. I'll not ask you again."

Now it was Morgan's turn to get angry. "I made you a business offer, nothing more. I made that clear from the beginning. I've not wanted your advances, so what right do you have to be angry with me? I have kept my part in our bargain."

Seth's face softened. His eyes, though, were still angry, his voice a harsh whisper. "You are right, you have kept your part."

There was a look of sadness about him now. "As old as I am, I never learn — there are two kinds of women, my silly sisters and the calculating Cynthia. Somehow I thought you were different, but now I know just where you fit." His voice lowered. "I will see that you get your beloved Trahern House, and I will bother you no more."

Her hair was loose, her dress unbuttoned, showing the shadow of a breast. Abruptly, he turned and left the room.

Morgan stared at the door, tears gathering strength.

Nora was disturbed the next morning to see the coolness between Seth and Morgan. Jake noticed it too, but neither said anything.

Tearful goodbyes were said, and both Nora and William forced money on the reluctant Morgan.

At last Morgan sat on the wagon beside Jake, while Seth rode ahead on his horse. Jake talked incessantly about New Mexico, about Kansas City, about anything that came to his head. Morgan listened and bounced on the wagon seat, and watched Seth's broad back. Morgan realized that no matter how big the horse was, Seth would probably make it look like a pony. "It would probably take a draft horse to look big in proportion," she muttered.

"What was that?" Jake looked toward her.

"I was looking at Seth," she answered, blushing.

Jake smiled, showing his three teeth, and began to talk about Seth. "Sure glad that boy got married. Tired of running that ranch myself while he keeps going into town for a woman." Then it was his turn to be embarrassed, "Uh, sorry, Mrs., uh, Morgan."

Morgan hadn't thought about the possibility of another Cynthia waiting for him in New Mexico. "Jake, does Seth have a girl in New Mexico?"

"Well, there is one that seems to have set her cap for him. A young lady whose father owns quite a bit of Santa Fe." Jake looked at Morgan and grinned. "She'd fill out that big dress of yourn and half of another one like it. You sure are a mighty *little* thing."

Jake was so natural that Morgan felt no resentment. "I guess Seth likes women like that — big, I mean."

The smile vanished from his face. "I can't say as he *likes* any women. He seems more to use them than anything. Oh, he's nice to them, and they sure like him, but he never seems to think anything about any of them after he leaves them." He paused. "Now me," and his grin returned, "I've been in love so many times." He laughed and slapped his thigh. "I remember a gal in Louisville once, had black hair and eyes. I was so in love with her that I couldn't eat for three weeks. Thought I'd die without her." He seemed to enjoy just thinking about the woman.

"What happened?" Morgan asked.

"Oh . . . she left me for some rich guy, but she'll never forget me, that much I know."

Morgan was quiet awhile.

"You don't think Seth's ever been in love?"

"Well, I used to work for his daddy, and I've been around Seth since he was about nine years old, and as far as I know, he ain't never been in love. Too bad, too. You miss a lot in life when you don't fall madly in love at least once a year."

Morgan was quiet after that, just sitting, listening to Jake and watching Seth move to the rhythm of his horse.

The first days were easy. At night they stopped at local inns where a hot meal and warm, clean beds awaited them. Seth always made sure Morgan had her own room, while he and Jake had another.

Seth and Morgan stayed away from one

another as much as possible, speaking only when necessary.

A few days before they reached Kansas City, Jake began to tell Morgan about someone named Frank. Jake seemed to have a lot of respect for Frank and was glad Frank would be traveling with them.

"Will anyone else be going with us?"

It was a minute before she could understand Jake's answer.

"Joaquín. What a nice name."

Jake muttered something unintelligible.

Kansas City was much more rustic than Louisville, and Morgan liked it. The people all seemed to be dressed for necessity rather than for fashion.

"Seth!" A man as big as Seth came up behind him as Seth was tying his horse in front of the hotel. They shook hands vigorously, obviously glad to see one another. "And Jake, you little old toad, you're still as ugly as ever." His eyes stopped at Morgan.

Seth followed his eyes. "This is my wife, Morgan." Seth's voice held no warmth.

Frank reacted immediately to Seth's voice. He knew something was wrong. Frank held out a tentative hand and helped Morgan from the wagon. "I am pleased to meet you, Mrs. Colter."

Morgan smiled, lighting up her face. "Jake has told me a lot about you — everything except your last name."

He smiled back at Morgan. "It's Greyson, but everyone calls me Frank."

"If you call me Morgan, it's a deal."

Smiling, they started into the hotel. As they were signing in, Seth said to Morgan, "My shy little wife sometimes loses her shyness. Do you think she saves it just for her husband?"

Morgan was startled by the hostility in his voice, but before she could say anything, he had turned to talk to the hotel manager.

Jake had overheard Seth and whispered to Morgan, "He's jealous," and then followed Frank up the stairs.

Seth turned back to Morgan, taking her arm and leading her away from the desk. "They have no adjoining rooms. In fact, they have only one room left in the hotel. I could bunk with Frank and Jake."

Morgan's eyes went to Seth's. Somehow, she did not want everyone knowing the truth about her relationship with Seth. She would rather people thought theirs was a normal marriage.

Seth was talking. "Jake already knows. But if you'd rather Frank didn't, just say so and I'll arrange something."

Morgan lowered her eyes. "I'd rather he didn't know." Maybe it was her imagination, but she thought she saw relief on Seth's face.

Seth escorted her to a small but clean room with one rather narrow bed which took up most of the space.

Morgan sat on the bed, as there was nowhere else to sit. She watched Seth. He ignored her and began to undress.

"Seth, what are you doing?"

"I am planning to wash some of this trail dust off me before dinner." He turned toward her. "You don't have to watch if you don't want to, you know."

She moved to the other side of the bed and looked out at the busy street, but she had difficulty concentrating.

He had hardly spoken to her since the last night at his parents' house. She tried to picture Trahern House, but saw only Seth's angry eyes. She heard Nora's voice saying that Morgan would fall in love with Seth.

"Morgan?"

She turned. Seth was standing so close to her. She felt like crying. Unwanted tears gathered in her eyes.

Seth dropped to his knees beside her. She was such a child. "What's the matter, little one? If you don't want me to stay here, I won't. I'll find someplace else."

His voice was so gentle . . . She *couldn't* be in love with him! She'd known him less than a month. Why was Seth's image so clear, and the image of Trahern House so blurred?

The tears started, and she couldn't stop them. She turned and buried her head in the pillow and began to let out the tears that had been locked inside for so long.

Seth knelt by the bed. After one puzzled look, he lifted Morgan into his arms and sat on the bed, leaning back against the headboard. He just held her and stroked her hair while she cried. After a while, as the sobs began to subside, Morgan began to hear Seth's voice.

"Shh, *mi querida,* be still. You are safe. No one will harm you. I won't bother you again. You have nothing to fear."

Morgan raised her head to look at him, but he gently forced her head back onto his chest and began to hum a tune. It felt so warm, so sweet to be near him, to be protected. Maybe, if she loved him, he would love her in return one day?

When Morgan awoke it was daylight, and she was in the bed, fully clothed, with a blanket over her. The last thing she remembered was lying in Seth's arms hearing him sing to her.

As she washed her face and combed her hair, she realized she was ravenously hungry.

Jake knocked on her door, and they started down the stairs together for breakfast. She wanted to know where Seth was, where he had slept, what he was doing.

At the foot of the stairs was one of the handsomest men Morgan had ever seen. His blue-black hair was perfectly ordered. His clothes were impeccable and in the best of taste. He looked like a picture Morgan had once seen in a magazine of Aunt Lacey's, a picture of a man for whom a young woman had left her husband and children. Of course, the man in the magazine had turned out to be bad. But this man was smiling up at her and was now extending his hand to her.

"Ah, this must be the lovely bride."

Morgan felt Jake's arm stiffen under her hand.

Ignoring Jake, the handsome man took Morgan's arm as if they had known one another for years.

"Allow me, Morgan. I may call you that, seeing that we are to be such close companions."

"I . . . uh," Morgan stammered. The man

certainly was charming. Morgan found herself standing a little straighter.

He laughed slightly, showing perfect white teeth. "Excuse me, I am Antonio Joaquín Santiago de Montoya y García, at your service. You may call me Joaquín." He took her hand from his arm, just as they were entering the dining room, and held it to his lips, his eyes never once leaving hers.

Morgan had not yet said a word. The man's eyes had a hypnotic effect. A loud laugh that she recognized as Frank's reached her, and she turned toward the sound quickly. Seth looked at her with malice. Why was Seth looking at her like that? She moved to the table and seated herself.

Frank laughed again. "Well, Joaquín, it looks like you won another of the ladies. But I reckon you better stay away from this one. If you don't, you'll be tangling with ol' Seth here."

Seth looked at his empty plate. They had waited for Morgan before ordering. "I don't put chains on my wife."

Joaquín was very calm, showing no awareness of the tension at the table. He looked at the four other faces. Seth and Jake were angry, Frank laughing, and Morgan was looking at Seth's bent head with an expression of puzzlement and helplessness.

Joaquín thought, "So that is how it is. For some reason, there is a very willing wife but a not-so-willing husband."

A keen observer of people, Joaquín liked to file bits of information away for future reference. Right now, he needed to know more about Seth.

"Seth, you must tell me where you met such a pretty young woman. Ah, but then you have always had such incredible luck."

Seth seemed to regain his composure, but he lost none of his furious look. Morgan did not know whether his anger was directed at her or at Joaquín.

"Morgan's father lived in New Mexico for years." Seth deliberately turned the conversation to a safer topic.

The three other men all turned interested eyes on Morgan.

"I haven't seen my father since I was a baby. I only heard recently that he had died."

"It's too bad he had to go before seeing his lovely daughter again." Joaquín raised Morgan's hand to his lips once more. "May I offer my sincere sympathy?"

Jake, who had been quiet through the whole awkward scene, nearly jumped at Seth. "What's the matter with you, boy!"

Seth leaned back against his chair and

smiled at Morgan. It was a cold smile, and it did not spread to his eyes. "My little wife is quite capable of saying no to a man when she chooses to."

Morgan rose, very slowly and steadily, avoiding Seth's eyes. "Excuse me. I don't think I am hungry after all." She turned and left the room after assuring Joaquín that she needed no escort.

By the time she reached her room, she was so angry that her entire body was shaking. She sat on the bed. There was a great deal of thinking to do. Nothing was going as she had planned.

Morgan spent the day in the shops while the men loaded the wagons. She paused before a window, taken by a shiny dress that caught the sunlight. She was drawn inside, hypnotized, her eyes never leaving the dress.

"May I help you with anything?" a soft voice asked.

Morgan was startled, embarrassed at having been caught staring. The dress was scarlet, the neckline was cut very low, and there was an inch and a half of very fine burgundy lace across the bodice. What wasn't entirely revealed by the low neck would be just barely covered by the open-work lace. Above the waist, just under the lace bodice, was a satin ribbon that tied in the back in the Empire style. The thin fabric was tightly fitted below the ribbon until it reached the waist, where it tapered into a long, flowing, bell skirt. The sleeves were puffy and reached only to the middle of the upper arms.

The woman followed Morgan's eyes and began to visualize how the blond young woman would look in the elegant red dress. It would suit her perfectly. The woman continued staring at Morgan for another moment. "I am Miss Satterfield. That dress was made for you."

Morgan heard the earnestness in her voice. "Yes," Morgan whispered, "yes."

Recovering herself, Miss Satterfield said, "That dress has the strangest history. Last year a young woman came in here and asked for a job as a needlewoman. Of course, I couldn't hire her without seeing some of her work, and I told her that. She seemed really excited when she left, and came back in a couple of hours with this dress. I could see her needlework was excellent, even if the dress was forty years out of fashion. She said she had copied the style from a book. I never did understand where she got such fabric as that, but I do know she tatted the lace herself."

Both women stared at the dress for a moment. "Would you like to try it on?" Her eyes gleamed.

Morgan, who had never cared much about clothing, remembered wondering, on the night of Cynthia Ferguson's ball, how she would look in red satin. She was certain the dress would fit.

"No, I don't think I'll try it on. But I would like it wrapped, please, very plainly. I'm leaving on a wagon tomorrow, and the package can't be too large."

"All right."

As Morgan left the store, she wondered what had caused her to do such a thing. She could never wear the dress. All the way back to the hotel, she told herself she should return the dress at once.

Morgan had lunch with Frank and Jake. Seth and Joaquín were busy in town. She was glad, as she didn't want to see either one of them.

At dinner, Seth avoided her eyes, and she was kept busy trying to avoid Joaquín. He was so charming, and seemed so concerned with her welfare.

Seth didn't come to their room that night. She lay awake, gazing out the window at the stars, wondering where he was sleeping.

CHAPTER FIVE

Everyone told Morgan that the first part of the trip was the easiest, but to her it was unbelievably difficult. The days were long and hot, and the nights were too short. The first week she was so tired she could hardly speak. Always, someone made a bed for her under the wagon. She never knew who it was. She was usually too tired to eat, even to wash. She wanted only to lie down and be still, to quiet her body after the jolting of the wagon. But the hard, cold ground gave her no relief.

By the eighth day she began to become aware of her surroundings. She became used to the long days and the hard bed. For the first time, she sat by the fire and drank a cup of Jake's coffee.

"Well, it's nice to see you back with us." Frank smiled down at Morgan.

Morgan returned his smile.

"It is always nice to have a beautiful

woman near, no matter where one is."

Joaquín's flattery made Morgan uneasy. She couldn't help being pleased, but Seth always seemed to be scowling in the background. As Seth tossed down a load of firewood, he growled, "Well, maybe my wife will be able to help with some of the work around here now rather than letting the men wait on her."

Morgan gave him what she hoped was a very sweet smile and said, "Of course, Seth, I'd like very much to help." She wasn't going to allow his gruffness to upset her.

Seth tossed the blankets at her. "Then you make the beds tonight."

At her puzzled look, he motioned her to the wagon. He showed her how to make the blankets into a passable bed. This was her place. She knew it was because she had crawled under the wagon between the blankets to sleep for the last several nights. She watched silently as Seth spread another bed under the wagon hardly a foot from her own sleeping place.

"What — ?" she started.

Seth grinned at her. "That is your husband's bed. You have been asleep each night when I came to bed, but you've slept very close to me every night." Suddenly his grin faded, and he left her abruptly.

That night, Morgan was very aware of Seth's big body spread out so close to her own. She could hear his slow, deep breathing. The sound made her feel safe.

The days began to form into a pleasant routine. Seth was still cool to Morgan, but his hostility had lessened. Joaquín always seemed to be near Morgan. Whenever she needed anything, there he was.

They stopped early one night at a place called Council Grove.

"Can you shoot a rifle, Morgan?" Seth asked her.

"No."

"You're going to learn. You may need to know how later on."

They made their way through the trees to a little clearing. Seth marked a target on the tree, and then stepped back.

"Now, put the rifle into your shoulder like this," he demonstrated.

"I didn't realize it was so heavy."

"Here, I'll show you." Seth stood in back of her and his powerful arms encircled her, his hands covering hers.

His body felt good to her. He had not touched her since they had left Kentucky. Feeling his warmth, she snuggled against him.

Seth bent his head next to hers to show

her how to sight the rifle. Her hair was sweet, her neck was slightly damp from the heat of the day. As he looked from the rifle to her, he felt her move against him and involuntarily he felt his breath quicken. Her small, round bottom pressed against his groin caused his manhood to stir.

"Damn you!" He abruptly dropped his arms and stepped away, turning his back to her.

"Seth?" She had no idea what had made him so angry. She went to him, put her hand on his arm. He jerked away from her touch.

Angrily, she turned from him. "My mother was right. Men are incomprehensible creatures. One minute I think we can be friends, and the next minute you're cursing me." She started back to the camp, each step quicker than the last, each step angrier than the one before.

Seth, recovering himself, reached her in a few long strides. His eyes and voice were as angry as hers. The hand on her arm hurt her as he swung her around to face him, the sun blazing behind him.

"Your mother! If your mother had been any kind of mother at all, she wouldn't have poisoned your mind. If she'd had your interests in mind, she would have taught you about men and women, rather than imprisoning you in that big house like a nun."

She jerked her arm from his grasp. "How dare you!" She spat her fury at him. "And your behavior proves she was right in everything she told me about men. I can't talk to you, I can't even be near you without you becoming angry with me for no reason." She started quickly down the path toward the wagons.

Again Seth was next to her, even more angry. He stood in front of her. Through clenched teeth he said, "You're damn right I can't be near you. What do you expect when you wiggle against me?"

"Wiggle? What are you talking about?" She looked at him with hatred.

Quickly, his big hands reached out and encircled the back of her head, pulling her lips to his. His kiss was gentle and searching. Morgan had the drowning sensation again. She felt her body go limp and at the same time she could feel every part of her react. She reached out, her hands touching his waist, feeling the firm, hard muscles of his stomach with her thumbs.

Gently, he drew back from her and looked down at her closed eyes, the delicate blue veins showing through the lids. Her eyelashes were long and thick. His voice was a whisper. "Your mother should have explained about men being very sensitive. That's why I can't be near you without being angry at not being able to have you."

Her anger was gone now, but many years of training by her mother cried out in her head. The anger was replaced by a look of determination and arrogance. "My mother was correct when she told me that men could not love, that they cared only for horses and business and that they used women. Since I have met you, Mr. Colter, you have shown me less consideration and friendliness than you show your horse. Now, if you'll excuse me, I have some work to do at the wagons."

She left him standing alone.

"What is it, my pretty little dove?" Joaquín's voice was soft and very close.

Morgan was leaning against a tree, trying to fight the tears that threatened.

She sniffed and smiled nervously up at Joaquín. "I guess I don't understand men."

"Ah, but men are very easy to understand. It is women who are mysterious. It is women who control men."

"*Control* men! I don't even seem to be able to talk to one."

"A lover's tiff. Soon you will make up, and then you will be happy again."

She took Joaquín's arm and he escorted her back to the wagons.

The next day Frank took over Morgan's shooting lessons. Seth avoided her.

One day as Joaquín and Morgan returned from a spring, both laughing, Seth met them on the pathway. His eyes showed amusement.

"My little wife seems to enjoy your company, Joaquín. She is usually not so friendly with men."

Joaquín looked from one to another. "Morgan is an enjoyable person. I envy any man with such a wife. Excuse me, I have some things I need to do before our journey tomorrow."

Silently, Morgan started down the path. Seth walked beside her.

"Look at that!" Seth pointed to the trees.

"I don't see anything."

Seth moved behind her, his hands on her shoulders, and turned her to see a brilliant, red cardinal sitting quietly on a branch. They both smiled.

"I was just going for a walk. After all day on a horse, it feels good to stretch my legs. Want to come?"

She smiled up at him. He stretched his hand to her and she took it.

"Come on, then." They ran, Morgan stumbling along behind to keep up with him.

"This greenness reminds me of Kentucky. But we'll leave it behind soon enough."

"Tell me more about New Mexico. Is it really flat and barren?"

"It's not flat at all. To some people it seems barren, but I don't think of it that way. The deserts and the mountains have always seemed like enchanted places to me."

They rounded a curve in the stream to a secluded area where the trees overhung the banks.

"That water looks good after the dust of the trail. I think I'll take a swim. Like to join me?" His eyes twinkled.

Before she could answer, Seth had removed his boots and shirt. His muscles were enormous and stood out easily. Morgan watched, fascinated.

As he started to remove his pants, she gasped, "Seth . . ." He smiled, "Remember, *mi querida,* we are married. I see nothing wrong in undressing in front of one's wife. Anyway, you could turn your head."

She turned to stare at a tree trunk behind her until she heard a loud splash.

"The water's so warm. Sure you won't join me?"

She longed to get into the water, to get rid of the trail dust. Sponge baths in the wagon never got her really clean.

"No, I'll just sit on the bank and put my feet in." She watched as Seth swam a ways down the creek. His back and arms were powerful in the water. She could see him clearly as he glided across the water: his arms and back, and then tapering to his buttocks and the tops of his thighs. Morgan shivered as she watched. She did not go in. Seth returned a bit later, and she walked ahead as he dressed.

"It's all right. You can come back now. I won't shock you any longer." His hand reached out for hers. "Sit down a minute — I'd like to dry off." He had not put his shirt back on but was using it to towel his wet hair.

She sat down, leaning against a tree. Seth sat beside her, then turned and lay his head in her lap. He closed his eyes.

"Seth, talk to me about you. You know so much about me. Jake has told me about you, but I want you to tell me about yourself."

His hands were crossed on his chest. She moved a hand to remove a leaf from his stomach and then left her hand there. His skin was so warm. Her other hand twisted a curl of his hair, now very gray in the sunlight.

"What did Jake tell you about me?" Seth was keenly aware of Morgan's hands.

"He said he didn't think you had ever been in love, that you only used women." She paused. "And he said there were lots of women who wanted you to marry them."

Seth smiled. "I guess that's true. But I figure most women want to get married. I just happened to be single." He snuggled his head deeper into her lap, and his hands covered hers, both pairs of hands lying on his chest.

"What about the other part — *have* you ever been in love?"

He took a minute to answer. "I guess not. At least I've never met a woman I wanted to be with for the rest of my life. I usually grow tired of a woman after a very short time." He raised her hand to kiss her palm, his eyes still closed. He felt Morgan jump slightly at the touch of his lips.

"What about your girl in New Mexico?" He looked at her, then closed his eyes again. His cheeks showed long dimples from trying to suppress his laughter.

"Jake told you a lot, didn't he? Marilyn's

very pretty and very . . . uh . . . obliging, but no, I'm not in love with her."

Morgan leaned her head against the tree and smiled, feeling very happy.

"Seth, you said my mother was wrong — that she should have taught me about men and women." She paused. Seth remained silent, but listened closely. "I don't understand about men. And I don't understand you at all. You are sometimes so kind, and then sometimes you look like you hate me. Then again, there are times, like now, when I feel I've known you all my life."

Seth's eyes were serious. "Yes, little one, sometimes I don't understand myself. Sometimes I hate you, and sometimes I want to pick you up and toss you in the air. Right now, I just want to be still." He closed his eyes again.

Morgan relaxed against the tree again and then she whispered, "Do you ever want to toss Marilyn into the air?"

Seth roared. "It would take a bigger man than me to toss Marilyn Wilson in the air. I can see you're not going to let me rest. Let's go and see what Jake has for supper."

He turned over and studied her for a minute. "God, I hate the way you hide your hair." He reached behind her, unfastened the knot of hair, and pulled it forward over her shoulders. "That's better."

He stood up, took Morgan's hand, and pulled her up beside him. She gazed up at him with complete trust.

"Oh, Morgan," he groaned, "how am I going to keep my hands off you for a whole year?"

Morgan smiled. "That's easy — if you can't catch me, you can't touch me!" she called over her shoulder as she ran down the trail.

Seth paused to grab his shirt, stuffing it into his belt, and took off after her.

Just before they reached the wagons, Seth sent one long arm shooting out to encircle Morgan's waist. She struggled, kicking and hitting against him while laughing uncontrollably. "Can't catch you? You're no bigger than a mosquito," he teased.

He lifted her above his head and turned her around in the air several times. Morgan screamed, "No, no," repeatedly, choking with laughter.

Seth then threw her over his shoulder, slapping her firmly on the behind when she struggled. He walked into the camp carrying her this way.

Jake and Frank looked up from the fire.

"I thought maybe we was being attacked by Indians." Jake frowned. Seth just grinned.

Embarrassed now, Morgan whispered into Seth's back, "Seth, put me down."

As Seth crossed in front of them, going toward the wagon, Morgan heard Jake tell Frank, "At least that boy knows how women ought to be handled."

No one saw Joaquín standing in the shadows, a scowl on his face.

Seth put Morgan down on the far side of the wagon, away from the campfire. Her back was against the wagon, and one of his arms was on each side of her, closing her in.

"Seth, that was awful. What will Jake and Frank think of me?" She tried to scold, but she was too close to laughter to sound sincere.

He moved his face closer to hers. "Keep looking at me like that, and I may do more than throw you over my shoulder."

She hadn't realized how she had been looking at his bare chest, the soft, curling hair on the bronze skin. She blushed and looked away. As she did so, he bent and kissed her on the ear. His lips, so moist, so sweet, caused her to turn toward him again.

"Morgan, sweet one," he whispered. His arms closed around her shoulders, and she put her arms around his waist. He held her, without speaking, for some minutes.

Morgan could feel his skin against the side of her face, could feel his hand gently stroking her head and tangling into her hair. Her mind was blank, she felt only security and contentment while being so close to this man.

He was the first to pull away. "You're a witch, you know that?" His voice was husky. "Go out there and get me something to eat, like a good little wife."

"Aren't you coming?" She didn't want to leave him.

"Morgan, you have a lot to learn about men. I'll stay back here a minute or so until I'm more presentable for company." He glanced downward.

Morgan followed his eyes to the large bulge in his pants. "Oh," she murmured, unnerved, and turned and walked quickly to the campfire.

Joaquín was very quiet that night. He usually managed to sit close to Morgan and always found ways of slipping compliments to her. But tonight Morgan had no ears for Joaquín. He noticed that every look, every gesture, was directed toward Seth.

Once, Seth glanced at Joaquín and was startled to see a look of undisguised hatred. At Seth's glance, Joaquín quickly recovered his countenance. For a few seconds, Seth puzzled over what he had seen on Joaquín's face, but soon dismissed it. Many things about the Spaniard were strange to him.

Joaquín Montoya was the head of a very wealthy ranch south of Seth's more modest ranch. Seth seldom thought about Joaquín except for an occasional feeling of distaste for his too-smooth manners. Of course, Joaquín's beautiful sister, Lena, was another matter. The first time Seth kissed her, she bit his lip nearly through, and then threw back her head and laughed. Making love to her was like making love to a wildcat. His back had been sore for a week, and her teeth had made a wound on his shoulder that had taken two weeks to heal. Seth did not think about the Montoyas very often.

Seth stayed around the campfire to talk of plans for the trip, while Morgan went to her bed under the wagon. She lay with her hands behind her head and looked up at the underpinnings of the wagon. She thought of the day, and the remembrance of Seth, laughing with him, touching him, being so near all day, made her skin glow and her breath come deeper and quicker.

When Seth came to his bed, so near to hers, she stretched out a hand to touch him.

"Oh, no, *mi querida,*" he whispered. He kissed her fingertips, and put her hand by her side. "I don't think I could stand any more kissing and touching today. I am only human. Go to sleep now, and don't test me anymore." He turned onto his stomach, and before long Morgan heard his quiet, even breathing.

The next night they camped at Diamond Springs. Seth took Morgan's hand and led her to see the spring flowing from a large, hollow rock. The water was clear and cool. They lugged the heavy water barrels back to camp, laughing at one another.

Morgan washed her hair in buckets of the clear, cool, spring water. As she sat in front of the fire, turning so her hair would dry, the four men watched.

"I never saw hair like that in my life," Jake murmured.

"My little girl has hair almost that color, but not so much of it," Frank added.

Seth grabbed a handful of the hair, jerking Morgan around. "I think I should get you out of here before I have to fight for you." Seth pulled Morgan to her feet.

"Seth, you're hurting me."

"If I didn't know better, I'd think you weren't a lady. That's a nice trick — to sit by a fire and spread all this around you." His hands were buried in her hair.

He led her into the dark woods, away from

the camp.

"Seth," she said angrily, "I don't know what you're talking about."

"I don't either. I guess it's just that you look better to me every day. I'm beginning to think about you a lot. I can't even take a trip to the bushes without wishing you were with me."

Morgan felt her heart beat harder. "Seth . . ." She lifted her arms to him, and their lips met. He set off a fire in her. Her lips moved with his, feeling his tongue touch her own. Her arms pulled him closer. One of his legs parted her own, and she could feel his thigh, so hard and so exciting.

He kissed her neck, and she could feel his teeth making small nibbling bites on her skin. Chills went up her spine and down the backs of her thighs.

From a long way off, she heard Frank calling for Seth. Neither of them wanted to hear it.

"Damn him!" Seth muttered in her ear. "I have to go, sweet. Maybe Frank is your guardian angel."

"Maybe he's the devil," Morgan whispered under her breath.

Seth drew back, surprised. Then he chuckled. "I think I'm going to like spending a year with you." He kissed her on the forehead and left.

Morgan walked closer to the camp and stood, watching Seth as he talked to Frank. She didn't want to think, but she knew she wanted him to come back to her in the cool forest. Maybe I do love him, she thought. I wonder if it is possible to fall in love so quickly.

After waiting some minutes, she gradually became aware of the chill in the air and returned to camp.

A rider had come to their camp, and Seth was leaving that night with him to scout the area ahead, to find the best way of crossing Cottonwood Creek.

As he packed his gear, he told Morgan he'd see her at the crossing in two days.

He held her in his arms a few moments before leaving, and kissed her gently. "Think about me while I'm gone?" His eyes were laughing.

"Maybe." They smiled happily at one another, and then he was gone.

At supper that night, Joaquín was especially attentive. "Possibly you would walk with me after supper. I'm sure my old friend Seth would want me to make sure his wife was entertained."

"Morgan needs to help me clear up the camp," Jake snapped.

Joaquín turned cold eyes on Jake, "I don't believe Morgan usually does that, and I don't see why she should now. May I escort you?" He offered his arm to Morgan.

They walked silently in the moonlight for awhile. "How did you come to marry Seth, Morgan?"

Morgan was startled. She had hoped that no one other than Jake knew of the marriage arrangement.

Before she could answer, Joaquín continued. "I ask because I am an observer of people, and I see that there is something wrong between the two of you. I know that each night Seth sleeps away from his little bride." He touched Morgan's cheek. "If I had a bride so lovely, I would not have ridden away from her, no matter how many creeks were in danger of flooding."

She jerked away from his touch. "Don't say anything about Seth! I owe him a great deal and he is good to me."

"I am sorry. I only meant to be your friend, to tell you that if you need someone to talk to, I will listen."

She looked at him closely. His slim, smooth handsomeness was so different from Seth's huge maleness. "I'm sorry for getting angry, Joaquín. Thank you for the offer. I will remember it."

■ ■ ■ ■

Seth rode all that night, thinking of Morgan's softness, her eager returning of his kisses. He shook himself out of his reverie and spurred his horse on. He wanted to get back to Morgan.

Joaquín was never far from Morgan's side for those two days. He asked no more questions about Morgan and Seth's relationship. Instead, he concentrated on being a pleasant companion and on making Morgan forget Seth.

Joaquín and Morgan went to gather water. Morgan gazed into the water and remembered the day before, when she had sat by the stream and held Seth's head in her lap.

Joaquín laughed quietly. "You look like a nymph by the water, looking for her lover. Tell me, little Morgan, what is on your mind?"

"I was just thinking about the water and its coolness." She smiled and looked away from him. "Joaquín, have you ever been in love?"

He scrutinized her carefully before answering. "Yes. Once when I was very young."

"Did it change you a lot? I mean . . . did

you seem to forget everything and everyone else except the one you loved?"

"Yes. It was like that." His eyes clouded as he looked away.

They were silent a moment. "But Jake said you weren't married."

"No." His voice was low. "She was killed in a riding accident a few days before our marriage." His voice had hardened. In a whisper, he said, "I died with her."

Morgan was embarrassed by something in Joaquín's voice, and remained silent.

"Morgan, we are too serious. It is a beautiful sunset, and I am alone with a beautiful woman, and yet I talk of serious things."

"Joaquín, I'm not beautiful. Surely you can see that." Her voice was teasing and light.

"I have seen many women, and I know you could be beautiful. The last few days I have seen a look in your eyes that has changed you. Too often you are sad, and you try to hide it."

Seth had ridden most of two nights to return to Morgan. He was not used to the feeling he had. He longed to see her, to hold her in his arms, to see her run to him.

He thundered into the camp and jumped off his horse, throwing the reins to Jake.

"Where is she?"

"At the stream." Seth ran down the path toward the stream as Jake watched. Jake had never seen such a look on Seth's face. "That young 'un has finally fallen in love," he muttered and grinned. Then his smile changed to a frown. "God, I hope that Montoya isn't up to some of his tricks with that little girl."

As Joaquín was telling Morgan that she could be beautiful, he put his fingertips under her chin, lifting her lips to his, and bent his head to hers.

Seth entered the clearing just as Joaquín kissed Morgan. It took a second for him to take in the scene. He turned and left.

Morgan turned to see Seth's broad back retreating into the woods. She forgot Joaquín.

"Seth!" She was surprised when he did not respond. She gathered up her long skirts and ran after him. Again he did not turn when she called. She caught up to him, grabbed his arm and planted herself in front of him.

For a second Seth nearly grabbed her to him. Then he jerked his arm from her grasp and angrily started down the path.

Morgan did not see Joaquín looking on with an amused smile.

"Seth! What's wrong with you?"

135

He turned toward her with a look of hate. His voice was low as if he were controlling a great rage. "What's wrong with me! I rode for two nights to be here with you and what do I see?" He jerked his head toward the stream. He paused and took a deep breath. His outward anger seemed to recede, but his eyes still blazed.

"I am sorry. It is my fault. I should have expected nothing. You offered nothing more than any other woman." He extended a hand and cupped her breast, hidden under so much fabric. He was momentarily surprised at its fullness.

She inhaled quickly and jerked back from his touch.

"Isn't that what you want, my dear, if not from me then from your handsome friend back there? It's such a shame that I found you out — you are such an accomplished actress. You almost had me believing in your innocence."

He turned and left her then. Morgan was totally bewildered. An actress? She remembered how she had run to him, eager for him. And then she remembered Joaquín's kiss. Was *that* what had made him so angry? She must go to Seth, reassure him that Joaquín meant nothing to her.

Seth was unsaddling his horse.

"Seth . . ." her voice was gentle, "let me talk to you."

"We have nothing to say to one another."

"No, Seth. I realize why you are angry. You saw Joaquín and me, didn't you?" Her voice had a pleading note. "It meant nothing, Seth. Not like when you kiss me."

He turned to her, his lips snarling, his eyes cold. "As I have said before, I have no chains on you. You may kiss whomever you wish. As for comparing my kisses to Joaquín's, that is the trick of a whore." His laugh was ugly. "Stay away from me. I want no more part in any of your games."

CHAPTER SIX

"Jake, what's a whore?"

Jake nearly dropped the skillet of bacon. "What . . . ?" he stammered.

"I've heard the word before, and I wondered what it meant." It had been two days since Seth had called her that. Having lived alone with her mother and then in the very sheltered company of her Aunt Lacey and Uncle Horace, she had never before been exposed to such talk.

"Well . . . it's a woman who gives her . . . uh . . . favors to a lot of men," was Jake's embarrassed reply. "Why'd you want to ask me that?"

Morgan couldn't tell him about Seth's remark. "I just heard it somewhere and wondered." She sat by the fire mending a tear in Seth's shirt. She had seen very little of him in the last two days. He and Frank had spent a lot of time fishing for catfish, and Morgan had begun to gather buffalo chips for the fire. There were no more trees now, only the plains. Morgan found the countryside ugly and hoped New Mexico wasn't as flat or as barren as the prairie was.

The next day they crossed Turkey Creek. Morgan watched as Seth removed his shirt and struggled with the horses to get them up the steep, muddy bank. She was fascinated by the magnificence of his enormous body. She remembered his arms around her, the way he had so easily lifted her and spun her around. She trembled, remembering.

That afternoon the rain started. It came down so hard that Jake could hardly see to drive the horses. Morgan sat on the wagon seat, drenched.

"Get inside the wagon, you little fool!" Seth's shout could hardly be heard. Water dripped down his hat and across his poncho.

"No!"

He lunged at her, and she quickly went through the opening into the dry wagon. She could see drops of water that had formed on the underside of the canvas.

Now that she was inside the wagon, she was very glad that Seth had made her come in. She removed the big dress and dried herself. It felt good to rub her skin until it glowed. She looked for something warm to put on and found a robe of Seth's in the bottom of a trunk. The robe was enormous on her but very soft and warm. She stretched out on the narrow wagon cot and was soon asleep.

Voices awakened her. It was night, and the wagon had stopped rolling, but the rain was coming down as hard as ever. She heard Seth's voice shouting, very close to the mouth of the wagon. The end of the wagon canvas was opened, and Seth climbed inside.

"Get up, wife, and perform some of your wifely duties." His voice had a leer in it.

She hurried to obey, nearly tripping on the long robe as she did so.

"What do you have on?" he demanded.

"It's your robe. I hope you don't mind, but it was cold."

He looked at her, his blue eyes clear in the lantern light. "Help me out of these wet clothes. I'm so tired I'm not sure I could get them off by myself."

She was glad to be near him, glad to have him speaking to her again. As she removed his boots and then his wet socks, she kept asking herself where her pride was.

She dried his feet briskly, massaging the toes until some warmth returned to them. She unbuttoned his shirt.

Seth leaned back on his hands and suffered her ministrations as if he were a small boy. The front of the robe gaped open and he saw the rounding and the cleavage of her breasts. Her hair fell now, cascading around her shoulders and down her back. It glowed in the dim light.

As she finished unbuttoning his shirt, she put her arms around his waist so she could pull the shirt free of his pants. He looked down at the top of her head.

When she had removed his shirt, she began rubbing him with the towel, briskly so that he was warmed by the action.

Morgan was trying not to think of what she was doing, trying not to look at Seth's massive arms and the mass of dark gold, curly hair on his chest. She rubbed the towel over his hard, flat, stomach muscles and on his back.

As she finished, Seth began unbuckling his belt to remove his pants.

"Seth," she said hesitantly.

He grinned at her, knowing what she was about to say. "All right." He took the towel from her.

Morgan sat on the bed as Seth removed his pants and began to dry off. His back was to her, and she tried not to look, but his body was beautiful, like the Greek statues of athletes she had seen in a Louisville museum. But Seth was about twice the size of the statues.

As she looked him over, he turned toward her, and she found herself staring at his manhood, something she had never seen before. She quickly looked away.

"My innocent little bride is quickly losing her innocence. Since you've told me whose kisses you like better, tell me — whose body do you like better?"

She had always tried to be friends with him. A few days ago she had thought maybe she could be in love with him. Now, because of one silly, accidental little kiss, he taunted her cruelly. All right, she could hate too.

"I like a gentleman better than an animal who can't even be civil," she spat.

"Well, the little girl drops her cloak of shyness. Tell me, miss, is there twenty-five thousand dollars to be collected for this marriage, or is that just another one of your stories? Possibly it was a ploy to get me to give a name to someone else's bastard?"

"I don't know what you're talking about!"

"It seems to me that ever since I met you, you have been teasing me, leading me slowly to your bed. You profess innocence, yet your kisses have a passion that belies innocence. It just occurred to me that maybe you are carrying a child, and that this little whore's game of yours is a way to convince me that I am the father."

Morgan listened in total astonishment. She said softly, "You have been around women like that too long. I will tell you this again, and if you do not believe me, then I cannot help it. I asked you to marry me so I could collect my inheritance, and for no other reason. I kissed you with such passion because, for a while, I thought I could love you. I am sorry I was such a fool. At the end of this year you will get your twenty-five thousand dollars, and I never want to see you again. Until that time, I suggest we stay away from one another as much as possible." She turned from him.

"You are right. I don't believe you. I think there is another reason why you trapped me into marrying you." He took a step toward her, a towel about his hips. He grabbed her hair in his hand and jerked her head back. "From now on you will perform your wifely duties for me."

She stared at him with hate and not a little fear. "Keep your hands off me."

He laughed and released her head. "I wouldn't touch you if you were the last woman on earth, but you are my property, and for the next year you will obey me. Now lie down."

He laughed again at the fear in her eyes, but not as viciously as the last time. "Did you think I planned to sleep outside in this rain?"

She lay down, as far on the side of the cot as was possible. He removed his towel and stretched out beside her, naked. He pulled the blankets over them, and soon the rain lulled them to sleep.

Seth woke first in the morning. As he looked at her sleeping figure he smiled, and then remembered all he had said the night before. He wanted to kiss her, to hold her close, to make love to her. Then he remembered her with Joaquín. Feeling Morgan snuggle closer to him in her sleep, he slipped out of bed and dressed quickly.

Outside the air was wet and the ground muddy after the heavy rains. After a cold breakfast, they started the day's miserable journey. Morgan gathered chips for the fire.

Joaquín met her in the twilight. "Ah, Morgan, I have been noticing that you look sadder than ever today. Is something wrong?"

Joaquín made her feel good. He noticed her, and cared about her moods.

"Here, let me help you with that." He took the bucket of chips from her. "Remember, I am your friend."

She looked at him and smiled. "Thank

you. Everyone has been so kind, you and Jake and Frank and . . ." She finished uncertainly.

"Your husband is a man of many conflicts. I'm not sure he knows how to love."

"Montoya!"

They both turned to see Seth standing a few feet away.

"If you want to keep that dapper little body of yours in one piece, then you'll stay away from my wife!"

Joaquín's eyes flashed hatred for an instant, and then they cleared to hold amusement. "Goodnight, señor, señora." He smiled at Morgan and left.

Seth glared at Morgan. "It seems I can't leave you alone even for seconds." He extended a hand and caressed the back of her neck.

His touch made her skin come alive. She closed her eyes and leaned into his touch. Seth groaned softly and removed his hand. "Let's eat. Tomorrow we come to the Arkansas River, and we'll need plenty of rest before crossing it."

Seth told her that there were beginning to be signs of Indians, and he thought she'd be safer in the wagon. They'd all start taking turns soon with night watches.

Morgan undressed hurriedly and slipped

into the voluminous nightgown. Seth walked in and caught a glimpse of his wife in front of the lantern, the light from which made the gown transparent. He had a sight of slim legs and a small waist, and then she slipped beneath the covers. He frowned and looked away. "Someday I'm going to tear off her damn clothes and see what she looks like," he muttered under his breath.

"Did you say something?" Morgan asked from under the quilt.

"Just go to sleep." His voice was gruff.

The Arkansas River was wide and shallow with no trees on either side. Yet there was an island in the middle covered with cotton-wood trees.

They stopped early that night, ready to cross the river the next morning. Morgan began to think of a bath and washing her hair. She visualized herself in the water, feeling thoroughly clean for once.

Seth and Frank had gone ahead to look for signs of Indians. Only Jake and Joaquín were left with the wagons. If she hurried, she could have her bath before Seth returned.

Quickly she got soap and a towel together and then told Jake where she was gonig. She saddled a horse and left.

Seth and Frank returned to the camp some time later.

"No sign of Indians, yet," Frank said in answer to Jake's question, "but a lot of buffalo trails. You'd better get your frying pan ready for some buffalo steaks."

"Where's Morgan?" Seth stepped from behind their wagon.

Jake looked up from his cup of coffee. "She went over to that little island to take a bath." He returned to his conversation with Frank.

Seth quickly made sure that Joaquín was in the camp. He was sitting a little aside from the fire, polishing the silver on his ornate saddle. When their eyes met, Joaquín gave Seth a knowing look.

Quickly, Seth straddled his horse and started toward the island. He made his way across the water slowly. He knew there wasn't any danger now, but the idea of his little wife being alone so far from camp made him uneasy.

He led his horse across the sandy island to the far side and tied him near a clump of sweet grass. Morgan's horse was closer to the shoreline. He smiled as he looked down and saw her clothes in a heap on the shore. He saw her a few feet away, standing waist-deep in the water, her back to him. Her hair was full of soap suds. He stepped back into the trees, in a shadow of the fading sunlight.

The sunlight glowed on her skin. It was the color of pale honey. He could hear her humming as she lathered her hair. She turned quickly and extended her arms to the water, and then went below the surface. Seth jerked upright from leaning against the tree, and his breath caught at his first glimpse of Morgan's nude body.

No clothes on earth could hide a body like that. It must be a trick of the setting sun. Morgan had said herself that she had a boy's body. That's just the way she looked sometimes, too, like a young boy in a woman's clothes. How could this lovely creature be his plain Morgan?

Seth stopped thinking when he realized he had not seen Morgan surface. Quickly he ran into the water toward the spot where he had last seen her. He saw one small hand above the surface. He dived under the water and caught her small body in his arms. Her foot was entangled between two logs. He twisted it and it came free.

He carried her to the beach and stretched her out on the sand. As she coughed up the water she had swallowed, she lay in his arms with her eyes closed, half-conscious and breathing jerkily.

She began to awaken, and found herself lying in Seth's arms. It seemed to her, in that moment, that every time she needed help, Seth was there. She smiled up at him and snuggled her head closer to his chest. Seth was too astonished to smile back.

Something in Seth's manner made her realize her situation. She sat up, trying to cover her breasts with her arms. "What happened? Seth, go away!" Her voice was frantic.

"Little wife, you need not try to cover anything — there's nothing I haven't seen." Then, releasing her, he said, "I think you had better get dressed now, because you are very close to losing something other than your life."

They slept in the wagon again that night.

Morgan remembered how she had felt today, awakening beside the water in Seth's arms. For an instant she had felt warm and safe. But she realized now that all he had cared about was seeing her without her clothes. As she drifted off to sleep, she wondered what Seth had thought when he saw her nude. "Probably thought I looked like a boy compared to Cynthia Ferguson," she murmured, before she fell asleep.

In sleep, his arms enfolded her and held

her close to him. Morgan was getting used to having his body near hers, to feeling his breath close to her ear.

Joaquín was the first to notice Seth's and Morgan's new attitude toward one another. He had seen several changes in them already. At one time they had looked at one another with an expression akin to love. Now they never seemed to look at one another at all, though Joaquín had noticed Seth staring wistfully at Morgan a few times.

From the moment Joaquín saw Morgan on the stairs of the hotel in Kansas City, he had known she was beautiful. He had been surprised that it was not treated as a fact, and generally accepted by everyone. It amazed him that all men couldn't see her beauty just because of ill-fitting clothes, and that rather sad look about her. There were times when that expression left her face, and she held her head up, and her shoulders didn't drop. Ah! Then she really was beautiful.

Colter, thought Joaquín, you've had everything all your life, but you won't have it all much longer. No, Nuevo Mexico will soon belong to us again. His lips curled. He lifted his coffee cup to Seth in a simulated toast.

■ ■ ■ ■

After crossing the Arkansas, the group had taken on a tension that hadn't been there before. Seth or Frank constantly rode ahead to check for signs of Indians. Each night the campfires were smaller, and there was little conversation. At the snap of a twig, someone jumped toward the sound with a rifle or gun.

They were over halfway there now, and Morgan longed for the jolting days to stop.

"Morgan, I'm glad to see you holding up so well under the strain," Frank told her one night.

She managed a smile. "My father seemed to think New Mexico was worth all this." Her hand swept toward the blackness outside the little camp.

"Oh, yes, Seth mentioned your father. What was his name? Maybe I knew him."

"Charles Wakefield. He had a ranch somewhere around Albuquerque, I believe."

Joaquín listened carefully. Seth was on watch, and Jake was on the other side of the wagons.

"Charley Wakefield!" Frank nearly shouted, and then quieted his voice. "I knew your father — no wonder I liked you from

151

the moment I saw you. Your father was a hell of a man. It really made me sad to hear he'd left us. Seems like a lot of the good ones die young." He looked at Morgan with a puzzled expression. "I always wondered why Charley never married."

Morgan had never heard her father mentioned in favorable terms before, and she wanted to hear more. She stared at the fire. "Tell me what he was like."

"He was a good man and a hard worker. I didn't know him until he'd been around for some time, but I heard he built up his ranch from practically nothing. It'd take a man a week to ride the borders of his land." Frank smiled. "I worked as a hand for him some years ago. Charley wasn't like most of those rich boys; he joined right in and worked alongside us. He could rope a steer with the best of 'em." Frank stared at the fire in silence. Then he added, "Sure never heard him mention a wife or little girl, though."

"My mother took me back to Kentucky when I was very young." Morgan's response was stiff. It was difficult to feel kinship with a man who had made her marry and leave her home against her will.

Frank sensed Morgan's hostility and wondered about it. "You sure missed a lot by not living out here. This country's got more excitement in one day than the East has in a year."

A bit later on that night, she slipped to the side of camp to sit on a rock and stare at the stars. Joaquín's voice startled her.

"There are no stars in the East like there are out here, are there?"

"No, I guess not. But it seems a high price to pay for stars."

Joaquín smiled, his teeth white in the moonlight.

"I was raised out here. To me the East is too unchanging. There is no surprise, no adventure."

"You have a ranch, too, like Seth's?"

Joaquín chuckled, and there was a tone of contempt in his voice. "I have a ranch, yes, but not like the Colter one. The Montoya ranch is several times larger than his, and it has been in my family for generations."

"Do you live there alone?"

"No," Joaquín answered, "I live with my sister, Lena." When one of his riders had told him about Lena and Colter, he had wanted to kill her. All she had done was laugh at him. He had vowed then to avenge himself on Colter one day.

"Tell me, Morgan, do you hate our West so much?" His voice had a slyness that Morgan missed.

"Yes!" was her vehement answer. "I hate this dust and the constant danger and . . . and . . ." Her eyes involuntarily went to the west where she knew Seth was on watch.

"And your husband?" Joaquín's voice was very low.

"Yes." Her voice was resigned, and Joaquín realized that she was close to tears.

"Morgan, I told you once that I was your friend. If you want to tell me anything — if you want a shoulder to cry on, I am here."

A tear rolled down Morgan's cheek and then another. She sobbed into her hands. Joaquín waited. Her first words were almost inaudible. "I don't know why he hates me. I wanted to be friends. I wanted to be like we were in Kentucky. We rode together and talked and laughed together. Then he kissed me." She shivered as she remembered Seth's kisses.

"Sweet Morgan, I am your friend." Joaquín's hand caressed the back of her head, but he did not try to touch her beyond that. "Why did he ask you to marry him?"

Morgan's sobs shook her body even more. "He didn't. I asked him to marry me. I didn't want to. My father willed that all the money went to my uncle unless I married and lived in New Mexico for a year. I offered Seth money to marry me." She continued crying softly and Joaquín sat back to digest this.

This explains a lot, he thought. Yet, he knew that as soon as both of them got over their anger, they would realize that they cared for one another a great deal. Joaquín had seen the way Seth protected Morgan, and the way her eyes followed him around the camp. He smiled in the darkness, very glad to have heard what he had been told.

"Not all men understand a woman's gentler feelings. Some men only use women. I am afraid you have married a man who may be like that." He changed his voice to a seductive tone. "I wish you had asked me to marry you. I would gladly have done so, without money. It would be a pleasure to be in the company of so beautiful a woman." He raised her hand to his lips and looked into her tear-filled eyes.

"I'm not beautiful, Joaquín," she whispered.

His smile was soft and knowing. "But you are, and someday you will know it. It would have given me great pleasure to show you how beautiful you are. I would like to dress you in satins and silks."

Morgan felt herself blush at Joaquín's words.

"Little Morgan, when you know you are

beautiful, then you will be beautiful."

They sat together in silence awhile, thinking of different things. Then Joaquín said, "Let's go back now before people start wondering where we are." He took her arm and led her back to the wagon. "Goodnight, my fair princess," he kissed her hand again. "Sleep well."

Joaquín left Morgan at her wagon and turned to be met by the hostile stares of Frank and Jake. He smiled and bowed toward them, then went to his own wagon.

"Somebody ought to do something about that little dandy," Jake muttered.

"Yeah, and I know who ought to do it." Frank looked toward where Seth was standing.

Crossing the Cimarron River was a nightmare for Morgan. The area around the river was crawling with rattlesnakes. The men kept shooting at them to keep them away from the horses. By the end of the day, everyone was tense and exhausted.

The next few days after crossing the river were just as tiring as the first days of the journey had been. At Middle Spring, Morgan had her first glimpse of tarantulas. She had not minded the rattlers as much as these huge, hairy spiders. Willow Bar was a welcome relief with its sand and willows.

Another relief was that Morgan had almost become used to undressing in front of Seth. And their attitudes toward one another were softening. Several times she had caught him smiling at her, and she had found herself smiling happily back!

Early one morning Seth rode ahead of the wagon train. "I'll meet you at Rock Creek in two days with some fresh game," he told Morgan as he packed his saddlebags.

Both of them remembered the last time he had gone away. The memory brought tears to Morgan's eyes, and she kept her head lowered so he couldn't see.

"What's this, little one?" his tone was mocking, "Will you actually miss your husband?"

She kept her eyes on the ground.

He said quietly, "It seems you and I always say the wrong things to one another, doesn't it? Let's try to start over again, when I get back. All right?" He smiled at her and made her smile back. "Could you spare a kiss for a lone knight?"

Before Morgan could think, she was in his arms. "Seth . . ." she whispered. His lips touched hers gently at first, and then they both felt the longing of the last weeks. Morgan drew him closer while kneading the muscles in his broad back and sides.

"No, sweet, we're going to go *slowly* this time. Both of us need time to learn to trust. I'll see you again soon, and we can start all over."

He touched her cheek briefly and then leaped into the saddle and was gone.

CHAPTER SEVEN

That night Morgan lay in the wagon, half asleep, pictures of Seth floating through her mind.

"Lookee here what I found, Ben." A stranger was climbing into her wagon! She pulled the blanket close to her chin in fear. "Lotsa yella hair, too."

Another man appeared at the end of the wagon. "Bring her out here, Joe." His voice had a strange, rough quality.

"Ah, let me get her now. She's no good to us. Let me have her." He was pleading.

"You get out of here and let me see if she's worth anything or not." The first man left the wagon, and the second entered.

"What are you doing here? What do you want?" Morgan's voice shook with fear.

"Nobody's going to hurt you. Just get up and let me see you." His voice gave Morgan chills. It was rough, but at the same time it was a sly voice, the voice of a person who could not be trusted. "Come on now, get up."

Morgan obeyed.

"Now, I'll just stand here, while you find a lantern and make some light in here." Morgan was shaking as she found the lantern and the tinder box. If a snake could talk, she thought, its voice would sound like that.

"Cat Man!" The voice came from outside the tent. "What we gonna do with these two?"

Morgan jumped — a cat! Yes, that's what his voice reminded her of.

"I'll be there in a minute. Just hold on and don't bother me again."

Morgan heard low, throaty guffaws from the men outside the wagon. There seemed to be at least two others besides the creature in the wagon with her.

Cat Man sat on the cot. "Now," he said when she had the lantern lit, "let me look at you. Come close to me."

With her first glance at Cat Man, she let out an involuntary gasp. His face fit his voice. His eyes were an exaggerated almond shape, long and thin, and his nose was wide and flat. His mouth was small, thin-lipped, practically nonexistent. She almost expected to see long whiskers above his upper lip.

Cat Man smiled at her, a knowing smile that made his eyes even more catlike. "Come here," he repeated.

Morgan inched slowly toward him. He seemed to enjoy her fear. When she was close to him, and while still holding her eyes with his own, one long, thin arm darted out and tore her nightgown from her.

Morgan covered her body with her arms.

"No." His one word conveyed his meaning, and she dropped her arms, staring off to the side of the wagon.

"Ah, yes, you'll do. Nice. Get some clothes on and come outside." He left the wagon.

Without hesitation, Morgan did as she was told. She didn't feel that Cat Man was usually disobeyed.

"What happened to all that purty hair I seen? Did she cut it off?"

"No, it's still there. Now you two get them tied up, and then let's get out of here."

"What about her? We gonna take her?" This was from another man.

"Yeah. Now get busy!"

Morgan saw the other two men, both rather tall but thin, pulling Jake and Joaquín from the side of the wagon.

"What you goin' to do with her?" Jake's voice was angry. "Her husband'll come after you. Don't take her, she's just a little girl."

161

One of the two men hit Jake across the head with the butt of his revolver.

"No!" Morgan gasped and started toward the fallen Jake, but Cat Man's grasp on her shoulder, his thin, steely fingers biting into her flesh, halted her.

"He is a foolish old man. Now look at your other friend there. He's more sensible." She followed Cat Man's slanted eyes to Joaquín, who was, as always, slightly smiling! He nodded his head faintly toward Cat Man. They seemed to understand one another.

In that one second Morgan had an insight into Joaquín. She realized that his only friend was himself, and that he didn't care any more about her than about the dirt under his feet. Her face must have betrayed her feelings, because his smile widened and he tipped his hat to her. She shivered. Any hope of being saved from these men was lost.

"Did you go through all the wagons?"

"Yeah," said one of the men. "And there ain't nothin' here. Just some old furniture, no money or nothin'."

"Well, we're not going away completely empty-handed," Cat Man stroked Morgan's neck. When she pulled away from him, he let out a low, throaty sound.

"Get her horse saddled, Ben, before this husband of hers returns."

Morgan wished more than anything in the world to see Seth riding in now, to get her away from this awful Cat Man and the two tall, thin men who came with him.

"Get on the horse."

Morgan's skirt caught under her leg as she straddled the horse, exposing a large expanse of calf.

"Woowee, gonna like that!" Joe nudged Ben in the ribs as they leered at Morgan's smooth leg. The party started away.

"What happened?" Jake held his head in his hands and looked up to see the four riders go off into the moonlight. "I've got to go after them," he began.

"Untie me first," Joaquín's voice floated up to Jake, and he stumbled toward the dark man and slowly untied the ropes binding his arms. Jake stumbled, still stunned from the heavy blow to his head.

"Careful, old man, you get too excited and we'll never find anyone." Joaquín put a helping hand under Jake's elbow.

Jake jerked from Joaquín's grasp and straightened his aching body. "It'll be a long time before I need help from the likes of you."

Joaquín watched, amused, as Jake painfully made his way to Frank's body.

"Well, you ain't dead yet, so I guess you're too mean to kill." Jake's voice showed his relief as he held Frank's head in his arms. "You!" his voice held the contempt he felt for Joaquín, "help me get him back to the wagons."

As Jake cleaned Frank's head wound and his own, Joaquín began gathering the horses that the bandits had dispersed.

"What happened, Jake?" Frank moaned.

"They took the little girl."

Frank started up from the cot. "I've got to go get her. You know what they'll do to her?" His voice cracked with the effort of talking.

Jake pushed him back down. "You couldn't swat a fly, and I can't see well enough anymore to go trackin' them, and that heathen out there ain't gonna help. So that leaves the boy." To Jake, Seth would always remain a boy, the closest thing he had to a son. "I'm gonna go now and find him."

"Jake, you can't go. Send Joaquín."

Jake spat on the wagon floor. "I wouldn't trust him not to spend his time staring at the stars. No, this is a man's job, and I'm sending a man I can trust — me. I'll see you as soon as I can manage."

He turned and left the wagon, saddled one of the horses, and left the camp, his destination unknown.

It took Jake all that night and into the next before he saw Seth's campfire. He called into the camp before he entered. "Seth, it's me, Jake. Are you there, Seth?"

Jake was nearly exhausted and Seth helped him from his horse. "What's wrong, Jake?" he demanded.

"It's Morgan," he gasped out. "They took her."

"Morgan! What do you mean, old man? Who took her?" He grabbed Jake's shoulders.

"Three men, one they called Cat Man . . . looked and sounded like a cat, too. They came to rob us. Frank was on guard, but they knocked him out — bad wound, too. Then they got me and Joaquín. They took the little girl with them and headed due west."

"When? When did they leave?"

"Last night about this time. I been lookin' for you ever since. Frank was too bad hurt to go after her, and I figured my old bones wouldn't hold up. So I came straight to you instead."

Seth began saddling his horse and packing his saddlebags.

"There's game strung up in that tree. Take it back with you. Then when Frank's better, take the wagons and go on to the ranch. I'll get Morgan, and then I'll meet you at the ranch." His voice was grim. As he straddled his horse, he looked into the horizon and then back to Jake. "I'll get her, Jake, and they better not have hurt her." His eyes were cold.

He rode off toward the west and was soon out of sight. "I hope for their sakes that they haven't hurt her," Jake muttered before he turned back to the fire. He had been without sleep for thirty-six hours, and he collapsed onto the ground.

Morgan had been on the horse for two days and two nights before they stopped and made camp. Until then, they had stopped for only brief periods to rest their horses. They had eaten pieces of dried beef while traveling. She had become proficient at sleeping on her horse. Cat Man held the reins while she slept.

At first Morgan wasn't even fully aware that they had stopped. She sat on her horse while the three men began to build a fire.

"Gonna enjoy this night." Joe motioned

toward Morgan. "Sure am gonna have a good time."

Morgan, still on her horse, her head drooping with exhaustion, felt someone near her. "Get down," Cat Man's voice was low. Obediently, she moved one painfully aching leg across the saddle and slid to the ground. She saw a bedroll spread out by the small fire. Cat Man's long finger extended in a gesture toward the blankets. Morgan stumbled toward the skimpy covers, dropped to her knees, and then lay down, so very grateful to be able to stretch out. She was asleep instantly.

Voices woke her and she heard them through a haze, as if they were a long way off.

"I seen her first! She's mine!"

"It don't matter who seen her first. She's mine, 'cause I got the gun out." Morgan heard a click.

"You ain't gonna shoot me, 'cause I'm gonna shoot you first."

"You and who else?"

"Stop it!" This was the cat voice that Morgan had grown to hate. "Nobody's gonna have her. Now make something to eat." His voice was calm and assured. Morgan had her eyes closed, but Cat Man must have walked out of the camp, because she heard the crackle of underbrush and rocks.

There was silence around her, and she began to drift back into sleep. Then the whispering seemed louder than the arguing of a few moments ago.

"It'll take him a while out in the woods. If we're quick, we can both get it done before he gets back, and he'll never even know."

"What if she tells him?"

"She won't. We'll just tell her she better not."

"I'm with ya. Who goes first?"

"Let's flip for it."

Morgan heard a low chuckle and then, "Damn!"

"You hold her and I'll stick her." The voices were very near.

Morgan turned over quickly to look into the two leering faces. She managed a gasp, before a hand closed over her mouth and then another held her two hands. She began to kick as she felt other hands on her ankles, then sliding up her legs to her thighs.

"Skinny little thing, ain't she?" Both men chuckled greedily.

Then, just as her skirts were tossed over her head, her legs were released and she felt something heavy fall across her right leg, below the knees.

"You didn't have no call to hurt Ben,"

whined one of the men. "We was just gonna have a little fun. We wasn't hurtin' nobody."

"Let her go."

Morgan was humiliated to her soul. Why was she lying here, pinned to the ground, her body exposed to men she hated?

When Joe released her, she immediately pulled her skirts from her face and covered her legs.

Joe grabbed Ben and dragged him away from her. As Ben began to recover his senses, Cat Man jerked both of them in front of him by the fire. Although Cat Man was very slim, he had a great deal of power in his spare frame.

"Now listen to me, you two, and listen good. This woman is a present to Boss, and Boss doesn't want leavings. I want her untouched and I want her treated with respect. If I leave her here for you to guard, that's what I expect you to do. Is that clear to you two thickheads?"

"Yes, Cat Man." Their voices were contrite. "We didn't know she was a present. You didn't tell us."

Cat Man's lithe body relaxed, and he smiled that strange, malignant smile of his. "Well, boys, now that you know, don't forget it. Now get me somethin' to eat."

"Yes, Cat Man, yes." They stumbled

against one another in their attempts to obey.

Cat Man walked to Morgan. "They won't bother you now."

Morgan was beside herself with rage. "What gives you the right to give me as a 'present' to anyone? I'm not something you can own." She kept her teeth clenched, trying to control her anger.

Cat Man looked at her in puzzlement for a few seconds and then laughed his peculiar laugh. It flashed through her mind that he worked at it, that he tried to look and sound like a cat.

He said quietly, "You are a woman — something to be owned, something to be bought and used. You'll make a pretty little ornament for Boss." He turned and left her before she could reply. "Give her some beans, Joe."

Joe brought her a plate of pinto beans, but she could hardly eat, because anger had made a lump in her throat. She climbed back under the covers to resume her sleep.

The next thing she felt was a hand on her shoulder, shaking her awake. She smiled as she thought of Seth and snuggled under the covers again. It wasn't even morning yet, so why was Seth trying to wake her? A hand on the side of her breast made her eyes fly open, and she looked into Ben's grinning, vacant face. His eyes were glittering. She shivered and jerked away from him.

As she sat up, she realized that the shoulder of her dress was torn at the seam, and as she looked at it she remembered the previous night's happenings. Joe and Ben watched her as she rolled up her blankets, as Seth had taught her, and strapped them to her horse.

I must keep my sanity through this, she thought. I must remember Trahern House and Kentucky and . . . Seth. Yes, Seth. She clung to her image of him.

They rode hard all day, stopping only once to water and rest the horses. Morgan splashed her face and hands. The water was so cool and good after the long, hot days. She was less sore than she had been the day before, but the insides of her thighs were raw from the saddle.

"Let's go."

"Ah, Cat Man, why do we have to keep runnin'? There ain't nobody followin' us."

"Yeah, I'm gettin' tired. What you say me or Ben go back a ways and see if we see anybody, and then if we do, we'll kill 'em?"

Morgan gasped and put the back of her hand to her mouth.

"Looks like the woman thinks somebody

is following us." They all turned to stare at her standing by the water. "Who do you think is following us? Couldn't be that old man, and the young one didn't seem to care if we took you or not. Ben, here, near killed the one on watch, or did you finish the job, Ben?"

"I don't know, didn't look to find out." Ben smiled at Cat Man.

"Well, then the only one left is this husband of yours. He was away, but I don't think there were other men with him — too small a train. If someone had taken my woman, I don't think I'd go miles in the opposite direction trying to get help. No, I guess I'd ride out for her myself. Is that what you'd do boys?"

Ben and Joe grinned idiot smiles at him.

"So, little lady, I figure there's only one man following us, and I reckon the three of us can take him on. You agree, boys? Tonight we'll stop early, and one of you can ride back a ways and see if you can find this husband of hers."

When she again mounted her horse, Morgan had something to worry about besides her own problems. She prayed that they wouldn't be able to find Seth. She never even questioned her certainty that Seth was following.

In the late afternoon they rode over a ridge to see a little adobe house nestled against the back of a hill. It was the first adobe house Morgan had ever seen, and she wondered at the flat roof. In Kentucky, the rain and snow would eat through the roof in a few years. Yet this house had the look of having been there for a long time.

As they stopped to look down at the house, a woman came out the side door, gathered an armload of wood from a pile, and carried it back inside the house.

"Cat Man! Maybe we can have a little fun with that one, huh?"

Cat Man smiled at Joe. "Let's go see if maybe they'll give us something to eat."

Ben grinned. "Yeah . . . and then the woman."

As they started their horses down the steep hill, Cat Man turned toward Morgan and gave her a malevolent look that she knew was a warning.

"Good afternoon, ma'am." Cat Man's voice seemed kind as he called out to the other woman, and Morgan looked at her with wonder when she showed no fear of the four strangers.

The woman *was* usually more cautious of strangers, but since they had a woman with them, she relaxed.

"Afternoon." She smiled at them timidly.

"Who is it, Meg?" A man came to the door. He also showed fear for a few seconds, until he saw Morgan. Then he smiled. "We don't get many visitors up here, so we have to be pretty cautious." Morgan saw the rifle in his hand. She glanced at Ben, who had moved his hand to his sidearm.

"Won't you come in and set a spell? Meg can rustle up some grub, and you can tell us any news. We don't get out of here very often."

"Well, that's right neighborly of you. We sure appreciate that." Cat Man's voice sounded sincere. He got off his horse, and then helped Morgan from hers. Again he flashed her a warning look.

After the four of them had washed at a small stream, they sat down at a large table covered with the strangest food Morgan had ever seen. She wondered how anyone could have prepared so much food so fast, until she realized that each dish had the same basis — a red sauce and pinto beans.

In spite of her situation, she enjoyed the food. Her favorite was a roll made of a kind of corn bread, but very flat and thin, wrapped around a mound of mashed pinto beans. It was covered with onions and the thick, hot, chili sauce, and then sprinkled with white cheese.

"This is very good," she murmured.

Cat Man laughed. "My wife," he watched her intently lest she contradict him, "is new to this country and our food."

Don't trust him! she wanted to scream to these people, these generous people who offered him hospitality.

"You sure can cook good, ma'am," Ben said. He pushed his plate away, having filled it three times.

Morgan helped the woman clear the table, and as they went to the end of the room where the washtub stood, she tried to manage a way to warn the woman. But she constantly felt Cat Man's eye on her. Maybe they'll just go away, maybe they won't hurt them, she offered a silent prayer.

When the dishes were done, she returned to where the others were sitting and smoking home-rolled cigarettes. Cat Man pulled a chair close to his own, smiled at Morgan, and patted the seat of the chair. To all the world it must have looked like a loving gesture between a husband and wife. With her back to the others, she allowed her face to show all the hate she felt for him. That secretive, catlike smile never faltered.

"Where was it you said you was headed?" the man asked Cat Man.

Before Cat Man could answer, Morgan saw Ben look at him with questioning brows. Cat Man nodded slightly toward him, and Morgan gripped the arms of the chair until her knuckles were white. If it was going to start, it would be now.

In an instant, Ben's arm reached out and grabbed the woman, Meg, around her ample waist. She was a large, strong woman, and she began to fight Ben with success.

Her husband reacted instantly, quickly crossing the room to his rifle. The second his fingertips touched the rifle barrel, a shot exploded beside Morgan, and she saw him crumple. Ben and Joe stopped to stare at the man lying in the corner. Meg jerked free and ran to him.

"John, John," she whimpered.

"I'm all right, Meg." His eyes caught hers, and motioned to the rifle at his side.

"Touch the rifle, and he won't live another minute." Cat Man had dropped the fake-sincere voice and returned to the lower, sly voice Morgan knew so well. "I didn't mean to kill him. I thought he might like to watch the boys here in action."

Both John and Meg looked at Cat Man with horrified eyes. Morgan whispered, "No, no."

Cat Man turned to her. "Sit!" he ordered,

"unless you want to see them both dead."

Shaking with fear, she sat down again, turning her head to the wall.

"She's yours, boys," Cat Man said with a sneer.

As Joe and Ben advanced on Meg, she began to scream. John raised himself up, holding his bleeding thigh, and started again for the rifle.

Ben kicked the rifle away and then started to kick John.

"No!" Cat Man told him. "Tie him up and gag him — so he can watch."

At the sound of tearing cloth, Morgan jerked her head around to see Meg's large body exposed. Ben held her arms, while Joe fondled her large, sagging breasts and turned to grin at Cat Man.

John writhed under the ropes and gag, but his eyes remained fixed on his wife. Meg stopped fighting and stood as if she were made of stone, staring at the ceiling.

Morgan couldn't stand it any longer. "No," she screamed, "you can't do this! You're animals! Stop it!"

Cat Man slapped her hard against the mouth. "Shut up, or I'll let them have you," he growled.

He sat down and pulled Morgan into his lap, putting a thin hand across her forehead, holding her head toward the sight of Ben and Joe holding the woman. "Look," his voice was soft. "Look at what I'm saving you from."

Ben roughly lowered the woman onto a rag rug. Morgan looked away, but it was difficult with Cat Man holding her head in his steely grip.

Joe pulled his pants down and mounted the woman. Morgan closed her eyes and ears to the sight. She tried not to think, but Cat Man's rapid breath in her ear made it impossible for her to escape the reality.

"Me next." Ben's voice was as excited as a five-year-old's.

As Joe left the woman and Ben removed his pants, Morgan looked at Meg, her head turned away from her husband, staring at the wall by Cat Man's feet. Her eyes were glazed, like a dead person's.

When Ben gleefully climbed on top of the prostrate woman, Cat Man's hand stole to Morgan's right breast and began to fondle and knead it. She tried to pull away, but his iron grip held her.

"Like a rabbit! You finished faster'n a rabbit," Joe laughed at Ben.

Joe's ugly jeer made Cat Man drop his hand. His breathing returned to normal. Morgan jumped from his lap. He grabbed at her, catching her skirt and tearing it at the waist. He smiled at her, narrowing his eyes.

"Ben, look for any money and pack some food."

"I was thinkin' about goin' agin." He looked down at the nude woman on the floor. She hadn't moved since they had put her there. Ben turned at a sound from John, and Morgan saw his eyes were pleading. She knew that John's look of entreaty was more likely to encourage their cruelty than to stop it.

Morgan grabbed a quilt from the back of a chair and covered Meg, and then put her arms under Meg's shoulders to lift her up. It was like holding a rag doll. Tears sprang to Morgan's eyes. "I'm sorry, I'm sorry," she whispered to the unresponding woman.

"Leave her alone. We got to go. Ben, you find any clothes to fit . . ." He looked at Morgan and grinned. "I don't even know your name."

She wanted these people to know their names, his name as well as hers. In a cold voice, she said, "It's Morgan, Cat Man." Perhaps this would help Seth to find her.

His eyes shifted to the man on the floor at his feet. He knew why Morgan has used his name. It didn't matter to him. He liked

179

people to know who he was. He liked it when his name caused fear in people's eyes.

"Find some clothes for Morgan," he called, his eyes never leaving hers.

"What about these?" Ben held up a pair of boy's jeans and a plaid shirt. Joe held a pair of boots.

"Good, I think they'll do real well. Now go outside and get the horses ready. I'll be out in a minute."

"Can't we see the little girl put the clothes on?" Ben whined.

"No! Now go do as I say." The two men hurried to obey.

When they were gone, Cat Man turned back to Morgan. "Now get dressed."

Reading her reluctance correctly, Cat Man quickly drew his gun and shot close to the head of the man against the wall. He hardly even looked where he was shooting. Meg, at Morgan's feet, turned her head to look at her husband, but she did not move otherwise.

Morgan began to remove her clothes. When she was totally naked, she stood straight up to stare at Cat Man, who was holding the clothes she was to put on.

Cat Man had seen her nude before, but now that he saw her body in daylight, he began to regret his decision to give her to

Boss Martin. Her skin was flawless, her waist so small, and the curve of her hips made him ache to touch her.

Cat Man tossed the clothes to Morgan. "Put these on — fast."

The pants and shirt were made for a young boy, and were too small on Morgan's curvaceous body. The pants fit over her hips and legs like a second skin, and the shirt strained across her breasts. It was one more cause for misery. How much longer could she bear this?

Seth had been tracking them for three days. He knew they were traveling fast, because he had found only one campfire in the three days. For a while he seemed to have lost their trail. Now he looked down on a cabin nestled against a hill. There were animals in pens around the place, but no sign of human life. Cautiously, Seth made his way down the hill toward the adobe house.

A rifle shot rang out, and Seth felt it whiz by, close to his left ear. Quickly, he turned his horse and was soon out of sight of the house.

He had followed the trail of Cat Man and Morgan to this cabin, and he meant to find out what they knew about his wife. He decided to wait until dark before going to the cabin again. He found a circle of piñon trees that gave privacy and shelter, and he stretched out on the fragrant needles to obtain some long-needed sleep.

When he awoke, the moon was high, and gave eerie shadows to the trees and shrubs around him. Quietly and stealthily, he made his way down the ridge to the back of the little house. About fifty yards from the woodpile, he tied his horse and then approached the house. He didn't know how many people were in the cabin, and he didn't want to take the chance of walking into a hostile group.

As he ran to the woodpile, he heard a noise from the door and watched to see a tall, slim man open the door slightly and look out. Holding a rifle in front of him, he limped slowly to the woodpile, looking around constantly.

When he seemed satisfied that he was alone, he propped the rifle against the stack of wood and began to fill his arms.

Seth sprang over the mound of cut logs, and before the man could even turn, Seth had a gun in his ribs and one powerful arm around the man's neck.

"Don't hurt us, mister. We been hurt enough," the man pleaded.

"I have no cause to hurt you. I just want

to ask some questions. Did three men come by here just recently, with a woman?"

Before the man could answer, the door to the cabin opened. Both men turned toward the sound.

"John . . . John, are you all right?" Her voice was full of fear.

When she made out her husband's form in the moonlight, and then Seth's much larger form holding him, she screamed and began crying hysterically, incoherently.

"Let me go to her. I'll answer your questions, but just let me go to her."

Seth released the man, and he went to comfort his wife. As he held her in his arms, he looked up at Seth, his face sad.

"I don't mean you any harm," Seth said quietly. "I'm just trying to find my wife."

John nodded his head. "The little blond woman?"

"Have you seen her?" Seth's voice was jubilant.

"Meg, it's all right." John's hand stroked his wife's hair. "He's not here to hurt us. Why don't you go inside, and I'll be in in a minute?"

Sobbing, Meg went back into the house, and John shut the door behind her.

"Yesterday, about sundown, three men rode up. They had the woman with them."

His hands were clenched into fists at his sides.

"Did they give you any idea where they were going?"

"No." Seth could not help but wonder at the hatred in the man's voice.

"Had they hurt her?"

John remembered Morgan standing nude, but he also remembered that Cat Man had not touched her, and that he had forbidden the others to bother her.

"No, they hadn't hurt her, but that Cat Man is evil."

"Did they do that to your leg?" Seth motioned to a wound that still seeped blood onto John's pants.

"This is the least of what they did to us." Seth's eyes followed John's to the cabin, and understanding passed between the two men. "If you catch them, mister, I hope you kill them."

"I plan to."

Seth returned to his horse and mounted to leave.

"They dressed her in boy's clothes," John said. "But she'll still be easy to find when it's known that she's riding with that Cat Man." Quickly, he described the men and their horses.

As Seth prepared to leave, they shook

hands and exchanged names. "I hope you get 'em," John called after Seth.

"I sure as hell do too," he whispered into the darkness.

Days later, as they came over a ridge and looked down at the little town, Morgan knew it was a mistake to even call the place a town. There were only five or six buildings, each looking as if it might fall down at any minute. A little apart from the other buildings stood a large white house. They started down the hill before she could see any more.

"Cat Man! Good to see you again."

"Joe, honey, where you been so long?"

Morgan looked around. The woman who had called to Joe was lounging in the doorway of a derelict, faded building. Her reddish hair was matted and filthy. Her dress revealed most of her sagging breasts. Morgan guessed that at one time the dress had been red and gold, but now stains and several unmended rips obscured the material. The woman returned Morgan's stare boldly.

"What you got here, Cat Man? Pretty little thing. Can I have her when you're done?"

Morgan felt a rubbery palm on her leg, and looked down to see a short, fat man, with a large nose and thick, protruding lips, staring at her. His greasy hand was caressing her thigh. Quickly she jerked her leg up and out to kick him hard in the chest, just at the base of the neck.

Unprepared for the blow, he landed sitting in the dust and refuse of the street. In front of her she heard Cat Man's low chuckling.

"That serves you right, Luke. Keep your hands off from now on. She's the Boss's woman."

Morgan heard laughter from the other people as they watched the fat man pick himself up from the dirt. She shuddered at the hate-filled look he sent her.

Several people had come out to see the little procession, and they all seemed to know the three men. There was much interest in Morgan.

"You say she's for Boss? I bet Boss's Nancy ain't gonna like that."

The four riders rode out of the tiny town to the white house that Morgan had glimpsed briefly from the hill. The townspeople did not follow them to this house.

It was two stories high and very well kept. A porch ran around two sides of the house, and the second story had a large, round turret on one corner, with a conical roof.

Everything was trimmed in brilliant green, making a sharp contrast with the stark surroundings.

At a motion from Cat Man, Morgan threw one leg over the saddle and slid to the ground. She was so tired that it seemed as if none of this were really happening to her. She moved automatically, and felt very little.

The front door was unlocked, and Cat Man led Morgan into a spacious entryway and up a wide, carpeted stairway. She had a brief sight of carved furniture and lush red curtains.

To the right at the top of the stairs was a door, and Cat Man opened it to reveal a large, bright room. Against one wall was a spacious fourposter bed, draped in a silky, white fabric. There were sprigs of sea-green flowers all over it. The carpet, walls, and the rest of the room echoed the colors of the pale green and white. The room was refreshing and inviting.

At Cat Man's hand on her arm, she stiffened. His cat-laugh sounded low in her ear, and he jerked her to a mirror over a chintz-covered dresser. She was startled by the sight of herself. She was as dirty and unkempt as the woman she had seen in the town. Her face was smudged, and her eyelids drooped. But what caused her to gasp was the sight of her own body in the tight pants and shirt. Her breasts strained against the fabric, and her nipples stood out taut and rigid. There was a gap between two buttons exposing the curve and roundness of her breasts. The pants fitted sleekly over her thighs, and the belt showed off the roundness of her hips.

"Like yourself, don't you?" Could Cat Man read her mind? His hand caressed her thigh. "Too bad I said I'd give you to Boss," he murmured. "But he's not too happy with me now, and I know what he likes." His hand lightly cupped her breast, and the thumb moved over the already taut peak. "I think he'll be real grateful to me."

He moved his face close to hers as if to kiss her, and she turned her face away. She heard his warning growl in her ear.

"That's all right, little princess. You think you're so good now, but a few months with Boss Martin will change your mind."

He moved away from her. "We'll stay here two days. Then we leave. I want you to get some sleep. Tomorrow you'll have a bath. If I took you to Boss now, he'd think you were a polecat."

She looked for something to throw at him.

"Don't." His voice was deadly, and after the last spurt of energy, Morgan realized how tired she was. She had been insulted too much to let another taunt hurt her.

"Now get some sleep, and don't try anything." His eyes went to the open window. "If you should get out, you'd be facing Luke, and I don't think he'd treat you with respect."

Morgan felt chills on her back as she remembered the fat, dirty man pawing her leg. Cat Man had made his point.

When Cat Man left the room, all ideas of flight left Morgan. The room was cool, and the green-and-white bed beckoned. She removed her boots, her pants, and then the tight shirt. As she crawled into bed, she marveled at the difference between men's and women's clothing. Women had to wear so much more than men.

The sheets were cool and clean, and felt good to her bruised and chapped body. She was so tired that she didn't even mind the dirt on her body. Cat Man was right — she did smell terrible. Just before she drifted into an exhausted sleep, she saw Seth's smiling face, saw him standing with his arms extended to her.

When she first awoke to the sounds of Ben and Joe's voices just outside her door, she thought she had been asleep only a few minutes. The sun was low in the sky and slanting across the thick, green carpet.

"Watch where you're goin'! You hit me in the leg with this thing."

"I don't see why we have to carry this up here anyway. Who the hell wants to take a bath?"

Morgan still wasn't awake when the door opened to admit Joe and Ben carrying a large copper bathtub. Morgan turned over on her side, pulling the sprigged sheet to her neck.

They put the tub down in the center of the room and turned toward her. At the sight of Morgan's lush curves, covered only by a sheet, the frowns left their faces.

"I sure would like to climb in there with that little girl." Joe took a step toward the bed, but Ben grabbed his arm.

"Let's go get the water."

In a few minutes they came back with four large buckets of hot water, and poured it into the tub. When the two men left, Morgan nearly ran to step into the steaming water. She lay perfectly still for several minutes, allowing her body to luxuriate in the hot water. Gradually, she became aware of her surroundings again, and began to scour her body and hair. As she scrubbed, she noticed that clean, fluffy towels had been placed in the room, and that her shirt and pants were clean, and had been draped across the end of the bed.

Now she realized that she must have slept for twenty-four hours, an entire night and day! Her mind was less cloudy. She began to think.

Somehow, she must escape. What would Seth want her to do? He would probably tell her to stay where she was until he could come for her. But she wasn't really sure that he could find her.

The door opened, and Morgan turned quickly toward the sound. An old woman came in and stood with bowed head at the foot of the tub.

"What do you want?"

The little woman kept her head lowered. Her dark hair was greasy, her dress torn and unwashed.

"What do you want?" Morgan asked again. When the woman didn't answer, Morgan shrugged, stepped out of the tub, and wrapped herself in a large, white towel. Silently, the old woman began filling buckets with the bath water. After several trips downstairs, she had emptied the tub.

Morgan sat in front of the mirror over the dressing table and combed the tangles out of her clean hair. "Seth, please come," she whispered to her reflection.

Quickly she dressed in the clean shirt and pants. The soft cotton fabric felt good against her skin. As she looked at herself in the full-length mirror, she wondered what Seth would think of her in the shape-hugging clothes. She ran her hands down her body, watching the points of her breasts come alive.

The sound of the door opening startled her. "Ben'd be real good to you, honey."

Morgan jerked the door open wider and stepped past Ben into the corridor. One dirty hand caressed her hip as she hurried past him.

"You look so much better now, little Morgan." Cat Man smiled at her. "Now my gift will be appreciated." His slanted eyes devoured her body, and Morgan felt her face growing hot. He ran a thin finger down her cheek. She turned her face away.

"Why don't you let me go? I've never harmed you. Let me go." Her voice was pleading.

Cat Man was dressed in black, and the color emphasized his yellow eyes. He took her hand and led her into the dining room, where a table was set with a large meal. He pulled out a chair for Morgan, and when she was seated, he took a chair beside her.

"You will find, Morgan, that often beautiful women's lives are ruled by their faces and their figures more than by their own minds. You are a woman to be owned — a woman to love, a woman to fight for, possibly to die for."

"You talk nonsense. I'm not beautiful, and I never will be. All my life people have told me how plain I am. Why do you talk this way?"

Cat Man's eyes widened for just a second. "It's difficult to imagine that anyone could be so blind." He reached for a buttered roll. "But then, I have seen you with a look of great sadness. Possibly your expression, the dress you wore at first, and the way you did your hair have all concealed your beauty. But it is difficult to believe, even so."

Cat Man continued eating. "The food is excellent. Would you like some wine?" he asked, as he filled her glass. She realized she was ravenous. Without another word she began eating the largest meal she had ever consumed.

Seth watched the town from the ridge above it. He had been tracking Morgan's captors for seven days, and now that he knew he was so close, he decided to rest awhile before he attempted her rescue. He needed strength. He knew from the looks of it that he'd get no help from anyone there.

There were no riders coming into the town, and Seth knew that his appearance would cause some speculation. He had followed the outlaws to the town early that morning, and knew they could not have arrived much before the previous evening. As he pulled his hat over his eyes and went to sleep, Morgan also slept. It would be hours before she woke to a hot bath and dinner with Cat Man.

He awoke when the sun was low, and he quickly made his way down the hill into the town. As he had conjectured, his appearance caused a stir. Casually, he tied his horse to the post in front of the saloon. He ordered a beer, and made his way to the back of the dirty room to an even dirtier table.

After a few moments of staring, the group began to lose interest in the stranger and returned to their own talk. Seth leaned his chair against the wall, sipped his beer, and watched.

He listened carefully to a group in a corner near him. He heard the name "Boss" mentioned several times, and then "Boss's woman" and loud laughter.

"You mind if I sit down, or you savin' this seat?"

Seth looked up to see a woman with red hair staring at him. Her eyes and lips were heavily painted, and she smelled strongly of perfume over her unwashed body. She could have been thirty or fifty. She eyed Seth with wariness. Seth wondered what could have caused her such fear.

"I'd be pleased to have you." At the gentle tone of his voice, the woman's look of caution increased. "Could I buy you a beer?" Mutely, the woman nodded.

"Barkeep! A beer for the lady."

The others in the bar turned toward Seth. They laughed. "You sure are a stranger, mister. Janie's a lot of things, but she sure ain't no *lady*."

"You don't know nothin' about a lady, Luke. That one yesterday sure set you on your ass," the woman beside Seth answered.

"Why, you!" The fat man came out of his chair toward the woman. She rose also, hands and fingers made into claws.

"I'd hate to have to defend the lady's honor." Seth's eyes narrowed, and his voice was steel. The fat man stopped and appraised the stranger.

"Come on back, Luke. She ain't worth a fight."

Luke relaxed his shoulders and smiled. "You're right, boys. Sorry to have bothered you, mister." He didn't want to fight with the enormous stranger. He turned his back on Seth, and returned to his table. "You're right, that whore ain't worth anything," he tossed over his shoulder like a child who had lost an argument.

"Thanks a lot, mister." Her eyes were adoring now.

"I just don't like to see a lady's name maligned." He emphasized the "lady."

The bartender brought Janie's beer, and she drank half of it down in one noisy swallow. She wiped her mouth with the back of her hand and looked at Seth. "You stayin' here long?"

"That depends."

"On what?" Her eyes and voice were eager.

"I've been hearin' that there's a big outfit working out of here, and I might be interested."

"You a lawman?"

Seth laughed derisively, held out his hand, and ran a finger across the curves of her breasts. "Do I look like a lawman?"

Janie had had her first man when she was twelve years old, and had long ago lost any feeling about the things men had done to her body. Yet, once, when she was sixteen, there had been a boy, a big, strong, clean, farm boy who had been good to her. He had wanted to marry Janie. He would have, too, if his mother hadn't found out how Janie had been supporting herself for four years.

Janie remembered the boy with affection, and Seth's kindness to her made her feel a sensation she had thought long dead.

She gazed up at him, hunger apparent in her eyes. "I reckon you don't look like a lawman." She paused. "I sure do like big men."

Seth leaned closer to her, seeing more clearly the cracks in the heavy makeup she wore. "Well, I got me a partiality to women — all of 'em." She opened her mouth to speak, and Seth smelled the stale odor of her breath.

"Anything you want, mister, and it's yours. It'd be my pleasure." She fluttered skimpy eyelashes at him.

Seth smiled knowingly at her. "What about this Boss I keep hearin' about?" He motioned his head slightly at Luke and the other men nearby.

Janie looked around to make sure no one could hear. She leaned toward Seth. "Boss Martin's the leader. He don't come to town much, but when he does, he stays in that big white house at the end of the road."

"Well, Janie." He put his hand on her arm. "How could I get in touch with this Boss Martin?"

Janie put her hand over Seth's big one. "Cat Man rode in yesterday, and is stayin' at the Boss's house."

"Cat Man?"

Janie shivered, "Yeah, he looks like a cat — real slanty eyes. Walks like one, too. None of the girls like to go upstairs with him. I thought he was goin' to kill me one time." Janie smiled. "But this time he brought his own woman. Dressed her up like a boy and took her down to Boss's house. She's a real snooty bitch, but nobody deserves what Cat Man does to a woman."

Seth worked the muscles in his jaw. "This woman he brought — what'd she look like?"

Janie frowned and looked at Seth, but he was staring across the bar, away from her, his eyes seeing nothing. "Yella hair . . . little, like a kid. What you want to know for? You interested in her?" Janie's voice was hostile.

Seth turned to her and smiled, showing his even, white teeth, and the long dimples in his cheeks. "I was just wondering what somebody'd bring into town, when they already had so much here."

Janie smiled back at him, showing a broken tooth on the left side of her mouth.

Seth drained his beer. "I got to be goin' now."

"Don't go yet, mister. I don't even know your name." She followed him to the door, hanging onto his arm. "I told you I'd give you whatever you want." She smiled up at him, coquettishly. "Tell me, is all of you as big as your arm?"

"It sure is, honey." He pinched her earlobe and left her.

Seth rode out of town past the big, white house. There were two men on the porch, both drinking and arguing loudly. Neither fit the description of Cat Man.

Seth tied his horse not far from the back of the house, hidden halfway down the side of a deep arroyo. When it was completely dark, he made his way down to the house.

"I don't know why Cat Man has to take so goddamn long, and why one of us ain't enough to stay with the little girl. What are you laughin' at?"

"I's just rememberin' that woman in the cabin — on the way here."

"Yeah, she warn't bad. Not bad at all."

Seth listened carefully. It seemed that there were only the two of them in the house. He listened a while longer to their bragging, and knew they were very drunk. Silently, he stepped through an open window. Through the open doorway across the hall, he could see both of the men in the lantern light. Remembering his promise to the raped woman's husband, he regretted not being able to kill the men now, but marked them well for a later fate.

Seth figured Morgan would be kept upstairs. He cautiously crossed the hall to the stairs and began making his way to the second floor.

"What was that?"

Seth froze on the stairway.

"I didn't hear nuthin'. Give me that bottle and quit worryin'. Ain't nobody goin' fool with Boss Martin's property."

Joe laughed. "You're right. Give me the bottle back."

Seth found only one door locked upstairs. He couldn't risk the noise of trying to break it open, so he entered the bedroom next to it. As he had hoped, there was an adjoining door, also locked, but a quick search of a night table revealed a key.

Quietly he entered Morgan's bedroom and saw her snuggled under the sheet, her long, golden hair spread around her, making a halo. He smiled his relief.

To keep her from crying out, he put his hand over her mouth. Instantly, her eyes flew open in terror. When he saw recognition reflected there, he removed his hand. Her arms flew around his neck, the sheet falling away from her nude body.

He held her close, burying his face in her clean, soft hair.

"I knew you'd come, Seth," she whispered tearfully. "I knew it. They said no one could find us, but I knew they were wrong." She pulled him closer. "I'm sorry for all the mean things I've ever said to you." She kissed him on the neck.

"Morgan, sweet, we've got to get out of here. Get dressed, and don't make a sound."

Her face showed her fear. "Seth, they're horrible. You don't know. They've done horrible things. I don't like to remember." Her eyes were full of tears.

"There's no time for that now! Get dressed!"

Quickly, she put on the tight pants and shirt.

"Let's go," he hurried her. "Follow me, and no noise."

Quietly and easily they made their way past the two drunken men and out of the house. Soon, they reached Seth's horse. He mounted and pulled her up to the saddle in front of him. He kissed the top of her head, murmuring a quick prayer of thanks for her safety. Then he nudged his horse up the hill.

CHAPTER EIGHT

They rode all night. Morgan snuggled against Seth and slept part of the way, safe with his enormous arms around her.

At dawn, Morgan awoke to a very different countryside than that surrounding Boss Martin's white house. The trees were tall here, straight, with white bark. They looked eerie, since they had markings that looked like eyes. The leaves were nearly round, and the gentle breeze made a rustling sound through the trees. It was quiet here, and cool, and somewhere in the distance she could hear the sound of running water.

"Where are we, Seth?"

"We're in the mountains of New Mexico. I came through here years ago and found the place where I'm going to leave you. There aren't many white men who have been there."

"Leave me?" She turned to look up at him. The sunlight shining through his hair made it seem very blond. His skin was tanned, and there were little lines at the corners of his eyes. "You're not going to leave me alone somewhere, are you?"

"I have to for a while. Cat Man and those two buffoons will be following us." He grimaced. "I don't believe he'll let you escape without trying to find you. I have to go back and find them first."

"No. They might hurt you. Please don't leave me. Let's just go on and get away from them."

"Little Morgan, how long do you think two of us can ride on one horse? We can't possibly lose them." At her worried look, he kissed her forehead. "Don't worry. I'll be back soon, and then I'll take you to my ranch."

She smiled up at him. "I want to see your ranch. Is it as pretty as this place?"

"No, it's not this high. There are no aspen trees there."

At the foot of a wall of growth, they dismounted. Seth tied the horse, then led Morgan between some trees. Now she could see an ancient trail, nearly overgrown with brush, spiraling upward. They climbed, Seth holding her hand and guiding her.

After several minutes, they came to a flat, worn place in a sheer rock face. There were several steps, and then they saw the village. There was an opening in the face of the rock about one hundred feet long and about forty feet high. Set back under the protection of the overhanging rock were ancient mud buildings. Some were crumbled, but others were still whole.

"What is it, Seth?" Morgan whispered, awed by the ghostlike city.

"It's an old Indian ruin. Frank, Jake, and I came down here years ago, and an old cowboy showed us this place. You'll be safe here."

Morgan left him to peer inside the nearest house. It was tiny. There was barely enough room for her to stand up. The ledge in front of the houses was bright and sunny, but the houses were cool and dark. She didn't feel as though she and Seth were alone. It seemed the spirits of people long dead were still there, watching. She smiled. She felt the spirits were protective.

"I like it here. The people are good."

Seth looked at her strangely, and then returned her smile. "You're right. They'll take care of you while I'm gone."

She ran to him, throwing her arms around his waist, burying her head against his chest. "Seth, let's stay here. They can't find us here. We'll wait a while — a week — and then when they're gone we'll leave."

He lifted her chin. "I want no more tears. I am going back. That's it."

She smiled and wiped her tears away.

"Do you have any kisses left?" he asked.

She stood on her toes and her arms slipped around his neck. His kiss was gentle at first, and then they both gave in to their need for one another. He kissed her cheek and then her neck. "Sweet little Morgan. I hate to leave you."

Abruptly, he held her at arm's length. "I have to fill the canteens. I'll be back in a few minutes."

For a second, Morgan was startled by his brusque way of leaving her, but then she smiled and hugged herself. She wanted to dance and laugh and cry all at the same time. She began humming and whirled around the shaded courtyard doing a waltz step. She would buy beautiful clothes, and she'd wear her hair loose. Or any way Seth wanted. Anything her beautiful, darling Seth wanted was his.

"May I join in?" Seth took her in his arms, and they glided gracefully to the music in their heads. Laughing, they collapsed on the floor, and in an unconscious gesture, Seth put his arm around her shoulders and drew her head to his chest.

As they looked into one another's eyes, their smiles faded and their lips met in a quiet, searching kiss. Gently, Seth lowered Morgan to the floor and began caressing her body. Expertly he unfastened the buttons of her shirt and exposed her warm, full breasts to his touch.

She returned his kisses with ardor, her tongue and teeth gently massaging the muscles of his neck and the open part of his shirt. She began to writhe and arch against him in the ancient manner of women. She rubbed his lean, hard thighs, searching. Gently, she kneaded the bulge she found between his legs.

An animal sound broke from Seth's throat. He rolled off her, his heart pounding and his breath coming in gasps. He sat up quickly and held both her hands in front of her. His eyes were glazed and his hair was rumpled. Silently, he buttoned her shirt. "Not now, little one." His voice was low and husky. "When I make love to my bride, it won't be hurried, it'll be when there is plenty of time."

He took a deep breath. "Stand up and listen to me. I have quite a few things to tell you before I go."

She listened. She was not to leave the ruins for any reason, not even to sit in the sunlight in front of the houses. He left her food, water, and blankets.

"Now, if I don't return within three days, try to make it east. About four days from here is the cabin where Meg and John live." At the question in her eyes, he said, "Yes, I met them. They will help you."

She put her arms around his neck and held him, desperately. "Please stay, Seth. I don't want to lose you again."

"You'll have time to think. I want you to be sure about us."

She looked at him. "What about you, Seth? Do you want me?" Her eyes hardened as an ugly thought crossed her mind. "Maybe you don't want me. Maybe you just want to enjoy your year as a husband before collecting your reward money."

The words were out before she realized, and she was frightened. Seth's reaction astonished her. He threw back his head and laughed and then picked her up in his arms and twirled her around. "Sweet little Morgan. Do you know so little about me that you think I'd marry for money? I think I must have fallen in love with you when you flashed Cynthia Ferguson that first look of hate. You were so sad in that ugly brown dress. The way you hung your head wrung my heart. But then, just for a second, your eyes lit up. And I was trapped." Laughing, he, kissed her.

"Do you really mean that, Seth? You do love me?"

"Always."

She frowned slightly. "Then why didn't you tell me before?"

He laughed again. "And have you tell me off? You wouldn't have believed me if I had told you." He kissed her thoroughly. "I must go now, love. You'll do as I say and stay here?" At her nod, he continued. "I'll be back soon. Will you still love me . . . or will you have changed your mind again?"

"Oh, no! Seth, I won't. I do love you." She stopped, eyes narrowed. "You're laughing at me!"

He smiled and hugged her close, then set her on the ground. "I'll think of you every moment, my love." He turned, grinned, and was gone.

Morgan listened intently to the quiet sounds of Seth's horse trotting away. When it was silent once again, she turned to face the wall. It wasn't as warm now as it had been when Seth was there. She felt small and very alone.

The tears began to run down her cheeks. "No!" she said aloud. "I won't cry, because

Seth will be back soon, and there's absolutely no reason to cry."

After a few moments she decided to explore the ruins, and thus fill up the long period of waiting for Seth. The back of the village seemed to have been a waste area, and she found many pieces of pottery and bones.

After two days she grew bored with the village and its great numbers of broken pots and scraps of ancient fabrics. Her clothes were dirty, and she had unwisely drunk nearly all of the water Seth had left her.

Cautiously she began to make her way down the worn stone steps to the bottom of the canyon. She made sure that she was always hidden under trees or brush and never exposed to the full view of anyone in the canyon or on the ridge above.

She followed along the stream and found a little pool surrounded by cattails and boulders. She removed her clothing and stepped into the clear, cold water. After bathing, she washed her cotton pants and shirt, and spread them on a rock to dry. She lay down on a rock and dozed in the fading sunlight. The sensual pleasure of the heated sandstone against her bare flesh made her remember Seth even more vividly.

Smack! The sharp pain on her bare buttocks made her eyes fly open. Quickly turning over, she saw Seth towering above her, his eyes blazing.

"I told you to stay out of sight! What are you doing down here stretched out for the world to see?"

She frowned, becoming angry herself, and opened her mouth to speak.

"I don't want to hear one damn word from you. I heard you come down that path like a buffalo."

His eyes were furious. "Anyone on that ridge could have seen you taking a bath. And now here you are stretched out, inviting trouble."

The fury she had felt left her, and she barely suppressed a giggle.

"What the hell are you laughing at! I try to make sure you're safe, while I risk my life to keep you that way, and you lie there and laugh!"

She smiled up at him, falsely innocent. "If you heard me coming down the path, why didn't you come to me then? Why did you wait until I'd finished bathing?" She turned on her side, her nude body tantalizing him. "You said I was inviting trouble. What kind of trouble were you thinking of?"

The tension left his body, and he gathered her to him. "Damn you, Morgan! You shouldn't have left the ruins. You weren't safe coming down here." He was serious.

"But what could happen to me now that you are here?"

He laughed. "I ought to spank you here and now, but I'm afraid you'd enjoy it." His voice lowered, and he said flatly, "I worried about you a lot. Please don't take chances like that again."

She was sorry she had caused him worry. "No, I won't again. Seth, is everything . . . finished?"

He stroked her hair, her head on his shoulders. "Yes. It's done now, and we won't speak of it again. I sent a message on to the ranch, to let them know we're all right." He drew her head back to look at her, his eyes teasing. "I met a woman in the saloon, and she was very friendly. I got the idea that if I ever wanted to go back, I'd be welcome."

"What do you mean, go back? And who is this bitch anyway?"

"Bitch! My, my, you have certainly learned a lot in the last few months. I could almost think you're jealous."

She said coolly, "I don't think she would be so interested in you if she knew your wife of four months was still a virgin." She turned to look at the water, idly running her fingers through her damp hair. "Of course, we did have geldings back home. Maybe she'd understand."

Seth's quick intake of breath was audible. "Lord! You would think that at my age I'd learn not to try to tease a woman. Come here, viper." He kissed her and ran his hand freely over her nude flesh. "Tonight you are my bride."

"Seth . . ." she began.

"What's this? Fear? From someone who has just called me a gelding?" He laughed and crushed her to the granite hardness of his chest. "Don't worry, my little one," he whispered. "I love you too much to hurt you."

He held her silently for a moment. "That water looks inviting. Help me out of these clothes, wife!"

In an instant they both were nude: two golden bodies drenched in the dappled sunlight. One body was big, strength showing in every contour, the other was small and delicate. Morgan stretched out a tentative hand to touch the steely muscles of his chest. "I like you like this," she whispered.

Seth smiled down at her, then quickly jumped in to bathe in the clear pool. This time Morgan watched him unabashedly, glorying in the way the water glistened on his magnificent back and arms. She sat on the edge of the pool and briefly wondered at the changes that had occurred in herself in the last few months. As Seth stood up, the water sliding over his glistening body, she thought, I'm in love now, and love changes everything! She stood up and ran to meet him, his arms enclosing her.

He led her to a grassy spot near the pool, sat down, and pulled Morgan beside him. At the nearness of her, and the sight of her perfect body, his manhood rose with an iron strength. He pulled her to him, and she felt his throbbing strength against her thigh. Her searching hand found him and held him in a firm grasp. Seth emitted the low moan that she had heard earlier. The size of him startled her, and she was afraid.

Seth sensed this. Gently, he kissed her lips, her neck, her breasts, teasing the pink tips with his tongue. His mouth traveled farther, while his hands stroked her inner thighs. Her legs separated of their own accord, as his tongue touched her most secret place.

His mouth found her lips again, and gently she felt him probing her. Slowly, he entered her, until she felt he filled her entirely. He lay still until the first, sharp pain faded and she began to move her hips. Following her lead, careful not to hurt her, Seth began to move with her, very slowly. Then, unable to contain himself, he moved more quickly until he lay quietly on top of her, supporting his weight on his elbows.

Morgan felt Seth's warm breath in her ear. What she had just experienced was so different from what she had imagined. It made her feel good to give pleasure to Seth, the man she loved. He hadn't hurt her, but neither had she felt the mounting excitement that he had, and then the quick relief.

"Did I hurt you, *mi querida?*" he whispered.

She hugged him closer, her arms not reaching across the broad expanse of his back. "No." She didn't want to tell him that she didn't find making love the joyous experience she had expected it to be.

Seth rolled off her, and rested his head on his elbow. He smiled at her. "Don't worry, little bride — it will get better."

She was startled by his understanding.

"What's there to eat around here? When a man changes from a gelding to a stallion in one day, it makes for hunger."

He laughed at Morgan's blush. Quickly she stood up and began to look for her clothes. "Here!" He tossed her his shirt. "I'm not ready to cover all that up, yet."

In minutes she returned from the cliff dwelling with Seth's saddlebags of food. He had started a fire in a sheltered copse of the canyon. Together they heated beans, and Morgan made baking-powder biscuits.

"If only Jean-Paul could see me now," she laughed. "We spent a week on white sauces, and now I am making crude biscuits over an open fire."

After the meal, Seth spread blankets. And as he held her close, she could feel his desire rising. As he kissed her and touched her body, she began to lose herself and feel a new urgency. Seth spent a long time with his love play, before he heard her soft moans and felt the movement of her body with his own.

When they made love the second time, she felt no pain. Her body felt good. She wanted this new feeling to go on forever. She was surprised at Seth's mounting passion, and was disappointed when he rolled to her side, spent.

He held her close, and was soon asleep. Morgan stayed awake for a few minutes. For some reason, she felt like running until she dropped from exhaustion. But the soft call of an owl finally lulled her to sleep.

They awoke together in the dawn. "Seth," she whispered.

Seth was smiling. She held out her arms

to him, and he came to her quickly, his needs meeting her own. He held back, until she clawed at his back and held his buttocks, pulling him deeper into her. Her desires met his, and they collapsed together in one another's arms, sated.

Morgan slowly recalled her abandonment of the moments before. She was embarrassed, and turned her head away from Seth. She had acted like an animal.

"What's this? Morgan, what's wrong?" He looked into her tear-filled eyes. "Tears, from my little wildcat?"

She began to cry more. "I'm not a wildcat. I'm a *woman,*" she sobbed.

He laughed. "So that's it. It's that damned mother of yours. Sometimes I wish I could have met her. But I'd probably regret what I would say to her." He kissed Morgan's damp cheeks. "Your mother had some wrong ideas about what makes a lady. I love you, and you love me. What we do between us isn't wrong." His eyes twinkled. "Didn't you enjoy this morning?"

"Yes."

"Then that's all that matters." He stood up, took her hand, and pulled her up to him. "Come on."

"Where?"

"We're taking a bath. I've smelled buffalo

more pleasant than the two of us."

She looked at his hair and noticed it was wet with sweat, as was her own. Seth was right. She had enjoyed their lovemaking . . . more than enjoyed it. She needed it. And she wasn't going to let anyone interfere.

"Race you," she called as she ran to the pool.

CHAPTER NINE

They spent four days in the canyon of the ancient ruins. Seth introduced Morgan to the joys of lovemaking, and after her initial fears were over, she learned to return his love with an abandonment that surprised them both.

"Morgan, sweet, it's time to go." Seth's voice was a whisper in the early-morning stillness.

"Go where?" She snuggled closer to him, still groggy with sleep.

"Today we have to start for home. We've been here long enough. I want to take my little bride back to my ranch."

It was a minute before Morgan reacted, and then she sat up, throwing the blanket from her body. The sight of her golden skin with the full curves of her breasts and hips always made Seth's body react. He reached out one large hand to caress her and pull her back to him, but with lightning quickness, she was already standing out of his reach.

"Hey," he called softly, "why don't you come back to me for a little while?"

She ran to him, pulling his head to her chest. "I want to go. I want to see your ranch, and I want to meet Lupita, and I want to be your wife."

"My wife? That's just what I want you to be right now." His hand reached inside her cotton shirt.

She laughed and pulled away from him. "Oh, no, Seth Colter, I know you. We'll make love, and then we'll sleep, and then we'll make love, and before long the day will be gone. You'll never take me home until I'm old and ugly and you don't want me anymore."

Her reasoning made sense to him. "You're probably right. So why don't we just stay here for a few more years?" He made a grab for her. "I promise to take you home when I'm tired of you." At the look in her eye he said, "All right. I'm getting up." As he put his clothes on, Morgan heard him muttering something about being henpecked so soon.

The journey east and north to Seth's ranch took over three weeks. They stopped often to rest the horse, which was overburdened with the weight of two people. There had been places where they could have purchased a horse, but Morgan had protested. This was her honeymoon, and she liked the feeling of being so near Seth.

Seth had said that they would reach his home within the next two days. She twisted in the saddle and unbuttoned Seth's shirt to kiss the bronzed skin of his chest.

"Can't keep your hands off me, can you, wench?"

Morgan giggled and then sighed, her chest against his cool skin. "Seth, do you think I'll fit in? Do you think the people on your ranch will like me?"

He kissed the top of her head, warm from the sun. "As long as I like you, then that's all that matters. Besides there aren't many others. You know Jake, and Lupita will adore you. For years, she's been trying to marry me off to every female relative of hers from fourteen to fifty. Paul runs the place while I'm gone."

"You've never mentioned Paul."

"He's been with me about two years. Between Jake, Paul and me, we keep the place going. In the spring we hire a few men, but then they leave again in the fall. I hope you're not disappointed, sweet, but

221

you are not married to a wealthy man."

"Seth," she leaned against him, enjoying the feel of his muscles against her back, "What will happen to your father's plantation? Wasn't he angry when you came out here to live, rather than run the plantation? You're his only son."

"He was at first, but then I think he envied me my freedom. He married and then I was born, when he was still very young. He had to support his family, and couldn't go off to new territory to start a life that offered no security. The plantation will go to my sisters and their husbands."

"It seems strange for a rich man's son to give up everything and start all over again, poor."

"But my ranch in New Mexico is mine, not handed to me. My son will be able to choose where he wants to live, too."

"Son!" Morgan murmured, and felt her belly. She would be glad to get home, to a home in this enchanted land for her, Seth, and their children.

It was late afternoon of the following day, when they saw the house. Even from a distance, it looked enormous to Morgan. "Well, when a house is built of adobe, I guess you can afford a big one."

222

It was low and sprawling, with fences and low walls surrounding areas off the rooms. In back were four other buildings, houses for Lupita, Jake, and Paul, and a sort of barn for horses and Lupita's dairy cow. There were several cottonwoods around the houses, and here and there chickens scratched in the dirt.

Other than the chickens, Morgan saw no signs of life. When they were about a hundred yards from the house, Seth dismounted, emitted three low whistles, and suddenly he was surrounded by dogs. They were glad to see their master, and leaped to greet him.

Smiling up at Morgan, still on the horse, Seth told her, "They're the worst watchdogs in the world, but I couldn't possibly get rid of them."

"Señor Colter! You are home!" A short, plump woman ran to Seth and threw her arms around his waist. Seth picked her up, swung her around, and kissed her heartily on the cheek.

"You're so skinny!" she laughed, wiping away tears. "They have no *frijoles* in that place, no *tortillas?*" She stopped when she saw Morgan.

"This is my wife, Lupita," Seth announced proudly, as he lifted Morgan from the horse and held her in his arms like a child.

"Put me down," she whispered to him, embarrassed.

Lupita laughed happily. "Jake has been telling me about you. I am so happy to meet you. I have been telling this buffalo a long time it is no good to live alone."

"Well, Lupita, she's only second best." Seth could feel Morgan's eyes on him. "I wanted Lupita, but she wouldn't have me."

Seth ignored Morgan's struggles and pulled her closer. "I seem to remember an ancient Roman custom, where the husband carries his bride into the house."

Lupita glowed as she saw the obvious love between the two. She had not expected this, not after what Jake had told her about the constant bickering during the journey. She loved Seth as the son she never had, and she knew this tiny bit of a woman that he so easily held was going to be her daughter. Maybe soon there'd be lots of babies for her to take care of. She laughed aloud.

"See, Lupita approves of my carrying you." Morgan relaxed against her husband as he started walking toward the house.

"Seth!" Morgan turned her head to see Jake running toward them. "What the hell took you so long? Frank's been over twice to see if you were back yet." He grinned his toothless smile and took Seth's outstretched hand in both of his.

"Well, I see you got the little girl back."

Seth pulled her close and said, "I would have been back sooner, but this little wildcat kept me holed up in a canyon for a week. Wouldn't let me go."

"Seth!" Morgan hid her reddened face in Seth's shoulder. Through clenched teeth she issued threats against his life, but he happily continued carrying her and ignored her protests.

When he reached the house, he paused at the threshold and sought her lips. He kissed her as he carried her into the house.

Sensing their need for privacy, Jake and Lupita walked around the house, leaving the newlyweds alone.

Seth enjoyed showing Morgan his house, and she immediately fell in love with it. There were few rooms in the house, but each one was enormous. The kitchen was in the center, with an open porch on one side and a long, narrow room with many windows on the other side. The living area was L-shaped, and she saw that Jake had already set up the furniture Nora had given them.

The only other room was a huge bedroom with big double doors leading onto a little walled-in courtyard. The bed was set against one wall, and was encased in a crudely but ornately carved bedstead. There were several rugs on the floor, of boldly patterned designs in bright colors. Every room except the kitchen had an open fireplace shaped like a beehive.

Morgan sat on the bed. "I love it! It's a beautiful house — not at all like what you described."

"Well, I didn't want you to be disappointed. It's not exactly like Trahern House." He looked at Morgan sideways, watching her reaction.

She didn't turn, but replied nonchalantly, "Trahern House? I don't believe I've heard of that place." She turned to him and smiled invitingly. She tested the bed with her hands. "Nice bed," she murmured.

Seth embraced her. "I want this to be your home. I want you to be happy here."

"I could never be any happier than I am right now. I love you so much."

Seth tangled his hands in her hair and pulled her back with him on the bed. "You know, I've never made love to you on a bed before!" He kissed her lips and her throat as she moved her thigh between his legs.

The following week was blissful. Seth was gone during the day, and she was content to stay in their house and perform the many chores there. At noon she often rode out to Seth and took him a lunch. More often than not, they made love under the piñon trees.

Lupita had loaned Morgan some embroidered blouses and full, bright-colored skirts. These fit her as poorly as the clothes from Kentucky. Lupita had said she should go into Santa Fe and get clothes to fit her, but Morgan didn't want to leave the ranch even for a day.

But Lena changed things.

She came one morning, riding a beautiful black stallion. Morgan was outside feeding the chickens, dressed in a particularly drab dress, with one of Lupita's old aprons tied around her waist. She held the apron in front of her, filled with chicken feed.

The sight of Lena astonished Morgan. Never had she seen anyone so beautiful. Lena's riding suit was entirely black, with a small patch of white lace at the throat. Her legs were encased in tall boots of soft black leather. Lena's blue-black hair was intricately arranged in soft, lustrous curls on top of her head and gently flowing down her back to her waist. Cocked over one eye was a tiny little hat with a slim red feather curling around the brim.

"Señorita Montoya!" It was Lupita's

happy voice behind her as Morgan stood as still as a statue. "Long time since you come. How have you been? Come and meet Señor Colter's wife. You will like one another."

Lena smiled down at Lupita and slowly, gracefully, dismounted. Lena kissed the older woman's plump cheek, and Morgan saw that Lena was small, like herself.

"Yes, I have heard about this little beauty of Seth's. Where is she?" At the question, Lena looked around and saw Morgan a few feet from them. She stared for a moment, and then confidently walked to Morgan and around her.

"Oh, yes . . . I can see what Joaquín meant. Yes. You do hide your beauty very well." She turned quickly to Lupita. "What do you mean, allowing the lady of the house to work like a *péon?*"

Lupita threw up her hands. "She does what she wants, and that husband of hers lets her. She cooks, she even scrubs floors, and no matter what I say, she does it. Maybe you can talk to her."

"Yes, I think I'll have to." She turned back to Morgan and possessively put her arm around Morgan's shoulders. "Now, drop that," she sneered at the chicken feed Morgan still held in her apron, "and let's go inside. By the way, I'm Lena."

Lena had always been spoiled, and she grew up believing she was the center of the world. She had never had any reason to suppose differently.

Morgan was shy around the beautiful woman who seemed so at home, so confident. Lena asked questions about their return trip to the ranch. Morgan briefly told the story of Cat Man.

"I think you were very brave and very smart to keep quiet and wait for Seth. Me — I would have killed the man myself."

Morgan shivered as she remembered Cat Man's eyes.

Lena, sensing her reluctance to talk further of the horrible episode, dropped the subject. "Well, Morgan, we have a lot to do to get ready."

"Ready?"

"Yes. Didn't I mention that the reason I came was to invite Seth and you to a party at the Montoya ranch in three days? No, I guess not. Joaquín said that there was some mixup in your clothing, that for some reason you had none of your own and had to take things from Seth's sisters."

"Yes, it was a . . ."

Lena watched Morgan carefully. "No matter. You and I will leave now for Santa Fe, and in two days Mrs. Sanchez can make you several dresses."

"Leave? Lena, I can't leave now. I still have too many things to do. The cow needs milking this evening, and I have bread that has to be kneaded and . . ." She couldn't bear the idea of being away from Seth for three whole days.

"*Qué tontería!* Bread and cows!"

"Seth. I don't want to leave Seth." Morgan's voice was quieter.

Lena's laughter rang out. "Ah! Now *that* I can understand. And Seth — such a beautiful man! I would not want to leave him either, if he were mine."

Morgan felt her jaw clench, and she shot Lena a look of fire.

"Morgan, let us be friends. Let us be honest with one another. I have been somewhat in love with that good-looking husband of yours for years, but he has turned me down." Lena did not mention that he had turned down her hints at a permanent relationship, but not her offers of lovemaking.

"Don't worry," Lena continued. "You and I will be friends. But tell me, honestly, would you like to go to my party in that dress?"

Morgan compared her own dress to Lena's elegant riding habit.

"I thought not. Now, I will ride out to tell Seth Colter myself. It will do him good not to see his little bride for a few days." She looked at Morgan critically. "When I get through with you, he will be even more in love with you than he is now."

Instantly, she was gone, and when Morgan heard the sound of the stallion's hooves, she collapsed in a chair. Lupita's laugh rang behind her. "That one! So full of fire. Do not worry, Señora Colter, she always gets her way. When Lena wants something, she lets nothing stand in her way."

"What about Seth? She wanted Seth. She's so beautiful, Lupita. What will Seth say when he sees the two of us together?"

"He will not even notice there is anyone else in the room except his wife. You had better pack some clothes, because if I know Señorita Montoya, you will be leaving very soon for Santa Fe."

Morgan knew she was right and went to the bedroom to get ready. For some reason, she was frightened at the idea of leaving the ranch. She looked around the room at the fireplace, the rugs, the big bed she and Seth had shared for so few nights.

"This is silly," she said aloud. "I'll be back in just a few days, and then Seth will be happy to see me and . . ." She shivered again. On impulse, she pulled a trunk from the corner of the room and dug deep into the bottom of it until she found the red dress. She held it up to the light and marveled again at its texture and the beautiful handmade lace across the bodice. She had never shown the dress to Seth because she had wanted to save it for a very special occasion. When she saw him again, after having been away from him for days, she'd wear the dress. Her eyes misted as she quickly packed the silky fabric beneath her other plain dresses.

"Morgan!" A thrill of joy ran through her. She ran to him and clung to him. It seemed much longer than three hours since she had last seen him.

"I missed you, too, little one." He kissed her hair, caressed her back and held her close. "What's this about your leaving me?"

"I don't want to go, Seth. I don't need any new clothes." Why did she feel such fright at leaving him?

Seth held her at arm's length and looked at her. "Lena convinced me. In fact, she's made me realize how selfish I've been, keeping you here all to myself." He smiled at her, and Morgan ached with love for him. "Don't look like that, it's only for a few days. In three days I'll come to the party,

232

and then I'll take you home. I couldn't live without you longer than that."

Lena watched the two of them together. Such a fuss over being separated for three days! Then she looked at Seth's enormous back and shoulders and she remembered how he felt, close to her, her arms around him. For that one, perhaps I, too, would cry over three days' separation.

"All packed?" Seth asked as he saw the little case on the bedroom floor.

Morgan nodded.

"You won't forget me?" Seth teased.

Morgan looked at him pleadingly. "I love you, Seth. I love you more than life itself."

He held her close to him. "I love you, too. More than I thought possible." He kissed her, and she returned his kiss urgently.

"If we don't leave now, Lena may have a two-hour wait."

Quickly, he ushered Morgan outside, and Jake led her horse next to Lena's beautiful black stallion.

For miles, Morgan kept turning to look back to see if she could still see the house.

"Santa Fe is not what you have been used to in Kentucky, but it is a pretty little town, and Mrs. Sanchez is a magician with a needle. I just show her a picture, and she can make a copy of the gown." Lena did not seem to notice Morgan's silence. "Of course, now that they've discovered gold in California, everything is changing. I heard that they're opening a stage line all the way from St. Louis to San Francisco. Already, more and more goods are coming into Santa Fe as the traders stop here on their way to the coast."

Lena continued talking as they rode.

It was nearly sundown when they reached the town. The buildings were like Seth's ranch house, made of adobe with long poles protruding from under the roofs. There were few stores, but the town seemed busy as the people moved around under the broad porches.

Lena led them to the hotel. The room was large and comfortable. Lena ordered a bath for Morgan as she left to get Mrs. Sanchez and some of her own clothes, which she always kept in town at Mrs. Sanchez's house.

Morgan was luxuriating in the hot tub when they returned. Mrs. Sanchez was a stout woman, dressed in black. "Here she is," said Lena. "She'll take your measurements and start on some clothes. Here, dry off so we can get busy." Morgan smiled as she took the towel from Lena. She was getting used to the way Lena ordered everyone around.

Lena gasped as Morgan stood up. "My brother told me you were beautiful under your ugly clothes, but he could not have known how much of the truth he spoke!" Quickly, Mrs. Sanchez took Morgan's measurements. Then she and Lena discussed Morgan's new clothes. After the seamstress left, a waiter brought their dinner. Lena went to her own room, and Morgan sank into the empty bed. It was the first time in weeks she had slept without Seth's arms around her, and she had to exercise control to keep from crying herself to sleep.

By midmorning of the next day, Mrs. Sanchez returned with a completed dress. Morgan looked at the woman's red-rimmed eyes, and she knew she had worked on it all night.

As Morgan slipped on the dress and then looked into the full-length mirror, her spirits lifted. The dress was beautiful. It was a brilliant blue, the color of her eyes, and it fit her curves perfectly.

Lena was watching her in the mirror. "It is strange what a beautiful gown will do for a woman."

"Lena, it is beautiful. I've never had a dress like this before. Do you think Seth will like it?"

"A woman in love! How very tiresome they can be. Of course, he will like it, and the women will hate you."

Morgan smiled at her own reflection.

"Now we will fix your hair, and soon we will be ready to show Santa Fe its newest citizen."

An hour later, Morgan stood before the mirror again, hardly recognizing herself. The mirror told her she was beautiful, and she held her head high. She laughed.

"What amuses you?"

"I was thinking about an old girlfriend of Seth's. Cynthia thought she was going to marry Seth. I wish I could see her now."

Lena laughed also. "I knew there was more to you than what I first saw scattering feed for the chickens. You would like to show off in front of your husband's admirer, would you?" Her eyes danced mischievously. "I think we could take a trip to a certain store in Santa Fe before dinner. You might find something to interest you there."

On their way from the hotel to the store, people turned to stare. Lena was attired in a maroon dress with thin bands of ruby-red trim. Morgan began to enjoy the way the people looked at them, and as they reached the store, she realized she was happy she had come to Santa Fe.

"Good afternoon, Marilyn. We came to see some yardgoods. My friend would like to have some shirts made for her husband."

At the mention of Marilyn's name, Morgan knew who the woman was. She was pretty, and her figure was generous, but Morgan guessed that in a few years she would be fat. This was Marilyn Wilson, the woman some people thought Seth might marry.

"Yes," Morgan said, "I would like some very fine cotton and silk, if you have it." She looked at Lena and acted as if she were suppressing laughter. "I will need several yards of each. You see, I'm very new at this and my husband is . . . a very large man." She gave an embarrassed laugh. "You know how it is, I'm sure, Mrs. . . . ?"

"Miss Wilson."

"Well, yes, you will learn in a short time, I am sure." Morgan patted Marilyn's hand. "Let me introduce myself. I am Mrs. Seth Colter. My husband and I have just journeyed all the way from Kentucky, and I find his wardrobe sorely depleted." Morgan walked to the counter, piled with bolts of fabric, pretending to be unaware of the woman's astonished stare.

Marilyn fairly exploded. "Seth!"

Morgan whirled to face her, her blue eyes wide in innocence. "Do you know my husband? But of course you would. My dear Seth is such a rogue, is he not? Why, even back home I sometimes had trouble with other women. Of course, Seth and I have been engaged practically since we were children."

"Engaged! You mean all the time he's been out here, he was engaged to you?"

"But of course. Didn't he mention me to you?" Morgan gave her a look of sympathy. "I'm so sorry, my dear. Seth has always been such a tease. I hope he hasn't caused you any distress? Lena, I think we should make our purchases some other time." She paused again to pat Marilyn's hand. "Why don't you come out to the ranch sometime for a visit? We'd love to have you."

Outside the store, Lena and Morgan walked together in silence for a while.

"Morgan, I am glad you and I are friends, because I would certainly hate to have you for an enemy."

Morgan smiled. She had only been protecting what was hers.

Chapter Ten

The Montoya ranch was enormous. The main house itself could have housed a small army. In fact, the shape of the house suggested that it had been made to hold off an attack. The house enclosed all four sides of a large garden and courtyard.

Everywhere there were servants. There were always men working in the garden, and every room had one or two women cleaning and polishing. Lena had introduced Morgan to two young girls whose sole job it would be to take care of Morgan. Morgan soon found that she liked being pampered.

The party would start in a short time. Lena had already gone downstairs to stand beside her brother as they greeted their guests. Morgan had not seen Joaquín yet and had, in fact, given him very little thought.

Seth had not come yet.

"Señora Colter, he will be here soon. You

are so beautiful that he will be very sorry he took so long."

"Thank you, Margarita."

The dress was of shimmering red silk. It was cut low in front and exposed Morgan's creamy shoulders. She was not used to the tight restrictions of the laced corset, but she liked the way it pushed her breasts above the restraining fabric. Her golden hair was piled on top of her head, with great masses of curls cascading down her back.

There was a knock, and Morgan, expecting Seth, eagerly stepped toward the door as Margarita opened it. Her face fell as she saw it was Joaquín.

"My beautiful little Morgan, is your old friend such an unwelcome sight after all we have shared together?"

She smiled at him and took his extended hands. "No, Joaquín. I am glad to see you. It's just that I expected Seth."

"He was always lucky with beautiful women." Morgan missed the slight edge to his voice and the passing look of hatred that fired his eyes.

"But let me look at you." Still holding her hands, he appraised her every curve until she felt the blood rising to her face. "I knew you were beautiful, but I did not realize how beautiful." He dropped her hands and reached into his inside coat pocket. "Lena told me what you were wearing, and she thought I might lend you some of the Montoya jewels." He opened a small leather case to expose a sparkling chain of sapphires surrounded by tiny diamonds. There were earrings to match.

"Joaquín, they're beautiful! But I couldn't wear them."

"Why not? They are not a gift, only a loan for one night. Surely you would not turn down a loan between friends? If you would like, think of them as coming from my sister. I am merely her messenger."

Morgan laughed. "Joaquín, I believe you could charm butter into cream with just your words."

Joaquín smiled, his eyes devouring her. "I wish that were so, because there are some things I would like to have. Seth is a lucky man."

There was an embarrassed silence until Morgan broke it by asking the maid to help her with the jewels. Joaquín took them from her instead, and as he fastened them around her lovely neck, Morgan had the distinct impression that he was about to kiss her. Somehow the moments she spent with Joaquín always became awkward. She wished Seth would hurry.

"There! They are nearly as lovely as you are."

"Oh, *señora!* They are really beautiful on you. Your husband will know you are the most beautiful woman in all of *Nuevo Mexico!*"

"Do you really think so, Margarita? I hope he likes me."

"Likes you?" Joaquín smiled. He had heard from Lena how they had clung to one another in parting. He himself had seen only the way they had acted on the trip to New Mexico. As he looked at Morgan, breathtaking in the silken gown, he ached to take her in his arms. "Morgan, little one, no man will be able to resist you at all tonight. If that husband of yours does not fall at your feet, I will shoot him myself." Joaquín's roaring laughter at his own comment caused Morgan to look at him curiously.

"Since your husband does not seem to be here yet, may I have the honor of escorting you downstairs?"

She really wanted to wait for Seth, but since Joaquín had been so nice about the jewels, she took his extended arm and they went downstairs to the party.

"Morgan! There are so many people here who want to meet you." Lena lowered her voice. "There are going to be a lot of women here who will hate you." She laughed at Morgan's startled expression. "Seth has been the most eligible bachelor around here for years. He and Joaquín have been pursued by every woman with a marriageable daughter within two hundred miles of Santa Fe." She touched Morgan's silk dress. "Isn't silk nicer than chicken feed?" They laughed together.

Lena had been right in telling Morgan that she would feel hatred from some of the women. Morgan felt that some of the people had come only to see her, to judge Seth Colter's new wife. As she shook hands with seemingly endless numbers of people, she overheard remarks from all sides.

"No wonder Colter waited so long. He was holding out for the best."

"Of course, if I had allowed my Katherine to dress like that, she would have had several men around her, but I prefer modesty and a certain respectability."

Morgan turned at this remark, obviously intended for her hearing. She saw an overweight matron glaring at her. Close behind the woman was a tall, thin girl with protruding teeth and a sharp nose. Morgan smiled at the girl and remembered herself, shy at a ball, less than a year ago. That had been the most fortunate night of her life. She had met Seth that night. She looked again toward the door for the thousandth time.

"You don't look as if you are having a very good time."

She smiled at Joaquín. "I just wish Seth were here. I hope nothing has happened at the ranch."

"You are the talk of everyone here tonight. There isn't a woman at my house now who wouldn't sell her soul to be as beautiful as you are. Yet you stand here and worry about problems on the ranch. Smile, sweet Morgan. Laugh and enjoy yourself. Come, dance with me, and let's give them more to talk about."

"You're right, Joaquín. I'll have to stop worrying."

Joaquín led her onto the dance floor, and Morgan was again glad her Aunt Lacey had arranged for dancing lessons.

"Who would have thought you could be so beautiful? There is a woman making her way toward us who has the most incredible look of hatred directed right at you."

Morgan turned to see Marilyn Wilson staring at her. She was escorted by a slim man with a pencil-thin mustache. He seemed almost as young as Morgan.

"Why, Mrs. Colter! What a pleasant surprise."

"Hello, Miss Wilson. Are you enjoying Lena and Joaquín's party?"

"Oh, yes." She looked up at her partner and then at Joaquín. "But I would have thought a bride would be dancing with her husband." She smiled. "At least for the first few weeks."

Morgan smiled back sweetly. "My husband was detained tonight, but it is nice to be a bride, don't you agree, Miss Wilson? Oh — *pardon* me. Of course, you wouldn't know, would you? Joaquín, could we get some champagne? I seem to be suddenly very thirsty."

At the long table set against the wall, Joaquín gave Morgan a glass of chilled champagne. "You are deadly to your enemies, are you not?"

"Oh, yes, I guess," Morgan was distracted as she glanced toward the door again.

"Come little one, I am not used to women who find me boring."

"Oh, Joaquín, it's not you; I'm just worried about Seth."

"Come walk with me in the garden. The fountain is lovely in the moonlight."

She looked at him apprehensively.

"I promise not to molest you or even to

kiss your lips."

She smiled at him, took his extended arm, and walked out through the open door with him into the moonlit garden.

Seth entered in time to see his wife, her body clad in red silk, smiling up at Joaquín. She took his arm and they stepped into the moonlight.

Seth's impulse was to run after her and knock the little Spaniard down. He'd like to have seen Joaquín on the floor, blood running from his nose. Damn her! I leave her alone a minute and she runs off with someone else.

"Seth! It's good to see you." Marilyn followed his eyes to the open door. She had also seen Joaquín and Morgan leave together. "Well, aren't you going to ask an old friend to dance?"

"Marilyn." He had just realized she was there.

"Seth, honey, would you like some refreshment? You look like you've just had a shock."

He allowed himself to be led to the table. After three straight shots of Joaquín's twelve-year-old bourbon, he felt stronger.

"Feel better now, honey?"

"Yes, I do." He looked at Marilyn. Her large breasts were nearly spilling over the top of her dress. In the last few months he hadn't looked at any woman other than Morgan. After another shot of whiskey, Marilyn began to look even better to him.

"Would you care to have this dance, Miss Wilson?" he asked sweepingly.

Marilyn felt good being in Seth's arms again. None of the other men she had ever had made her feel the way Seth did. Most men cared only about themselves, but when Seth made love to her, he made sure she enjoyed it, too.

"I met your wife a few days ago." She had his attention. "It seemed so strange to me that she was a new bride, yet running around the countryside with that Lena. You know what Lena's like. I thought it was odd then, and here she is tonight flirting like a . . . like a . . . Well, I'm sure you understand my distress." She cast him a sidelong glance to make sure he was listening. "And that Joaquín Montoya, of all people!" She smiled when she felt Seth's arm muscles tighten. "Yes, everyone is talking about them, about how they keep standing in dark corners, giggling and drinking champagne together. I'm sure if I had a husband, I wouldn't —"

Seth dropped his arms from around her and quickly left the room, out the same door Morgan and Joaquín had used a few minutes earlier.

A few people turned and stared, and Marilyn nearly laughed aloud with joy. Little bitch, she thought, I'll teach her to snub me.

The first thing Seth heard was Morgan's laughter.

"Well, it looks like my little wife is enjoying herself."

"Seth!" She ran to him and threw her arms around his waist. "I was so worried. You're so late."

He disengaged her arms, holding her from him. "Yes, I can see how worried you were."

"Seth! For Heaven's sake, you're not going to be jealous, are you? Joaquín and I walked out into the garden together for a few minutes. That's all. You are not going to spend our entire married life getting angry every time I speak to another man, are you?"

Seth looked at Joaquín. "No," he said quietly, "I don't think I'll spend all our married life getting angry, because we may have had all the married life we are going to have. Now, if you will excuse me, I believe I can find other things to occupy myself than trying to keep my wife from her lover — or is it lovers? Goodnight."

Seth was gone before she could react to

his accusations. She started walking toward the house after Seth, but Joaquín caught her arm. "Morgan, you cannot think to pursue him after he has treated you as he has. No, you must wait for him to come to you, to apologize and to beg your forgiveness."

She stared at him. "I don't understand why he should be jealous. He's the only man I've ever cared about. How *could* he accuse me of the things he did?"

Joaquín put a comforting arm around her shoulders. "He was wrong, and soon he will know it. He'll come back to you and everything will be all right. Now, cheer up. A lover's quarrel is not the end of the world. We will go back inside, dance, and show the world we do not care."

She jerked from his arm, not seeing the frown on his face. "But I do care. I care more than you'll ever know. I love him more than my own life, and he must know that. I must find him."

Quietly, Joaquín agreed. "I will help you. We will go to my stables now, and we will find this ignorant husband of yours, and you may explain all night if you like."

"But, Joaquín, your guests."

"Pah! Lena is the one who loves parties. She will not even know I am gone, and she will be glad that your beauty is no longer there to compete with hers."

It seemed they had traveled for hours when Joaquín stopped at a little house Morgan had never seen before. Joaquín began to dismount in front of the house.

"Joaquín, what are you doing? Seth isn't here."

"We must rest the horses, and I, for one, am very thirsty."

It was very dark now, but she could see the look of determination on Joaquín's handsome face.

The interior of the house was unexpected. There were mirrors everywhere, and the walls were covered with crimson silk. In front was a tiny living room and then an enormous bedroom. The furniture was gold and white, while the bed was draped in a sheer version of the crimson silk.

"What is this place, Joaquín?"

"Can't you guess?" She turned quickly at the peculiar tone in his voice. His eyes were hard. He stared openly at her body. Involuntarily, her hand went to cover her breasts.

"Joaquín, why are you looking at me like that?"

He moved closer to her and took her hand, kissing it. "I have wanted you from the first moment I saw you. That husband of yours did not even see your beauty. I was glad when I saw how the two of you fought constantly and glad when he did not spend the night with you in the wagon."

She backed away from him, beginning to be very frightened. "But, Joaquín, I love Seth."

"Seth, Seth, Seth! That is what I hear from too many women — my own sister, and that cow of a woman, Marilyn Wilson. Do you think that one must be as big as Colter to be a man? I assure you, it is not so. Come, little Morgan, and I will show you tenderness. I will show you the fine art of lovemaking, not the crudeness of these Americans."

"Joaquín, I'd like to go now." She started firmly for the door.

"Oh, no." He grabbed her arm, pulling her to him, clasping her body close to his. "I've waited a long time for this." His lips on hers made her shudder. They were too soft, too moist. They didn't make her feel as Seth's lips did.

She twisted in his arms, pulling her mouth from his. "No, Joaquín." His lips moved down her throat leaving a damp trail, like a snail.

"No!" She fairly screamed the word and

pushed against him with all her might, catching him off guard. He nearly fell. She looked into his eyes, and the hatred she saw there made her realize the danger she was in.

"So, you refuse me. You teased me on the wagon train, yet you meant nothing. You do not use a Montoya and get away with it. Now you will be punished."

She screamed when he came to her and tied the gag around her mouth. She fought him, but he was surprisingly strong and held her easily.

"Remember this, little one — you have chosen your fate. We could have been such lovers, but now —" He finished tying her hands and then her ankles and tossed her on the bed. "Now that husband of yours will die because of your teasing." He laughed as he saw Morgan's eyes widen in horror.

He walked to the doorway. "I will be back in a few hours, and then I have some plans for you."

After one last searching look at her, he turned abruptly and was gone.

CHAPTER ELEVEN

When Seth left the Montoya party, he rode hard for an hour until he realized what he was doing to his horse. He stopped and rested. The first blind rage was gone, and the cool night air helped to clear his head of fury and liquor.

Gradually, he began to remember the way Morgan's face had lit up when she saw him, the way she had run to him. Damn that Montoya! Seth had played right into his hands, and Joaquín had enjoyed every moment of it.

Morgan, sweet little Morgan. She was so innocent that she probably didn't even realize what Montoya was like. He had been a fool to leave her there alone. He mounted his horse and started back to the Montoya ranch. He was so lost in his thoughts that he didn't hear the approaching rider. A shot rang out and the bullet slammed into his shoulder.

Before he could get to his own gun, the rider took it, then grabbed the reins of his horse. Silently, he led Seth back toward the Montoya ranch, blood dripping from his wound, each step increasing his pain.

When Joaquín returned to Morgan a few hours later and removed her gag, she tried to reason with him. He smiled at her, and she wondered why she had never understood the coldness of his smile before.

"It would do no good now to try to save yourself or your husband."

"What have you done with Seth? Where is he?"

"Ah, sweet little noble Morgan, would you like to save the life of your husband? If you could save his life, what would you do for me?"

Her eyes looked straight into his. "Anything," she whispered.

"Yes, I believe you would. Too bad Colter had such a woman as you and never realized it. But you can save his life, and very easily, too. All you have to do is write a letter."

"A letter?" A new fear was growing in her stomach.

"Yes. You see, I have been trying for a long time to get Colter to sell his ranch to me. I thought I had succeeded, but then he brought back a wife. A wife makes a man settle down."

"Why would you want Seth's small ranch when yours is so large?"

"A good question, my little pretty one, but your husband's ranch has the source of water for my ranch. At any time, he could cut off all the water to my home and my cattle."

"But Seth wouldn't do that."

"Who can say? I do not like to trust my fortune to someone else."

"So, you think Seth will sell the ranch to you if I am gone?"

"Yes. Exactly. But first I plan to make him never want to see the place again. That is important, and that is where your letter comes in."

The fear inside her increased.

"I want you to write a short note saying that you and I are going away together, that we had planned it for some time, ever since we were on the wagon train together."

Morgan's eyes widened in horror. "No," she whispered. She could not do this. If she ever did find Seth again, he would hate her. Even if she escaped, he wouldn't want her again. He'd believe the note. Joaquín must know that.

"No? A moment ago you said you'd do

anything to save his life. I guess I'll tell the men to kill him." He turned toward the door.

"No! I'll do what you ask. Don't hurt him. Please."

"That's much better. Now I will get a pen and paper."

Morgan wrote the note with trembling hands. She knew she was writing the end to her marriage. Seth would never want her again.

Quickly, Joaquín took the note from her, retied her hands, and replaced the gag. As he removed the sapphire necklace and earrings, he kissed her neck and she flinched. His eyes hardened, and he raised a hand to strike her.

"No. I will not mar your lovely skin. I have plans for you. I am sure there will be many men who will do more to that lovely body than just strike your cheek."

Her eyes had gone dead. She didn't look at him, but held her eyes on the note he carried in his hand.

He left. Morgan felt that her life went with him.

Joaquín's two men led Seth west, away from the Montoya ranch. The pain in his shoulder had intensified, and the loss of blood was making him weak. Eventually they came to the walls of a crumbling adobe hut. Here the two men dismounted, and painfully Seth did also. It was close to dawn, and the sky was beginning to lighten. He stuffed a handkerchief against the wound to try to stop the blood.

The two men said nothing. They just watched him, pointing a revolver at him continually.

When he saw Montoya riding up in the faint morning light, he used his rapidly draining strength to rush at him.

"Where is she? What have you done with her?"

Roughly, the guards pulled Seth to the ground. One of them kicked him in the ribs. He raised his foot to strike again but Joaquín halted him.

Seth regained his breath and pulled himself into a sitting position, leaning against the mud wall.

"Such concern for your little wife. Too bad she does not return that feeling for you. You see, she and I have been planning this, er . . . meeting . . . for a long time."

"I don't believe you," Seth's voice was hoarse. Breathing hurt, and he knew his ribs were cracked.

"Somehow, I knew you wouldn't. So I

brought you a little note from my beloved. Read it."

Seth winced. He read the note twice. It said very simply that she had always loved Joaquín and that she was leaving with him.

Seth remembered the time on the wagon train when he had seen her kissing Joaquín. Yet he also remembered the four days they had spent in the canyon, and the weeks since then. How could anyone have been such an actress? He had believed she loved him. He crumpled the note.

"I see you sense the truth of her note," Joaquín sneered. What fools these *gringos* are, he thought. Colter couldn't see that the woman lived only for him. She adored him and the dolt was blind to her devotion.

"Now I will take your horse and leave you."

Seth put his hand to his bleeding shoulder. As he did so, Joaquín noticed a ring on Seth's little finger. It was surely a woman's ring.

The three men mounted their horses. When they had ridden a few yards, Joaquín turned, aimed his pistol at Seth's head, and fired. Seth's head slumped forward onto his chest.

Joaquín turned to the man on his left. "He has a ring on the little finger of his left hand.

Bring it to me."

When he had the ring, the three of them rode toward the east. After Joaquín had given the two men exact instructions, he rode to the little house where Morgan was.

For hours, she had worked at the rough rope fastenings until her skin was raw and bleeding. The sound of the opening door set her heart pounding.

"Well, little one, I see you are still here." He removed the gag from her mouth. "It is too bad to have to cover up such a lovely mouth." He bent to kiss her and frowned when she turned her head away.

He slumped in a chair, ignoring the tight ropes that held her wrists and ankles together. "It's over," he sighed.

She turned fear-filled eyes toward him, too afraid to ask what he meant.

"Oh, yes, I have something for you." He rose and untied the bindings on her wrists. As she rubbed her numb wrists and hands, he held out the ring. Instantly, she knew what Joaquín meant. Her eyes flew to his.

"I believe you recognize the ring? I seem to remember seeing it on your lovely little hand when we were on the wagon train." He tossed it into her lap and returned to his chair.

Gingerly, she picked up the ring. Her

mother had given it to her just before she had died. After she and Seth arrived at the ranch, Jake had taken it into Santa Fe and had it made to fit Seth's much larger finger. Seth had never taken it off since she had put it on his finger. That Joaquín had the ring meant that Seth had believed her note.

"He believed it," she whispered, more to herself than to Joaquín.

"More than that, sweet Morgan. It seems that your husband met with an unfortunate accident and is no longer a problem to anyone."

"Accident?" Morgan was uncomprehending. "Accident! What do you mean? You said if I wrote the note you wouldn't harm him — you'd let him live."

"Morgan, you must learn not to trust everyone." His voice was heavy with sarcasm. "I couldn't very well leave him alive when he knew I had taken his wife away, now could I? With the owner of the Colter ranch dead and his new little bride nowhere to be found, it should be easy to obtain his ranch. But even if I didn't want the ranch, I would have killed Seth Colter." His eyes gleamed with hatred. "I would like to kill all the Seth Colters."

Morgan screamed and lunged at him, her fingers curled into claws. She would kill him herself. As her bound feet caught her and made her fall helplessly to the floor, she screamed her rage and cursed him.

"Such language from such a pretty little bird." He caught her hands behind her. She twisted her head and sank her teeth into his arm. He groaned and hit her across the face, sending her head reeling. He retied her hands and the gag and set her back on the bed.

His teeth clenched as he looked at her. "My men are making arrangements for you now. I will return for one last visit in a few hours." Then he was gone.

Seth was dead. Joaquín had killed him after all. The world was full of Cat Men and Joaquíns. Even the nearly five precious weeks she had spent with Seth had been marred by his jealousy. Now he was dead, and he had died thinking she had betrayed him.

"That her?" The voice was deep with a heavy accent.

Morgan had lain there for hours, tears soaking the gag. There were no more tears now. She wasn't even aware of the numbness in her feet or the blood on her wrists. When Joaquín entered, she showed no interest in him or the men with him. He was startled at her expression. It was as if she were dead, she as well as her husband.

When he unfastened her bindings, she remained motionless. "I liked you better when you were raging at me, my love." She failed to respond and did not even rub her chafed wrists and ankles.

"Trop petite." The man who had spoken first now made his contempt clear. He was a short man, very stocky, and his clothes were a mixture of rough cottons and animal skins. His hair was matted and reached past his shoulders. There was a gold earring in one ear.

"I do not like them so little. They do not last on the journey to the coast. And these blond ones — it is too much trouble to keep the Indians away from them. They like light hair." He grabbed a handful of Morgan's hair and jerked her face up to his. "This one — something has killed her spirit. It will be hard to keep this one from doing herself harm."

"All right, Jacques, what do you want? More money?"

"She will be a great deal of trouble."

"Here!" Joaquín thrust some bills into the Frenchman's calloused hand.

Jacques grabbed Morgan's hair again, pulling her to her feet. "She must have something else to wear." With a swift jerk, he tore the red silk down the front.

Joaquín heard his own sharp intake of breath. He took a step forward. Then he stopped himself.

"Skin and bones! This one will be much trouble, but if she survives the trip over the mountains, she will bring a good price at Madame Nicole's." He uttered something in a guttural language to a tall, sinewy man who was standing in the doorway. The man was the first Indian Morgan had ever seen. He had on a long tunic, once white, over leather leggings and high moccasins.

Morgan stared unfeelingly at the sight. She had made no effort to cover herself. Now she saw the Indian leave and quickly reappear with a bundle. He tossed it on the bed.

"Get into that!" he ordered Morgan. When she didn't respond, he slapped her. He thrust the bundle at her. Mutely, she rose and stepped out of her dress, and the Frenchman deftly used his knife to cut the bindings of her corset and the back of her chemise.

Morgan felt as if she were already dead. She paid no attention to Joaquín's avid interest in her body. Slowly, deliberately, she stepped into the leather shirt and pants.

She pulled on moccasins that came to her knees. The clothes were too big for her, and hid her curves.

The group moved outside, and one of the Indians tossed her onto the saddle of a shaggy pony. The Frenchman took the reins of the little horse and led her away. Morgan did not think about where they were taking her.

They rode through the hot New Mexico sun for hours. Morgan's face was burned, and her back ached from the long hours on the horse. Only once did the Frenchman pass her a canteen of water.

Neither the Indians nor the Frenchman talked, and Morgan was left to dwell on Seth's death.

The sun was low when they arrived at a large camp. Morgan was vaguely aware of people around her and of dogs barking. She was pulled from her horse and dragged, stumbling, to a crude shelter of sticks and dried grasses — a wickiup.

She fell against the back wall of the hut, the tiredness in her body numbing her to the sharp sticks pressing into her skin. As her eyes adjusted to the dim light, she saw three other women in the hut. Two were watching her and one huddled in a corner, her face turned away from the others. The oldest of the women left the hut and returned with a dipper of water. Quietly, she held this to Morgan's lips, cautioning her to drink slowly. Then she spread a heavy blanket on the floor and gently guided Morgan to lie down on it. She covered her with another of the patterned blankets.

"You get some sleep now, honey. They'll be movin' tomorrow, and you'll need your rest." She stroked Morgan's forehead, and Morgan was soon asleep.

In the morning Morgan could hardly move for the stiffness in her body, but the woman who had helped her the night before told her she must cooperate or else Jacques would hurt them all. Morgan could not miss the pleading in her eyes.

Unspeaking, she followed the woman's directions for dismantling the wickiup and fastening the poles onto a travois that was then lashed to a horse. An Indian motioned for her to mount one of the scruffy little ponies.

They traveled in a long column for two days, stopping for only a few hours at night. The woman, continuing to befriend Morgan, rode beside her and urged her to eat the strips of dried meat she offered and to drink the water.

At the end of two days, they made camp again, hastily erecting the crude shelters. As Morgan was lashing some dried grass to the roof of the hut, Jacques stopped beside her.

"My scouts have just returned to tell me that no one is following us. The little Spaniard said he had killed your husband, but I would not trust such a one as him. *Eh, ma petite?*" She stared at the Frenchman as if seeing him for the first time. He was a short, thick man with a scar across one eyebrow and a belly that hung over his belt. He looked very old, as though every single event in his life had etched a line on his weather-beaten face. He stuck out a dirty hand and caressed Morgan's breast. Involuntarily, she jumped backwards.

"Ah, so — *la petite* comes alive. They usually do. You are lucky now. On other trips, I have let my Apache *amis* take their pleasure of the white women. But they are not gentle and one of the women died. I lose money when one of my women dies. Other women showed up at Madame Nicole's with Indian babies in their bellies. My old friend does not like this. She says the white men are such silly creatures that they do not like to go where a redskin has gone before." He cupped Morgan's chin in his hand and studied her. "Yes, Madame Nicole will like you," Morgan tried to move her head from his iron grasp, and the Frenchman laughed.

"Such spirit from one so little! Be careful, Golden Hair, or I may take special notice of you myself." He turned and was gone.

Morgan stood for a few seconds glaring at his back, her eyes blazing with hatred. Then she went into the hut and was soon asleep. For the first night since she had been taken from the Montoya ranch, she dreamed. She saw Seth in her dream, and she ran to him, her arms open. When she was close enough to see his eyes, they were sad and he turned his back on her and began to walk away. She called his name, pleadingly at first, and then her cries became more and more desperate.

She awoke, her body drenched in sweat, to feel a hand pressed firmly over her mouth. "You're all right now. I'll take care of you. Just be quiet or they'll hear you."

Morgan felt herself being cradled. It was good to have an older woman's comforting arms about her. In the three days she had been a prisoner, she had paid little attention to her surroundings or to her fellow captives. Now she felt she desperately needed this woman's comfort.

The woman talked to Morgan as she held

her. "My husband and my little boy and me lived up on the side of a mountain, about three days east of where they picked you up. It wasn't an easy life. The winters were hard, and Bobby was always out with the sheep." Her voice was toneless.

"The three of us had just set down to eat when the door busted open and the Frenchman and two of his Indians walked in. Without a word, they killed Bobby and little Jimmy. He was only three years old.

"They looked me over, like I was an animal. I made a jump for Bobby's gun, not to kill them but to kill myself. I didn't want to live after what they did to my baby. They caught me. So here I am."

"Why?" Morgan asked through her tears. "Who is this Madame Nicole? What does he want with us? Why doesn't he just kill us? If he killed us, then I could be with Seth."

"Seth is your husband?"

Morgan nodded.

"I'm not sure, but I believe he deals in white slavery. He doesn't keep all women." She shuddered. "Only the ones who pass his inspection."

"A slave?" Morgan asked. "I don't understand. You can't sell white women."

"Well, it seems he can and is going to. I

heard them mention San Francisco."

"Just be glad you're little and pretty." Morgan turned to another woman. Although it was dark in the hut, she knew the woman was young, with bright red hair — pretty in a brassy way. Her mouth was too wide to be really beautiful. "Her mother wasn't so lucky." She inclined her head to the girl in the corner, quietly sobbing. "They raped her mother and then killed her. The girl had to watch." The girl in the corner was only about sixteen years old.

"My name's Jessica," said the red-haired woman, "but everyone calls me Jessy."

"And I'm Mary," said the woman who still held Morgan. It seemed understood that they would not use last names.

Morgan murmured her own name.

"Morgan? Strange name for a girl," Jessy said. When Morgan held her silence, Jessy continued. "The girl over there is Alice." She turned again to Morgan. "How'd they get you? What happened?"

Mary interrupted Jessy's questions. "Don't bother her now, Jessy, she needs rest. It's too soon for her to talk about it."

Jessy continued, "I can guess how you feel, but I figure for me anything's better than my old man. They killed him, too, but I don't feel no regret. In fact, I'm almost glad to be goin' to San Francisco. Been itchin' to go ever since I heard about the gold."

"Let's go to sleep now." Mary put an end to Jessy's story. "They'll want us to start soon enough. Let's remember, though, that we're in this together."

The next night they set up camp again. Morgan was beginning to be adept at taking apart and setting up a wickiup. The three women felt a good deal closer, and for the most part, they worked well together. The girl Alice still spoke to no one, and went about her work awkwardly. Morgan joined the other women in covering Alice's errors and slowness.

Morgan set the last bundle on the ground by the wickiup. As she straightened, she felt a hand on her hair. She knew it was one of the Indians. She had seen them staring at her as she hastily braided her hair each morning. In spite of herself, she felt a scream rising in her throat. As her mouth opened, a hand closed over it, a hand tasting of smoke and horses.

Morgan felt her body shiver with fear. She did not like the Indians. They never showed any feeling.

Gently, the Apache unfastened her braid and held the blond silk up to form a curtain that caught the sunlight. He uttered some guttural words and seemed pleased as he rubbed his hand in the softness of the hair.

A shot rang out close to their feet. The Indian dropped his hands from Morgan and reached for his knife. She turned to see Jacques holding a rifle, aimed at the Apache behind her. The two men exchanged a few of the guttural sounds and the Apache turned and left, angrily.

Jacques went to Morgan, her body shaking with fright. The Frenchman grasped the uncoiled braid of her hair and let it twine around his fingers.

Her eyes holding his, she asked, "Where are you taking us? Why have you kidnapped me?"

Still holding her hair, the Frenchman laughed, a deep, rumbling laugh. "I don't like my women so thin, but with your eyes and hair a man could be tempted." He moved his face closer to Morgan's, and she instinctively moved back. "You ask me questions. I will answer them, *ma petite*. I dealt in furs for a while, but that is hard work. I met Madame Nicole and we worked out our business arrangement. I bring her pretty young women, and she pays me for them." He smiled at Morgan's shock.

"You can't *sell* people!"

271

"Oh, but I can, little one. Madame Nicole finds unwilling women often please her customers more than the ones who readily agree to their whims. Bah! There are no real men left in this new country. I do not need to fight a woman to prove I am a man.

"One thing . . . do not tempt me to anger, pretty one. Madame Nicole will pay me well for such a one as you. I would not like to lose the money." Abruptly, he left her alone to stare after him.

"I thought as much." Jessy was standing beside her. "I've heard of some of these houses in San Francisco. A girl can live in luxury there."

Morgan turned to stare at Jessy. The events of the last few days were suddenly too much for her. Blindly, she began to run. She stumbled over dogs that ripped at her, but she hardly noticed. There was only one thought in her mind, one overwhelming desire — to escape, to get away from her captors. Reason had left her.

She halted as Mary caught up to her, jerking her arm painfully. "Morgan! Stop it! Look around you. You can't escape — they'll kill you first." Mary's fingers bit into the flesh of Morgan's upper arms. "Look at me and listen. This is not the way to escape. How long do you think you could survive in this land?"

"I don't care. I just want to get away. Even if it means my death, I can't face going on without Seth. I can't face what they have planned for us. I cannot."

Mary's eyes were hard. "Of course, you can face it. No matter what they do, we are still alive, and we need to survive."

Morgan's eyes had a faraway look as the tears quietly rolled down her cheeks. "Do you know what they plan to do with us? They plan to sell us as whores. Whores! Did you know that a few months ago I didn't even know what that word meant? Now I am to become one! That's funny, isn't it?"

Her voice grew louder. "Five weeks ago I was a virgin. Now . . ." She began to laugh loudly.

Mary looked up to see the Indians surrounding them, pointing at Morgan. Behind them she saw Jacques making his way over to them, an angry scowl on his face. She began to shake Morgan. "Stop it! Stop it! You'll cause more trouble if you call attention to yourself. Now come into the wickiup."

Morgan followed Mary, and the older woman was relieved to see the Frenchman turn and walk away from them.

In the hut, Mary turned to Morgan. "Why

don't you help her?" she asked, nodding toward the girl Alice. "Jessy and me can't seem to get through to her. Maybe if you help someone else a little, you won't be so wrapped up in yourself."

Quietly, Morgan sat by the unseeing girl. Mary was right. She was not the only one here. She took Alice's limp hand into her lap.

"I sometimes think that if I cry enough or if I wish hard enough, I'll open my eyes and this'll all be gone. Then I'll be home with . . . Seth." The name brought fresh tears to Morgan's eyes.

"Do you know how I got here?" Morgan continued. "A neighbor, a friend, wanted me to sleep with him. I said no, so he killed my husband and paid Jacques to take me. All my life my mother told me men were horrible, wicked creatures who cared little about women. Then I met Seth. I fought my feelings for him for a long time, but then I realized how much I loved him. Seth is . . . was . . . the most handsome man imaginable. He was so gentle and so good. Everyone on the ranch loved him. He even had some old dogs who were so lazy they wouldn't even bark until a stranger was practically inside the house. Seth was too kind-hearted to get rid of them."

She stopped talking. Alice was staring at her, tears glistening in her soft brown eyes. Morgan put her arm around the girl and pulled her head to her shoulder.

There was only two years' difference in their ages, but Morgan felt old enough to be Alice's mother. They sat in silence for a while, and then Alice began to talk, very quietly.

"My father went to the gold fields and said he'd send for us when he struck it rich. But after he left, my mother said she couldn't live without him, so we packed up and started west. We were going to join a wagon train in Santa Fe, but we never got that far. There were four wagons. They . . . they killed everyone, all the men. They took Mother and me with them.

"When we got to the camp, Jacques tore our clothes off. He had an Indian hold me while they . . . while they . . ." She couldn't finish her sentence and buried her head against Morgan's soft shoulder. After a few minutes, she began again. "They made me watch. She told me she loved me just before she died."

Morgan stroked the girl's brown hair. "We must stay alive."

"Why? So they can do to us what they did to my mother?"

"I don't know, Alice. I thought I wanted to die, but my life must be worth something. I know Seth wouldn't want me to die. I know that if he were here, he'd tell me to live . . . no matter what."

The days turned into weeks. They traveled every day. The trip from Kentucky to Santa Fe had been luxurious compared to travel with the Indians. Morgan learned much about the Frenchman's Apache followers, a rugged group. The women took care of all the work on the trail, putting up the shabby grass huts each night and tending to the food. One of the Indian women, Little Flower, had a new baby strapped to her back, bound onto a cradle board.

After the one attempt to touch Morgan, the Indians left the four white captives alone. The captives were given dried meat and roots that the Indian women gathered on the long, grueling trip.

Morgan took over the cooking for the four of them. Little Flower, who was about the same age as Morgan, showed her how to grind corn and cook it on top of the stews made from the game the men caught. Gradually, they began to understand one another through signs and a few words exchanged in the two languages.

At the night camp, Little Flower took her son from his cradle board and let him play on a blanket while she cooked. Morgan gestured to Little Flower to ask if she could hold the child.

"What are you doing with that heathen child?"

Morgan turned to see Mary's angry face. "Don't you realize that it might have been his own pa that killed your precious Seth?"

Morgan was calm, looking at the baby who had extended a chubby hand toward her golden braid. She smiled at him and he gurgled in delight as he caught the soft hair in his fingers. "White men killed my husband, but it wouldn't have made any difference. Babies are innocent, no matter who their parents are."

"Not when they're Indians!" Furious, she turned on her heel and left Morgan and the baby.

"Don't mind her." It was Jessy. "She just can't bear to look at another kid since hers is gone. Now me, that's somethin' I hope I never have." She looked with contempt at the child in Morgan's arms, happily putting her braid in his ever-open mouth. "Either they're squalling or their other end needs attention." She cocked her head and stared at Morgan. "I reckon you'd like one though.

Maybe you're carryin' one now?"

Morgan's head jerked up. The thought of Seth's baby made her body glow. Her face lit up. "Yes," she said quietly. "I'd like that. I'd like very much to have a baby . . . Seth's baby."

Jessy went back to the wickiup, and Morgan stayed with the baby. Morgan had hope now, and as the days passed, she began to pray fervently that she was really carrying a child and that, if she were, it would survive the trip.

Chapter Twelve

Jake had been riding for three days when he first saw the circle of buzzards. He removed his hat, wiped the sweat from his brow, and spurred his tired horse forward. At the bottom of the arroyo he saw the ruin and next to it a large dark form. He shot at the birds, scattering them. Something inside of him knew it was Seth there, lying so still, the hot New Mexico sun beating down on him. He was unaware of the tears that began to roll down his cheeks. He had one goal, and even his blurring vision couldn't keep him from it.

Seth was on his stomach, blood forming a halo around his head and across his shoulders. Carefully, Jake turned the big man over, cradling his head in his arms. His sobs were louder now and he rubbed his sleeve across his nose.

"Seth, boy. You hear me? It's Jake. I come to take you home."

It seemed an hour before Jake could still his own heart's frantic beating long enough to listen for Seth's. When he felt a slight pulse, he raised his tear-filled eyes skyward and offered a prayer of thanks.

He lay the wounded man's head down on the ground and went to his horse for his canteen. Slowly, he poured a few drops of water onto Seth's parched, cracked lips. Seth rolled his head and groaned.

"Just be still now, boy. You'll be all right. Drink slow, now."

"Morgan." Seth's voice was a harsh whisper and his breathing was ragged.

"Don't talk none. Just let ol' Jake take care of you. Like I done since you was a little boy."

Jake wet his handkerchief and began to wipe Seth's face. There was no way at first to tell the extent of his wounds, because his entire body from the waist up was covered with patches of dried blood. Jake used nearly all the water he had in his two canteens cleaning the nasty wound on the side of Seth's head.

"Got to get you home now, so's we can take care of you." The older man smiled down at Seth's enormous body. "You always was too big for your own good. Now I bet you wish you was just ordinary size, something ol' Jake could handle."

Jake used his sleeve to wipe his tears. "Got me bawlin' like a baby. Always did care too much for you." Jake looked around at the scrawny trees on the side of the arroyo, judging them for size. He stroked Seth's forehead. He was flushed, showing signs of fever. "We're gonna get you out of here Injun-style."

The knowledge that Seth was still alive gave Jake new energy, even after the three long days in the saddle. Slowly, carefully, he fashioned a travois from two young trees and strips of blanket from his bedroll. It took several hours, because he needed to make it strong enough to carry Seth's enormous body without any mishap.

His horse was tired and protested loudly when Jake fastened the travois to the saddle. The sun was just setting, turning the horizon red and orange. Jake knew he and his horse should rest, but if he waited until morning, it would mean traveling under the hot sun.

It took all of Jake's strength to get Seth onto the travois. Seth made no sound, hardly even opened his eyes, yet Jake could see the pain on his face as he tried to move. He was still semiconscious, and Jake knew Seth was using all the strength he had to control the pain. His shoulder wound re-opened and began to bleed again. The ugly wound on the side of his head was puffy and looked as if it might be infected.

"That's good, boy. The hard part's over. Now we're going to take it real slow and get you home."

They traveled all night. Jake led the horse most of the time rather than riding it. That way he could see more clearly and lead the tired horse around rough spots and mes-quite bushes. Jake stopped often and bathed Seth's face with cool water. Seth seemed to realize that he was being taken care of. He began to relax and let the pain take over.

The fever increased and he began to lose consciousness. He mumbled Morgan's name over and over.

"We'll find the little girl. Just as soon as we get back to the ranch, we'll find her for you. She's probably there now, worried sick about you."

When the sun began to rise, Jake started to look for a place to spend the hot part of the day. He didn't dare travel with Seth exposed to the sun.

He found a muddy-bottomed arroyo, and after digging a hole about two feet deep, he had enough water to bathe Seth's wounds. Under the shade of an old piñon tree, he cut away Seth's shirt and began to examine the wound. The bullet had gone through, making a large but clean hole.

For the first time since he had found Seth, his joy at finding him alive began to turn to anger. "Why would anyone want to hurt my boy?" Seth's breath whistled through his clenched teeth.

"I'll kill whoever did this. Shot a man and then left him to die in his own blood. They didn't even make sure he was dead, just left him to rot in the sun. A man wouldn't even treat a dog like that."

As he pulled Seth to one side to cut away the rest of his shirt, Seth's face blanched, and Jake saw the pain in his glazed eyes. Carefully, Jake felt along Seth's side and knew the ribs were broken. He removed his own shirt and tied it around Seth's ribs, binding them.

Jake covered Seth's body from the drafts, and the big man slept. Jake didn't even have a shirt to cover his bony body from the sand burrs and needles of the ground, but he lay close to Seth's travois, and slept.

It was late afternoon when he awoke. Seth's breath was shallow and fast, and when Jake felt his forehead, it was cool and his fingers were cold. He was beginning to try to move, to kick the blankets off, but at the same time clutching them closer.

"Easy, boy. Quiet now."

"Morgan . . ."

"We're going to her. We'll find her. Just be quiet and she'll be with you soon."

They traveled many hours, and Jake became increasingly worried about Seth. Walking beside the tired horse, he began to piece together what he knew of the few days before Seth was hurt. And by the time he came to the Colter ranch, he knew that Joaquín Montoya was responsible for this.

Lupita hadn't slept much since Morgan had ridden to Santa Fe with Lena. Somehow she had known that things were going to turn out badly. When neither Seth nor Morgan returned the day after the party, she was sure that something was wrong. Paul had laughed at her, but Jake worried as much about Seth as she did. They had waited all that day and night, and early the second morning he had set out to find Seth.

"You'll be embarrassed when you find them nestled in some cabin somewhere. The way they act around here, they may not be back for weeks," Paul had teased Jake.

Jake's mouth had been set, clamped over near-toothless gums. "I'd rather be caught with my hand in the pot than be here when the boy needs me someplace else."

Paul doubled up with laughter. "Boy! Seth's gonna love this! You're half that boy's size, and I don't think he's gonna need any help with that little wife of his."

Jake had ignored him and finished saddling his horse.

Lupita had been nervous and on the alert ever since then, so when the first sounds came to her, she was ready in seconds. When she first saw the tired figure of Jake outlined in the moonlight, she started toward him. The sight of the travois stopped her. She turned and ran toward Paul's cabin.

Within minutes the young foreman was dressed and running ahead of Lupita toward Jake.

Jake motioned toward Seth, and Paul went to him. Now that Jake had brought his beloved boy home, his own strength was going.

Silently, the three of them carried Seth into the house and put him into the big double bed that he and Morgan had so recently shared. Lupita deftly began to cut away Jake's makeshift bandages, removed the rest of Seth's clothes, and began washing him. His body was hot now, and he moaned when the cool cloth touched his fevered skin. Lupita gradually became aware of loud voices in the next room.

"You can't go anywhere, old man. You wouldn't even make it to the corral."

"Just who the hell do you think you're callin' an old man? It was me that brought him back." Jake raised his fists toward Paul.

"What's going on here? Isn't there enough to worry us without you two fighting? And why are you still here? One of you should go . . ."

Jake lowered his fists and checked his gun. "That's just where I'm going — to kill that Montoya."

"Jake, you've got to let the sheriff handle this. You can't just ride into the Montoya ranch and kill Joaquín."

"Sheriff! Kill!" Lupita fairly screamed. "There's one man in there nearly dead, and you two talk of more killing! Before anyone kills anyone, I want a doctor here!"

Both Paul and Jake stared blankly at Lupita.

"Jake, I'll need your help here." She knew how tired the little man must be. "Paul, go into town and get the doctor, and then get the sheriff — but a doctor is what we need most." She turned toward the bedroom, took a few steps, and then turned back to the two men. "Does a man have to *die* to get you two to move?"

Quickly, Jake followed Lupita and Paul left the house.

In the hours that followed, Seth began to talk, mostly saying Morgan's name over and over. As Lupita continued to wash Seth, she noticed his left hand always clenched into a fist.

"Jake, what does he have in his hand?" It took the two of them to pry open his fist. Jake read the note from Morgan first to himself and then to Lupita.

Jake sat down in a chair heavily. "How could she have done this? How could she leave Seth for a man like Montoya?" He looked at Seth, the tears forming in his eyes again. "She did that to him, as much as if she'd pulled the trigger herself."

"No," Lupita's voice was a whisper, "I do not believe it. No." She looked up at Jake. "It is a trick of some sort. She loved him. She could not pretend so well."

"We have proof that she aimed to run off, and the proof involves Montoya, too."

Lupita's eyes held Jake's. "You may believe your little piece of paper, but I will believe what I know to be true. Señora Colter was very much in love with Seth, and she would not leave him of her own free will."

Jake turned his back on her. "We'll see

what the sheriff says," he mumbled.

It was nearly daylight when Paul returned with the sheriff. Jake had finally dozed off in the big chair beside Seth, but he was quickly through the doorway, showing the sheriff the note.

"Hold on, Jake. I know how you feel, but I can't just shoot the man. We went to the Montoya ranch first and Señor Montoya had witnesses who said he was there all night. This note mentions Joaquín, but we can't even be sure when it was written."

"I don't care how many witnesses the little bastard has! He nearly killed my boy!"

"All right. We'll go again. We'll face him with the note. The doctor should be here any minute. He was out in Pecos, so it'll take him a while. Paul, you ready?"

Helplessly, Jake watched them go. An hour later the doctor came.

He complimented Jake for the care he had given Seth on the rough trail, and after he had examined him, said there was nothing else to do but wait and see if the fever broke. He wrapped the broken ribs tightly, to keep him from breathing too deeply and putting one through his lungs.

Seth's fever raged for days. Lupita and Jake took turns sponging his perspiring body and forcing broth down his throat. He talked a lot about Morgan, and how he loved her, how he wanted her. He kept calling for her, asking where she was, sensing even in his delirium that she wasn't there. With every mention of her name, Jake's hatred for Morgan grew.

After nearly a week, Paul and the sheriff returned to the Colter ranch. They had been searching for Joaquín and Lena Montoya all that time. They had returned to the Montoya ranch the morning after Jake had brought Seth back and found the servants closing down the house. Joaquín and Lena had left immediately after the sheriff's first visit.

"They didn't plan on Seth still being alive," Jake yelled in frustration.

"Someone should try to find the Señora Colter." The three men turned to stare at Lupita.

"But she's the one who caused all this. She and Montoya had their escape planned. It probably wasn't Montoya's sister who left with him at all."

"Jake's right." Paul's voice was calm and tired. "I think we should leave this up to Seth. When he's well, he'll decide whether he believes his wife's note or not." Paul's expression left in doubt none of his feelings toward Morgan.

With a sigh of resignation, Lupita went back to Seth.

It was two more weeks before the fever broke.

"Lupita?"

Lupita turned from gazing out of the window. She whirled toward him. "Señor Colter. You are well." Her voice held both joy and relief.

Seth grinned weakly at her. "I don't think I'm well of anything yet. Everything hurts. How long have I have been ill?"

"Three weeks now."

"Three weeks! Where is everyone? Where's Morgan and Jake and Paul and . . . food! I've never been so hungry in my life. Tell Morgan I want some of those little dough-nuts of hers and one of those cheese and bacon things in the crust." He grinned as Lupita hurried from the room. "Tell Morgan I want her *now!*" he called toward the door.

He lifted himself up and grabbed a pillow to prop behind his head. He ran his hand over the welt on the side of his head and felt where the scar ran under his hair. His ribs and shoulder hurt, and his legs ached. "Three weeks!" he murmured. "I'll bet

Morgan had her hands full, but I'll make up for lost time."

He grinned at himself. Smells from the kitchen reached him and he wondered where the hell she was. What was taking her so long?

He put his hands out in front of him, stretching his muscles, easing some of the stiffness that three weeks in bed had caused. "Three weeks in bed," he laughed. "I bet I spend the next three weeks in bed, too, but not for the same reason. And not alone! Where is she?"

It was then that he noticed the white spot on his little finger. Morgan's ring! Where was it? And then, in a flash, he remembered everything, every ugly detail.

He put his hands over his eyes, rubbing the heels deep into the sockets, trying to block out the images . . . Joaquín and Morgan in the garden . . . Joaquín giving him the note . . . Joaquín aiming the pistol and firing. "No," he whispered. "Please, God, no!"

"Here is food and lots of it. Jake and Paul will be here in a minute. They will be so happy to see you well. They have both worried themselves sick over you." She bustled into the room with the tray of food, but the smile left her face when she saw Seth. She knew then that healing his body had been easy compared to what it was going to take to heal his spirit.

"It's all true . . . what I remember. Isn't it?"

Lupita would have sold her soul to be able to tell him that it all had been a dream, that his lovely wife was running to him, would be here in a moment. "I do not think it was true. The little *señora* would not do such a thing. I think someone should go and find her."

"Well, I don't." Seth and Lupita turned to see Jake in the doorway. "We found the note. I say let her go. If she wants to leave here, let her."

The pain in Seth's eyes was more than Lupita could bear. "She loves you. She loves you very much. She could not have acted like she did and not love you. The day Lena came for her, she did not want to go. She wanted to stay here in her home. She was so happy here."

"Stop it!" Seth fell back onto the pillows. "To me . . . she is dead. I never want to hear her name again. We will not refer to her again, in any way." His eyes were cold, but both Jake and Lupita could see the pain behind them. "I think I'd like to sleep now."

"But your food! You need to eat."

"No, Lupita, I don't feel hungry now."

Jake silenced Lupita's protests with a stern look. "That's right, boy, you just rest and get well. The food'll be waitin' for you when you wake up."

Seth's recovery was slow. He didn't seem to mind staying in bed, and he showed no interest in anything. Jake tried to ask his opinion about what he and Paul were doing on the ranch, but Seth hardly answered him. Eventually, he began to move around the room a little, going only from the bed to the chair. He sat and stared at the walls. Lupita encouraged him to sit on the little patio by the bedroom, but he didn't seem to care where he was.

As the pain left Seth's body, the pain in his mind increased. He was continually reminded of Morgan.

She seemed to be everywhere. He started sleeping on the couch in the living room because he couldn't stand the bed they had shared. One day he rode out with Jake, and it seemed she was even outside. A clump of trees recalled a time when she had brought his lunch to him and then run from him, laughing, unfastening her clothes as she went. Even the sunlight recalled her hair and skin.

The snows began and he remembered how he had planned on long snowy days of lovemaking. With Christmas coming, Lupita decorated the house with chilis and popcorn. Seth watched lethargically as Lupita, Jake, and Paul decorated the little piñon tree.

On Christmas Eve, Seth remembered the music box he had packed in Kentucky. It was to have been a Christmas present for Morgan. It had been weeks since he had been in his own bedroom, but he went now and found the box. He wound it and listened to the tune. How she would have loved the delicate carving!

"Why, Morgan, why? He couldn't have offered you more love than I did. It isn't possible!" Tears blurred his eyes as he brought one powerful fist down on the little box and smashed it.

He glared at the broken little box, and through clenched teeth, he swore, "If I ever find you, Morgan, I'll kill you!" With one sweep of his arm, he knocked the remains of the box to the floor.

He left the room and announced to the others that in the spring he would leave the ranch for the California gold fields.

In March, 1850, when the snows were barely gone, Seth set out for California and the gold fields. After the heavy use of the previous year, the trail was well defined. He was only a few miles out of Santa Fe when he met the Chandlers' wagon train.

CHAPTER THIRTEEN

It took the little band — the Indians, the Frenchman, and the four women captives — five weeks to reach the mountains. After a week of grueling travel, everyone's temper was short. The nights grew cooler, and the nip of autumn was in the air. Morgan figured it was somewhere around the first week of October, 1849, and she knew now that she was not carrying Seth's baby.

"I don't know why I always seem to do most of the work around here." The closer they got to San Francisco, the angrier Mary became. She took her fear and hatred out on everyone.

"What with Morgan doing all the cookin', I don't see how you can think you're doing most of the work." Jessy's happiness and excitement were obvious.

"Please, can't you two stop fighting?" Alice pleaded with them tearfully.

"It's just these Indians! They're always

around. A body can't even step into the bushes without one of them watching. I'm always ready to scream."

Jessy looked across the camp at one of the Apache braves who returned her stare. "Indians ain't all that bad. That Yellow Hand's not a bad looker at all."

"You filthy little slut! I ought to tear your hair out!"

"You and who else?"

Mary raised clawlike hands and started for Jessy's face. Morgan quickly stepped between the two of them. "Stop it, you two! They may decide we're not worth the trouble and kill us now."

"Death just may be better than the life they have planned for us." Mary's face was twisted as she sneered at Morgan and Jessy.

Alice's whimpering carried across the campfire.

"Oh, Lord! Is she going to start that again? That girl is afraid of her own shadow." Jessy rolled her eyes.

Alice's sobs increased, and Mary went to her to comfort her. "If you had any feelings, you'd realize she's just a child."

"Child, hell! It may interest you to know, Miss Mary-Know-Everything, that that 'child' and I are the same age."

Both Mary and Morgan turned startled

eyes to Jessy. There was an ageless quality about Jessy that made her seem anywhere from fourteen to fifty. Neither of them had ever considered her true age. "That's right," she laughed. "I just turned sixteen on my last birthday, sometime in June. My pa never could remember the exact date." She turned and left the three staring after her.

"I'm older than her," Alice whispered.

Along the Gila River, the trail was so narrow that the horses were frightened and skittish. The nerves of the four captives were even further strained.

After the river, they came to a wooded area. Jacques told them to take advantage of the water, because it would be the last they'd see for a long time. In another couple of days they'd start the long trek across the desert.

"May we take a bath then, before we start?"

Jacques touched her cheek with a large, coarse hand. Morgan bravely met his eyes. She didn't even move away, as much as she wanted to. "You are a temptation, *ma petite*. Of course, you may bathe. All of you may splash and play in the water all night." He smiled at her, and his eyes swept down over her buckskin-clad body. His hand dropped from her cheek to her shoulder to her arm, his thumb caressing the soft curve of her breast. Her eyes held his, and she controlled the inner revulsion she felt.

Jacques turned and left her, and she could hear his deep, throaty laughter as he walked away.

"I'd like to have a knife at his throat for a while," Mary hissed.

"Never mind him. Get Jessy and Alice. We're going to take a bath!" She hurried to the wickiup. "A real bath. Clean hair and skin. I don't think I've ever looked forward to anything quite so much." She paused inside the cool, dark, empty wickiup. "Except you, Seth," she whispered. "You were the only thing that really made me happy. Now I look forward to such silly things. Oh, Seth. *Why* did all this have to happen? Why do I have to go on living? Why can't I die and be with you again?" She fell to the dirt of the floor and cried.

"Morgan, is it true what . . ." Jessy paused as she saw Morgan. She knelt by her and took her in her arms. "Ah, Morgan, you're the strong one among us. Don't you give way. If you give up, we won't have anything to hold onto."

"Seth is on my mind constantly, every second. Everywhere I look I see things that remind me of Seth. Even trees, Jessy! Even trees remind me of Seth. He was huge, the biggest man I ever saw. Not awfully tall, but big. His arms were as big around as my waist. And he was so handsome." Morgan smiled and the tears began to clear. "I had to fight women off him constantly."

"What's wrong with you two?" Mary's querulous voice sounded through the wall.

Morgan wiped her eyes. "I'm all right now. Let's go take a bath." She turned to smile at Jessy. "Thanks for listening to me."

"Morgan, I've decided this Seth of yours never existed." Her face was serious. "No man could be both kind and good-lookin'."

Morgan flashed her a brilliant smile. "Seth is special." Happily she raced toward the water, leaving Jessy to notice that she had said "is," as if her husband were still alive.

Jessy was the last one to the water and was surprised to see all of the Indian men, Jacques, and some of the Indian women standing there with the three white women.

Jacques's deep laughter came to her. "My Indians do not take baths, and they are very much interested in someone who does. They want only to watch."

"Well, I ain't takin' my clothes off in front of no Indians." Mary turned back toward the camp.

Jessy laughed. "What about you, Morgan? I think bugs have nested under my skin, it's been so long since I took a bath. I'm not gonna let a few staring Indians keep me from getting clean." She sat on the ground and began to pull off the tall moccasins. Seconds after she stood up, she was completely naked and ran happily into the cool water.

The other three women had watched speechlessly. The Indians and Jacques began to laugh as Jessy happily dived under the water, her smooth round buttocks coming to the surface.

"It feels great," she called.

"She's a fool besides being a slut," Mary muttered. "These animals need no more temptation. I wouldn't be surprised if one of them attacked her."

Alice clung to Mary, her face fearful.

"You sure you won't join me, Morgan? I can feel two months' worth of dirt and bugs floating away. Toss me my buckskins, will you? Might as well get them clean."

Morgan picked up Jessy's clothing and started to throw them to her.

"You know . . . if they wanted to, they could tear our clothes off at any time. What difference does this bath make?"

"You're right, Jessy." Quickly, Morgan

undressed and walked into the water.

"Lord, Morgan! I think you've started a fight." Jessy gestured toward Jacques, who was smiling at one of the Indians. The Indian made an obscene gesture that even Morgan understood, and she turned away.

Jacques laughed and called to her. "Did you hear that, Golden One? Running Bear offers me six horses and four blankets to let you be his third wife. Would you like that? It is a good price, and he is a brave warrior."

Morgan looked at the Indian, his hair heavy with grease and his face stained with remnants of paint and food. Involuntarily, she shuddered. Recovering herself, she met Jacques's eye. "Do you think Madame Nicole will offer only six horses and four blankets, or do you think I am worth more?"

Jacques looked at her full breasts rounding above the surface of the water, her small chin and flashing eyes, and the great mass of golden hair cascading about her. He threw back his head and laughed. "You will bring a great deal more from Madame Nicole — I will make sure of that."

"Morgan, you have more guts than any three people put together."

"Not really, Jessy. It's just that I don't really care. If I can get to San Francisco, maybe I can escape and get back to Seth's ranch. At least there I'll be close to him."

"No matter what, Morgan, you're lucky — lucky to have had a love like that, even for a while. Just once I'd like to fall in love with a man and have him love me in return. I mean real love, not like those men that paid my pa."

"Paid your father!"

"Don't tell Alice or Mary, but my father put me out to whore when I was thirteen. You can see why I felt no regret when the bastard died."

Too stunned to speak, Morgan stared.

"I shouldn't have told you," Jessy said quietly and began to swim away.

"No," Morgan caught her arm. "I was just thinking how I always hated my father, and I never even knew him. I guess we never know what we should be thankful for. If it hadn't been for my father, I'd never even have known Seth." She stopped and her eyes opened wider. "If I hadn't met Seth, he would still be alive."

Jessy's fingers dug into Morgan's flesh. "Morgan! You've got to stop blaming yourself! You can kick yourself for the next fifty years, and you still won't change the past. Remember Seth with all the love you have for him, but stop hating yourself."

Morgan frowned at Jessy. "Are you sure you're only sixteen? You sound more like ninety."

Jessy laughed. "Let's get out of here before they change their minds about leaving us alone."

They finished their baths and washed their hair and clothes. They put the wet buckskins on their bodies to dry. The sun was barely visible on the horizon, streaked with brilliant colors. As Morgan sat by the campfire in front of the wickiup, trying to smooth the tangles from her hair with only her fingers, Little Flower came to stand beside her. Absent-mindedly, Morgan smiled at the young Indian woman. Little Flower left and returned in seconds holding a beautiful tortoise-shell comb. She gestured to Morgan and Morgan nodded. Little Flower sat behind the blond woman and began combing her long tresses, while Morgan held the baby.

"What do you think you're doing, letting that animal touch you?"

Morgan hardly noticed Mary's anger, preferring to ignore it. Mary turned away in a huff.

When Little Flower had finished, Morgan asked to borrow Little Flower's knife. After a second's hesitation, she gave it to her.

Morgan cut off a thick golden curl and tied it with a long piece of grass. She put the piece of hair into the fastenings at the top of the baby's cradle board.

Immediately, Little Flower grabbed the cradle board and ran to show the other Indian women and her husband.

"What's going on? What's all the noise about?" Jessy asked.

Morgan laughed, looking down at the baby pulling at the thong ties on her shirt. She told Jessy about the piece of hair.

"Well, it must mean somethin', 'cause here comes the bossman himself."

Jacques explained to Morgan that the piece of hair was considered a great gift and she was to choose a gift in return.

"I'd like my freedom."

"That is not Little Flower's to give. Choose something else."

"I don't want a gift, just her friendship."

"She will be insulted that you do not accept a gift from her." At the look of puzzlement on Morgan's face, he turned and spoke to the pretty Indian woman with a few soft words. Her face brightened and she ran to her wickiup.

Quickly, she returned and handed Morgan a silver and turquoise bracelet. The turquoise was a work of art, worked inside the metal in hundreds of little ovals, like daisies going round and round. The bracelet was surprisingly delicate.

"It was taken from a Zuñi warrior. They make beautiful things, no?"

"Tell Little Flower it is beautiful, and I thank her very much."

When Jacques had repeated her words, Morgan leaned over and kissed the Indian woman's cheek. Little Flower said something.

"She says you are now sisters."

"Sisters! Bah! Sisters to these filthy wretches! I'd rather be dead!"

Jacques turned to Mary's scowling face. "For you, that may be arranged very soon."

Later, Morgan always hated to remember the trip across the desert. Never had she imagined such a horrible place existed. They broke camp before full daylight and camped again before the hottest part of the day. There were no more campfires. The rich stews they had enjoyed were now memories. They ate dried meat and dried cornmeal. Water was strictly rationed, and the dry food stuck in their throats.

Morgan clamped her hands over her ears to block out the whimpering of Little Flower's baby. His mother did not have enough water to replenish her milk supply, so the baby was hungry. Morgan shared her water with Little Flower until Jacques found out.

"Do you think I go to all the trouble of bringing you across the mountains just to have you blow away? If you give more of your water away, I will kill the squaw and then the baby will have no milk at all."

One good thing came of the journey across the desert. Jessy and Mary stopped quarreling for a while, neither had the energy for it. During the hot afternoon, they lay in the scanty shade, barely able to breathe the scorching air. The horses were kept under crude shelters, rigged each day.

Eventually, gradually, they began to encounter green plants and they knew that San Francisco was near. Morgan felt the ring she kept on a rawhide thong around her neck, and dreamed of Seth.

Early one morning, Jacques and two of the Indians saddled horses for the four women captives, and, leaving the other Indians in camp, they began the last leg of the trek into San Francisco.

CHAPTER FOURTEEN

After three days of hard riding, they arrived in San Francisco in the dead of night. Jacques led them down alleys to the side of a three-story frame house. The women were too tired to notice much about their surroundings. A small, pretty mulatto girl opened the door.

"Get Madame Nicole right away. Tell her Jacques is come."

The girl scurried away, and quickly a large-breasted woman with masses of coal-black hair appeared in the doorway. Her skin was beautiful, flawless and unlined. She might have been beautiful, except that she weighed nearly two hundred pounds. Surprisingly, she carried her weight as if she were a young girl. Her walk was graceful and her movements were delicate.

"Jacques! How good to see you!" Her voice was pretty and young. There was a slight French accent that was very becoming.

Jacques threw his arms around Madame Nicole and lifted her enormous body off the ground. The woman blushed like a schoolgirl. "Jacques — you devil! How I have missed you!" She slid down across his body to plant a kiss on his mouth. After several seconds, they broke their embrace.

"There aren't many real women left," he said, giving the large woman a knowing look. "So I brought some of those skinny little gals those half-men of yours like. I think you're really going to like one of 'em."

She looked at him quizzically. "I am not about to lose you, am I, Jacques?"

He smiled at her, looking her up and down. "It'd take all four of them to make half the woman you are."

She smiled at him, a smile of pure joy. "Later we will find out if you mean your words. But first, business." Immediately, she changed from lover to business-woman, and assessed each of the tired, dirty women.

"The blonde, *oui?*"

Jacques winked his reply. "Could hardly keep my Apaches from her. Real looker when she's clean."

"Good! They are just in time for Christmas. We are going to make four men very happy this Christmas."

Madame Nicole clapped her hands twice, many bracelets flashing. Instantly, four serving girls appeared. She gave orders, and Morgan found herself escorted up some narrow stairs to a bedroom. The sight of the bed, the first she had seen in months, held her entranced. She walked toward it as if hypnotized.

"No, no!" The girl took Morgan's arm. "Madame will not allow anyone so dirty to sleep in her clean bed. Carrie will bring water. You must bathe first." She led Morgan to a chair and moved a screen to reveal a large, red porcelain tub on gold claw feet. The girl, Carrie, arrived, and soon the tub was full of steaming hot water. Morgan allowed herself to be undressed and then she stepped into the tub.

The water seemed to soak through her body, even to her bones, and she enjoyed the rough scrubbing the girls gave her skin and scalp. She was stepping out of the tub into a heated towel when Madame Nicole entered.

The large woman appraised her as if she were a piece of furniture. "Ooh la la! You are by far the best of the four. In fact, you may be the best I have ever presented. You will bring a very high price."

Morgan stared at her in contempt. "What right have you to sell anyone? I am a person, not an article of merchandise."

The big woman threw back her head and laughed. "So, a crusader. I sometimes forget that such as you still exist. So often the women Jacques brings me have lived in poverty all their lives. They find all this" — her hand took in the room — "a dream. They like the luxury and the cleanliness."

Morgan clenched her teeth. "But your people kill their families! My husband was killed."

"Oh, yes, that is necessary." She dismissed the subject. "We cannot have angry relatives coming after our women. I would lose all my clients. Anyway, men are easily replaced."

"Not all men!"

"So you had not been with your lover long enough for the bloom to wear off. After your hands had cracked from the lye soap, and your body had worn out from bearing his children, you would be glad to trade for a life like this."

"No matter what, this is a whorehouse! I won't be used!"

"The women Jacques brings me, I do not use here in my house. They are sold to very wealthy men. They often marry well later,

311

or if their lover tires of them, he settles sums on them that leave them comfortable for the rest of their lives." She paused and stared at Morgan. "Yes, you will do very well. You are even prettier when you are filled with rage."

Nicole took a few steps to the mirror and watched as the servant girls finished drying Morgan and dressing her in a pink gown. "You see, I like to know my girls, and I try to pick men who will fit their types. Your Jessica already loves it here. It will be easy to find a man for her. And Alice . . . we will find her an older man, one who will protect her and pet her, and she will be very happy. Mary needs a man to hit her now and then.

"And you, Morgan? What type are you?"

Morgan glared at her. "I am not any 'type.' I am a person and I cannot be put into a category."

"Ah, but you have just described yourself. You need a man who will tell you his problems. One who will listen to you and to whom you can listen. And as a lover, you need one who will let you plan the moves sometimes, one who will let you control him sometimes, but not too often."

Morgan stared at her in astonishment. She was too close to the truth. Embarrassed, she turned away from the woman. She saw too much.

Nicole laughed. "You see, I am right. Every woman and every man fit into little niches. The world is too old for anything to be new. Come now, get into bed. We want you pretty and fresh tomorrow. There are a lot of things to do to prepare for our Christmas special."

In spite of her anger, Morgan fell asleep instantly.

For three days, Morgan lived amid a flurry of dressmakers. After a while she got used to standing nude in front of several women and even an occasional man, as they wrapped fabric around her and pinned things in place. She was not allowed out of her room or to see the other three captives. She missed Jessy and wished they could talk.

After the first three days she was left alone, but was still not allowed to leave the room. She found the door unlocked, but when she started out the portal, her way was barred by an enormous black man who held a whip coiled in his hand. Madame Nicole informed her later that Samson would always be there. He seemed never to sleep.

They gave her one of Mrs. Weston's latest romantic novels to read, but she angrily tossed the book aside after a few chapters. She could not read about flowers and romance when her own life was so harsh.

When the first of the dresses was finished, Madame Nicole informed Morgan of a tea to be given in their honor. There they were to meet some of the eligible young men of San Francisco.

Morgan marveled at the woman. She seemed to have no contact with reality as Morgan understood it. An outsider would have thought the four women were Nicole's beloved daughters instead of her slaves.

Morgan was led into a room of gold and white. The chairs and couches were covered in white velvet and there was a white rug on the floor. All the wood, including the mirror frames, was intricately carved and gilded.

"Morgan!"

She and Jessy ran to one another, their arms extended. "You're beautiful!"

"Ain't I though!" Jessy's red hair had been toned down with, Morgan guessed, a color rinse. Her lean body was beautifully enhanced by a soft violet dress. "It's her, though, that's done the most changin'," she whispered to Morgan.

Morgan was startled to see that meek little Alice was hardly recognizable. "She's been standin' in front of the mirror since she came in. Mary's havin' fits because the girl will hardly look at her. After all Mary did for her on the trip."

Alice held her chin high, barely nodding toward Morgan. She kept twisting one way and another to see herself from every angle. Mary was on the verge of tears, pleading with Alice to come sit by her.

Jessy and Morgan exchanged looks, Jessy rolling her eyes to the ceiling. They both covered their mouths to suppress their giggles.

"They been treatin' you good, Morgan? This is the finest place I ever even seen. Decked out like this, I look like a lady. Madame says all the men who come here are gentlemen. I'd sure like to get me a real gentleman."

"I don't really care, Jessy."

Jessy looked at her friend in sadness. "I never saw nobody pine over anybody as long as you have."

The door opened and Madame Nicole entered, followed by two very handsome young men. "Ladies, may I introduce Mr. Leon Thomas and Mr. Joel Westerbrooke?"

Morgan considered laughing. Was this an ordinary afternoon tea?

Mary's voice reached her. "We're held

here as prisoners against our will. Would you help us? Get the sheriff!"

The two young men turned away, their faces crimson. Immediately, Samson appeared from nowhere. Mary was taken away.

Later, Morgan could remember little of the conversation. Alice and Jessy had talked to the young men eagerly. Morgan watched it all with little interest, and was glad when it was over.

Nicole came while Morgan was eating dinner in her room. "You were smart to be quiet this afternoon. Men dream of a quiet, beautiful woman. It is by far the better game."

Morgan worked hard at controlling her anger. "I was not playing any game."

Motherly, Nicole patted her shoulder. "Already San Francisco is hearing about Madame Nicole's little celebration, and it is rumored that a sensational beauty is to be offered. I thought I would reassure you. The sale is by invitation only. All these men have impeccable taste and a great deal of money." She smiled at Morgan.

"I doubt if you would be smiling if *you* were about to be sold like an animal."

Nicole laughed aloud, a deep laugh. "How ever do you think I got into this business? Actually, *chérie,* the sale is very exciting. I would give a great deal to be as young and as beautiful as you. To be auctioned off, to be fought over by many handsome young men — yes, that is very exciting. It happens only once. You should enjoy it."

She looked again at Morgan's furious face. "The young! They are so full of causes! This one would like to miss showing her beautiful body to men who will appreciate it. She would rather share it with only one man, one who will soon grow used to it and be bored by it. You are so lucky, Morgan, and you do not even realize it. Youth vanishes so quickly. Use it! Enjoy it!"

She realized that her sentiments meant nothing to Morgan. "Bah! Youth is wasted on the young. Goodnight."

The day before Christmas, Morgan was left alone. She napped and dreamed of Seth. All day her thoughts of him were especially strong. Late in the afternoon, she heard a music box playing and turned toward the sound, to the dresser. In the mirror she saw not her own reflection, but Seth's. He was staring at her with hatred, his features contorted. She stood frozen in horror. Then there was a muffled crash. The tinkling music was gone, and Seth's face vanished.

She was still locked in her place when

Madame Nicole and two servant girls entered. Instantly, the large woman knew something was wrong.

"Morgan! What's wrong? You're shaking." She held Morgan's shoulders, but the young woman continued to stare at the mirror. Nicole turned to the mirror and saw nothing. She put herself between Morgan and the glass.

"Tell me."

"I saw . . . I saw . . ." Morgan's voice was a harsh whisper.

"What did you see in the mirror? Girls! Make the water *very* hot." The three women undressed her and put her in the tub.

Gradually, Morgan began to lose her vacant stare and Nicole breathed a sigh of relief. "What did you see in the mirror?" she asked quietly.

Morgan's voice held no emotion. "My husband."

"But Jacques said he was dead. You only thought you saw him." Her eyes caught Morgan's and held. Something in them told her the truth: this vision been no wishful imagining. *"Mon Dieu!"* she exclaimed and crossed herself. Abruptly, she left the room.

Tonight, when Madame Nicole opened the sealed bids, she knew who would win Morgan. If only he *would* bid. This night she would say her rosary many times before sleeping.

The two young girls were quieter than usual as they dressed Morgan. Her clothes were especially fine, the lace on her chemise handmade. Her corset was satin and embroidered with tiny rosebuds. The dress was also satin, a rich emerald green. It was simply cut and unadorned, but very low in front, exposing her lovely shoulders.

The girls worked long on her hair, arranging it high on her head in loose, fat curls and waves. They kept checking the number of pins to hold it up, trying for as few as possible. Twice they removed all the pins and watched their artwork fall down her back in beautiful disarray. After the third try, they seemed satisfied. Their mood lightened as they became more deeply involved in their task, and they giggled often.

"Madame Nicole is very pleased with you. She says you may be the best girl ever offered. The men will be very happy."

"We'll show you off just right. Carrie and I have done this lots of times, but never with anyone as pretty as you. Sometimes we use makeup on the body, but you don't need it at all."

As Morgan's silence lengthened, they

stopped talking.

"Now you just stay right here while we go get ready. Don't do anything to muss yourself."

It seemed only minutes before the two girls reappeared. Morgan gasped at their costumes. Their dresses were black with tight long sleeves and very low square-cut necks. The gowns were pulled in very tight at the waist, and the skirts flaring out dramatically. The dresses ended at midthigh. The girls' legs were covered only by sheer black silk stockings. Each had on black high-heeled pumps.

Morgan had never seen a woman expose her legs before. If the dresses had reached even to just the ankle, they would have been indecent. But this was beyond her imagination.

"These are our special dresses for the sales. Aren't they pretty?"

"But so much of you is exposed! How can you appear before men like that?"

"Like this? Honey, you're going to expose a lot more tonight."

Morgan stared at the girl. "What do you mean?"

"Carrie didn't mean a thing. Now you come along." Over Morgan's shoulder she gave Carrie a stern look.

Morgan met the other three women in the hall, each attended by two servant girls dressed exactly like the two beside Morgan. The four captives barely nodded to one another, each apprehensive about the events to follow.

They were led to a narrow backstage area. They could hear the muffled coughs and voices of men — many men — on the other side of the curtain.

Madame Nicole rushed to them. "Girls . . . be careful they do not muss their dresses. It will be Mary first, Jessy, Alice, and last" — she looked adoringly at Morgan — "our Morgan." She was gone, and soon they heard polite applause.

As Nicole addressed her audience, her voice purred. "My dear gentlemen: The first lady is Mary. Mary will need some taming to overcome some of the unpleasant aspects of her personality. But as our Mr. Shakespeare has noted, there are ways to tame a shrew." Polite laughter. "I apologize for the need for Samson, but I hope you will agree with me that Mary is well worth the extra effort."

They heard the soft sounds of an orchestra.

"What do you think is going on?" Jessy leaned toward Morgan.

They heard Mary's voice from the stage. "No!" Then the crack of Samson's whip.

Alice looked anxiously at the other two women, quickly losing some of her recently acquired courage. They heard Mary sobbing. After a few moments the music stopped and they heard the tearing of paper.

"Mr. Thomas Millsant has just made a purchase," Nicole called out cheerfully.

There was a rustle of curtains at the other end of the stage, and the three women turned to see Mary, her face buried in her hands, her body gleaming in the dim light.

"Oh, my God! She's naked!" Alice seemed ready to faint.

Before Jessica could speak, her maids were hurrying her to the other side of the curtain. Morgan had a glimpse of Jessy's frightened face before she disappeared.

Again Morgan heard Nicole sketching the personality of one of "her" women. She exclaimed over Jessy's sweetness and complaisance. Again there was music, but there were no screams of protest from Jessy. There was polite, interested applause when the music stopped.

Morgan did not look at the opposite end of the stage when Jessy left it. She tried to make her mind blank, to will it somewhere other than where it was. She knew now what was to happen to her. Alice walked past her. Only vaguely did she hear Madame Nicole expounding on Alice's virtues and virginity.

It seemed only seconds had gone by when she heard applause, much louder than before, and Madame Nicole's voice announcing the winner.

Her two servants helped her stand up. They smoothed her hair and dress. Morgan heard Madame Nicole.

"Now, gentlemen, the one you have waited for, the one all San Francisco has heard about. I must warn you now that if the bids are not high enough, I will reject them all. Now we will show you our jewel."

The music began and Morgan was led out onto the stage. She was glad there was so much light in her eyes, because she could not see the men in front of her. She tried to concentrate on something pleasant, but could find nothing.

The girls walked her back and forth across the stage and then, as she knew they would, they began to undress her. As they removed each layer of clothing, they turned her around to show off all the parts of her. Morgan was aware of low, quiet male voices.

Her body was bathed in the pink light the hundreds of candles gave off. It took the assistants nearly half an hour to remove

Morgan's clothes. Finally, she stood clad only in high-heeled pumps and black silk stockings, held in place by lace garters just above her knees. The girls turned her around and removed the pins from her hair, allowing it to cascade down her back.

It was then that the applause broke out. It seemed thunderous, as if hundreds of men were out there. She heard chairs moving back, scraping the floor. She wanted to run, to hide, but the girls held her arms and Samson blocked the exit.

They led her off after what seemed hours. They had walked her back and forth again, while her hair was down.

The girls put her arms into a robe and she collapsed into tears on the bed in her room. Madame Nicole came in close behind her. "You were sensational! My sale will make history! A standing ovation!"

"You got what you wanted. It's over for you, but for me it is only just beginning. I'm sold to God only knows who. To some man who will use me in any way he pleases."

Nicole loved her girls in her way, and it hurt her to hear the venom in Morgan's voice. She took her in her arms, Morgan sobbing on the woman's ample breast. "No, *chérie,* I am not without feeling. For years I held these sales in New Orleans. This is only my second sale in San Francisco, and because of you I am already a great success. You have made a new name for me, and I am grateful."

She held Morgan's shaking shoulders. Looking into her tear-filled eyes, she explained, "I was young once. I do know what it means to love someone, truly love someone. I have given you a new chance in life. I did not take the highest bid, and I pray no one will find this out. Your benefactor will suit you well while your broken heart mends. When you are well again, when your mind is as beautiful as your body, you will be able to begin again, to look for another love."

Morgan wiped her eyes. "I don't understand what you're saying, what you mean."

Nicole stood up. "You will, and I hope that someday you will not hate me. It is not easy to sacrifice a good profit. Girls! Get Morgan's traveling outfit. Mr. Shaw has a carriage waiting." She gave Morgan a nod of farewell and left.

"Mr. Shaw! Such a handsome man." Carrie rolled her eyes.

"Madame Nicole will tan you if she finds out what you're saying." Both girls giggled.

"Why are you acting like this, first Madame Nicole and now you two? What's wrong with this man, this monster she's sold me to?"

The girls looked at one another and dissolved in giggles. Their fingers were shaking so that they could hardly finish the closings on Morgan's chocolate-brown cape.

"Get out of here — do you hear me?" Morgan's voice was low, but getting louder as her panic rose. "Get out!"

Quickly, the girls left the room, clicking the door closed behind them. Immediately it opened again. Morgan didn't look up, but continued staring at her hands. "I told you to get out. I've had enough of . . ."

She looked up into the eyes of an extremely handsome man. He was probably in his forties, but his skin was clear and youthful. His hair was blond and waved back from his head. His eyes were blue. His shoulders were wide and his chest thick, tapering to slim legs.

Morgan stared, speechless. He seemed too perfect to be real. He motioned for her to look in the mirror. What she saw startled her. Their reflections were very similar. Their hair and eyes were surprisingly alike.

"It's as if we were brother and sister, don't you think? I was startled at the resemblance myself, when I saw you inside. Turn around and let me look at you." He took her chin in his hand. "Mmm, yes. I was afraid Nicole had used makeup to cover flaws, but I can see there are none."

Morgan jerked her head from his hand. "I assume you are Mr. Shaw."

"You do not have to say that as if I were an insect. Yes, I am Theron Shaw. You may call me Theron."

"Well, Mr. Shaw," she emphasized the words, "what do you have planned for your slave?"

"My slave? Well, I guess you would feel some hostility after that rather vulgar performance of Nicole's. But I do have plans for you. It's rather late now and I am tired. Tomorrow is Christmas Day, and we can spend the entire day discussing your future. Shall we go?"

"My wish is your command."

"I can hardly wait for you to stop this ugly sarcasm. You will stop it, won't you? I mean, it's not your normal personality to be so cynical, is it?"

She didn't answer, but he was beginning to puzzle her.

"Just let me say goodbye to my friend." Morgan heard Jessy's voice behind her and turned to hold out her arms. "I got me a pretty man. My girls say he's really rich and a real lover, too."

Her smile showed real happiness. "They told me the trick Madame Nicole played on you. I'm real sorry, Morgan, you deserve better."

"Are you coming, Jessica?"

"Be there soon, love."

"Hear that? He calls me Jessica. You cheer up and maybe we can visit each other soon. Goodbye." They kissed one another's cheek once more and parted.

Theron helped Morgan into an elegant carriage. They didn't speak until they had stopped in front of a simple, white, two-story house. It was new but unadorned, unlike many of the new houses.

The inside was unlike anything she had ever seen. Theron looked closely for her reaction, and her surprised gasp pleased him.

"So you like it?"

"It's beautiful. I've never seen anything to compare with it."

"Well, you see, this is my business. I am an importer and a collector. Most people decorate their houses in whatever is in fashion at the time, but I choose whatever I like from any period of history I like. That is why you see Chinese porcelains mixed with carpets from Morocco. That blue chair is Italian, late seventeenth century. I was told that it was made especially for a king, but the dealer wasn't sure which king." His eyes laughed.

Theron ushered her to a beautiful staircase, the curving handrail held up by carvings of flowers and vines.

"This staircase came from your own South. The house burned down, and this was one of the few things left undamaged. Are you familiar with Renaissance paintings? Brueghel, Rembrandt, and a new man — Ingres. I like the curve of this woman's back, don't you? Physically impossible, of course — but a lovely line."

Morgan was having difficulty absorbing everything.

"Morgan, you're tired. Please forgive me. Here is your room. I'm afraid you will have to take care of yourself tonight. I had no plans to bring a guest home tonight. Jeannette will take care of you in the morning. Is there anything I can get you? Something to eat?"

Mutely, she shook her head. He bade her goodnight, leaving her standing at the closed door, her little bag of night things on the floor.

The beauty and taste of the house had been a shock to her, but the bedroom was breathtaking. The walls were covered in a pale blue silk, lightly patterned. The ceiling was white. The floor was a highly polished parquet, with white rugs scattered about. The bed was enormous, hung in the same material as the walls. There was a low dressing table, a highboy, and a glass-fronted cabinet, all of the same honey-colored wood as the floor. The cabinet held several intricately carved jade statues. There wasn't one article in the room that didn't look as if it had been made especially for this room.

It took a few seconds for her to regain her senses, to know that Theron would soon be coming to the room to exercise his rights as her owner. Quickly, she took off the brown traveling dress and stepped into the pink gown Madame Nicole had given her. The gown looked sleazy in the lovely room.

She brushed her hair with the brush she found on the low table. There was a matched set for nails and hair, about twelve pieces made of a rich green marble. She climbed into bed and blew out the lamp. She waited expectantly for a few minutes, planning what she'd say to convince Theron to give her back her freedom. The day proved too much for her, though, and she fell asleep quickly.

When she awoke, it was morning and the sun was streaming in through two French doors. A young woman in a black-and-white maid's uniform was smiling at her, showing even, perfect teeth.

"Good morning. Mr. Shaw said I wasn't to wake you, but since you are awake, I'm sure he'd like you to join him for breakfast."

"I'm sure I have no choice in the matter," Morgan muttered.

The maid looked at her with a puzzled expression. "I am Jeannette. Mr. Shaw says you are to be his new assistant."

It was Morgan's turn to look puzzled. "Assistant?" She saw Jeannette frown slightly at her cheap whore-house gown.

"Excuse me, ma'am. I will find you a robe." Jeannette was back in seconds with a brilliant blue satin robe, trimmed with marabou at the neck and around the bottom. "Lovely, isn't it? Mr. Shaw has exquisite taste."

Theron was seated at the breakfast table reading a newspaper. When he saw Morgan, he rose and took her hand to escort her to the chair beside him. "I hope you slept well."

Morgan was now wary of this man. When the butler stepped from the room, Theron turned to her. "Really, Morgan, there is no need to look like a scared rabbit and cringe from me. You will have every servant for blocks talking about how I beat you."

Before she could think of what to say, the

butler returned with a plate covered by a matching porcelain dome. He set it in front of her, removing the lid.

"Oeufs demi-devil!" Morgan exclaimed. "It's been a year since I had eggs prepared like this." She took a forkful as she looked into Theron's astonished face. "Delicious! Your chef must be complimented."

"You know French cooking?" Theron obviously thought this was too much to hope for.

"Yes. I studied for some time with a French master chef."

He smiled, and his face resembled a Greek god's. "We are going to get along splendidly."

Their talk was about food and cooking for the rest of the meal. Morgan had time to notice the gleaming white tablecloth, the blue-and-white Limoges china, the silver accessories, and the blue-and-white carnations floating in a silver bowl.

"Jarvis, we will have coffee in the conservatory."

Morgan took Theron's arm as he led her through an archway at the end of the living room. The room was half of a dome with rounded panes of glass set in strips of dark wood. It was filled with lush greenery and orchids of every color. In the middle of the room stood a white marble statue of the classical Greek man, his body perfect. It could easily be a statue of Theron. Morgan turned toward him.

"I see you notice the resemblance. I found it in Greece." He turned away to stare at a cattleya orchid. Morgan realized he was embarrassed at the apparent vanity in having a statue so like himself.

"You were going to explain my future to me today?"

"Yes." He was relieved to have the subject changed. "I have already told you that I am an importer of fine art objects. I have lived and worked in New York most of my life, but when I heard gold had been discovered here, I knew there would be a need for my business. When men discover gold, their wives need ways to spend it. First, they have their husbands build them enormous houses, and then they fill them up. That is where I come in. I supply things for them to buy — lovely, beautiful, expensive things. I also make suggestions as to what to buy. Unfortunately, money is not often accompanied by good taste."

Morgan sipped her coffee. "Where do I fit into this?"

"In Europe or in New York, my job would pose no problem. There, people understand

333

me. But here! This new gold takes a farmer or laborer and makes him a millionaire overnight. With all his new-found wealth, he is still ignorant. He dresses his fat, sweating wife in purple satin and thinks she is a lady — he thinks every man wants her." He paused. "I'm sorry, I am getting too emotional about this.

"I have learned that I need a companion, a woman to assist me when I talk to these ignorant people. Alone, I seem threatening. Also, the husbands are more likely to go along with their wives' extravagances when a beautiful young woman is in the room."

"Is this what you want me for? Your assistant?"

"Yes," he said simply.

"But I don't understand. Why did you have to buy someone from a brothel? You could hire someone."

"You make it sound very simple, but it is not. You have not caught the gold fever. You haven't seen what it does to people. The women who come here come with their husbands or fathers, and they don't want jobs — they want to spend their days in the sun shaking little pans of rocks. It's very difficult to hire anyone for a steady job these days. Besides, as you see, I cannot bear ugliness. Farmers' daughters rarely appeal to me.

"I had an assistant for a while, but she left me for one of those loud drunkards who had a few hundred dollars' worth of gold dust in his dirty pockets." His voice held contempt.

"I don't usually attend such things as Madame Nicole's human auction. But a friend of mine, Mr. Leon Thomas, remarked on the resemblance between the two of us, and I was intrigued. Madame Nicole offered me an invitation. I buy things for a living . . . beautiful things. And when I saw you, I made an offer."

"But you can't buy people!"

"Please!" He lifted his hand in protest. "Let's not go into that again. Madame Nicole said your husband was dead and that you are alone. I need an assistant and you need a home. Couldn't we just call this an intelligent business arrangement?"

"A business arrangement?" Morgan whispered. Tears came to her eyes as she recalled saying those same words to Seth, less than a year ago.

"Excuse me. I believe I've said something wrong again."

"No, it's not you. It's an old memory, but still very fresh in my mind. I have not gotten over my husband's death yet. Sometimes I am afraid I never will."

There was an embarrassed silence.

"As I was saying, you could work for me and learn my business and stay with me until your purchase price is paid. You will have every luxury."

She considered this for a moment. She could go back to New Mexico to her father's ranch. She knew that under the circumstances, she would qualify to inherit the estate. But what would she do alone on a ranch? Perhaps it would be better to work for a living.

"What is included in this business arrangement of yours besides decorating?"

He smiled at her, looking so much like the marble statue. "If you mean do I plan to become your lover, the answer is no. Though you are beautiful, you do not interest me in that way."

A sudden memory of her mother's chef, Jean-Paul, came to her. She understood, and returned his smile. Madame Nicole had indeed done her a favor. "Yes, I'll accept your job."

"Good! Now we can start to work. Jeannette says the clothes you brought with you are atrocious. I can imagine Madame Nicole's taste." He shuddered delicately.

"Since we are so much alike in coloring, I know what colors suit you best — rich, bright, vibrant colors."

"That's just what my mother-in-law said. No pinks or beiges for Morgan — reds and blues and blacks."

Theron put her arm through his and patted her hand. "We're going to make a team, you and I. We'll be talked about everywhere. Look." He paused before a full-length mirror and she was startled again at the similarity between them. Streaked blond hair, gently curling . . . brilliant blue eyes . . . the same full lips. "Of course, I'm probably old enough to be your father, but I somehow doubt that I am." His eyes twinkled and she laughed.

"I think we're going to enjoy our partnership."

The following weeks were almost a fairy tale. Theron was a pleasant companion and a wonderful observer of people. Together, they laughed at the posturings of the *nouveaux riches.* Theron's impeccable taste enhanced Morgan's beauty. Soon she was a celebrity in San Francisco. Heads turned toward them wherever they went. There were constant invitations.

Men encouraged their wives to hire

Theron to help them spend their wealth. Many times Theron had to rescue Morgan from the grasp of a too-ardent husband.

Jessy sent Morgan an invitation to lunch with her at a fashionable new tea shop. It was one of the few times Morgan had ever been anywhere in San Francisco without Theron.

Jessy and Morgan hugged one another, glad to be together again. Morgan noticed that Jessy's cheap taffeta dress was frayed and stained, but the happiness in her eyes overshadowed any money problems.

"He's been havin' some bad luck in the gold fields lately. Made too many bad investments."

"But you are happy, Jessy? That's what matters."

"Oh, sure. Me and Tom still get along swell. I got me a new lover on the side, too. Now don't look so shocked, Morgan. I'm not like you. I never could love one man at a time. Tell me about you. I was upset when those two girls told me what kind of man Madame Nicole sold you to. Maybe you got a lover by now too?"

Morgan laughed. "Jessy, I need you around all the time. Sometimes my mind gets lost for days in Louis XIV furniture and French enamels. You always seem to know just what you want."

"I do know that furniture, no matter how pretty it may be, is no replacement for a man. Now answer my question — you got a lover yet?"

Morgan was serious. "There's only been one man in my life and that's all I want. No one will ever replace Seth. Jessy, don't look at me like I'm crazy. I am happy, as happy as I can be without Seth. Theron and I are friends. He is good to me and I enjoy decorating."

"You're right, I do think you're crazy. But as long as you're happy, that's all that counts. I need to go, or Tommy'll decide I've left him and throw my things out. You know, I couldn't tell him I was meetin' you. If he ever found out I knew the famous gorgeous Morgan, he'd nag me to my grave to get to meet you." They parted laughing.

In May, when Morgan had been with Theron for nearly five months, the new wagon trains from the East began pouring in, each loaded with people aiming to try their luck in the gold fields. The Chandler wagon was among these.

CHAPTER FIFTEEN

The Chandlers had already had a long, hard trip from Vermont. They were driving two wagons, one filled with farm implements and some basic mining equipment, the other carrying household goods. Ed Chandler was glad when he met the big man, Seth Colter. It had been all he could do to take care of a wife and two rather active young ladies all by himself. His daughters were pretty, and it seemed that every young man on the twenty-six wagons in the train was courting them.

Mr. Colter had said little about himself, just that he was heading west. Ed had offered him a job immediately. If he'd help with the stock and the wagons, he'd have his meals cooked by Ed's wife and daughters, and someone would care for his clothes.

Ed laughed to himself as they shook hands on the deal. Seth looked at him questioningly. "I'm not sure I've done you such a favor, Mr. Colter."

"Why's that, Mr. Chandler?"

"I have two daughters, both experts at breaking hearts. I'm afraid they may cause you some problems."

Seth's face was serious. "I don't think I have to worry about a broken heart."

Ed Chandler frowned. There was something far too serious about this young man.

Early the next morning, Seth rode out to the wagon train and met the Chandler women. Ivy Chandler's eyes were forever darting around, watching her daughters. The girls, Gladys and Sudey, were both pretty. They were tall, big-boned girls with beautiful auburn hair. Gladys was seventeen and Sudey eighteen. When their father introduced Seth, they stared and nodded. Seth tipped his hat and left them.

It was a minute before the girls recovered, Gladys first. "Papa, why didn't you tell us about Mr. Colter?"

"I did, yesterday." He smiled. He knew exactly what they meant.

"Where does he come from?"

"Is he married?"

"Girls! Please. I know next to nothing about Mr. Colter. I met him just yesterday and offered him a job."

"Do you think that's wise, Ed? I mean, we really know nothing about him, and we will be spending three months very close to him."

"Three months!" Gladys sighed.

"A stranger. A tall, handsome stranger!" Sudey joined.

"Girls! I want no more of that. Mr. Colter is an employee of your father's. Even though we are in the wilderness, there is no excuse for unladylike behavior."

Both girls adopted looks of shame and contrition. The second their mother's back was turned, they turned to one another and grinned. Watching, their father could hardly contain his laughter.

"Don't encourage them, Ed," Ivy whispered to her husband.

During the day, Seth often rode ahead of the wagons to look for fresh game. At night the new settlers circled their wagons into a fortress against danger.

"Could I get you some stew, Mr. Colter? I made it myself."

Seth smiled up at the girl, giving her his full attention for the first time. "Yes, I'd like some, especially since you made it yourself."

Gladys glowed from the compliment and smiled as she saw Sudey frowning at her.

"Coffee, Mr. Colter?" Sudey asked.

Ivy Chandler watched her two daughters warily. At night when she and her husband were alone in the wagon bed, she talked to him. "Ed, you have to speak to your daughters. They're too forward. Since Mr. Colter came, they're not even speaking to the other boys on the train. They pester the poor man till he can hardly get his work done."

"Ivy, they're not causing any harm. I remember when we were courting. You seemed to turn up everywhere I went."

"Edward Chandler! Are you saying I chased you?"

Ed laughed. "No, dear. It was all just co-incidence, I'm sure. But Mr. Colter seems sad. Even in the middle of several people, he seems alone."

"I've noticed that, too."

"I think two pretty girls fighting over him may be just what he needs."

Both Gladys and Sudey had made many efforts to get Seth's attention, but they both felt their failure.

Gladys was pleased when she saw Seth walking away from camp alone. She let him get a few yards ahead and then began running after him, calling his name. When he turned toward her, she bent her ankle under her and fell.

343

Quickly, Seth was kneeling by her, taking her foot in his large hands. As he kneaded the foot and ankle, he watched her face for signs of pain. There were no such signs, but Seth didn't mind. He had known only one woman who hadn't played games to get him. He did not expect to meet another.

"Does it hurt?"

"Oh, yes," she cried, trying to squeeze out a tear.

"Let me help you up." He put his arm around her shoulders and she leaned against him. She took one step and collapsed to the ground.

"I'm so sorry, Mr. Colter. I don't seem to be able to walk at all. Maybe you could get my father for me and he could carry me back to the wagon." She looked coyly up at him through her lashes.

Easily, chuckling to himself, he bent down and picked up the large girl.

"Mr. Colter! You don't have to carry me. I'm much too large to be carried."

"You hardly weigh more than a bird, Miss Chandler," Seth lied.

Ed Chandler was upset at first to see his daughter injured, but when he noted the smile on Seth's face, he guessed Gladys's trick.

Sudey was furious with her sister. At night

in the wagon, she viciously grabbed her sister's ankle. "You weren't really hurt. You had no right to act like that!"

"And who says I have no right?"

"He's mine. I've wanted him ever since I first saw him!"

"Well, so have I." She turned to her sister, smugly. "You can't imagine what it's like to be held in his arms. He's so *very* strong."

Sudey leaped at Gladys, catching some of her hair in her fingers.

Their screams brought their mother.

Ivy Chandler lectured the girls for some time on their behavior toward Mr. Colter. She reminded the girls that they knew very little about the man, that it was possible that he had a wife and several children somewhere.

The girls stayed away from Seth for a week. Sudey looked out from the wagon one night and saw Seth sitting alone by the dying fire. Quietly, she left the wagon and joined him.

"I couldn't sleep," she explained.

"Coffee?" He poured her a cup.

She rubbed her upper arms. "Nights in the mountains get awfully cold, don't they?"

Seth stepped to his horse and got a blanket from his bedroll on the ground. Sudey stood up as he put it around her shoulders and lifted her face to be kissed.

Instinctively, he kissed her. She molded her body to his. Her lips were very receptive, but Seth felt nothing.

Angrily, he pushed her from him. "I think you'd better get back into your wagon."

Sudey smiled up at him, happy, oblivious.

Seth watched her go, his hands clenched by his side. Damn you! Damn you, Morgan! He went to his bedroll and stretched out. He tried to remember Sudey's kiss, but all he saw was Morgan. He compared every girl to Morgan. Sudey had yielded to him, but all he thought of was Morgan's body. It was a long time before he went to sleep.

After the kiss, Sudey became very possessive of her father's helper. She took care that his shirts were mended and his plate was always full. But the longer they spent on the trail, the more Seth stayed by himself.

When Ivy Chandler questioned her daughter about this new possessiveness, Sudey told her of Seth's kiss.

They were coming close to the edge of the desert when Ivy confronted Seth with Sudey's admission.

"I just want to know what your intentions are, Mr. Colter. My daughter is very young and very forward, I know . . . but I'd like to know where you two stand."

"I'm sorry, Mrs. Chandler. I did not mean to take advantage of your daughter. I'm sorry it happened. As for intentions toward your daughter — I have none."

"Are you married, Seth? Do you have a wife somewhere?" Her voice was gentle. She saw the pain her question caused.

"Yes, I have a wife somewhere. Though, at the moment I don't know where."

She put her hand on his shoulder. "You carry a heavy weight with you. I hope you will find peace someday."

Ivy told her daughters of Seth's wife. They were both upset, but they finally decided to turn their interests elsewhere.

Crossing the desert was more of a hardship than anyone had imagined. Everyone on the train turned his thoughts to dreams of water. It was a tired, ragged group that arrived in San Francisco in May of 1850.

CHAPTER SIXTEEN

"Remember, if you ever need anything, just look us up," Mr. Chandler called to Seth.

The girls watched him walk away, leading his horse. "Whoever his wife is, she's a very lucky woman."

"I want to marry a man just like him, big and quiet, who walks just like that." Both girls watched Seth, then giggled.

"If Mama heard you, you know what she'd say."

"I know, but it's hard for Mama to understand — she was never faced with a man like Seth Colter. Any woman who would leave him must be crazy."

Seth tied up his horse and walked into the saloon. An explosion of laughter came from three well-fed men in business suits at a near table.

"Ol' Charlie here paid three thousand dollars for some Chinese wallpaper just because the little gal said she would personally supervise its hanging. Three thousand dollars for three days' company! Pretty expensive, huh?"

The man with the red face laughed. "Of course, he *did* get to keep the wallpaper."

"That's *all* he got, though. He sure didn't get anything else."

Again, the explosive laughter.

"The smartest thing that pretty boy ever did was buy the little lady from Madame Nicole. My wife loves that fella, but I never could abide him. He's so pretty. I thought he belonged on the mantelpiece instead of walking around. But with that sweet little Morgan, he can spend all the time he wants at my house. Course it sure costs me a lot for the opportunity of lookin' at her."

"Hey, mister, we say somethin' to interest you?" The man's tone was slightly belligerent.

Seth smiled, slow and easy. "I was just listening. Heard the name Morgan. Used to know a girl named Morgan."

"Come set down with us and tell us about your Morgan. I can't believe there could be another woman like San Francisco's Morgan Colter."

Seth tried to hide his emotions. It *was* Morgan! And the little bitch had the gall to

349

use his name. You'd think she'd at least use another name. "Seth . . . Blake's my name." The three men introduced themselves — Charley Farrell, Joe Beal, and Arthur Johnston.

The-red-faced man was Joe. "Our Morgan's a real beauty. A little blond thing, big blue eyes and a body — wooeee." He grinned and looked to the other two men for agreement.

"Couldn't be the Morgan I knew. The one I knew was probably not as pretty as your horse." He grinned and took a sip of his beer. "This Morgan of yours sure sounds like something. What's the chances of getting a, shall we say, private showing?"

The three men all started to talk at once and Charley quieted them. He leaned back in his chair. "Well, Mister Blake, this little gal comes real high. I mean real high." He gave furious looks to the other two men to quiet their protests. "You see, she used to work at Madame Nicole's place, a real classy cathouse. You practically have to show your teeth along with a carriage full of gold just to go look at one of Madam Nicole's shows. Well, this little Morgan was the star at Madame Nicole's place — used to go on stage and have two girls undress her for everybody to see. Of course, that was a special-invitation show only." Again he gave warning looks to the two other men, both of whom were staring, open-mouthed, wondering at this fantastic story.

"Now she's left Nicole's and works for this blond feller. He's so pretty, and he looks like Morgan. They're a real pair, struttin' around town, goin' to the opera. Well, as I was sayin', this little lady is expensive. She and this feller sell you things for your house. If you've got enough money and buy enough stuff for your house, you get a little extra on the side. You know what I mean?"

Seth managed a smile, one that didn't quite reach his eyes. "I guess I do know what you mean."

Charley continued. "Art, here, just finished decorating a whole house, and it was a real pleasure, wasn't it?"

Arthur nodded, silently.

"See, me and Joe are still workin' on our houses. So far, I've only spent three thousand dollars, and that ain't near enough for me to enjoy it yet."

Art coughed nervously. "You come to try your luck in the gold fields, Mr. Blake?"

Seth drained his beer. "Yes, I think I will." He turned back to Charley. "Whereabouts does this Morgan live?"

Charley could hardly contain his laughter.

"Boy, you won't have a chance dressed like that. Even at Madame Nicole's she wouldn't entertain no goldminer. You need fancy duds like these." He gave Seth directions to Theron's house and Seth left the saloon.

Charley waited until the big man was out of the building before he allowed his laughter to escape. "The man'll try everything to get her. He'll see her and think she's for sale and . . ." He realized the other two men weren't sharing in his laughter.

"Come on, men. Don't you see the joke? Can't you see ol' Theron's face when that big dumb cowboy makes an offer for his little jewel?"

"Charley, Miss Colter is a lady, and you know about Nicole's sales. Morgan Colter didn't entertain in no whorehouse and you know it. I don't care about the cowboy, but if Morgan or Theron heard, they could do us damage."

"And besides, I like the little gal. She's a nice lady, and she keeps to herself. And nobody's even seen the inside of her room, even though everybody's tried."

"Oh, hell! Can't a man have a little joke? I was only funnin' the man." He finished his beer. "Let's get out of here. Charlotte's got Morgan and her pretty boy comin' to tea and she wants me there." He looked at the other two reproachfully. "A man can dream, can't he?"

Seth's senses were reeling. She was here! She was in San Francisco. A real classy cathouse, the man had said. Did she leave Montoya, or did he get tired of her?

Without conscious thought, he followed the man's directions to Theron's house. He stood staring at it for a long time before he saw the door open.

"Theron, shouldn't we take some of the upholstery samples? Charlotte may want to change her mind about that awful brocade."

"Morgan, will you never learn? That woman would never change her mind, not unless you held a gun on her. We could try that, couldn't we? 'Lady, either you pick what we say, or you die,' " he mocked. "How's that?"

"Oh, Theron, sometimes I wish we could. What is it with these people and purple?" She was smiling and turned in Seth's direction an instant before he disappeared around a building.

Her knees gave way and she grabbed Theron's arm for support.

"Morgan, what is it? Jarvis, go to the Farrells' and tell them Morgan is ill, that we can't make it." Theron picked Morgan up and carried her upstairs to her room.

Seth watched from the street, his rage mounting by the second. He turned and left the area.

"*Seth.* It was Seth, Theron. I saw Seth."

"But Morgan, Seth is dead. It must have been someone who looked like him."

"Theron!" Her eyes blazed. "It *was* Seth. He's alive. I have to find him." She started up from the bed.

"Not now you don't. I don't like your color. Jeannette, get Morgan some tea." He looked at Jeannette knowingly and she nodded.

"Theron, you have to understand. There is a reason that I have to find him now, without delay. He may hate me. He may think I left him for another man. He was told I did."

"How could he believe that? Morgan, you don't realize how much you talk about that man. I'd really like to meet him, because I'm sure he has a golden halo and his feet are supported by little clouds. If something is good . . . anything — art, food, wallpaper paste — you compare it to Seth. If it's bad, then it's not like Seth."

"Theron, please!" She looked at him in desperation.

"Here's your tea." Again, he and Jeannette

exchanged looks. "Drink this and then we'll talk about finding your Seth."

Morgan sipped at the tea and then, at Theron's urging, drained her cup.

"Now, let's go." She swung her legs off the bed, then put her hand to her forehead.

"Theron! You put something in the tea. How am I going to find Seth? How am I . . . He hates me . . ."

"She's asleep. Good."

"Mr. Shaw, what's wrong with her? I've never seen her so upset. Do you think she really saw her husband?"

"I don't know, but I plan to make a few inquiries while she sleeps. A man with sandals and a white robe should be easy enough to find, don't you think?"

"Sandals?" Jeannette looked puzzled and then smiled. "Mr. Shaw! You shouldn't say things like that."

"If she wakes up, try to keep her calm. I'll be back soon."

Theron spent the afternoon and part of the evening trying to find Seth. He knew very little about him except that he was large. The bartender at one saloon seemed to remember a man like that, but he wasn't sure. Two wagon trains had arrived in San Francisco that day and he'd been pretty busy. It was well into the night when Theron returned home.

Morgan met him at the door, but she knew from his face that he'd been unsuccessful. She sank to her knees, dissolving into tears. "Seth. Seth." Her cries were close to hysteria.

Theron held her, rocking her gently. In the five months they had lived together, they had become very close. Theron thought of Morgan as his little sister. He enjoyed teasing her and, at times, protecting her.

"Morgan, sweet, don't cry. We'll find him. If we have to turn the town upside down, we'll find him. I'll send men into the gold fields to look for him. Whatever it takes, we'll find him. Now, please calm yourself. I can't stand to see you cry."

When Morgan couldn't stop her tears, built from months of loneliness and longing, Theron carried her back to bed.

"Morgan, please, I'm getting too old to keep climbing those stairs," he teased. Morgan's unresponsiveness sobered him. "If you'll rest, I'll go out again and look for him. Now."

Theron left her, worried about the frantic look in her eyes.

It took Seth only a few seconds and the

flash of some gold to get the little tailor's promise to have a suit altered in a few hours.

It was night when he left the shop. No longer did he fit in with the tired, dirty prospectors in from the East. The charcoal gray suit and white shirt set off his hair and tanned skin.

His long strides took him to the rather quiet, unassuming house on First Street. A carriage pulled up and two men went to the door. A tall butler opened it, smiled, and ushered the gentlemen in.

Seth knocked on the door. The butler looked him over carefully. "Yes?"

"I am new to San Francisco, just arrived today, and I heard that some enjoyment might be had at Madame Nicole's."

"Just a moment, sir, and I will see." He closed the door. Within moments it reopened and Seth saw an enormous woman with beautiful black hair.

"Madame Nicole, of course." Seth bowed slightly. His eyes raked over her, making her feel as beautiful as her vanity allowed. "Seth Blake at your service, ma'am."

"Well, Mr. Blake, Edwards tells me you'd like to visit my humble establishment."

He smiled at her, showing deep dimples.

"Mr. Blake, I declare you can certainly charm a girl." Her eyes swept down his massive chest "I believe I just may keep you for myself." She possessively took his arm and led him into the large drawing room.

"Will you be in town long, Mr. Blake?"

"I'm not sure yet. I have a ranch in New Mexico. I thought I might try my hand in the gold fields."

She led him to a table covered with various hors d'oeuvres and wines. When Seth refused refreshment, she asked him more questions.

"Tell me, Mr. Blake, what would interest you tonight? Nicole has a wide variety of beautiful young women."

"Well, I saw one today that interested me. I believe she once worked for you — a little blonde, blue eyes. I believe she now works with an importer?"

"Ah, Morgan," Nicole smiled. "She was here for a while, yes. But she was sold right away."

"Sold?"

"Yes, twice a year I have a sale of beautiful young women. The highest bidder wins the lady. Morgan was the most beautiful woman yet offered in San Francisco."

Nicole did not see the muscles clenching and unclenching in Seth's jaw. He had hoped it wasn't true, that the men had lied. "So she did work here then?"

Nicole did not want to tell the handsome and possibly rich young man that she had never had such a beautiful girl work for her. Her reputation might suffer.

"Yes, I have many beautiful young women working for me. Let me show you a few." She clapped her plump hands and three women in thin, nearly transparent gowns entered the room.

Nicole had been around men for many years and could sense their needs. Something was troubling this young man, something deeper than simple need for a woman. He hardly looked at these. Nicole raised her hand and dismissed them.

"Seth, I don't know you, but I think I know your problem. You're in love."

Seth raised one mocking eyebrow.

"Go to her. Tell her you love her. Take her by force if you need to, but let her know how you feel."

Let Morgan know how he felt! Yes, he'd tell her. He'd tell her how much he hated her. He smiled. "Yes, I think you are right. Goodnight, Madame Nicole."

Nicole laughed when he was gone. She wished she were that young woman. It would be wonderful to hold that man in her arms.

■ ■ ■ ■

Jeannette blew out the light in Morgan's room, glad to have finally gotten her to sleep. She closed the door quietly and went downstairs to her own room.

Seth made no sound as he opened the French doors and stepped into the room. Even by moonlight the beauty of the room was obvious. He walked to the dresser and touched her brush and comb, taking his time making his way to the bed.

Her hair was spread all around her and tangled in one fist. She made a little hiccough as she slept, as if she had been crying.

He reached out a hand and touched a golden tress with one finger. It was so soft. He hadn't remembered how soft her hair was. She moved, kicking the covers below her waist. She had on a satin gown of deep, rich apricot. The ties were loose in front and the fabric gaped open to expose the soft curve of her breast.

Too many things flashed before him: Morgan sunning herself on a rock in the canyon, Morgan cooking his breakfast and then sitting in his lap to feed it to him.

And then the note. Those few words, telling him she loved Joaquín.

Seth's eyes lost their softness. He put out his hands to clasp her neck, but then stopped. He had loved her, loved her from the first. He had stood back while she made up her mind whether she wanted to be a woman or not. He had waited and watched, for a long time. He had killed three men for her. Cat Man and his two cohorts had been sitting peacefully by their campfire. He had not even given them a chance to go for their guns. He had killed them and ridden away. For her!

He began removing his jacket. When he had removed all his clothes, he lifted the light blanket and climbed into bed with Morgan.

Gently, he began caressing her soft breast. He brought his lips to hers, barely touching their sweetness, then delicately nibbling at her lower lip. In her sleep, Morgan felt the longed-for touch of Seth. She moved against him, parting her lips. The tip of his tongue traced the outline of her lips.

His kisses traced a sensuous path across her cheek to her earlobe. His teeth nipped the tender piece of flesh. "Morgan," he whispered. She nuzzled closer to him. *"Mi querida."* Her eyes opened slowly, languidly, her arms going up to encircle his broad shoulders.

She opened her eyes fully and then opened her mouth to scream. Seth silenced her lips with his own. Her eyes were wild and she began to struggle.

Quickly, he put his fingers over her lips. "Don't you know your husband?"

She looked at him with astonishment for one long moment and then tears rushed to her eyes. "*Seth.* I knew it was you. I *knew.* Oh, Seth! What happened?" She pulled him to her. "Seth, I love you. I love you so much." She couldn't see his jaw clench, his eyes freeze. "Seth . . . did Joaquín finally admit that he —"

His hand covered her mouth. His eyes were dark with passion. "Later, sweet. Later you can tell me all about it."

Doubt flickered a warning in her mind. But he was so urgent.

"Have you missed me? Did you think about me?" His hands moved across her body, making her ache with longing. Her arms pulled him closer and she arched against him.

"Yes, oh yes," she whispered into his ear as she kissed it, pulling the earlobe between her lips.

"You're eager for me, aren't you, Morgan?" Again, she had the awful feeling, the doubt. What was strange about Seth?

He removed her gown. Her body screamed for him to take her. His caresses were tantalizing, making her lose her senses. It was as if she were only a body, only desire.

His lips traveled down her neck, the weight of his body pressing on her. Her fingers pulled him closer. He felt her urgency and this made his kisses even slower.

"Seth, Seth," she moaned over and over.

His lips traveled down her body, across her breasts, one hand holding hers to keep her clutching fingers still, the other softly kneading her inner thigh. His lips traveled down and down, touching all of her.

When he reached her feet, he kissed each of her toes, raking the soft fleshy part against his lower teeth. "Please, Seth, now, now."

Abruptly, he turned her over, his teeth and tongue and lips making a trail across her smooth, perfect skin.

When he reached her neck, he turned her over and began to make love to her. He kept his lips on hers to still her loud moans. They reached their peaks together.

They lay quietly for a moment, wrapped in ecstasy. Their bodies were one, and inseparable.

Seth moved to lie beside her. He kissed

her neck, her eyelids.

Morgan's body was on fire. Her fingertips were extremely sensitive, the nerves wonderfully alive. They sought Seth's body, searching the length of his broad back, feeling each muscle and the texture of his skin. She kissed his neck, running her tongue along the muscles, the sinews.

Her fingers entangled in the hair on his chest, her lips following the sensitive path of her fingers. Her hands found his maleness and lingered, gently stroking until she heard low sounds from Seth's throat.

She climbed on top of him and this time, slowly, they came to new heights of desire and finally collapsed in one another's arms, sated.

Content, Morgan slept, her cheek against Seth's chest, the hairs tickling her nose. Seth's low voice woke her from the first happy sleep she had had in many months.

"Did you do this with the men at Madame Nicole's?"

"Mmmm?" she snuggled closer to him. Seth was here, alive and in her arms. She kissed his chest.

"Was Joaquín a good lover? Did he make your hips move and your hands claw?"

Her eyes flew open. "Seth, must I tell you . . . ?"

He roughly pushed her from him. "No, I must tell you. I know about them all. I know about Madame Nicole."

Her hand flew to her mouth, her eyes were wide. "No."

He stepped out of the bed, reaching for his clothes. "Tell me, did you react for all of them as you did for me? No wonder you're such an expensive whore. Tell me, how much do you share with your 'partner'? Does he set you up or do you find your own men?"

"No," she whispered, the tears coming to her eyes. She was on her knees in the bed, her damp, tangled hair falling about her. "No, Seth. That's all wrong."

"Well, ma'am, you are certainly fetching like that. I don't imagine you'd pleaded with many men. Does it hurt your vanity to find that you can be walked away from? I know you are used to doing the walking."

Her sobs were choking her, her body shaking.

Seth almost reconsidered, but quickly he picked up his hat and walked to the French doors. "I remember some time ago, when you left a light in the window so I could climb to your bedroom. It's ironic, isn't it?" He paused and reached into his jacket pocket and withdrew several gold coins. He tossed them to the floor beside the bed. "You can share that with your decorator friend. Goodbye, *wife.*" He made the word sound ugly. And almost instantly, he was over the balcony.

When Theron found Morgan an hour later, his patient was calm, sitting quietly against the back of the bed. Something was very wrong. He preferred her hysterics to the icy calm he saw in her eyes now. He sat by her, took her cold little hand.

"What's happened?"

She turned to him and smiled. It was a smile Theron had never seen before, and it made chills run down his spine. "I have just had a visit from my husband, the man I've loved so long, the man I've dreamed of day and night." Her voice was flat.

"After he had used my body and made me react, he taunted me, accused me of having many men."

"Morgan, I really don't understand any of this. Why would he want to hurt you so? Doesn't he understand our relationship?"

She laughed. "I don't believe my husband understands anything. He wouldn't allow me to explain. He saw only the wrong side of everything." Morgan began telling Theron of her marriage to Seth, how she had asked him to marry her, had fought her feelings for him. She told of Seth's jealousy and Joaquín's treachery.

"He never even asked you if the note was true? It never occurred to him that you had been taken against your will?"

"It is ironic, isn't it? He has tried, judged and hanged me — and I am innocent. I don't believe I want to talk anymore, Theron."

The look in Morgan's eyes frightened him. Always, she had a kind word. Always, she smiled. But now her lips curved into a snarl.

"Maybe we could find him. Find him and tell him the truth of what has happened to you — that none of it was your fault."

She turned on him, eyes flashing. "I should go to him and tell him that I am innocent? What should I do, plead with him, beg him to forgive me — for nothing? I loved him and he should have been able to see that. I told him so tonight, but he chose to ignore it. He believes I was one of Nicole's whores. What if I had been? What if his pure little Morgan *had* been tarnished by other men? Should I kill myself in that case? He didn't care enough for me to even listen to me, to find out what had happened to me all this time."

She took a breath and leaned back against the pillows. "He was not the man I thought he was. I never want to hear his name again."

"Morgan, please listen . . ."

"I would like to sleep now. I believe Mrs. Farrell will want us to spend the day discussing her dining room, and I need strength to face that woman's taste. Goodnight."

Theron kissed her forehead, blew out the lamp, and left the room.

Morgan fell asleep, remembering Seth's back as he disappeared over the balcony.

Morgan became more and more involved in her work with Theron. In the next months, she tried constantly to keep herself from thinking of Seth, from fully realizing that he was alive. Did he have a mistress? Was some other woman taking care of him?

All she had to do was find him, tell him that Joaquín had forced her to write the note, that she had not had any other men . . . No! How dare she even think of pleading with him! He was a vain, arrogant man and she wouldn't lower herself.

Gradually, Theron's customers noticed the difference in Morgan. Before, she had met the men's advances with smiles and jests.

Now she tended to sneer at them. She no longer returned their flirting with friendly jibes.

The evenings she spent with Theron often turned into brooding silences. Before, they were hardly ever out of one another's sight; but now Theron spent some evenings alone.

"Take it away, Jeannette. The very sight of food nauseates me."

Jeannette took the tray and set it on the dresser. Then she held her hand to Morgan's forehead.

"Stop it! There's nothing wrong with me. I just don't feel like eating."

Jeannette was calm. Theron had told her about Seth's attack on his wife. "No, ma'am, there's nothing at all wrong with you. I'd say that, in a few months, you'll be perfectly all right."

"Months! Don't be absurd! I'm just not feeling well. A few days' rest and I'll be fine."

"I should say in about six months, you should be quite yourself again."

"Six months! Jeannette, will you stop raving like a lunatic and take that food away? Even the smell of it makes my stomach turn and . . ." Her face drained. She met Jeannette's stare.

Smiling, the maid picked up the tray and

started to the door. "I'm sure Mr. Shaw would want the doctor to check you, to confirm the time. But I think he'll say six months."

When Morgan was alone, she leaned back in the bed. "No. It can't be," she whispered. Her hands went to her stomach. It was hard, but had a slight new roundness. "A baby . . . what will I do with a baby? A baby whose father hates his mother?" She remembered her own fatherless childhood. It had hurt her in many ways, being raised without a man around.

The doctor's visit confirmed what Jeannette had known for some time and Morgan hadn't even guessed at.

Theron was delighted with the news. "A baby in the house! Delightful! Wondrous! We'll make the guest room into a nursery. Chinese décor, don't you think? Of course, I'm very partial to Chinese. Or how about Italian, some clean lines, very fluid? Color. We can do oranges and siennas, or the cool colors."

"Theron, please. I've just found out about this. I don't know what I'm going to do yet."

"Going to do? Well, of course you're going to stay right here. Jeannette and I will take care of you. Come along, Jeannette, let's let Morgan rest for now. We'll see you in the morning. I'm rather tired, too. This has been a very exciting day."

Alone, Morgan's thoughts whirled. A baby, her own child. She smiled. Yes, she wanted this baby, very much. She needed someone to care for, to care about.

But how should she or he be raised?

Her life with Theron was pleasant, but a baby needed more than a mother who decorated people's homes, a mother whom the townsmen took great delight in trying to pinch. What if her child found out this mother had been sold in a public auction at a brothel? What about Morgan's inheritance? She had not thought about it in a long time, but if she had a child, she wanted him to be raised in security.

She would go to Albuquerque and meet with her father's lawyers. Then she'd take her child and go back to Kentucky, and Trahern House.

The thought of Trahern House brought tears to her eyes. Many times when she'd been so happy with Seth, she had laughed at Trahern House, thinking how lonely and barren it would seem to her after her life with Seth. Ah, but now she wouldn't be alone. She'd have her child.

It took Morgan a week to convince Theron

of the wisdom of her plan. She would return to New Mexico and then to Kentucky.

"Morgan, how can you leave? You're like my little sister. What would life be like without you? Please stay."

It wasn't easy to think of leaving Theron or the luxury he provided for her. When she left him, she'd be enitrely on her own, taking care of herself and responsible for another life as well.

A stage line had recently been started, connecting the Santa Fe Trail with the gold fields of California. It was on this stage that Theron booked Morgan's passage.

The goodbyes were tearful. "If you ever need anything, you know where you have a friend," Theron told her as she mounted the high steps into the stagecoach.

The return trip to Santa Fe was awful. The coach swayed and bounced with every rock the wheels hit, and there were thousands of them.

They stopped only long enough to change horses, the passengers being forced to grab whatever they could and to eat in the coach. The windows had pieces of canvas that rolled down over them, but a closed coach, with the six unwashed and sweating people, was unbearable. They talked at first, one man in particular trying to get Morgan's attention, but after the first few days they were all too tired for conversation. In the beginning Morgan had tried to keep her face and hands clean, but when she rubbed her neck and dirt rolled off in her hand, she gave up.

When they arrived in Santa Fe, she was too tired, hungry, and dirty even to remember why she had come. Her legs were cramped and she could hardly stand.

"Here, let me help you with that." Someone took her hand baggage and she turned to meet a pair of familiar eyes.

"Frank!" she cried, the weariness of her body making her vision blurred.

"Morgan!" Frank picked her up and swung her around. "Last time I saw you, them outlaws had carried you off."

Her eyes clouded. "An awful lot's happened since then." She turned away, frowning. If he thought of her as Seth did, he'd hate her, too.

"Hey, little gal!" He squeezed her again and set her down. "Don't you go lookin' like that. I heard every word of the story from Jake. I don't know your side of it, but I sure don't believe you left Seth for Joaquín."

"You don't?"

"Hell, no. Anybody could see the way you two followed one another around. I never saw two people so stubborn as you two. Both of you head over heels in love and neither of you admitting it."

"Oh, Frank! Thank you."

"Let's get you out of here. I bet you want to clean up. I'll take you to the hotel, and then tomorrow, after you've rested, we can go to the ranch."

"No, I can't go to the Colter ranch."

"Just hush now and I'll take care of you. I won't put up with your bullheadedness. Tomorrow you go to the ranch. It's where you belong, especially with that young 'un you're carryin'."

Her eyes flew to his, open wide.

Frank laughed. "Always have had an eye for the ladies. Only thing that's changed about you is that curvy little belly. And with six kids of my own, I sure know what causes that."

Morgan was grateful to Frank for taking care of her. She was content to stand back and let him order her a bath and dinner in her room. Once alone, she scoured herself in the hot water and ate greedily. It was still only about six in the evening when she fell into the soft bed.

Late the next morning, Frank came for her with a buckboard. She had rested and she felt strong enough to protest about going to Seth's ranch, but Frank refused to listen.

"That's your home. Of course you're going there."

"But, Frank, I need to go to Albuquerque and see my father's lawyer."

"All right, you can visit there later, but first you go home. Lupita will be waiting with open arms and hot tortillas. You couldn't ask for more."

Morgan was grim. "What about Jake? And Paul? Will they greet me with open arms? The woman who ran off with another man? You don't even know for sure that the baby I carry is Seth's."

Frank grinned. "You're even more stubborn than I remember. I know that that little one you're carryin' is yours. That's good enough for me. If Seth Colter and you been in the same town for the last few months and he ain't the father, then there's something wrong with him, not with you. Now, if you've finished your lunch, we'd better be on our way."

As they made the long trip to the Colter ranch, Morgan tried not to think of what would greet her there. They talked of Frank's family, whom Morgan had never met, and of life in general in New Mexico. Morgan told Frank about the hundreds of people pouring into San Francisco each week. She talked about Theron and the work they'd done, making him laugh over her stories of the people and the wealth they didn't know how to handle.

Lupita heard the wagon long before she saw it. She walked slowly out to meet them. Since Seth and Morgan had both gone, a change had come over the place. There was no laughter anymore. Jake and she ate their meals in the big kitchen while Paul took his outside. Paul didn't like the gloom of the inside.

She recognized Frank instantly, and thought he'd brought his oldest daughter with him. But something about the small-ness of the form next to Frank made her start. "It couldn't be," she whispered. And then she began running toward the wagon.

"Señora Colter! You've come home!" The large woman practically lifted Morgan out of the wagon. She clasped her tightly in her arms, Morgan returning the hug.

"Lupita, you better be careful how you handle our little mother-to-be."

Lupita gasped, held Morgan at arm's length, and then hugged her again.

CHAPTER SEVENTEEN

"Frank, you must stay to help us celebrate Señora Colter's return."

"Please, Frank, I need your help. I need someone here who believes in me."

Both women looked up at Frank, their eyes imploring.

"No, Morgan, you don't need me. Not when you have Lupita fighting for you. I've got to get home. The wife'll want to know what kept me overnight in Santa Fe anyway. I may need *you* to come defend *me.* Jake's a hummingbird compared to my Louisa."

Lupita and Morgan watched as Frank rode off in the buckboard. When he was out of sight, they turned to one another.

"Lupita . . . I . . ."

"There's no need for you to explain anything. I never believed a word of it. Now, let's get out of this sun. If there's going to be a baby, then there are many things to be done."

"But, Lupita, I can't just come back here to live, not after all that's happened. Frank nearly forced me to come."

"And he was right. This is your home. This is where Seth's baby should be born."

Morgan stopped. "Seth's . . . How do you know? What makes you so sure it's his baby? I've been gone a long time."

"Señora Colter," Lupita laughed, "you do not have to explain anything to me. Jake and Paul will need explanations but I do not. Now come on inside or that baby will get a fever from the sun."

Morgan turned startled eyes to her rounding stomach. Her hand went to the mound. She had so recently learned that she was to have a baby that she hadn't had time to think of it much yet, to get used to its constant presence.

"Yes," she smiled up at Lupita. "We will have to take care of her."

"Her? Already you know what it will be?"

Laughing, their arms around one another, they walked to the house. It was cool within the thick adobe walls. The familiar rooms brought Morgan home at last. Everything had been good in this house. All the many happy memories came flooding back to her.

She turned to Lupita, her face reflecting joy at being home.

"You are right. This is my home. This is where Seth's daughter will be born." She watched as Lupita's grin widened. "Yes, it's Seth's child."

Lupita again ran to Morgan and hugged her tightly. "I knew you'd find one another. I knew it. When will the Señor join us? Why did he ever allow you to travel alone? I will have many words to say to him for this."

"No, Lupita. Seth doesn't know about the baby. He won't be coming here." She paused. "Now you will let me explain."

"No! It does not matter. What is between you two is your business. Come into the kitchen and let me feed you two girls."

"Two girls?" Morgan laughed when she realized Lupita's meaning. "Lupita, do you think we could make some *empañaditas* this afternoon?"

The rest of the day was blissful. It was good to remove the whalebone corset she had worn in San Francisco. Lupita's cool cotton blouse and skirt felt marvelous against her body. She brushed her hair, glad not to have a maid standing nearby waving a hot curling iron.

"Now you look like yourself. The chickens all ran and hid from you before."

"Yes," Morgan laughed. "I feel like me again. Like I've really come home. Lupita, no matter what happens, I have a right here, don't I? I want my baby born here." The tears came once again. "This is where I was happiest. Where Seth and I were happy."

"Yes, Morgan, no one will make you leave. Seth's child will grow up here."

"Look at me. Sometimes I think I've spent the last year crying. I think we ought to get started with the cooking. Does Paul still eat as much as he used to? Of course, it was always Seth who could eat more than the rest of us put together," she laughed. She wiped her eyes with the back of her hand. "It's not going to be easy, is it, Lupita? I know Jake believed Joaquín's story."

Lupita looked at her with sympathy. "No, it won't be easy. But soon it will all be worth it, Morgan."

As Morgan began putting flour and butter together, she said quietly, "I like being called Morgan by you."

That evening when Jake walked into the house and saw Morgan, he was torn. He wanted to kill her. And at the same time, he wanted to leave and never see her again. He stood rooted, staring at the young woman who had caused everyone so much misery.

Lupita spoke first. "Paul, you come in, too, and welcome Morgan back."

"Her! It's because of her that Seth left. It's not right when a man has to leave his own home. We should get the sheriff for what she's done. Get tired of your lovers, did you, honey?"

Defeated entirely, Morgan turned to leave. "It's no use, Lupita. I'll go." Then she saw the gun in Lupita's hand, aimed at the two men. "Lupita! No! It doesn't matter. I'd rather leave than cause all this trouble. Please."

"You're right. Get out! We don't want you." Jake took a step toward her, in spite of Lupita's revolver. "He almost died because of you. When he got over all the wounds, he was still sick. Sick over your treachery."

Lupita stepped between Jake and Morgan. "Jake, we have known one another a long time and I'd hate to use this, but one step closer to her and I'll shoot you in the leg." Lupita's eyes were hard. "She has a right to be heard, a right to tell her side of what happened."

"She has no rights! She almost killed him!"

"I mean it, Jake. Not one more step. Now you two sit there and listen." She gestured with the gun to the couch.

"Lupita, this isn't going to work. You can

see they hate me. No matter what I say, they'll never believe me."

"The note! We saw the note you wrote Seth. How could you run off with that Montoya when you had Seth?"

Morgan had turned to the bedroom, to get her bags. She just wanted out of the house, away from these people — two men who hated her unfairly and a woman who was ready to shoot someone for her. Jake's accusation brought her back to reality. It was the same as the night Seth had come to her room. She had begged him to listen to her, but he had been too selfish to bother. That night began to come back to her . . . all of it. She whirled on the two men.

"I've had enough of the Colter men to last me the rest of my life! You accuse *me* of treachery? Did it occur to you that your precious Seth ever did anything wrong? Yes, I wrote a note to Seth, a note I thought was going to save his life. Yes, go ahead and look at me in disbelief.

"I don't know why I bother with you. Yes, I do! I am sick of being accused of things I didn't do.

"The night of the party, I waited and waited for Seth. I hardly talked to anyone; all I wanted was for him to come to me." Morgan laughed.

382

"When he did come, he threw himself into a rage because I had dared step outside with Joaquín. You were right, Jake, when you said it was foolish to want Joaquín rather than Seth. I never even considered Joaquín. Never. I loved Seth and no one else. After Seth stormed out, I followed him. Joaquín went with me — to help me find him, he said. After several hours of riding, Joaquín took me prisoner in a strange house, tied and gagged me."

The first flush of Morgan's anger was gone now, leaving her weak. She sat down, staring at the empty fireplace. When she continued, her voice was quieter. "Joaquín said he'd kill Seth unless I wrote the note. He said that if Seth believed I'd run away, he'd hate the Colter ranch and sell it to him."

"Why? Why would Montoya want this little place?"

Morgan didn't look up. "Something about water rights. He said Seth could cut off the water from the Montoya ranch at any time." She missed the looks of confirmation exchanged between Jake and Paul.

"But after I wrote the note, he came back to tell me that he had killed Seth. I knew then that Seth had died hating me." She was silent for a while.

"What happened?" Jake's voice was gentle.

Morgan looked up at him and smiled an ironic smile. "Oh, very little, actually. Joaquín paid a Frenchman to remove me. The Frenchman took me and three other women across the country and sold us to a brothel owner in San Francisco. She auctioned us off to the highest bidder, after what you might call an unveiling ceremony."

Morgan laughed. Her speech became higher and more rapid. "I was lucky. A man bought me and was good to me. He never touched me. I was happy, after all the horror.

"Then Seth appeared. He was alive. He came to my room. He made love to me. I was so happy, happier than I'd ever been in my life. I told him how much I loved him. Then the accusations started. He believed Joaquín, not me. He would not listen to me at all. He wanted to know why Joaquín had left me. He found out about the brothel, but he thought I had worked there as a whore. He . . . he . . ."

Lupita was on her knees in front of Morgan, gathering her in her ample arms. "Get out and leave her alone. She's been through enough. And I hope you both feel what I think you feel."

Sheepishly, the two men rose and walked

toward the front door. Then Jake turned and went back to Morgan. He gently pushed Lupita away and took Morgan in his thin arms. His voice was husky. "We've all done you a wrong, Morgan. I know Seth and I know his father. Under their calm faces, they're jealous men, often given to yelling first and then asking questions. I'm right sorry we made the same mistake." He pulled away from Morgan and looked at her, his hands on her shoulders. "Can you forgive us? Will you stay here with us?"

Morgan smiled at the old man. "I don't know, Jake. I hadn't planned to come back to the ranch. Frank insisted that I . . ."

"Of course she'll stay. We have a baby on the way. A little boy just like Seth." Lupita smiled broadly.

"It's a girl," Morgan answered her. "A nice, sweet, little girl."

"A baby!" Paul was astonished.

Jake recovered from his own astonishment. "Yes, a young 'un, you numbskull. Morgan's going to have a baby. We'll teach him to ride a horse, brand cattle . . ."

Morgan laughed. "It's going to be a girl and I'd like to get her into the world before you start teaching her how to ride a horse."

"He'll learn to use a rope, too, just like his pa."

"*She* will learn to make pastry, just like her mother. Lupita, I'm starved."

Everyone laughed together. "Babies need lots of food for growing. Let's feed this one."

It was a happy group that sat down to dinner. Lupita quietly put the gun back in the cupboard where she always kept it for emergencies. It was good to have laughter in the house again. If only Seth would come back. She offered a silent prayer to her favorite saint for his safe return. "Maybe he will come before the baby is born," she whispered.

"But, Jake, I can't stay here. What if Seth comes back? I don't want to see him. I don't ever want to see him. Not after what he did. I begged him, Jake, begged him to listen to me."

"Now, girl, don't get so riled up. We'll cross that bridge when we come to it. First thing you need is for someone to help you with the baby. Who else you got?"

There was no one. She couldn't go back to her Uncle Horace and Aunt Lacey. Seth's parents would take her in, but that would be the same as staying on the Colter ranch.

"You see, you know there's nothing else to do. So stop worrying and eat somethin' for that boy."

"Girl," Morgan added absent-mindedly.

After the first few days on the ranch she began to relax. The house was familiar and the people cared for her. She began to think more about her baby. Her stomach seemed to stretch a little each day. She rubbed the mound often, glad of its presence.

"Cecilia. What do you think of that name, Lupita? I'm going to name her something very feminine. I get so tired of people's comments about my name."

"Cecilia is a good name. Another tortilla? They're hot."

"I don't know why I'm so hungry. It seems that no matter how much I eat, I just get hungrier."

Lupita smiled as Morgan coated the tortilla with freshly made butter. She poured her glass full of milk. "You're eating for two now."

"Yes, I guess so." Morgan's mouth was full. "I guess I should worry about getting fat, but somehow, I don't care. I feel sort of like a . . . a big pillow, just content to do nothing. I don't even worry about Seth coming. It seems nothing matters to me. I just want to have Cecilia."

Morgan looked up as Jake came into the kitchen from outside. "Are you still eating, girl? Did you know it's time for the noon meal and you're still eating breakfast?" He turned to Lupita. "She's going to pop her skin. Why do you let her eat so much?"

Morgan held up her arm and looked at it. Jake was right. The skin was tight and almost shiny. Her ankles and legs were the same way. Somehow she didn't care. She smiled up at Jake. "I'm glad it's lunchtime, because I'm hungry."

Jake watched her with growing concern as she ate constantly throughout the meal. After lunch, Morgan announced that she planned to take a walk. Jake was relieved to see her get away from Lupita's stove.

Later, as Jake was in the barn, he saw Morgan make her way slowly past the open door. "Morgan," he heard Lupita call. He watched in disbelief as Lupita fastened a cloth bag to Morgan's back. "In case you get hungry," he heard Lupita tell her.

Jake started to give his opinion of Morgan's food needs, but thought better of it. Whenever he spoke out, Lupita ignored him and Morgan smiled sweetly at him and then went on eating. She already ate more than the other three of them put together.

As Morgan's size increased, so did her placidity. She had not been so calm since she'd left Trahern House. Nothing bothered her. The emotions that had once raged inside her no longer concerned her. She thought of nothing but food and the baby's name. All of them were names for girls.

She spent mornings with Lupita. Whenever she forgot what she was supposed to be doing, and stared into space, Lupita quietly finished her task for her. After lunch, she walked. She walked for hours, very slowly and awkwardly. She never had a definite path in mind or even seemed to remember later where she'd been. Lupita always made sure her knapsack was filled with food, and Morgan always returned the sack empty.

As the weather grew colder, Jake tried to stop her from her long walks, but she never seemed to hear him. He couldn't understand her dreaminess, and he was worried about the way she looked.

Morgan's entire body swelled and stretched. After the first few months, she could no longer get her feet into her own shoes. Lupita brought her an old pair of *huaraches* to wear. Morgan still wore Lupita's clothes. The Mexican cotton blouse that had once swallowed her tiny frame now nearly burst at the seams. Her plump shoulders and bosom strained against the embroidered fabric.

One day as Jake and Paul watched her

heading toward the trees for her daily walk, Paul commented, "A duck. She looks just like a duck." They both laughed at the apt comparison. Morgan heard their laughter and waved.

"She's something'." Jake watched her go. "Even if you told her to her face she looked like a duck, she wouldn't care. Sometimes when you talk to her, she don't even hear you."

"Women! I never understood them, especially one that changes as much as Morgan. She's all sweet when Seth's here and then she comes back spittin' fire. Now she's like one of the hens, just settin' on her eggs."

Jake grinned, showing his near-toothless gums. "That she is, a hen on her nest."

January of 1851 was very cold, and there were some days when Lupita made Morgan stay in the house and forget her walk. Morgan was just as content to sit by the fire, nibbling on *bizcochitos* and *empañaditas,* as she was walking.

The baby became more and more active. Morgan rubbed her enormous stomach and was pleased with each kick. She never thought of the actual birth, only of the time when she'd hold her daughter in her arms.

In the ninth month, Morgan stopped her walks altogether. Her hands were swollen too badly to sew and her feet no longer fit the old *huaraches.*

Jake became more nervous with every passing day. "When's that baby going to be born?" he demanded.

Neither Morgan nor Lupita paid any attention to him.

"You women don't seem to understand that that child is very close to being my grandchild. I'm worried. I've seen lots of women going to have babies, but never one to gain as much weight as her."

Morgan smiled at him. "Lupita, you know what I'd really like to have? Strawberries. I can taste them, so red and juicy. In Kentucky, we used to have the sweetest strawberries. And peaches! The juice would run down your arm. I think I could eat a bushel basket of peaches. And —"

"See! That's what I mean. It just ain't healthy for a woman to eat that much, or even a man to eat that much. She's so fat now somebody has to help her in and out of the chair. That baby's going to smother to death. Lord! If that baby ain't born soon, I'm goin' to go crazy." He grabbed his coat and stormed out into the cold air.

As Paul watched him go, pipe in hand, he heard Morgan. "And blackberries. I'd risk a body covered in chiggers for a pint of blackberries right now." He laughed to himself.

Lupita had begun to sleep in the big house. When she heard Morgan stirring in the bedroom, she was quickly in the room with her. Morgan was trying to change the bedclothes.

At the sight of Lupita, she began her explanation. "I guess Jake is right — I do eat too much. My stomach hurts and when I finally did go to sleep, I woke up again to find I'd wet the bed. I hope you won't tell him; he'll worry even more."

Lupita went to Morgan and guided her to a chair. "Now sit down and I'll change the bed. Does your stomach still hurt?"

"Yes, it . . . oh . . . Lupita. The baby! Lupita, it's the baby, isn't it?"

"Yes. Very soon now you will have a new baby."

"I'm so glad. Victoria. How about Victoria?"

"What the hell's going on in here? I suppose she got up to get something to eat."

"Out! We are going to have a baby."

"Oh." Jake's face became somber. "I'll get the doctor." He turned toward the door.

"I need no doctor meddling in this. I have felt the baby and he is in the right position.

I've delivered too many to let some man tell me what to do. Now get out, both of you," she said as Paul came in the front door. "I'll call you when we have a new little Colter."

The delivery was easy. It seemed only minutes before Lupita was saying, "There's the head. Push again. Good. Slowly . . . ah."

Morgan fell back on the pillows, her hair damp with sweat. "Victoria. Let me see my little girl."

"Morgan, little madonna, your little girl is a boy. A very large and healthy boy."

Quickly she finished washing the baby and wrapped him in a clean cotton blanket. Morgan put her arms out to the baby. Lupita finished cleaning the mother and checking to make sure there were no complications with the afterbirth.

She could hear Jake and Paul in the next room. "They'll want to see you, now. Is it all right?"

"Yes. He's beautiful, isn't he, Lupita? Lots of hair, too. Look at his little hands."

Quietly, Jake and Paul looked down on Morgan and her new son. "He's going to be as big as his pa."

"What's his name? Cecilia?" Paul laughed.

Morgan smiled up at him. "Adam. My own sweet little Adam." As she said the name, Adam screwed up his face, opened his mouth and let out a lusty yell.

"The baby is hungry. You will have to leave now and we will quiet him."

"Hungry!" Jake was indignant. "He's been eating like a pig for nine months and now he's not ten minutes old and he's hungry!"

They all laughed while Lupita shooed the men out. Morgan and Lupita were alone with the baby. It was some time before Morgan's milk was enough for Adam's huge appetite.

In the morning, Jake was relieved to see that Morgan ate only a normal breakfast. Lupita laughed at him. "You think your little girl is going to look like me? No. It was only the baby wanting so much to eat. She will soon be as slim as she was before. You will see. Already Adam gives her much exercise. He is a healthy baby."

From the day of Adam's birth, he never lacked for someone to give him attention. It seemed to Morgan that sometimes she had to fight to get to hold her own son. At first she had been almost afraid of him, but she soon realized his strength. He loved water and happily drenched his mother when she bathed him.

For the first three months, Morgan was content to stay in the house and see to the needs of her young son. But after a while, she began to grow restless. Gone was the placidity of her pregnancy. She began to ride for a short time each day and the weight she had gained melted off her, leaving her body smooth and slim once again.

As she studied her body at night, she found very little change. Her breasts were fuller because she was still nursing him, but her stomach was again flat and her legs were slim. She remembered her pregnancy as if it were a long dream, and she shuddered to remember the enormous amount of weight she had gained. "Oh well," she murmured aloud, "at least there won't be any more children." The thought brought Seth to mind, and for the first time in months, she again felt anger and resentment. He had treated her unforgivably.

Lupita's cottons once again swallowed Morgan. So, on one of his trips into Santa Fe for supplies, Paul returned with Mrs. Sanchez and several bolts of fabric. For three weeks Mrs. Sanchez stayed at the Colter ranch, and the three women sewed constantly on Morgan's new wardrobe. There were two riding habits, several day dresses, and more dresses for shopping or visiting. Morgan had brought evening gowns from San Francisco.

Morgan wrote to Theron often, and he

was delighted with the news of the baby. Theron and Jeannette were well. He had not hired another assistant. His clients still asked about her. As always, Theron begged her to return.

His letters always made Morgan a little sad. Although she was surrounded by people she loved and who loved her, there were times when she was lonely.

By August, 1851, Adam was six months old. He was a happy child and liked everyone. Frank came to visit and Adam was immediately taken with him. Frank carried him about on his horse and Adam laughed happily. Sometimes Morgan accused Jake and Paul of making fools of themselves over the little boy.

In September, Morgan turned twenty-one. Lupita planned a party. Morgan wore a deep blue satin gown that Theron had bought her. When she tried it on, she was surprised to find it loose.

"You have lost too much weight. You do not eat enough. I have watched you and you are pining for something — or someone."

Morgan shook her head as the larger woman pinned the waist of her dress. "That's silly, Lupita. I'm perfectly happy. I have everything I need right here."

"Except a man."

"I have Adam."

"Yes, *señora.*"

"Lupita, don't use that trick. I am happy and I mean it, and stop playing the docile servant."

"Whatever the *señora* wants."

"Lupita!" But she was gone. Morgan smiled to herself. She's wrong, she thought, I've just lost weight because I try to keep Adam from crawling into the stove. Anyone would lose weight running after Adam. She kissed her sleeping son, his blond hair curling about his face. He moved and made a few sucking motions with his mouth. A deep dimple appeared briefly in his cheek. Just like Seth, she thought. Just like Seth. She tried to brush the idea from her mind and went outside to greet her guests.

Many of the people there that night were strangers, and Morgan was glad when the party was over. When she had removed her satin gown and slipped into her plain cotton nightgown, she gazed at the bed and began to cry.

"What's wrong with me?" she asked, "I have everything, but I want more." Her voice woke Adam, and she was glad to go and comfort him. It was a long time before she went to sleep.

The snows began early that year and the winter dragged on and on. Adam seemed to grow some each day, and she and Lupita were busy sewing clothes for him. Jake and Paul whittled wooden horses and cows for him, gradually creating an entire wooden ranch, complete with house, barn, fences, wagons, and men. Lupita filled the little toy house with furniture and food. She even made a replica of Adam. Adam rewarded everyone with squeals of laughter and a sometimes rather sticky hug.

Morgan's memories of Seth increased day by day and she began to be very restless. She wanted to go away from the ranch for a while. She worried about Seth's return.

In February, Adam was one year old. Lupita and Morgan baked an enormous cake, and Frank and Louisa brought their six children to share in the celebration. Adam was shy around the other children for a few minutes, but quickly recovered. Frank tossed Adam into the air. "Goin' to be as big as your pa, ain't you?"

Jake grinned. "Looks more like him every day. Doesn't seem to have his pa's stubborn streak though, or at least not yet."

Lupita watched as Morgan's face whitened at the mention of Seth. Lupita knew the memories tormented her and she felt the pain her little mistress felt.

Soon after Adam's birthday, Morgan wrote to her father's lawyer in Albuquerque. She stated briefly that she had fulfilled the terms of the will and would like to know about her inheritance. She hoped she and Adam could go away together, possibly even to Europe.

She waited expectantly for weeks for an answer to her letter, but none came. She thought she might write again, but Lupita told her to wait a bit longer. The mails in New Mexico were very slow.

Now when Morgan went for her morning ride, Adam went with her. Often they took a basket of food to make a picnic.

Neither of them saw the pair of eyes that watched them every day. As the sun was going down and Jake, Paul, and Adam walked around the house, none of them sensed their quiet observer. Once the horse Adam played near was stung by a wasp, and the horse reared. Only Adam saw the strong brown arms that pulled the unsteady toddler from beneath the iron-clad hooves.

It had been nearly two months since Morgan wrote the letter. She sat under a tree some distance from the ranch house, a place where she often brought Adam to play and picnic. The stream that watered the ranch flowed here, and the grass was green and the shade cool. Their horse, grazing nearby, whinnied, but for the moment Morgan was lost in thought. She decided to send another letter to the lawyer. Why hadn't he replied?

"Eat." Adam smiled at his mother as she lifted him from the horse.

"No, not eat. I'm mama, remember, Adam?"

"Ma ma ma."

"Yes, that's right. Look Adam, a butterfly." She pointed, but Adam continued to stare at his mother. He tried to form words, but none would come. His eyes lifted from Morgan's to an area just behind her head He laughed at what he saw there.

Morgan laughed with him. His dimpled smiles were infectious. Still smiling, she turned to look at what he saw. Her hand flew to her mouth in alarm. Quickly she stood up and held Adam behind her. He struggled to see around her skirts.

An Indian sat majestically on a black-and-white pony. He was slim, his hair straight and black, falling just to his earlobes. It glistened in the morning sunlight He was naked from the waist up. There was a rawhide strip around his neck which held a little leather pouch, decorated by black and red beads.

His legs were clad in buckskin with fringe down the sides. He looked exactly like the Apaches who had taken her to San Francisco. Her voice shook. "What do you want?"

The Indian dismounted fluidly. He stared at Morgan and at Adam and took a step closer. Morgan turned and picked up Adam, pulling him close to her. He pushed her away. He wanted to walk, not to be carried. Morgan pulled him even tighter.

"Go away. Leave us alone." Adam frowned at his mother. What was wrong?

"I'm really sorry to have frightened you so. Allow me to introduce myself. I am Gordon Matthews."

Morgan's eyes widened. The Indian's voice was deep, rather musical. It was refined. His words were carefully articulated and the endings sharply pronounced, unlike the Kentuckians Morgan had always known.

He watched her closely, as if waiting for something. When she pulled Adam closer, Gordon shrugged and sat down on the bank of the little stream.

"Yes," he said. "You do look like your

pictures." He turned and smiled up at her, showing even, white teeth. "I really shouldn't do this, I know. Uncle Charley used to say I played at being an Indian. It *is* really rather ostentatious of me, isn't it?"

"Osten . . ." Morgan loosened her hold on Adam, who had decided to remove the trim from her riding habit. She was confused.

"I really enjoy the game, and I get to play it so seldom these days. On the ranch the men like to forget that I'm half-Indian. So I like to dress up whenever I can. I have a great deal of trouble with my hair. You see, it tends to curl, so I have to use a little lard on it. I'm sure my ancestors would disown me for not using buffalo grease, but these are modern times, are they not?" He paused.

"Morgan, please sit by me. I may get a cramp in my neck if you keep standing."

Morgan took a step farther from him. "Who are you? How do you know my name?"

Gordon sighed and then stood up. "I think one needs to keep in better shape to play Indian." He rubbed his neck. "The name Gordon Matthews means nothing to you?"

"No."

"Your father never mentioned me in his letters?"

"My father? Letters?"

"Morgan, please. Stop being so frightened. I won't hurt you. Here, let me take Adam and then we can talk."

Morgan twisted her body so that Adam was farther from him.

"It's your decision, but he is ruining your habit. Adam — look." He held out the beaded pouch and Adam reached for it. Gordon held his arms to Adam and Adam lunged toward him. Gordon caught the sturdy boy. "Another year and he'll be bigger than you are, Morgan. Now, let's sit down."

Gordon sat down again, took off the pouch, and gave it to Adam, who happily toddled off with his prize.

"He's a very handsome young man. I believe he's going to look like his father. Seth is a large man, isn't he?" Gordon turned back to look at Morgan. "You know, you look very much like your father when you frown like that. All right, since you don't know, I'll explain. Uncle Charley always said I took hours to get to a point. My father always said my education had interfered with my thinking. They were probably both correct." He chuckled ruefully.

"I am serious, Morgan. Unless you sit

down, I won't explain one thing. My neck is really beginning to hurt."

Morgan's mind was whirling. This was preposterous. He looked like an Indian, one of the dirty Indians that had traveled with Jacques. But he sounded like an educated Yankee. She sat down on the bank, several feet away from him.

"I run the Three Crowns."

"Three Crowns?"

"You really don't know, do you? Your father and my father were partners in the ranch south of Albuquerque, the ranch called the Three Crowns. My father was killed in an accident three years ago."

Morgan saw a look of pain cross his face. Adam came back to them and pulled at the silver bracelet on Gordon's upper arm. Gordon smiled at the boy, removed the bracelet, and handed it to him. Adam promptly put it in his mouth, tasted it, and then walked away again, holding Gordon's possessions, one in each hand.

"He certainly is an energetic boy. I'll wager he never gives you a moment's peace."

"Go on with your story, Mr. Matthews."

"Gordon. I don't understand how you know nothing of your father when he knew everything about you. There are pictures, drawings of you, everywhere in the house. They show you at every age. A lot of them are of you on horseback, and some are of you peeping out a carriage window."

"No one drew pictures of me. How could they be of me? I never saw my father again after we left New Mexico. My mother refused to answer my questions about him."

"Hmmm. This is a puzzle! I guess you don't remember much about New Mexico. After all, you were about the same age as Adam when you left."

"I remember riding in a wagon and being very thirsty."

"That would have been the trip to Kentucky. Your mother was such a stubborn woman. When she made up her mind to leave, she did. She refused to wait for the guide your father hired.

"Of course, the ranch was really nothing in those days, just a little adobe shack. And your mother had to cook and clean for two men and me. She was expecting you then, and she was so clumsy. She hated the dirt and the dryness. Pa and I used to hear her complaining to Uncle Charley — that's your father — for hours each night about how rough her skin was, how tired she was, how she hated everything."

Gordon reached across the distance between them and took Morgan's hand. "Smooth, yet I know you do a fair share of work on this ranch."

She pulled her hand back. "How do you know what I do around here?"

"I've been watching." Gordon laughed at the astonished expression on Morgan's face. "I told you it's too seldom that I get to play at being an Indian. So when the chance arises, I take it. These rather suit me, don't you think?" He motioned to the buckskins covering his slim, muscular legs.

Adam toddled back to Gordon and his mother. He had trouble holding onto both his treasures, so Gordon put the pouch around Adam's neck and hung the bracelet on the leather thong along with the pouch. Adam grasped at a flower, and came away with only part of the head. As he dropped it in his mother's lap, he fell heavily backwards. He quickly got up and ran away, stumbling every few feet.

"You were so much like Adam when you were his age, but of course on a smaller scale. You had that funny streaked blond hair even then, curling around your face. You smiled a lot then and, like Adam, you thought no one was a stranger. I think I adopted you from the moment I saw you, when you were about twenty minutes old.

The day I came home and you were gone, I cried until I was sick. It was a week before I could eat again."

"Gordon . . . I . . . this is so new to me. The impression I have of the time I was in New Mexico is so different. My mother hardly mentioned it except to tell of the miseries she suffered."

"I know a lot about your mother, too. No" — he held Morgan's arm — "Adam needs to fall hundreds of times before he learns to walk. Let him be . . . We always assumed those letters were from you. The ones after Uncle Charley's death were from some man, some agency. I guess they were always from him."

"What letters?"

"About a year after you left, the letters started coming, one a month, very regularly. I never read one, but Uncle Charley told us in detail what was in them. It's funny to realize you knew nothing about us and we knew so much about you. I grew up hearing about little Morgan every day. Remember the time you fell off your horse when you were eight and cut your leg? When the doctor sewed it, you screamed so loudly that the groom had trouble quieting the horses in the stables."

"Yes, I remember," Morgan said quietly.

It was still impossible to believe that this man could know so much about her.

"Pa and Uncle Charley and I always looked forward to those letters, and the sketches. My favorite is of you taking your first jump, when you were about seven. Your little hat was mostly over your face."

"This is too much! My mother never told me about my father, nothing good, anyway. I grew up with little thought of him. Trahern House and my mother were my whole world. And then the will! I hated my father then!"

"Yes," Gordon looked away, embarrassed. "I tried to talk him out of that, but Uncle Charley said, 'That damned woman's made her hate men. If I don't do something, she'll rot in that big old house and dry up just like her mother did.' I suggested he stipulate that you come out here, but leave out the part about your having to get married. But he said that as soon as word was out about the will, lots of young men would be swarming around you. That's what he wanted for his pretty little daughter. He knew your mother had made you afraid of people, especially men. He just wanted them to come to you so you could choose any one you wanted. It wasn't meant to be an ordeal."

Morgan stared ahead at the little stream, lost in her thoughts. She had thought her father wanted to punish her for some reason. He had only wanted to help her. She *had* been afraid of men, afraid of everything, and he had known all about it. He had prevented her from retreating. He had cared about her, cared very much.

Gordon jumped to catch Adam as he nearly tumbled into the icy water. "There now, why don't you stay up here?" Unperturbed, Adam sauntered after more flowers.

"I was really surprised when you asked Seth Colter to marry you."

Morgan's head jerked up. "How do you know that?"

"Possessing a superior intelligence, I deduced it. After Uncle Charley died, the letters kept coming for a while. I was furious when I read what your Uncle Horace had planned. I was very nearly on my way to Kentucky when the last letter came and said that you had married Colter. I wrote a letter to one of Uncle Charley's old friends in Kentucky and got all the gossip, about how Colter was such a prize catch and he had eloped after meeting you only once. I knew that anyone who had been reared as you had did not captivate 'prize catches' in one evening. Besides, the agent had already told me how Horace dressed you. So I put two and two together. And I was right!"

"Yes, you were right. For a while it worked out well . . . Adam!" Morgan jumped to her feet, but Gordon lithely ran after Adam and again caught him before he fell into the stream. Gordon tossed him into the air and Adam laughed loudly. "I'm Gordon. Can you say Gordon?"

"Or."

"Good enough. 'Or' it is."

"Eat. Eat." Adam squealed.

"Good idea."

"Gordon, this is all too much for me to take in. You've upset all the beliefs I've had about my father, even my mother."

Gordon smiled. "Well, then, let's take Adam's advice and eat. I'd like to sample some of the cooking you learned from Jean-Paul. He cost Uncle Charley a *fortune.*"

"My father paid for Jean-Paul?"

"Of course. You don't think your mother would have let a man into her house without a great deal of persuasion, do you?"

Morgan spread out the picnic lunch. "There's something I've never understood. Why did my mother's father leave Trahern House to his son-in-law rather than to his daughter?"

Gordon put a tiny quiche in his mouth,

handed one to Adam, and laughed. "Old Morgan Trahern was a smart one. He knew how spoiled your mother was. He left everything to his son-in-law because he knew his daughter was too headstrong to control that much property. He also hoped to keep her from leaving your father. But Uncle Charley was too soft. He could have made her stay with him in New Mexico. He tried to get her to leave you with him, but —" Gordon filled his mouth again and shrugged. "— Uncle Charley never pushed anyone."

Morgan's eyes flashed at him. "Except me. He used his will to push me to do what he wanted."

Gordon smiled at her. His eyes sparkled. "Still angry, huh? Well, it looks like it came out all right." He rubbed his cheek on Adam's head.

They finished their lunch quickly. "Excellent, Morgan. Jean-Paul was worth it."

"Merci beaucoup, monsieur."

"Now! Let's go back to the house."

"Gordon, wait."

"No, I know what you're going to say. 'I wouldn't give you a plugged nickel for a dozen gol-danged Injuns.' That sound like Jake?"

Morgan had to laugh because Gordon's

imitation of Jake sounded so much like him.

"Watch this." Quickly, Gordon went to his saddlebags and got a bar of soap. Within minutes, he had soaped and rinsed his hair in the stream and then returned to his horse for clothing. He stepped behind some trees and a few minutes later emerged in a light blue cotton shirt and darker blue cotton pants. He looked nothing at all like an Indian.

He smiled at Morgan's astonishment. "Sky Eyes, the Comanche warrior, has changed into Gordon Matthews, ordinary but rather attractive white man."

" 'Sky Eyes'?"

Gordon looked at her fiercely, then rolled his eyes. "Sapphire-blue eyes that captivate women in four states, and you didn't even notice."

Morgan laughed, the first good laugh she'd had in a long time.

"That's better. Now you look more like the little girl who used to ride with me on my pony."

"Or. Or." Adam tugged at Gordon's pant leg, wanting to be picked up.

They all rode back to the house slowly, Adam riding in front of Gordon. Morgan had too many thoughts for further talk, so Adam and Gordon kept up a conversation between themselves.

Jake was waiting for them, close to the house, with a rifle. Morgan felt that, as much as anything, he didn't like another man so near Adam.

"This is Gordon Matthews. He and I are partners in the ownership of the Three Crowns. It's . . ."

"The Three Crowns! Glad to meet you, Mr. Matthews. I've heard about the Three Crowns since I first come to New Mexico. You say Morgan's your partner?"

Jake warmly clasped Gordon's hand. As they walked together toward the house, Gordon turned and caught Morgan's eye. He put two fingers to the back of his head and wiggled them, like feathers. Then he winked at Morgan before returning to the conversation with Jake.

Morgan laughed at Gordon's play. She felt better than she had for a long time. She hurried after Adam, who was trying to catch up to the two men.

Supper that night was fun. Adam decided he wanted his chair moved next to Gordon's. "Gor," he learned to say.

Morgan sat quietly with her own thoughts through the others' conversation.

"How many head of cattle you run on a place like that?" Jake asked. "What about

Injuns? Any trouble with them?"

Morgan felt Gordon's silent laughter at the question. After supper, the two of them walked outside together, Adam toddling behind.

"I can feel the difference between the altitudes of Santa Fe and of Albuquerque." As Adam's steps slowed, Gordon picked up the boy, who snuggled against his shoulder.

"Come live with me, Morgan."

She didn't move, but stared ahead.

"I know something's wrong here. No one mentions Seth's name, yet I feel he's still alive."

"Yes, he is," Morgan whispered.

"Whatever's happened is your business. I don't need to know, but I do know that your father would have wanted you to come to the ranch. I know I'd like for you to come. I'm a bachelor. My father's people are in the East. My mother's people are Comanches and, in spite of my games, I know little about them.

"There are too many memories for you here, Morgan. Come back with me. I'll make a home for you and Adam." He stroked the hair of the sleeping child.

"I don't know, Gordon. I really don't know you. But what you say about there being too many memories here is correct.

Let me think about it and give you an answer soon. Right now, I need to put my son to bed."

She walked ahead as Gordon followed with the dozing Adam. "Do you know that I've loved your mother since she was twenty minutes old? I don't care where your father is, because I plan to move heaven and earth to become your new daddy. Would you like that, son?" He kissed the dimpled cheek of the boy. "We'll go to the ranch. And inside of a year, I'll be your pa."

It took Gordon two days to persuade Morgan to go with him to the Three Crowns. The major opposition came from Jake; he couldn't stand the idea of Adam's leaving.

"I have to, Jake. What if Seth returns? I can't be here then. I don't want to see him."

Gordon could hardly control his elation as he loaded the wagon with Morgan's and Adam's clothes. "I'll send a hand back to return the wagon, and he'll let you know that we got there safely."

The goodbyes were tearful. "Send us letters. Tell us about yourself and the boy. The house will be sad without you," Lupita cried. Paul gave Adam two more carved wooden horses for his ranch house. Jake took it the worst, almost refusing to see them off.

Adam waved to them for a long time, enjoying the unusual pleasure of riding in a wagon. By the time they reached Santa Fe, he was fretful and Morgan was glad to stop. She wanted to purchase fabric for some new clothes for him. The days were getting longer and the afternoons hotter. Gordon had told her it was much warmer farther down the mountains toward Albuquerque.

Gordon had taken Adam with him and promised to meet Morgan by the wagon in an hour. Morgan's last stop took her to a new shop, one she'd never seen. It carried imported silks and velvets, handmade laces, as well as the sturdy cottons she needed for Adam. She didn't hear the footsteps behind her.

"Well, Mrs. Colter, it is such a surprise to see you here again."

"Miss Wilson." Marilyn Wilson was the last person Morgan wanted to see. "How have you been? Is this your shop?"

"I've been quite well, thank you, and yes, my father bought this shop for me about six months ago. I hear you came back alone from San Francisco."

Morgan clenched her hands into fists.

"Tell me, how is Joaquín Montoya? Wasn't it strange how he and his sister packed up and left for Spain that way, just a few days after their party?"

Before Morgan could answer, Marilyn continued, "All of Santa Fe thought it was strange how you and Joaquín rode off together right in the middle of the party. Of course, as I mentioned to Seth, you two had spent a great deal of time together already."

"You . . ."

Neither of the women heard the shop door open.

"Then, of course, all of Santa Fe knew Seth spent the winter alone on the Colter ranch."

"Ahem." Both women turned to see Gordon and Adam. Adam let go of Gordon's hand and ran to his mother to show her the little wooden trees Gordon had bought him.

Morgan picked her son up. "Pretty, aren't they? They'll go with the rest of your ranch. Oh — Miss Wilson" — Morgan acted as if she had just remembered the woman's presence — "let me introduce my son to you. Adam, this is Miss Wilson." Adam looked at the woman for only a second and then began jabbering to his mother about his trees. He smiled, showing dimples so like Seth's.

Gordon took Adam. "I guess it's time we left Santa Fe." He didn't like the lightning atmosphere between the two women.

As they got to the door, Morgan turned back. "I guess all of Santa Fe doesn't know about my son. I think you'll agree there's no doubt who his father is. Goodbye, Miss Wilson."

In the wagon, Morgan was quiet at first. Then, a few miles outside of Santa Fe, the tears began to flow. Gordon pulled the wagon over under some large cottonwoods. Without a word, he set Adam on the ground and then lifted Morgan from the wagon. He held her in his strong arms and let her cry. He sat under a tree and rocked her gently. Adam heard his mother and came to investigate. When he realized she was crying, he began to cry, too. Gordon tried to keep one arm around each of them, but the more one cried, the more the other cried.

It took him a few minutes to realize that Morgan was laughing. "What's so blasted funny?"

"You. The look on your face. Two people crying in your arms and you trying to comfort both of them. I never saw such frustration."

Gordon grinned at her. "I'll have to remember the look for the next time you cry, so I can make you laugh. Anyway, it was worth it for a chance to hold you."

Gordon's seriousness made Morgan realize her position. She quickly moved from his lap and gathered Adam to her. Adam was happy again when he saw his mother smile, and ran to explore a nearby sound.

"You want to tell me about it?"

Morgan shook her head.

"Who was that woman, anyway? You seemed to know one another pretty well."

"Know one another! I've only seen that . . . viper a few times in my life. And each time, she's caused me problems. Her vicious tongue helped break up my marriage!"

"No. It was Seth's temper and jealousy that caused the rift between you."

Morgan looked at Gordon in puzzlement.

"Jake told me the whole story."

"Jake told you! He had no right. Does he tell *everyone* he meets, or just overnight guests?"

"Calm down, Morgan. He thought I should know, and he's right. He said it was Seth's fault and that you had every right to be angry."

"Angry! I believe I feel an emotion a little stronger than anger! I never want to see him again, not after the way he treated me. When we get to the ranch, I'm going to have my father's lawyer arrange a divorce."

Gordon felt like doing his best Comanche war yell at this news. "Morgan." He lifted her chin and smiled at her, but her deep frown still remained. "Oh, no."

"What is it?"

"That's my best melt-the-girls smile, and it didn't even make you lose your frown. I must be losing my touch."

"Gordon," Morgan smiled, "what would I do without you?"

"I hope you never find out." His eyes betrayed his seriousness, and Morgan looked away, embarrassed.

They spent the night camping. It was the first time Morgan had slept outdoors since she had been taken to San Francisco by Jacques.

"Warm enough, Morgan?"

"Yes, I am. Gordon, thank you for taking Adam and me back to the ranch. I needed a change, and you came at the right time."

Gordon settled into his own bedroll. "Purely selfish, Morgan," he whispered to himself.

CHAPTER EIGHTEEN

"Hey, mister, watch where you're goin'!" The man, one eye twitching, squinted up at Seth. "You sick or something', mister?"

Seth stared at the man, unseeing. "What?"

"You hear about the gold out at Cypress Pass? From what I hear, it's the biggest strike yet. You goin'?" He stared up at Seth. "You sure you're not sick?"

"No, I'm fine. Where is this Cypress Pass?"

"No need to ask that, just follow all these people." He put out one grimy hand and gestured to the confusion around them.

Seth looked at the people in the streets for the first time. Work. That's what he wanted — work.

"These people are going to look for gold?"

"Boy, mister, where you been? Sure, that's what's goin' on. The whole country knows about the gold and here you stand in the middle of it and . . . Listen, bud, just go over there to the general store and get some

gear. The storekeep'll know what you need."
He watched Seth turn toward the store.
"And get some clothes. Those duds are too
fancy for the gold fields . . . You sure get all
kinds out here." He muttered this last
remark to himself.

As Seth walked toward the store, he
turned back. Morgan, his brain screamed.
I'll go back to her, I can't stand this. His
mind raged at him and he saw her face, the
tears running down her cheeks. He heard
her say, "I love you, Seth," over and over.
But after what he'd done, she'd never take
him back. What about Montoya? What
about this Shaw that she lived with?

He stopped walking. No, it was over. He
and Morgan were finished. She'd chosen
her life and it didn't include him. He'd had
his revenge on her and now he could go
ahead with his life. He'd mourned enough
last winter. He remembered Morgan's sweet
little body, her golden hair tangling between
them, the eagerness of her kisses. And "I
love you, Seth," cried out in his mind again
and again.

"No!" He clutched his hands over his ears.
A man and woman turned to stare at him,
then shrugged and continued walking.

It's finished. He turned again to the store.
Yes, he thought, I've had my revenge. But

why isn't it sweet?

The storekeeper barely looked up from his ledger. The sight of Seth, his impressive size, and the expensive suit he wore caused him to take a second look. "Help you, mister?"

"I need some things for panning gold."

The clerk sighed. They were all alike, young and old. The gold fever hit everyone. He reached under the counter, never leaving his stool. He caught the neck of a burlap bag and slung it onto the counter beside him. It rattled and clanged as it hit. "Fifty dollars, cash."

Seth counted out the money. "How do I find out how to use this stuff?"

The clerk returned his attention to his ledger. "Ask anybody at the site. Anybody over three years old can show you."

"Thanks."

The clerk watched the big man leave, shook his head, and looked back down at the ledger. He considered the panners fools. He'd made his own gold strike and had never had to break his back in the sun for months on end.

Seth went to the livery stable to get his horse. He changed from the expensive suit to his sturdy cotton work clothes. Contemptuously, he tossed the suit into a corner of the stall. It had seen too many bad memories for him to want to keep it.

The moon was up and the way to the new gold strike was easy to find. By the time he reached Cypress Pass, the sun was just beginning to lighten the horizon. It took Seth very little time to find a place in the stream and to learn to use the gold pan.

After several hours of bending, his back hurt and his neck ached. His head throbbed and he felt the burned skin of his back through his shirt. The pain was good; he hoped it would block out his vivid memories of Morgan. He attacked the pan with new energy.

He didn't really see the sun set, only noticed that he couldn't see the pan any longer. He looked around and saw a man entering a tent, carrying a lantern. He walked toward the man.

"Twenty dollars for your lantern."

The man looked up at Seth in surprise, then grinned. A front tooth was chipped and discolored. "Sure."

Seth returned to the stream. The flecks of gold glinted in the lantern light. When the sun came up, he was still at it. The other gold panners paid little attention to the newcomer. They all knew how it was when the fever first hit.

By noon, Seth was beginning to collapse. His eyes blurred and his head was light and he had trouble holding the pan steady. Only vaguely did he feel the hand on his arm, see the hand that removed the pan from his grasp. In the back of his mind, something whispered, "Morgan," but he knew it couldn't be.

"Here, eat this."

He sat down heavily. As the smell of stew reached him, he realized he hadn't eaten for a long time. He took the plate and ate greedily. The pan was filled twice more before he felt he had eaten enough.

There were no more trees in the ugly little camp, so he stretched out on his bedroll in the shade beside a tent. He was instantly asleep. The girl stared down at the big sleeping man and smiled. Although he was twice her size, something made her want to take care of him, like a little boy. She knelt down and caressed the hair at his temple. Then she started, and quickly looked to see if anyone had seen her. No one had. She went back to her parents' tent.

The sun was just going down when Seth awoke, the horizon pink. His first waking thoughts were of Morgan. It seemed he never remembered how things actually stood between them in those first drowsy minutes. He always reached out, expecting to find her near him. Then he remembered.

"I brought you some more food."

He looked up at the girl standing over him. Hair darker than Morgan's, not nearly as pretty, and . . . Damn it, Colter, don't compare every woman to Morgan.

Seth nodded his thanks to the girl and began to eat, slowly this time. "Did you bring me food earlier today?"

Shyly, she nodded, not looking up at him.

"I thank you. I'm afraid I lost track of time working out there. Another few hours and I might not have been worth saving."

Her eyes flew to his. They betrayed her opinion of his worth. She lowered her lashes when she saw him staring at her. "We're camped over there," she pointed. "There's Ma and Pa and Ben and me. Ben's my big brother." There was pride in her voice. "Ma and me cook for some of the men here, the ones who ain't got wives." She looked up at Seth questioningly.

"Well," he smiled at her, "I guess you can cook for me." The idea of a wife was too painful to Seth.

She smiled back at him. "I'm Lee Ann Coleman."

"Seth . . . Seth Blake."

She was beginning to lose her shyness.

"Don't you have a tent, Mr. Blake?"

"Seth. No, I don't."

She was quiet and seemed to be considering something. "I saw you working out there. You must be awful hungry to strike it rich, or else you're trying to kill yourself."

Seth was serious. "Maybe a little of both."

"I got to be getting back now, Mr. . . . Seth. I'll bring you breakfast in the morning. You better sleep now."

Seth watched her go. The old dress was faded and patched, but clean. It fit her too tightly, showing her stocky little body. He remembered Morgan's lush curves and he saw her again as she had looked in the bedroom at his ranch. Damn! he thought, will she ever get out of my mind?

Lee Ann was up early the next morning, heaping Seth's plate with fried eggs and fried bread. As she went to get a steaming mug of coffee, her mother caught her. "Why can't he come to the tent like the rest of the men? What's so special about this one?"

"Oh, Ma, he's . . ."

Corinne looked into her daughter's eyes and then smiled. So that's how it was. She'd been about Lee Ann's age when she'd met Larry. "Go on then and take him his breakfast. But hurry back, 'cause I need your help."

Corinne watched her daughter go. She knew Lee Ann would never be a beauty — her little face was too plain for that, and her sturdy little body would never be elegant — but she had a good heart. Sometimes when she looked up at you with those liquid brown eyes, she could melt your heart. Corinne had no doubt that this new man was in some kind of trouble. Not law trouble, more likely a broken heart. Lee Ann always loved the helpless ones. Corinne sighed. Too often, once Lee Ann had them on their feet again, they'd go running off. Lord, she prayed, let this one be different.

Seth was already working when Lee Ann got there. He stopped when he saw her. "I'm glad to see you. I could eat these flakes of gold, I'm so hungry."

Lee Ann sat beside the big man, her legs drawn up under her, and watched him eat. "I like to see a man eat. I just hate these puny little ones who eat three eggs for breakfast and call it a meal."

Seth remembered how Morgan and Lupita had always plied him with food and more food. He looked at the meal of Lee Ann's, the eggs and bread swimming in grease. It was a far cry from Morgan's brioches and cheese-filled omelets.

"You from around here?"

"New Mexico."

"We been through there once. Too dry for me. I like it better here."

Seth looked around at the dirty, barren camp. There were many tents and a few haphazard shacks. The trees had long ago been used for firewood. Even the stream was discolored with dishwater, cooking grease, soap-suds, and the leavings from hundreds of slop jars. He remembered the clean, clear hills and arroyos on his ranch.

Seth quickly finished his meal and went back to work. The more he worked, the more tired he was, the less he was able to think. Yet at night, under the stars, he often lay awake for hours remembering Morgan, every word they'd ever spoken, every caress they'd shared.

A month passed. The days began to run together. The other people in the camp had tried to be friendly, but Seth's sullenness made them withdraw. Only Lee Ann stayed by him, bringing his meals three times a day.

It was Lee Ann who got the tent for him. One of the diggers was giving up, selling out, going back east. She bought everything without even asking Seth. Seth told her to take what gold she needed from his ever-growing hoard. She marveled that he trusted her so much, but also wanted to scold him for not hiding his gold like her pa did.

When Seth fell onto the hard cot at night, he hardly noticed the difference between it and the ground he had grown accustomed to. He was used to Lee Ann's presence and took for granted that she kept his food hot until he was ready for it, kept his clothes washed, mended, and orderly.

One morning after Seth had been at Cypress Pass for two months, Lee Ann saw him packing his gear on his horse. His tent was already down and he was just rolling his blankets.

"Where you goin'?"

He missed the alarm in her voice. "This place is getting too crowded. Heard about a new place upriver and thought I'd try there for a while. The gold's played out here."

Lee Ann turned abruptly and started running back to her parents' tent.

Seth looked after her. He'd planned to stop and say goodbye to Lee Ann, but as he watched her go, he just shrugged. He didn't really care one way or another if he left the camp. He didn't really seem to care about anything anymore.

Lee Ann ran to her mother, breathless.

"He's leavin', Ma, and I'm goin' with him."

There was no need to tell who "he" was. Corinne knew her daughter had thought of nothing but Seth Blake for two months. Corinne opened her mouth to protest, but one look at Lee Ann's eyes made her stop. She'd felt this way about Larry, too. There was no use trying to persuade Lee Ann to wait and get the man to marry her. Corinne and Larry hadn't been married until after Ben was born.

"I have to, Ma," she whispered.

The tears gathered in Corinne's eyes. "I know." She hugged her daughter, a short fierce hug. "Well, let's hurry and get your things together. You'll have to take the mule."

"Oh, Ma, I can't. Pa needs him."

"That's all right. He needs his daughter, too. If he can spare one, he can spare the other. There, now, that's everything." They had hurriedly stuffed Lee Ann's two other dresses into an old carpet bag.

"You'll tell them for me, Ma?"

"I will. You be careful, now. And Lee Ann," she called after her daughter, who was already climbing onto the mule, "if anything happens, you come back, you hear?"

Lee Ann nodded and headed the mule

away from the tent.

She's so young, Corinne thought, and so happy. Please, Lord, let it turn out as good for her as it did for me.

Lee Ann caught up with Seth about a mile out of the camp.

He smiled at her. "Goin' into town?"

"No, I'm going with you."

He stopped his horse. "You're what? You can't go with me."

She smiled up at him. "I certainly can. You need me — to take care of you."

"What about your parents? And I don't need anyone."

Lee Ann continued smiling. "Ma understands. She ran off with Pa, just like I'm goin' with you."

Seth's eyes narrowed, his voice was stern. "*You* don't understand. I said I don't need anyone, and we're not going to be like your ma and pa."

Lee Ann's smile of confidence didn't dim.

"You have to go back. Don't you understand? I have a wife!"

Only for a second did a shadow cross Lee Ann's brown eyes. "If you have a wife, then why ain't she here? You need someone here with you now, and that's me."

"My wife . . ." Seth began. He could see

it was no use. There was a will of steel behind those soft eyes. "Don't expect anything from me, Lee Ann, because there's nothing left to give," he said quietly before he turned his horse toward town again.

As Lee Ann kicked her mule to follow, she thought, at least it'll be easier to fight a ghost than a flesh-and-blood wife. I'll make him forget. She was happy as she smiled at Seth's broad back, the bronzed muscles moving under the rough cotton shirt.

For months, Lee Ann and Seth traveled from one gold field to another. After the first few weeks, Lee Ann began to lose her natural happiness. Seth ignored all her attempts at any sort of a relationship. One night, when she had crawled onto his cot with him, he merely shrugged and turned away. In the morning, he had pulled her close to him and she was so happy she laughed aloud, the happiness spilling over her. The sound of her laughter made Seth look at her, shaking off the drowsiness of sleep. Abruptly, he pushed her from him.

She had thought he'd talk more when she lived with him, but if anything, he talked less. As the days wore on, she lost her smile, and went about her chores lifelessly.

Seth was aware of Lee Ann and it nagged

at him that she was unhappy. He'd tried to get her to go back to her parents, but each time he mentioned it, she'd cry. He'd finally dropped the idea.

On one of their trips to town for supplies, they met Johnny.

"Are you staying long, Mr. Daniels?" The girl was a pale blonde. She seemed to have no eyebrows or lashes.

"That depends, Miss Emory, on whether you're going to be around." He flashed even white teeth at her.

Lee Ann watched the scene absently. The young man was hardly out of his teens, not like her Seth, she thought. She looked to where Seth was studying new harnesses. *Her Seth!* He didn't even know she was around, half the time. She looked back at the young man. He was very handsome, and the three girls around him thought so, too.

"My pa's camp is not far away. Maybe you'd like to come for supper some night."

"That I would, Miss Cookson, but I'm sure my appetite would disappear with something as pretty as you so near me."

Lee Ann looked at Miss Cookson. Her nose was positively hooked! She turned away in disgust.

"Girls!" An older woman summoned the

three women. Reluctantly, they left, amidst flamboyant goodbyes. Lee Ann kept her attention on the groceries.

"Now, young man, what can I get for you?" The clerk addressed Mr. Daniels.

"I'm not sure. I've never cooked anything before. What do I need?"

Lee Ann felt her heart lurch at the need in the boy's voice.

"Beans, first of all." He handed the boy a bag of dried beans.

"Aren't they a little hard to eat?"

Lee Ann couldn't suppress a giggle. She was still laughing when she felt a hand on her arm.

"Allow me to introduce myself — Johnny Daniels, Miss . . ."

"Lee Ann." She couldn't give Seth's last name, and her parents seemed so far away.

"Well, Miss Lee Ann."

"No, just Lee Ann."

"All right, just Lee Ann, possibly you could explain how I make these" — he held out the dried beans — "fit to eat." Johnny's eyes sparkled and Lee Ann responded to the laughter in them.

Seth turned to see Lee Ann smiling into the boy's eyes. He had not seen her look like that in months. There had been times when Morgan had looked at him in adoration. He tried to wipe the image from his mind.

He walked toward Lee Ann and she introduced them. As Seth watched Lee Ann's face light up, he realized how much he owed this girl for taking care of him for so long. He was poor company even for himself, much less for this young girl.

"Why don't you invite Mr. Daniels to supper, Lee Ann?"

Both Lee Ann and Johnny were happy at the prospect. As they left the store, Seth heard Johnny whisper to Lee Ann, "Is he your father?"

Seth looked down at himself. He felt old. He didn't like what he had become. He remembered how happy he'd been in the few weeks when he and Morgan had been together.

All through dinner that night, as the three sat in the dingy tent, Seth watched Lee Ann and Johnny. The eyes were wide as they discovered mutual interests and explored backgrounds. Able to stand it no longer, Seth left the tent, needing the cool night air.

"Did we do something?" Johnny asked.

"No, he's like that. Moody. Tell me some more about your family."

Johnny frowned for a moment. He wanted

to ask Lee Ann just exactly what her relationship to Seth was, but he didn't know her well enough. Seth was a strange man.

Seth walked for a long while. Damn you, Morgan! Everywhere I look, I'm reminded of you. It's been nearly a year since I saw you, and still I haven't been able to get you out of my mind for even a few hours.

I want you! He stopped walking and stared at the moon. It was a revelation. No matter what you've done, I still want you, Morgan.

But how? He couldn't just walk into that fancy house in San Francisco and demand to see her. What could he offer her that she didn't already have? Why would she leave the wealth and luxury she had in California to return to a little dirt-poor ranch in New Mexico? He couldn't expect that of her. She had her choice of men. Already all of San Francisco worshipped her beauty.

Money! That was the answer. He would go to her when he could lay diamonds at her feet. His eyes narrowed. Or sapphires, like the ones she wore at Montoya's party. Whatever she wanted he would give to her. He loved her. It was time he admitted that to himself. He felt as if a great burden had been lifted from him.

Purposefully, he strode back towards the

tent. He had to see to Lee Ann. He owed her a great deal.

"Lee Ann." He burst into the tent. She and Johnny drew apart from their first tentative kiss. Seth knew then that he could use Johnny to repay Lee Ann. "Johnny, how'd you like to move in with us? Lee Ann would love to have you, and maybe the two of us could make a little money."

"Yes, sir."

Lee Ann stared at Seth. She had never seen him so animated. It had crossed her mind that he might be jealous, and she was willing to give up Johnny for Seth. What ever had caused the smile on his face now?

Lee Ann thought Seth had worked hard before, but it was nothing to what she saw now. The three of them worked together in the fields. No longer were Lee Ann's days taken up with just cooking and caring for Seth. Sometimes the three of them rode into San Francisco. Lee Ann and Johnny spent the days looking at the new shops and houses which seemed to spring up overnight in the rapidly growing city. But Seth never joined them.

Seth realized that San Francisco was going to grow. Hundreds of people poured into the town every day. The gold fever attacked them like a disease. Many of these people would eventually settle here. He began using the gold he found to buy land. He rented land to the gold diggers. He leased it to men to put up new buildings. But he never sold it. What he bought, he held onto.

Johnny and Lee Ann were content to let Seth use their money for them. But after eight months, they were tired of living in a tent. They wanted to get married and buy a little home of their own. Seth tried to persuade them to hold onto their land, but they wanted out. Seth bought their shares of land from them.

Their wedding was quiet and Seth envied them their joyful faces. How he wished he and Morgan could have met one another normally and had an ordinary courtship. They might still be together.

It won't be long, Morgan, he vowed.

Seth missed Lee Ann and Johnny. Without Lee Ann there to make sure he ate, he lost weight. And he worked even longer hours. He dedicated himself to panning more gold and to collecting his rents and buying more land. He noticed little else.

"Hello."

Seth looked up to see a woman with red hair and a too-generous mouth. Her clothes were dirty, but had once been good.

"Hello." He smiled back.

"Well. *Well!* Won't I be the envy of every woman in this here camp? Mr. Good-Lookin' hisself has spoken to me."

Seth looked puzzled.

The woman laughed loudly. "You ought to know, honey, that every woman in camp has been pantin' after you. Not only are you the best-lookin' man here, you make the other women's men all look lazy."

Seth liked her easy openness. "Well, I guess we ought to remedy that. How about if we get out of the sun and sit a spell?"

"Wowee. I sure would like that, Mr. . . ."

"Blake. Seth Blake."

"Seth?"

"What's wrong?"

"Nothing really. Just the name Seth reminds me of someone. My name's Jessy."

"Well, Jessy, I'm very glad to make your acquaintance."

Seth brought Jessy a tin cup of water, laced generously with whiskey.

"Real good water," she smiled. "Your woman about?"

"I don't have one. Not here, anyway."

Jessy propped herself on one arm and studied Seth. He sat on a wooden box and leaned against the tent pole. His massive

440

legs were spread in front of him. She imagined him without his clothes. She liked her imaginings very much.

"How'd you like to have a roommate?"

Seth looked at Jessy's unwashed hair, at the dirt on her neck. He grinned at her, showing dimples. "That's the best offer I've had all day, but I'm afraid I'm going to have to pass."

"Mmmm. Too bad. Maybe I could do a little cookin' for you?"

"Now that I'd like."

"Well, then . . . thanks for the drink and I'll be seein' you. Maybe we'll work out somethin', Seth. A man like you is too temptin' to give up after just one try."

Seth went back to his work. Jessy's visit cheered him. True to her word, she brought a heaping plate of indescribable stew. Lee Ann's cooking had been a royal feast compared to Jessy's.

"Could I get you anything else?" Jessy asked when he'd finished. "Maybe you could use a little company overnight?"

Seth laughed and thanked her for both the food and her offer, but declined.

Jessy hadn't been so attracted to a man since she'd been sold at Madame Nicole's. Jessy always remembered Madame Nicole's as the height of her career, for she'd made her body her career. She loved men, and they loved her open easiness, her willingness to laugh.

Jessy had been bringing Seth meals for nearly a month when she first mentioned Morgan.

"You know, I guess I'll always be partial to any man named Seth. I knew a girl once, a real beauty, who was married to a man named Seth. You never saw anybody so in love — *real* love, you know what I mean? Well, her Seth was killed, and you would of thought it was the end of the world. A neighbor, can you beat that, a neighbor, killed her husband and because she wouldn't bed the guy, he sold her to a Frenchman and his Apaches. That's when I met her. She cried all the way across the country for her Seth. The first few weeks she kept hopin' she was gonna have his kid. When she found out she wasn't, I thought she was gonna go crazy . . .

"Oh well, I'm boring you. I gotta go."

"No!"

Jessy turned to look at Seth. His eyes were fierce and he almost frightened her. His hand on her arm hurt her.

"Tell the rest of your story." His voice was harsh.

Jessy was puzzled. Maybe he'd seen Madame Nicole's show and knew enough of the story already to know who she was talking about. Jessy straightened up and ran a hand through her tangled hair. Maybe he remembered her being in the show.

"Oh, Lord. All kinds of things happened to us. The Frenchman sold us to a whorehouse, Madame Nicole's. It's a real classy place. Maybe you've been there?"

She watched Seth's nod.

"We didn't work there. They auctioned us off. Morgan brought the highest price."

Jessy failed to notice Seth's whitened face. "What happened to her, this Morgan?"

"Well, Madame Nicole sold her to a pretty-boy, you know what I mean? I thought it was a dirty trick, but Morgan didn't care. All she ever talked about was her Seth. Me, I'd rather have a live one than a dead one, no matter how great a man the dead one was.

"Hey, you all right? You don't look so good. My story do that to you, or my cookin'?"

"I guess it's the sun. I've had too much sun."

"Well, you don't look good at all, like you was taken sick. You better stay out of the sun the rest of the day. I really gotta go now.

You need anything, just holler." She touched Seth's forehead. "You are a little warm. I'll come back later and check on you."

"Oh, God! Morgan, what have I done to you?" He sat on the little camp stool, his head in his hands. "What ever have I done?"

He started walking, as he always did when he was upset, toward the top of the mountain. Memories began to flash before his eyes, more vivid this time than ever before.

He saw the Montoya party. Marilyn had told him that Morgan and Joaquín huddled together in corners. But he saw that in a new light now. He knew Marilyn, knew her well enough to remember that she lied and schemed to get what she wanted. Marilyn would have been angry about his marriage, would have wanted him to think his wife had lovers.

The note! Why had she written the note? Jessy had said Joaquín had tried to force Morgan into his bed. He could have forced her to write the note. But why? She must have known he wouldn't release her after what she had learned about him. But Morgan wouldn't know that. She had such trust in people.

Oh God! What she went through! Montoya sold her to some Apaches, to be used in a white-slave auction! Seth had heard of Madame Nicole's auctions. They were becoming famous in San Francisco. He'd heard, too, that sometimes the women purchased there were reluctant about their new jobs. It was whispered that Madame Nicole came by them in a rather mysterious manner.

Then there were the men in the saloon, when he'd first come to San Francisco. It was obvious now that they'd lied to a stranger, just to see him make a fool of himself over something they knew he could never have. Morgan was not to be had. That was the point. That had been the crux of their little joke.

What she'd been through! He remembered the night he went to her room, how he'd ignored her declarations of love. He sat down on a rock, his head in his hands. What had he done?

Morgan, can you ever forgive me? Can I ever make it up to you?

He stood up, staring at the sun. "I'll make it up to you, Morgan. I vow here and now that I'll find you and make it up to you. I'll never doubt you again, no matter where you are or what has happened to you. If it takes the rest of my life, I'll convince you that I love you."

Seth began walking down the mountainside, slowly at first, and then with stronger strides. Well, Colter, you've had enough time to feel sorry for yourself. A year — no! it was over two years since the night he had sneaked into Morgan's bedroom. He smiled cruelly at himself. Two years of his life had been devoted to self-pity.

But he was through with that now. He was going to go to Morgan and fight for her. If she hated him, it would take longer. But he'd make her love him again.

"Seth! Where've you been? I was lookin' for you. I was afraid my cookin' might have killed you off." Jessy looked up at Seth. He seemed ten years younger. "What's happened to you? You look like somebody died and left you a gold mine."

Seth put his big hands on Jessy's shoulders and, to her astonishment, gave her a resounding kiss on the mouth. It wasn't the passionate embrace she'd hoped for, but it was a start. She smiled up at him. His eyes were sparkling. She'd never noticed the deep blueness of them before.

"I don't know what's come over you, but I sure like it. Hey! What're you doin'?"

Seth was putting the saddle on his horse. "Jessy, I'll owe you till the day I die. No matter what I do, I'll never be able to repay you. Here." He took a plump leather pouch from his saddle bag and handed it to her.

Jessy felt the bag and knew it contained gold dust and nuggets. "What's this for? I don't understand what I did — but I know what I'd like to do." Seth's good humor was infectious.

Seth swung onto his horse. "Jessy, it's been a real pleasure knowing you."

"Wait!" She ran after Seth and he stopped. "What did I do? You have to tell me."

"My name's not Blake, it's Colter — Seth Colter."

"Colter! You're — *you're* Morgan's Seth? But you were supposed to be dead."

"Morgan thought I was dead, but it takes a lot to kill me." He laughed. "Morgan's Seth. Lord, I hope you're right. Goodbye, Jessy, and if you ever need help, come to Santa Fe, to the Colter ranch." He reined his horse and started toward San Francisco.

"What about your gear? Your tent?" she called after him.

"It's yours."

Jessy stood and watched Seth until she could no longer see his broad back. "I'll be damned. Morgan's Seth. Who would'a thought he'd be alive." She remembered the way Seth had looked at her. "No wonder she pined after him for so long. Lord! What I wouldn't give to be her right now and have a man like that gallopin' after me."

She turned back to the barren camp and shrugged. Jessy was not a dreamer, and she did not spend time longing after something she could not have. The gold Seth had given her, the tent, and his panning gear were more than enough reward for her. "Imagine that — Morgan's Seth," she murmured as she entered Seth's tent. It was good to have a place of her own.

Seth's first impulse when he reached San Francisco was to break down Theron's door. He laughed as he realized he'd already used cave-man tactics on Morgan. This time, he was going to go slowly. He would not push her. He was going to woo her, court her.

The first place he went was back to the little tailor who had made the suit for him two years ago.

Seth grinned broadly at the man.

"You certainly look nicer this time," the tailor said. "Last time I was afraid to speak, afraid my head would be removed from my shoulders."

"It might have been, too. Tell me, could you fit me with another suit?"

"Let me guess. You want it in three hours?"

"I think you and I are going to get along fine. You think this could hurry you along?" Seth dropped several gold coins on the table.

The tailor smiled at him. "Mr. . . ."

"Colter."

"Mr. Colter, it is a pleasure to do business with you. Let's get on with the measurements."

Later, when Seth was putting his rough cotton work clothes back on, the tailor said, "Mr. Colter, I am curious about something. When you were here before — what, a year and a half, two years ago? — you came in demanding a suit. Now it's the same thing. I know this is all caused by a woman, but I'd like to know if it is a different woman this time or the same woman."

Seth's laughter filled the room. "It's the same woman." He picked up his hat and was nearly out the door when he turned back. "And the woman is my wife."

The tailor laughed. It wasn't often a man was so particular when the woman was his wife.

Seth went to a hotel, ordered a hot bath, and impatiently scrubbed weeks of dirt from his body. He marveled at himself. For the first time in two years, he was alive. He had admitted long ago how much he loved Morgan, but nothing could have lightened his spirit like finding out that Morgan had really always loved him.

Seth spent another hour at the barber's and then got his suit from the tailor. "Good luck," the man called after Seth.

By the time Seth reached Theron's house, he was shaking. Damn! he thought. I'm like a bridegroom on his wedding night. Would Morgan slam the door in his face? A butler answered the door.

"I'd like to see Mr. Shaw, please."

The butler appraised him, and Seth seemed to stand up under his scrutiny. "If you will wait inside, sir, I'll see if Mr. Shaw is in."

Seth waited in the spacious hallway. So this is what Morgan had been living in for the past two and a half years! It was a far cry from the adobe house on his ranch. He was glad he had some money now, glad he could give her things like this.

"If you'll come this way, sir."

Seth followed the butler into a room of golds and rusts. He stared at the man coming toward him. He'd seen Theron once before, but had paid little attention to him. He was incredibly handsome, smooth and blond. His features and trim physique were almost too perfect.

"Mr. Colter, I believe."

Seth was surprised at Theron's use of his name.

"Oh, yes, Mr. Colter, I know who you are. In fact, I've followed your adventures all over the gold fields. I must commend you for your wisdom in buying land here. I believe you are on your way to becoming a very wealthy man."

"You have the upper hand, Mr. Shaw. I know nothing about you."

"Won't you have a seat, please? Anyone who has lived with Morgan has heard of the great and wonderful Seth Colter." Theron's voice had a slight sarcastic edge to it.

Theron walked to an oak cabinet against the wall. The front of it was carved in a high relief. It was very old. He pulled a knob, and the front lowered into a shelf, held in place by delicate chains. "Could I get you something to drink, Mr. Colter? A brandy, perhaps?"

Seth nodded and Theron handed him a large crystal snifter of brandy. They both paused and savored it.

"Now, what can I do for you on this beautiful afternoon?" Theron's eyes were cold. This was the man Morgan had cried for, had been ready to die for. Seth Colter had taken her devotion lightly, had flung it in her face, used it against her.

"I'd like to see my wife."

Theron put his glass down and walked to the window, hands clasped behind him. He must control his anger. This . . . Kentucky lout walked in here and demanded to see his wife. Where the hell had he been when she needed him? He hadn't even been with her when the baby was born. Little Adam! He probably didn't even know he had a son. He certainly didn't deserve Adam. Theron breathed deeply and turned back to Seth.

"Mr. Colter, it is my opinion that you have lost all right to your wife."

Seth toyed with the brandy glass. He smiled up at Theron, a cold smile. "As you say, that is your opinion. What is between my wife and me is our business alone."

He certainly was cool. "Morgan has been my close friend for some time now, and what concerns her concerns me. I believe you have lost your priority in her life."

Seth frowned into the glass. "You are right, Mr. Shaw. I've been so wrong. I've done some horrible things to Morgan. I'd like to start again. I'd like to say some things to her that I should have said a long time ago. A great deal of our trouble is the result of plain misunderstanding."

"Oh, so the long-lost lover has come to his senses at last and now rushes to his little bride's side. Well, Colter, you are too late. Nearly two years too late. Morgan's gone."

Seth was on his feet. "Gone? Where is she?"

"Did you think she'd stay here and wait patiently for two years while you made up your mind whether you wanted her or not?"

Seth sat down, heavily, clumsily, setting the brandy snifter on the table next to him. His voice was quiet. "Everything is my fault. I have always had such a temper. I am thirty-five years old, and still I've never learned to control it. I've never loved a woman before, not the way I fell in love with Morgan. I couldn't stand it when I thought she didn't return my love. I didn't think — I just flew into a rage.

"You mentioned my investments. I made those for Morgan. I decided some time ago that I loved her no matter what she'd done, even if she *had* worked in a . . . brothel. Even if she was your mistress. I decided I didn't care, that if she could be bought, then I would buy her. I set about making money.

"Today I found out what a fool I had been, what I had done to Morgan. She should hate me. I know she must, and I deserve it. But I still love her."

He looked up at Theron, standing by the window. "I want to make it up to her. No matter how long it takes, I want to prove to her that I do love her." He looked down at the floor again. The room was silent.

Theron took a seat across from Seth. "Morgan left here not long after your, *ah . . .* visit."

Seth moved uncomfortably, not meeting Theron's eyes.

"She says she hates you, and she has reason to, but I believe she needs you. She is living now at her father's ranch, the Three Crowns."

Seth looked up. "Yes. I know the place."

"She is living there with a sort of foster cousin — the son of her father's partner, a very pleasant young man — of whom I believe Morgan is growing increasingly fond."

Seth watched Theron intently.

"If you want her, I'd suggest you go quickly."

Both men rose and stood facing one another.

"I know I haven't deserved your consideration, but I thank you, and I thank you for taking care of Morgan. Jessy seemed to think you two liked one another."

"Jessy? Ah yes, Morgan's friend. Jessy told you Morgan's story, then?"

"Yes."

"I looked for you for a long time after that night, even though Morgan refused to mention your name. When I did find out about you, she was already in New Mexico."

"I have a great deal to do before I can leave San Francisco. I need to take care of my property. As soon as I can, I'll be off to New Mexico — to Morgan." He took Theron's hand. "You won't regret trusting me. I know you care for her."

Seth left the room and Theron stared after him. He wondered if he'd done the right thing. Morgan was happy at the ranch with Gordon and Adam. He didn't know if he should have broken into her peace. But he knew how much she'd always loved Seth. And, of course, there was Adam now. No matter what, Adam was Seth's son and Seth deserved at least to see the boy.

He smiled to himself. He'd like to see Seth's face when he discovered he had a son. And Morgan's when she saw Seth! He laughed aloud. It was almost tempting to make the journey to New Mexico. He shuddered. New Mexico was too ghastly to even consider. How could anyone want to live in that wasteland?

Oh, well, he sighed. Back to work. Mrs. Osborne needed some new drapes. Morgan would have loved these. They were several shades of Morgan's abhorred purple, and the figures on them resembled gargoyles rather than the young ladies they were supposed to be. He still missed Morgan's cutting little remarks and, he had to admit, the stir they caused when they went places together.

It took Seth a week to take care of his business in San Francisco. He found a young lawyer, Tim Bradbury, who was disillusioned and disgusted with the gold fields. Seth was his first client. With Seth's holdings to administer, he was able to set up his own law practice. He was grateful to Seth. To keep his gratitude, Seth gave him a share of the rents and a percentage of the profits from the sale of any land. Revenues were to be sent to a bank in Santa Fe.

His mind was clear when he set out for Santa Fe. He was free to give all his attention to his wife.

CHAPTER NINETEEN

Morgan was happily surprised by the ranch house of the Three Crowns. It was built in the Spanish tradition, like the Montoya ranch. It was enormous.

"What do you think?" Gordon asked her as they looked down on the spacious house from the ridge above.

The house was the same color as the surrounding countryside and seemed always to have been there. It nestled down amidst the piñon trees and the much taller cottonwoods.

"There's a river near the house." Gordon pointed to a strip of green not far from the house. "Are you surprised?"

"Very. It's practically a mansion. How many rooms does it have?"

"I've never counted them, but you'll have a lifetime to count them." Gordon looked back at Adam, who'd climbed into the back of the wagon and fallen asleep. "We'd better get Adam into a bed."

Morgan thought the inside of the house was even more beautiful than the outside. The rooms on the first floor were large and airy. They opened into a spacious courtyard, in the center of which was a tiled pool. Stone benches and statues were sprinkled among the trees and flowering shrubs.

"He's asleep." Gordon returned from putting Adam to bed. "Now, let's meet the servants and have dinner."

"Servants?" Morgan laughed. "I'm afraid I've become accustomed to doing most of the housework myself."

"This is your home and here, if you want to, you can sit and eat chocolates all day."

"Chocolates! I needed you when I was carrying Adam."

Gordon looked puzzled and then smiled. "Oh, yes, Jake told me about your unusual eating habits."

The servants were lined up in the foyer, at the bottom of the stairs.

"Roselle, our cook. Martin is our butler and general factotum. This is Carol, who takes care of the upstairs rooms. Donaciano, who is our groom. Carol's sister, Magda, comes in during the days to help with the downstairs rooms."

Morgan shook hands with each of them.

Roselle and Martin were married and had worked in the house since it was built. Carol was a young girl, in her teens, very plain and rather shy. Donaciano was just a boy, about twelve or thirteen. Morgan learned later that Gordon had adopted him when his parents drowned two years earlier.

Gordon escorted her into the room adjoining the foyer, the dining room. The pine table was enormous, with at least twelve large pine chairs. It was covered now with a snowy white linen cloth and set with the finest Limoges porcelain and crystal. The silver was heavy and ornate.

"Gordon! It's really beautiful."

Gordon smiled at her praise. He liked to live comfortably. "Roselle is an excellent cook, and I think you'll be pleased."

The meal was delicious, as Gordon had promised. Martin served the meal expertly. Gordon raised a glass of chilled champagne to Morgan. "To your new home. To the hope that you find peace and happiness here and that you stay . . . forever."

She smiled back at him. "I hope you're right."

By the time the meal was finished, Morgan felt her body drooping. Gordon put his arm around her and led her upstairs to her room. The room was feminine, a white lace bedspread on the bed. The covers were turned down to expose lace-edged pillows. Her nightgown was spread ready for her. Gordon left her and she quickly undressed and was asleep.

Gordon paused outside her door. "I love you, Morgan," he whispered.

Morgan awoke to the sounds of Adam's squeals of laughter outside her door. Hastily, she donned her dressing gown and went to investigate. Adam was perched on Martin's shoulders, gleefully banging him on the head with a wooden horse, screaming, "Eat. Eat."

Gordon followed closely behind Martin. "Morgan, we woke you. I'm sorry, but Adam was rather disturbed at waking and finding himself in a strange place."

Morgan smiled up at her energetic son. "Thank you for caring for Adam, Martin." She held up her arms and Adam tumbled into them, his weight nearly unbalancing her. Martin continued downstairs, rubbing his head.

"Now, where is this monster's room?" She smiled affectionately at her son as he grinned up at her, showing two large dimples. "You know, I have a feeling he is going to be even more spoiled here than he was on the Colter ranch."

Gordon smiled at her as he led her into Adam's room. As she began to dress Adam, she looked around the room. It was filled with toys and pictures of children. When he was dressed, Gordon helped the child onto a large rocking horse.

Morgan went to investigate the pictures — they were all of one little girl. She looked questioningly at Gordon.

"Don't you recognize her?"

"They're . . . that's me, isn't it?"

"Every one of them. These were your toys. When my father and Uncle Charley built the house, he had the pictures put into the room. It's been more or less a shrine. Your father spent hours in here. Sometimes, after a letter arrived, he'd lock himself in here for an entire day. I'm glad there'll be a little more life in here now."

Morgan laughed. "With Adam, you don't have to worry about any place being dull — or quiet. Adam!" She tried to be heard over his shouts of happiness about the rocking horse. "Let's go eat breakfast." Adam stopped rocking immediately and quietly climbed off the horse. Seeing Gordon's puzzled stare, Morgan explained: "Eat. That's a magic word with Adam."

Gordon took Adam to breakfast. Morgan

dressed in a sturdy cotton gown, one that fit perfectly and accented her curves. Then she joined them. Both Adam and Morgan ate heartily of the food Roselle prepared.

After breakfast, Roselle asked to keep Adam in the kitchen with her. Morgan consented, and while Gordon attended to the business of the ranch, she explored the house and gardens.

At lunch, Martin watched Adam constantly, and anticipated his every need. Morgan sighed, knowing that all the attention was not good for her impressionable son. When Adam began rubbing his eyes, Morgan took him to his room for his afternoon nap.

Gordon returned to the house and asked Morgan to go riding with him, to see some of the ranch. They rode along the little river and Morgan found an ideal place for picnics under a grove of cottonwoods. When she dismounted the mare Gordon had given her, she tripped and grabbed at her saddle to catch herself.

Gordon caught her in his arms, holding her close to him. "I'm sure that this will be the highlight of my day."

"Oh, Gordon," she laughed, as she stepped away, "you're always teasing, just like . . ." She left her sentence unfinished.

Gordon's eyes were serious. "Believe me, Morgan, I am totally serious." She turned away to hide the consternation that flooded her face. She wasn't ready yet. Seth was too real to her. When his memory faded, then she'd be able to look at another man.

The candlelight dinner, alone with Gordon, was pleasant and Morgan relaxed with him. "To my beautiful little foster cousin, who changed into an even more beautiful woman," he lifted his glass to her.

Early the next morning, she heard Adam in the hallway. She opened her bedroom door and her small son found his mother's room. She crawled back into bed, watching him wander about the room, looking at rugs, touching jars on Morgan's dressing table, and knocking on the door that connected Morgan's bedroom to another room.

"There's no one there, Adam." Morgan rolled over and found herself looking into Gordon's amused eyes. He was standing in her open doorway. "It used to be your grandpa's room, but now it's empty."

Morgan moved down in the bed, bringing the sheets to her shoulders.

"Do you mind if I take Adam with me today? I'd like to show him the ranch and show him to the men."

Morgan sat up, the covers falling away. Gordon was like an older brother. It was difficult to think of him in any other way, in spite of his protestations to the contrary. "Gordon, you don't want to take Adam. You don't know what he's like. There are times when he's more than I can handle. You'll never get any work done."

"Leave him to me. If it's all right with you, I'll take him."

Gordon stepped out of the room and returned with a little sombrero. It had a beaded band on it. "I bought this in Santa Fe. I think it'll fit." Adam loved the hat, jumping up and down at the sight of himself in his mother's mirror, the long nightshirt flying and looking very incongruous with the hat.

"Are you sure you're ready to handle that all day?" Morgan laughed.

In answer, Gordon swept the laughing boy into his arms. "My pleasure. Now, cowpuncher, let's get you into some other duds."

Morgan heard Adam's laugh all the way to his room. She leaned back against the pillows. Yes, she thought, this is very pleasant. It was peaceful here. No memories assailed her. Gordon was wonderful, too. It would be very comfortable to fall in love with him, yes it would.

With Adam gone, Morgan found she had too little to do. As always, she wandered toward the kitchen. Roselle was surprised when Morgan rolled up her sleeves and plunged into kneading a large mound of bread dough. They both soon forgot the notion that they were mistress and servant, and became just two women, cooking and talking together.

"Gordon has always been such a lonely fellow, even as a little boy. My heart cried for him at times."

"Lonely? But Gordon doesn't ever seem to be sad at all."

"He covers it with his jokes and laughter, but it is not easy to grow up without a mother."

"Didn't his mother ever live with him?"

"No. She left soon after her son was born, returning to her own people. For all the jokes he makes, Gordon takes his Comanche relatives very seriously. He has never spent much time with them. Once when he was very young, an uncle came to see him and Gordon followed him around for two weeks. His Indian uncle showed him how to dress like a Comanche and told him to be proud of his Indian blood. Gordon was very upset to find the Indian gone one morning.

Now he gets so upset over what the white man is doing to the Indians." Roselle cocked her head toward Morgan. "The men on the ranch try to forget he's half-Indian. They don't like the idea of an Indian boss."

Morgan nodded her understanding.

Lunch was lonely for Morgan, with both Gordon and Adam away from the house. She ate in the kitchen with Roselle and Martin, but realized that her newness in the household made them shy.

She went to her room to nap. For some reason, her thoughts of Seth were especially strong. As she removed her dress, she almost felt his hands on her body. The memory made her ache.

Gordon arrived later with a tired, sunburned Adam. Morgan, glad to be busy, washed the child and slipped him into a clean nightshirt. He was asleep as his mother finished buttoning the gown. As she kissed her son's cheek, she was reminded again of how much Adam resembled his father. She chastised herself for always thinking of Seth.

At dinner, Gordon was especially happy. "You should have seen them! I never saw grown men make such fools of themselves over anyone. All day they talked baby talk to him. Calhoun especially! 'Ooh wanta go for wide on horsey?' Adam just stared at them. Wouldn't go to a single one of them. Stayed with me." Gordon's eyes gleamed with pride.

Gordon put his hand over Morgan's. "I can't tell you how glad I am that you are here. I've been rattling around alone in this big house for years. Sometimes I slept in the bunkhouse rather than be alone in here. Roselle and Martin have been the true occupants."

Gordon kissed her check. He was handsome, easy to laugh, and Adam adored him. What more could she want? she asked herself. Gordon's goodnight kiss had not sent shivers down her spine as Seth's kisses did. Don't compare them! she told herself. As she climbed into bed, she thought again how comfortable it would be to be in love with Gordon.

The days began to fall into a routine, and Morgan was content, if not deliriously happy. Gordon often took Adam with him in the days, and in the evening he entertained her with stories of how the men tried to entice Adam from him. It seemed they never succeeded.

When Adam was gone, Morgan spent her mornings in the kitchen and her afternoons riding, improving her skills on the mare.

Adam and she often took a picnic lunch and spent the afternoons together by the river. It was a little greener, but otherwise a lot like the place where they had spent their afternoons at the Colter ranch.

They had been at the Three Crowns for three months when Gordon first mentioned the divorce. Seeing Morgan every day and not touching her was agony for him. He wanted to know how she felt about Seth. He wanted the way clear for himself, with no ghosts between them. He loved her enough to wait for her.

They were at dinner. "Morgan, have you made any decisions about Seth?"

Morgan looked up, startled. Even the mention of Seth's name made her stomach contract, the skin of her scalp tighten. "I don't want to discuss him." Roselle's *coq au vin* suddenly lost its appeal.

Gordon watched her closely. It seemed that what her eyes said and what her lips said did not match. "Would you consider a divorce?"

A divorce, a permanent separation from Seth, from Adam's father. She must be sensible. "Yes, I believe it would be appropriate. But I don't know where Seth is. I'm sure he must be found before there can be a . . . divorce." She hated the word, hated the whole idea. "I don't want to see him again."

"Then I'll contact John Bradley and see what can be arranged."

They were quiet the rest of the meal. They had coffee outside in the courtyard. Morgan was occupied with her own thoughts. Why is the idea of a divorce so distasteful to me? Because it makes me feel like a failure? She argued with herself over the absurdity of the idea, but she knew her answer was correct. Of course, it wasn't her fault, only Seth's. Seth and his temper.

"More coffee, Morgan?" Gordon interrupted her thoughts.

Gordon knew now it was going to be a tough fight. Morgan said she hated her husband, but he could see the lie in her eyes. Something had to be done.

When Morgan and Adam had been at the Three Crowns for six months, Gordon decided to have a welcome party. Morgan had met very few of the neighbors who sparsely dotted the countryside. She was glad to arrange the party, glad to cook, and to decorate the house. Gordon was happy to come home every night to Morgan and Adam. For the first time in his life, he wasn't lonely. His happiness would have been complete if he hadn't sometimes caught a glimpse of longing in Morgan's eyes.

CHAPTER TWENTY

It was the day of the party when Gordon saw the big man riding toward him. The easy, straight way he sat his horse showed unusual confidence. Gordon watched with interest as the stranger approached. He wasn't an ordinary drifter, and he was older than he appeared from a distance.

"They tell me you're the boss." The stranger's voice was deep, soft, very pleasant.

"I guess I am. My name's Gordon Matthews." Gordon extended his hand and found it engulfed in the man's larger one. It was hard and calloused from work.

"Dave Blake." He smiled and Gordon had a sudden flash of recognition. What was familiar about the man?

"I'd like a job."

"What experience do you have?" Gordon knew he was going to hire the man even before he answered.

"I used to run my father's plantation in the East, and I've worked out here about six years."

Gordon smiled back at him. "I can always use a good hand. You're on. That's Boyd, my foreman, over there. He can put you to work." He watched the man turn his horse and ride off. The way he moved his hands was naggingly familiar. Yet he couldn't remember having seen this man before.

The rest of the day, he watched Dave work. He wasn't like most new hands. He didn't wait to be told what to do. It was as if he'd been working on the ranch for years. The other men took to him quickly, liking the quiet way he stepped in. Yet they held him off, too, and did not bombard him with questions.

Gordon noticed one of the younger members of the crew asking Dave what he should do when he'd finished the task Boyd had assigned him. Gordon watched his foreman for signs of hostility. But Boyd, never an ambitious man, was content to let Dave take over where he could. On the ride back to the bunkhouse, Gordon sought out the new man.

"Dave, I watched you work today, and I want to say welcome to the Three Crowns."

Dave smiled at his employer, and again

Gordon tried to remember whom Dave reminded him of.

"We're having a little party at the house tonight. Everyone's invited. Plenty of beer and hard stuff and all the food you can eat."

Dave laughed, his laughter deep. "I'm afraid you might get more than you want. After a day like this, I could eat my horse — even the horseshoes. What's the occasion?"

"Morgan and Adam have been living with me for six months now, six very happy months."

"A party because two men have moved in with you."

Gordon was puzzled for a second, then grinned broadly. "Come tonight and meet my guests. I think you'll be pleasantly surprised." He left to return to the house. Dave was certainly going to be surprised all right, after thinking of Morgan as a man.

Adam was just running down the stairs when he saw Gordon. Morgan ran close behind Adam. The boy leaped, knowing Gordon would catch him. Gordon held Adam close and looked up at Morgan. She was beautiful. She had just washed her hair and it hung down her back, still slightly damp.

"One of these days, he's going to jump at someone and miss. How was your day, Gordon?"

"Now that I'm home, it's a beautiful day." He kissed Morgan's cheek, put Adam down, and the three walked to the courtyard to look at the party preparations. "I hired a new man today."

"Oh?"

"The strangest thing." Gordon had his mouth full, and Morgan looked up sharply.

"Gordon, stop eating those! I have them arranged in a design and you'll mess it up. Now, what was strange?"

"This new man I hired. I know I've never seen him before, but I feel like I know him. The way he walks, certain ways he moves. It's like I've seen them hundreds of times."

"Maybe you're just imagining it."

"I guess you're right. I'll go get ready now. You going to wear that?" He looked at her everyday cotton dress.

"Don't be silly. I have a dress you've never even seen before. The silk is from Italy and it is gorgeous."

"With you in it, it will be."

Morgan watched him go, smiling. Gordon was so pleasant. She constantly wondered at herself for not being in love with him.

■ ■ ■ ■

Dave walked into the bunkhouse and then busied himself while listening to the men talk.

"A real looker, ain't she?"

"Nearly bust my britches every day when I see her ridin' by on that horse."

"Maybe a good fairy'd give me three wishes and I'd give 'em all to be that saddle."

"I'd rather be the horse. She can ride me bareback."

As the laughter exploded again, no one noticed the new man leave the room. And no one noticed that he wasn't with them when they left for the party.

Dave returned to the empty bunkhouse to take his time bathing and dressing. The suit fit his body closely, emphasizing his muscular frame. The silk of the shirt offset the dark, nubby weave of the vest. He took his time, and when he started toward the house, the party had been going on for hours.

When Morgan came down the stairs, Gordon gasped. He had never seen anything quite so lovely. The emerald-green dress reflected in her eyes until they were the same color. Her hair was piled on top of her head in large, fat curls, while more curls cascaded down her back, all the way to her waist. Her delicate little ears were exposed where the hair swept upward, and she wore tiny diamond-and-emerald earrings that sparkled when she moved. The dress hung just off her shoulders and low across her breasts.

"Morgan, you're more beautiful then I thought possible. I don't know what to say."

"Do you like my hair?" She turned around and he touched a soft curl.

"It's lovely. I've never seen so much hair in my life." He looked at her questioningly. "Is that all yours?"

Morgan giggled. "Sir, it is not at all polite to ask a lady what on her person is real and what is not."

Gordon eyed her voluptuous figure. "At least I know some things are genuine."

Morgan laughed at his compliment. "Shall we go?"

Gordon took her arm and leaned close to her. "You smell nice, too." His lips touched her cheek and moved slowly to her waiting lips. His kiss was gentle, soft, and very pleasant. Morgan smiled up at him. She enjoyed his kisses, and might even grow to love them.

All eyes turned toward them as they entered the courtyard. For the thousandth time, Gordon wished Morgan's father had written his will to specify that his daughter must marry Gordon. He had hinted broadly, but Uncle Charley had laughed and said that feudal times were past, that the will he was writing was bad enough. He wanted to insure that Morgan would have her choice of several men.

For Morgan, the party was too much like the party at Joaquín Montoya's. The couples, all strangers, mumbled polite wishes as Gordon introduced her. He was so proud of her, he fairly strutted. She liked being beside him and felt comfortable on his arm.

Morgan hardly knew any of the ranch hands, having seen them only from a distance. After "good evenings" were exchanged, neither she nor Gordon noticed their conspiratorial looks.

Morgan had been standing for hours. She must have said "thank you" a thousand times. The faces of the people ran together and she had long ago given up trying to remember their names. She was considering going upstairs to check on Adam, but she had already used that excuse to escape twice.

She smiled at a large woman in a purple satin dress. Lord, but I hate that color, she thought. She saw Gordon coming toward her. Maybe she could persuade him to take her upstairs for good. She frowned slightly as she saw him veer off to the right, to the shadows a little behind her.

"Dave! I thought you weren't coming. I want you to meet the 'man' I'm giving the party for. Remember, I told you you'd be surprised.

"Morgan, I'd like you to meet the new hand I hired today, Dave Blake."

Gordon watched Dave's face for his reaction. "Dave, this is Morgan Colter."

He turned sharply at the crash of the punch glass. Morgan's face was totally without color. She was staring at Dave. "Morgan, what's wrong?" He looked from her to Dave, who seemed to be the cause of Morgan's distress. "Do you know Dave?" There was dread in his voice.

"No, I don't believe we've had the pleasure. Maybe I remind Mrs. . . . . Colter of someone she's met before."

"Is that it, Morgan? Does Dave remind you of someone?"

Morgan stood staring, speechless.

"I think I'll take Morgan upstairs. Something about you has upset her."

"Please do. I'm very sorry to have upset you, Mrs. Colter. Maybe you'll forgive me when you find I'm not the same man you think I am. Goodnight." He watched as Gordon led Morgan away.

Morgan still hadn't spoken when they reached her bedroom. Gordon picked her up and put her on the bed, her hair spreading around her.

"Morgan, what's wrong? Do you know that man? Does he remind you of someone?"

"Yes." Her whisper was hoarse.

"Who?"

"Seth." He barely heard her. Seth! My God! He had been afraid she was still in love with her husband, but if she reacted this way to a man who only resembled Seth! He stroked the hair on her forehead. "I'll send Carol up to help you undress. There's no need for you to come downstairs again. When everyone is gone, I'll come back."

Carol had come and gone, and Morgan lay in the bed in her nightgown. It had taken a long time before she could begin to think. Now the first shock of numbness was beginning to wear off.

Seth was here! She hadn't seen him since the night he had come to Theron's house. That horrible night when he had accused her of — She stopped. She didn't want to remember. What did he want here?

The shock of seeing him again had caused her more pain than she had thought possible. She had hoped that living with Gordon would make her forget Seth. She hadn't had enough time! She needed time to get to know Gordon, to forget Seth.

He can't do this to me! The tears collected in her eyes and ran down her cheeks. Adam and I are happy. We have a home now. Why can't he let us be?

She wiped away the tears as something occurred to her — she didn't have to let him upset her! No, she didn't love him anymore. She knew him for what he was. This time he wouldn't be able to charm her, because she knew now what lay behind his dimpled smile. She knew how to handle this. She would totally ignore him!

She sat up straighter in the bed, and smiled. Mrs. Colter, he called her. Well, Mr. Blake, you will be another hired hand, just as Boyd and the others are. No special favors, and no recognition, either. If he had come in spite, to punish her for crimes he believed she'd committed, he was going to be surprised. She wouldn't allow him to upset her. He no longer had any control over her.

She answered Gordon's knock. His concern faded rapidly when he saw Morgan's smile.

"Feeling better now?"

"Yes, much better."

"Morgan, I just wanted to tell you that you'll have to remember that Dave Blake is an entirely different person from Seth. Just because a physical resemblance is there doesn't mean they're at all alike."

"You're perfectly right. Mr. Blake is another man. It was such a shock, that's all. I don't know how I'll ever make it up to him. The poor man. He must have thought I was insane."

Gordon patted her hand. He was still shaken by Morgan's feelings for Seth. "I doubt that. You're much too beautiful for any man to take offense at anything you do."

Morgan laughed. "Did you know that at one time I was considered very plain?"

Gordon ignored her question. The idea was too absurd to consider. He kissed her forehead, blew out the light, and left her.

Before Morgan fell asleep, she saw Seth's smiling face. He hadn't changed at all. He was still very handsome.

Seth sat under the stars for a long time after the party ended. The carriages were gone and the bunkhouse was silent.

He had almost left the party when he first saw her. He had watched her for over an hour, being careful that she didn't see him. He had known right away that she was bored. Morgan had never liked a lot of people around her. She was happiest when there were just the two of them. He had seen the way Gordon hovered over her, always watching her, protecting her. It was obvious that Gordon was in love. That's what had made Seth want to leave. But as he watched Morgan's face, he knew she didn't return Gordon's love. He didn't know if he'd been joyous or sad when he saw that she was not in love with Gordon. Part of him wanted her to be happy, at whatever cost to himself, but the other part was selfish and wanted her to be his alone.

Where was this Adam that Gordon had mentioned? He'd said the party was for Morgan and Adam. Maybe she loved Adam. Adam! What was he like?

Seth rubbed his hands on his thighs. He felt he'd won one round in the battle for

Morgan, but it had taken a lot of his strength. He dreaded the outcome of the next round. This was a fight for his life.

It was still very early when Morgan heard her son banging on her bedroom door. "Mama, eat. Mama, eat. Horse."

Drowsily, Morgan left her bed and opened the door for him.

Still mostly asleep, Morgan stumbled back to the bed. Adam ran ahead of her, reaching it before she did, and began bouncing up and down on the mattress. "Horse. Horse," he shouted. "Gor, horse."

Morgan smiled at her sturdy son. "Well, my talkative little son, I take that to mean that you are ready for Gordon to take you on his horse?"

Adam smiled at her, pleased she had understood.

"You little imp! You may have everyone else on this ranch hanging on your every monosyllable, but not me." She lunged at him, catching the tail of his nightshirt. Adam collapsed on the bed, laughing helplessly.

Hearing the commotion, Gordon came to Morgan's open bedroom door to investigate. The sight of Morgan and Adam wrestling on the big bed made him laugh. Then he grew serious as he watched Morgan. She wore a thin muslin gown and it was wrapped tightly about her body to expose smooth, golden legs. As she pulled Adam to her, the outline of her breasts swelled, full and sensuous. He felt little beads of sweat on his upper lip.

Feeling another presence in the room, Morgan turned. She saw Gordon and followed his eyes to her exposed legs. Hastily, she pulled a sheet over her body.

"Gor! Horse! Eat!"

Even with the sheet pulled to her neck, Morgan was beautiful. Her hair tumbled about her shoulders in a disarray of fat golden curls, some honey-colored and some almost white. Her face was slightly flushed. Gordon recovered himself just in time to catch Adam as he jumped from the bed into Gordon's arms.

"Good morning," she murmured.

Gordon's face broke into a wide grin and he looked at Adam. "Good morning. You sure are a lucky man, Adam. I'd like to crawl in bed with your mama some morning."

Morgan gaped at Gordon. Never had he said anything like that to her before.

As Gordon turned to leave, Adam in his arms, he smiled back at her. "You really should close your mouth, Morgan, beautiful though it is."

By the time Morgan was dressed, Gordon had dressed Adam, packed some bread and cheese, and left the house. She ate breakfast alone, trying not to remember that Seth was somewhere on the ranch.

"Hey! Gordon's bringing Adam today!" Seth heard the men yelling in the bunkhouse. Well, she certainly has picked a popular man this time, he thought. As the men all left through one door, Seth quietly made his way to the other door. He wanted to postpone meeting Morgan's new lover as long as possible. His horse shied away from him when he angrily tossed the heavy saddle onto its back. Of course, she had every right to take on a new lover, after the way he'd treated her.

But she was his wife!

Whoever this Adam was, he was going to have to fight Seth for Morgan's love and Seth meant to fight any way he could.

"Dave, are you in here?"

Seth didn't want to talk to Gordon. Probably wants me to shake the bastard's hand. If he's a pretty little fop, I may put my fist through his face. Even if he's twice as big as I am, I may try to do it anyway.

"Dave! There you are. There's someone I want you to meet. This is the *real* boss of the Three Crowns. This man's word is law."

Now I know I'm going to hit him, Seth thought. Slowly he turned, jaw clenched. He saw only Gordon.

"Adam," Gordon looked down and then behind him. He laughed, turned, and picked the boy up. "This is Adam Colter. Like I say, he's the real boss of this ranch. Adam, this is Dave Blake."

Gordon looked from one to the other. Neither spoke. Man and child stared at one another with an incredible intensity.

Gordon had never seen Adam be still so long, or be so solemn. Then Gordon saw the resemblance. No wonder Morgan thought this man looked like the boy's father. They both had the same shade of blue eyes, the same wavy hair, though Adam's was honey blond while Dave's was darker. Adam would someday be as large a man as Dave Blake.

"Morgan's right."

Without moving his eyes from Adam's piercing stare, Seth asked, "About what?"

"Well, Morgan said you resembled the boy's father. You two could easily pass for father and son."

Seth looked at Gordon and grinned, showing dimples like Adam's. "Is that so? Well, I've taken a real liking to this boy. Do you mind?" He held out his arms to Adam.

"No, not at all, but he won't usually leave me. We're pretty good pals."

Adam fell into his father's arms with no hesitation. Seth held the boy, running his hands over his arms and legs, over the back of his head. He smiled at the boy and Adam returned a mirror-image smile.

"Yes, sir, I do like this boy."

Gordon straightened his shoulders. "Well, we need to get to work." His voice was cool. Don't be silly, he told himself. Maybe Adam just feels a kinship with the man because they look alike. It doesn't mean anything. He tried to calm himself. He turned to saddle his own horse, and another beast felt the brunt of someone's anger.

Seth carried Adam into the morning sunlight. "Well, son, you are certainly a surprise. And you're one more reason why I have to get your mother back. It's not going to be an easy task."

Adam smiled up at his father and put out a hand to touch his cheek. "Horse."

Seth returned the smile and kissed the small hand, so like his own. "No, son, I'm not a horse. Less sense than one sometimes, but I'm what is known as a daddy. Can you say 'Daddy'?"

"Da da." Adam laughed delightedly, always happy saying new words.

"That's close enough."

Gordon came to stand by them. "Adam, are you ready to get on the horse?"

Adam smiled at his friend, content with Seth. He made no move to go to Gordon. "Da da."

Gordon looked puzzled and then laughed. "His first attempt at 'Dave'. Morgan complains that no one except her tries to teach him new words. She'll be glad to hear this one."

"I hope so."

Gordon took Adam and put him on the front of his saddle and then climbed up behind him. They waited as Seth mounted. Adam took one look at Seth on the horse and lunged toward him. Seth caught him and put him in front of him. The saddle could barely hold the two of them.

Gordon had to laugh. "You know, it's not easy for me not to be jealous. For six months now, Adam has been like my own son. Sometimes he'd rather stay with me than go to his own mother."

Seth tried to make his voice sound light, and Gordon didn't notice the way the big man's hands tightened on the reins. "The mother! Now she's a beauty. It must have been like having her for a wife for the last six months."

Gordon laughed aloud. "I wish you were right. That's what a lot of men think, but Morgan has a mind of her own. She has . . . problems . . . concerning the boy's father. But some day — maybe. I'm going very slowly with her right now."

"I would have thought living in the same house with a beautiful young widow was the kind of situation men dream about."

"It's a dream all right, but that's all. Oh . . . and Morgan's not a widow. She's still legally married." He started to turn his horse away and then looked back. "I must be as silly as Adam. I don't usually discuss my private affairs with the hands."

"I thank you for the confidence."

"Well, here's where we part. You're to work with Boyd today and I'm leading another crew. Adam, are you ready to go with me?"

Adam pressed his back closer to Seth's chest. "Da da." Gordon shrugged.

"Well, it looks like you're stuck with him."

"My pleasure." His hand was on the boy's knee. "I can't imagine anyone I'd rather spend the day with."

"I'm not sure you know what you're asking for. When he's tired, he can really be a nuisance. Right now he's happy, but —"

Seth tousled the boy's hair. "There's no need to worry. I'll take care of him as though he were my own son." Seth reined his horse toward Boyd and the other men. His son's little body near his own felt comfortable and familiar, as if they'd known one another for years.

The other men looked up sharply as they saw the new hand with Adam in front of him. Gordon never allowed the boy out of his sight. But then they shrugged. There was something about Dave Blake that made a man trust him, something even the nineteen-month-old Adam must feel.

All day Seth stayed with his son. It was true that his work would have been easier without Adam to look after, but Seth had been by himself too long to begrudge a little extra work now. Whenever Adam stepped too near a skittish horse, a large hand was there to guide him to safety. Seth felt a peace that he hadn't experienced in a long time. He was content now to take his time with Morgan, to go slowly, to give her time to trust him. Now, he had Adam.

Morgan was nervous all day. As soon as she entered the kitchen, she cut herself. She stared at the cut unseeing. Roselle bandaged it for her. Later, when she was removing a hot tray of rolls from the oven, she forgot to use a potholder. Roselle smeared her palm with cool butter and told her to leave the kitchen. Morgan didn't understand.

"Mrs. Colter, something is wrong today. Go outside, ride your horse, read, but please stay out of the kitchen."

Morgan removed her apron and went to the drawing room. Roselle was right, something was wrong. Seth Colter had come back into her life. She knew he must have seen Adam by now. What did he think of his son? Maybe he didn't even realize Adam was his. That would be just like him — he'd probably think Adam was Joaquín's son, or Theron's.

She picked up *Jane Eyre.* She scanned pages, anxious for Jane and Mr. Rochester to get together again. As she read, she began to realize that she was seeing herself as Jane and Seth as Rochester. She remembered clearly every muscle of Seth's body. She put the book aside and wandered from room to room, checking to see if anything was out of order.

Lunch was a lonely meal, adding to her nervousness. She had Donaciano saddle her horse and rode to her favorite place by the river. She spread a blanket and wished Adam were there to keep her busy. The thought of Adam brought visions of Adam and Seth together to her mind. I wonder how Seth felt when his own son preferred Gordon? Adam would rather be with Gordon than with anyone else in the world.

It was hot, and the place was alive with dragonflies and numerous other flying insects. Morgan removed her riding boots and stockings, wiggling her toes, glad to be rid of them. It wasn't long before she fell asleep.

She awoke dazed, not knowing where she was, her body stiff from the hard ground. The sun was low. It was well past time for her return. Hastily, she tried to pin her hair back into its careful coiffure, but finally gave up. Pulling the pins and ribbon out, she thrust them into her pocket.

She rode quickly back to the house. Breathless, she tossed the reins to Donaciano. "I'm late. Would you give her a good rubdown, please? I need to go — Gordon and Adam will be here soon."

Donaciano was willing to do anything for his young mistress when she smiled at him like that.

She started running toward the house and then turned to call thank you to Donaciano.

She caught her breath as she ran into something; a hand caught the back of her head and tangled in her hair.

She looked up into Seth's sparkling blue eyes. His hand was burning her skin, causing chills down her back. Their eyes locked, each seeing only the other, oblivious to the rest of the world. Seth's hand moved along the back of her neck, fingers caressing the tendons, touching each muscle. Along the scalp, her hair was warm, almost hot. Involuntarily, Morgan's eyes began to close. It had been a long time . . . Her eyes flew open. He was staring at her with a slow smile, a smug smile. She jerked away from him but he held her easily.

"There you are, Dave. I wondered where you'd gone." Gordon looked from Seth to Morgan and Seth dropped his hand from her hair. Immediately Gordon felt the tension between them.

"Mrs. Colter ran into us, running from the barn."

Only then did Morgan notice Adam in his father's arms. The boy slept peacefully, his head cradled against Seth's shoulder. She turned startled eyes to Gordon.

"I know. It's the strangest thing. I never saw Adam take to anyone as he took to Dave. He spent the whole day with Dave, and no matter how many times I tried to get him to come with me, he refused to leave. The way they stared at one another, you would have thought they'd known one another all their lives."

"I'm afraid the boy's worn out. If you'll show me his room, I'll carry him to bed."

Seth's smile infuriated her. He was so smug, just because Adam liked him. Well, Adam was just a little boy. He didn't have much knowledge about all the dishonesty in the world. She smiled back at him, icily. "Mr. Blake, isn't it? I am quite capable of putting my own son to bed. Adam." She put her hands under the sleeping child's arm, trying not to touch Seth. Adam opened his eyes only slightly and saw his mother. He went to her willingly and she carried him into the house.

Gordon watched her go, astonished by her rudeness. "Dave, I really must apologize for Morgan. I've never seen her rude to anyone before. She's really not like that. Actually, she's a very warm person."

"That's all right. She just seems to have taken a dislike to me. Maybe I ought to forgo your invitation to supper."

"No, please don't. I owe you something for taking care of Adam. I know it's not easy to do a full day's work and keep an eye on a

494

toddler at the same time. By the way, my foreman says you do one hell of a day's work, and that you know exactly what you're doing, too."

"It seems I get along with animals and children a sight better than I do with women." They laughed together.

"Well, I trust Adam. Anyone he likes is all right with me. Now let's go wash."

Morgan began undressing her son. He was dirty and needed a bath, but she didn't want to wake him to give him one. She washed his face and hands and began to put his nightshirt on him. He frowned once and fluttered his eyelids when she jerked his arm too sharply.

"I'm sorry, sweetheart." She kissed his cheek and finished dressing him more gently. Damn him! Why did he have to come back? Now that he's seen Adam, he'll probably never give me a divorce. I'll never be able to lead my own life.

Maybe he wanted the money, the money she offered him to marry her. But, somehow, she didn't think that was it.

She tucked Adam into his bed, brushing the hair from his forehead, and kissed him. She sat a minute, looking at her sleeping son. He was always such a whirlwind of activity that it was pleasant to see him quiet.

She went to her own room to dress for dinner. She chose a filmy sea-green dress, a gift from Theron. She had chosen it to match the jade treasures in her bedroom. She began to pin up her hair and then, on second thought, left it down, adding a ribbon that matched the dress. Just the way Gordon likes it, she thought, as she studied her reflection. And Seth — No! She wouldn't think that way.

Tonight was Gordon's night. She would be especially nice to Gordon. She would forget Seth, forget his laughing eyes, forget his touch. Yes, tonight would be the beginning of a new relationship with Gordon, and Seth Colter would be out of her life for good.

She started down the stairs. At least tonight she wouldn't be troubled by Seth. She could relax, alone with Gordon.

"I'm sorry I'm late, Gordon. I had to get Adam to bed. He was so tired after being with that awful Mr. Blake."

"Morgan!" Gordon's tone was sharp. "We have a guest." His eyes sent warning.

Seth's large form was visible now, inside the dining room. His eyes were teasing. His smile was slight but his dimples were deep, betraying extreme amusement. Amusement at her embarrassment!

"I'm sorry, Mrs. Colter, if your son was so disturbed by my presence."

"I'm sure Morgan didn't mean that, Dave." He looked to Morgan for support. "It's just that . . ."

"Would you mind if we ate now? I am starved." Morgan's voice was honey-sweet and she looked at Gordon lovingly.

Gordon frowned. This wasn't Morgan at all. What was the matter with her?

She entered the dining room on Gordon's arm, turning her back slightly on Seth.

"I'm sorry we're still in our work clothes, but we got back too late to change."

"Mrs. Colter would put us to shame, no matter what we wore." Seth smiled at Morgan's look of fury.

"Yes, she would. I don't believe I've seen that dress before. Is it new?"

She looked a challenge at Seth. "No. My former employer, Theron Shaw, gave it to me."

Seth offered no response. He sipped his wine and smiled into Morgan's eyes.

So that's how it was: He didn't care at all. Well, she didn't care either.

They sat quietly as Martin served dinner.

"Tell us about yourself, Dave. You said you'd been in the West for some time."

"Yes, Mr. Blake, do tell us about your life. You must have done a great many *very* interesting things." Her voice was close to a sneer.

Gordon was embarrassed. She was really carrying her dislike too far. He would talk to her after dinner. He didn't like having a guest mistreated.

Morgan ignored the looks she was getting from Gordon.

"There's not much to tell, really. For the last two and a half years, I've been working in the gold fields in California."

"The gold fields! I've lost several men to gold fever. I considered going myself, at one time."

"It's not a pleasant way to live. Dirty, and the work's almost unbearable at times."

"You seemed to have enjoyed it. You stayed for over two years. That's a long time; a lot of things can happen in two years." She looked at Gordon affectionately.

"Yes, whole lives can be created in that amount of time."

She knew he meant Adam. He had not taken her meaning. "People can start new lives, if old ones are finished."

Seth merely smiled.

"Well, this conversation is becoming too philosophical for my poor Indian brain."

"Indian?"

"There now, I've told the house secret. My mother is a Comanche. But I know little about the Indian way of life. My mother left me when I was a baby and returned to her people."

Morgan looked up at Gordon, her eyes gentle. "But there are times when you make a very convincing Indian, Sky Eyes." Her voice was low, caressing.

Gordon was puzzled. You would have thought they were sharing a lover's joke. He laughed, but he was confused.

Morgan turned to Seth. He was smiling placidly, as if he hadn't even noticed.

Seth was now listening to Gordon, and Morgan was able to look at Seth, unobserved. His broad shoulders and thick chest were clothed in rough cottons. He was not clumsy at all, sitting amidst the silver and porcelain. When one large hand carried a fragile crystal glass to his lips, she wondered at the ease with which he controlled his strength so the glass didn't break. His shirt was open at the throat and showed blond curling hair on his chest. She remembered the color of his skin, a great expanse of dark honey and then lighter below his waist. His thighs were so muscular. She even remembered his toes. She shuddered.

"Morgan, are you cold?"

"No, not at all." She tried to make her voice light. At all costs, she must avoid Seth's eyes.

"What is this dessert?" Seth asked.

Gordon turned to Morgan for the answer. *"Babas au rhum,"* she murmured.

"Ah, yes, now I remember."

"Are you familiar with French cuisine, Dave?"

"Yes, somewhat. I had a brief encounter with the food once. I grew quite attached to it."

"Morgan plans all the menus and often cooks a lot of the food. You should taste her breakfasts — they are really delicious."

"I should love to share Mrs. Colter's breakfast." He looked at her across the top of a delicate porcelain cup. His eyes dropped from her face to her breasts.

Morgan stopped her hand midway before it flew to cover herself. He had no right to look at her like that! It was as if she were completely naked. She looked to Gordon for defense from the animal across from her. But he was busy with his dessert and had seen none of their exchange.

The meal was finally at an end, and Morgan realized her body ached from tension. She wanted to relax now, to be alone.

"Would you care for brandy and a cigar, Dave?"

"Yes, I would."

"Morgan, would you like to join us?"

"No. I think I'll have some tea in the courtyard. It's cooler outside. If you would bring it, Martin?"

"Morgan's right, it's a beautiful night."

"Then maybe Mrs. Colter would allow us to join her."

"Morgan, would you mind?"

There was no acceptable excuse. So, silently, the three of them entered the courtyard. There was no moon, and they could hardly see one another.

Gordon broke the silence. "The skies here are so clear, the stars so bright. If I liked nothing else about New Mexico, I'd love the night sky."

"You speak with some knowledge."

Morgan jumped. Seth's voice was near — too near. She could almost feel his breath on her.

"Have you spent much time in the East?"

"Quite a bit, unfortunately. My father sent me to Harvard."

"Really? You were probably the first Indian to graduate from Harvard!"

"I'm sure I'm the only one, but since they never knew about my mother, it's not something I can publicize."

Seth laughed, quiet and low, a laugh Morgan remembered well.

"I'm sure the people in the East feel the same about Indians as people do here."

"Yes. Every little man needs someone to hate. Dave, would you keep Morgan company for a few minutes? I'd like to go and check on Adam."

"I'll go, Gordon. There's no need —"

"I want to. After all, I didn't get to see him all day. Dave stole the boy completely away from me."

She watched Gordon go, seeing only his outline in the darkness. She grabbed frantically for words. "The first time we saw Gordon, he was dressed as an Indian. I was scared to death of him, but Adam wasn't. He liked him right away. Sometimes he'd rather go to Gordon than to me." Her voice was fast, high-pitched. She made herself stop talking and took a sip of tea. Why doesn't he *say* something? He came here to punish me. Now why doesn't he get it over with?

"He's a fine boy, Mrs. Colter."

Mrs. Colter! Why did he keep up the pretense when they were alone?

"I believe Gordon will return in a few minutes and I need to get up early in the morning. We're going after some mustangs tomorrow. So, if you'll excuse me . . . The dinner was delicious and the company delightful. Goodnight, Mrs. Colter."

Morgan stood alone, speechless, and watched Seth go. How very cool of him. Goodnight, Mrs. Colter, indeed!

What did he want here? Why had he come back? Why was he such a coward that he couldn't even come out and tell her what he wanted? She had never known another person so unfeeling.

She put aside her tea cup and left the courtyard for her bedroom. She began to undress. She'd fight Seth with all her strength, she vowed, slipping under the covers.

The knock startled her and her heart began to pound. "Come in." Her voice had a slight quiver in it. When she saw Gordon, she quieted.

"Are you all right, Morgan? When I got to the courtyard, you were both gone."

"I'm fine, Gordon." She looked away. Why couldn't her heart pound at the sight of Gordon? Why?

"He upset you, didn't he?" Gordon's voice held a tinge of anger. "Did he say something to you while I was gone?"

"No. He was a perfect gentleman."

Gordon studied her eyes for a moment and then relaxed. "Good. I like Dave. He's experienced and the men like him.

"Today a fight broke out between a couple of the men. Tim came to tell Boyd and me, but before we got there, Dave not only had stopped the fight but had the men laughing as well. Boyd never got the hands' respect like that. And Adam adores him."

"Please, Gordon, I'm tired of hearing about this man's virtues." Gordon was staring at her. He'd guess more than she wanted him to know if she weren't careful. "I'm sorry. I'm glad you and Adam like him. I just need a little more time before I trust someone completely."

Gordon smiled at her. "You can have all the time you want." He kissed her on the forehead. "I guess I should be glad you dislike him. I've always been afraid that if Seth Colter walked through the door, you'd fall right into his arms. It's good to see you dislike a man just because he resembles Seth. Goodnight."

Seth found it difficult to sleep. The few moments alone with Morgan in the dark garden had been hell. He had had to leave. He couldn't have stayed there another minute without taking her in his arms.

504

She was the same insecure little Morgan he'd met years before, but there was also a different air about her now. She looked people in the eye. She wasn't afraid of her own body. She didn't hide under yards of fabric. She was a woman now and, if possible, even more exciting than before.

Even so, it was not Morgan's lovely face that floated before Seth as, at last, he fell asleep. The face was much smaller, round, and distinctly dimpled.

Morgan was groggy when she heard the knock. She couldn't seem to open her eyes, and didn't really want to. She heard Adam's squeal in the hall, and then the door opened.

"Horse!" Her son's demands were unmistakable. She turned over and gradually focused on Gordon and Adam.

"I'll take you on a horse in a minute."

Morgan frowned. "He's never going to learn to talk if no one ever makes him ask for what he wants."

"You're certainly in a bad mood this morning."

"I am not. I just didn't sleep well." She started to get out of bed.

"You just stay there. I'll take care of Adam and send Carol up with a breakfast tray."

"Adam needs a bath and . . ."

"He'll just get dirty again around the horses. Morgan! Get back in bed or I'll put Adam in there with you."

Morgan smiled. "You win. No one needs to be tortured like that."

"Good. Now go back to sleep and Carol will be up in a couple of hours."

Morgan tried to sleep, but after a few minutes, she knew it was a useless effort. She got out of bed and hastily donned her riding habit. Gordon and Adam were just leaving as she entered the room.

"Going riding, Morgan?"

"Why else would I wear a riding habit?" She continued toward the dining room, then stopped. "I'm sorry. I didn't mean to snap. Yes, I thought I'd take lunch and a book, and go to the stream."

"That sounds like a good idea. Maybe you'd feel better if you were outside for a while."

"There's nothing wrong with the way I feel! I just —" She closed her mouth. Nothing came out of it right any more.

"I want to take Adam with me again today. That is, if he'll stay with me and not go to Dave."

She wanted to scream. Her life was filled with the doings of Seth Colter. He was already beginning to control Adam, and

Gordon liked him so much. She kept her mouth closed. No matter what she said, it would be wrong. Someone would defend Seth.

She turned to Martin. "Would you please have Roselle prepare a lunch in a basket for me?"

She kissed Adam goodbye, promising him a good scrubbing when he returned, and saw them out the door. She hurriedly ate breakfast and got her book, quilt, and the picnic basket. As usual, Roselle had packed enough for several people.

The air cleared her head and made her feel better. At the stream, she spread the quilt under the cottonwoods and settled down to read the rest of *Jane Eyre.* It was quiet, with only the sounds of the birds, the locusts, and the stream. She wasn't aware of it when she slept.

Gordon turned to see Dave riding toward him. Adam was slumped against the big man, his head down. Gordon sighed and wondered if he'd ever get used to the boy's preference for Dave.

"Gordon, I think you'd better take Adam back to his mother. It looks like two days in the saddle in a row are too much for him."

"Pull that rope a little tighter or you'll lose

him. I can't go right now; I need to stay here. I don't think Morgan's at the house, but I guess Carol can take care of him. Wait a minute! Morgan should be at the stream. Why don't you take Adam and leave him with her? It's closer."

Gordon gave him directions. He hoped that, if Morgan got to know Dave better, she'd like him.

Seth stopped on top of the ridge and looked down at his wife. Her head rested on one arm and the other was sprawled, palm up, across an open book. How could she possibly be anyone's mother? She looked only about six years old herself.

Carefully, Seth dismounted and picked Adam up. He secured his horse and walked quietly toward Morgan. He put Adam on the quilt on one side of his mother and then sat down on the other side. Adam turned onto his stomach. Just like his mother, Seth thought.

Seth wanted to stretch out beside her, take her in his arms. But he'd lost that privilege. He smiled at Adam. At least his son harbored no ill will toward him.

Seth tentatively touched a lock of golden hair, then stopped as he realized her eyes were open and staring at him. There was hostility in them, and wariness. His heart ached. How could he have caused such a look?

"I brought Adam." He nodded to the sleeping child on her other side. "He was too tired from yesterday to last today. Gordon told me where you were. I hope you don't mind my disturbing your peace."

Adam stirred. He rubbed his eyes and then went to his mother. She sat cross-legged, now, staring at Seth. Adam sat ungracefully in her lap. He looked up at Seth and smiled. "Da da."

Morgan was startled.

"He's probably trying to say 'Dave.' "

Morgan looked at Seth in total distrust, knowing he'd probably been teaching Adam to say "Daddy."

"Thank you for bringing him to me." She looked away, her heart pounding.

"Eat!" Adam saw the picnic basket. "Chi'en."

Morgan laughed. "I believe that's supposed to mean chicken. He learns new words every day, but sometimes it's not easy to understand them." She watched as Adam dug into the basket. He squealed when he found that he wanted. With great pride he displayed a chicken wing, a trophy.

Morgan avoided Seth's eyes. "Most children's first words are 'Mama' and 'no,' but Adam's first word was 'eat.' In fact, I don't believe he's ever learned to say 'no.' "

Finally she turned to him. His eyes were gentle. She felt her throat tighten. He turned toward Adam.

"I can't imagine a better word than 'eat.' "

Adam turned to Seth. He liked conversations with his favorite word. He handed Seth his prized chicken wing and beamed at him. "Eat."

"It seems you've passed the test, if Adam is willing to share his food with you."

Seth smiled, a delighted smile that Morgan often saw on Adam. "I'm glad to pass his test." There was a slight emphasis on "his."

She looked away. It was still too painful to be so near him. She would be glad of the time when he was just another man to her, when she could look at him and not remember how it was to kiss his neck, his eyes. "I guess you'll have to stay for lunch. Adam seems to want you, and he tends to be rather spoiled. He makes a fuss when he doesn't get what he wants."

Seth's eyes grew sad. Adam sometimes used the same trick on her to get what he wanted. She always melted when he looked like that.

"I'm glad Adam wants me."

She wanted to scream at him. Why did he play this politeness game? Why didn't he tell her what he wanted from her and then leave her in peace?

Seth opened the picnic basket and Adam made a grab for the tin flask held by his father.

"Say what you want, Adam."

Adam's eyes gleamed. "Milk."

Morgan had to laugh. "It's just as I thought. He probably knows the English language better than I do. He's just too lazy to say the words. I'm glad someone else forces him to talk."

Seth's eyes were proud. "I have a special interest in this boy."

Morgan remained quiet through the meal, listening to Seth as he taught his son new words.

Abruptly, Seth stood up. "I have to go back to work now. I thank you for lunch." He turned toward his horse, then looked back at Adam, who was watching him avidly. Seth dropped to his knees and put his arms out to the boy. "Give Dada a hug?" Adam ran to his arms and Seth kissed the boy's cheek. "You take care of your mama and I'll see you later."

Seth tipped his hat slightly to her, and his

eyes raked her body. Again, she felt naked under his gaze. Her hands flew to cover herself, but she caught them mid-way. Seth seemed to read her thoughts and laughed quietly. She and Adam watched as he walked up the hill and mounted his horse. The way Seth walked only added to her frustration. It seemed everything reminded her of days past.

She looked down at Adam, still watching Seth on his horse. He waved again. Her anger rose. Seth was trying to win Adam's affections in order to get to her. He thought that when he had the boy in the palm of his hand, he'd get Morgan again. Well, he was wrong.

Adam was content to stay with his mother after lunch. He stretched out on the quilt beside her and she read to him from *Jane Eyre*. He fell asleep quickly.

When Adam awoke, Morgan returned with him to the house. Adam decided he wanted to go back outside on a horse, and Morgan had her hands full persuading him that he was going to be given a bath. Later, when her son stood before her, clean and shining, he grinned at her. He seemed to know when he had given her an especially difficult time and just when to charm her. She tickled him until his squeals of delight were heard all over the house.

Roselle had dinner waiting for him and asked to be allowed to put the child to bed. By that time, Morgan was glad to let someone else take over the care of her active son.

At dinner, Gordon was full of talk about Dave. It seemed she was bombarded all the time with praise about Seth. She longed to scream out the truth about Seth Colter.

She was glad Seth wasn't sharing their dinner, but she kept looking across the table to where he had sat the night before. As Morgan took a bit of Roselle's *boeuf bourguignon,* she wondered if Seth was eating properly. The cook for the hired hands was a little man who reminded her of Jake. He generally liked pinto beans and fried cornbread. What did she care? Seth could starve to death. It would only serve him right.

She went to bed early and fell asleep quickly. She remembered Seth as he was on his knees with his arms outstretched.

Morgan did not see Seth for three days. She told herself that she was not getting enough rest, that that was why she jumped at the sound of a door opening. Her face fell when she saw only Martin, or Roselle, or even Adam at the door, but she thought it was just because she hoped to see Gordon. Yes

— that was it. She was falling in love with him. She ignored the fact that she felt just as disappointed whenever Gordon appeared.

She tried not to allow herself to think about Seth. But there were times when she caught herself staring into space, remembering the way he looked astride a horse. Then she would curse him and fervently wish he had never returned to interrupt her life.

At night she slept poorly, often reading far into the night. The strain was beginning to tell on her.

Early one morning, she was baking *madeleines* for Gordon and Adam. She had slept very little the night before, and there were bluish shadows under her eyes. It was hot in the kitchen with both ovens going, and Morgan's hair escaped from the soft arrangement into damp curls on her neck and forehead.

"Why don't you go outside for a while? Take your horse and go to the stream."

"I really can't, Roselle. There's too much to do, and I need to watch Adam."

"Adam is no problem. I've had five children of my own. I can certainly handle one little boy. Now you go outside. You don't look so good."

"A ride would feel good. I'll go and

change."

Roselle laughed and put her hands on Morgan's shoulders, pushing her toward the door. "You don't need a fancy riding habit. Go get on your horse and ride. This is New Mexico, not Kentucky. Women here do not own even two dresses, much less riding habits."

Morgan smiled in gratitude. "You're right. Thank you."

Donaciano was asleep in a stall when she got to the barn. Quietly, so as not to disturb him, she led her mare outside, taking a bridle from the wall. She stood on top of a barrel to mount the horse. She looked around carefully to make sure no one saw her and then tucked her skirt up into the waistband. It was good to be free, unhindered by long skirts. On impulse, she removed the pins from her hair and let it fall free.

She guided her horse to the place by the river. She had not been there since Seth had brought Adam to her, four days before. She wanted to return. She wouldn't let Seth keep her from doing what she wanted.

She slid from her horse, and quickly removed her shoes and stockings. She splashed icy water on her legs and thighs, face and arms, and unfastened her blouse to the top of her breasts. She had a sudden impulse to remove all her clothes and stretch out in the water. Instead, she leaned back on the bank, her hands clasped behind her head.

Roselle had been right to make her get out of the house. This was her favorite spot. She smiled up at the sunlight filtering through the cottonwoods.

"You really should tie your horse."

Morgan jumped to her feet. A few feet away, Seth was tying her mare's reins to a branch.

"If something scared her and she ran, you'd have a long walk back to the house."

"What are you doing here?"

"I come here often in the mornings. I liked it when I was here before, so now I come whenever I have the chance." His eyes went to her unbuttoned blouse. "I find the scenery especially beautiful."

She felt the blood rush to her face. "What do you want here? What do you want from me?" The anger she had been holding back for so long threatened to erupt.

Seth's voice was quiet. "I want nothing from you that you are not prepared to give."

"Give? I gave you everything I had and you —"

Seth's eyes were sad. "I'm sorry. I'll leave.

516

I didn't mean to disturb you." With a few quick strides, he was gone.

Morgan sat down heavily. Somehow, she felt defeated. Why couldn't he rage at her, or drag her into his arms? Anything but this constant politeness, this self-effacing manner of his. She angrily wiped away her tears. What was wrong with her? She had planned to ignore him, but she was the one who was being ignored. She mounted her horse and rode around, directionless, for an hour before she returned to the house.

She heard Gordon in his study. He sounded angry. Morgan had never known Gordon to be angry. "Damnation! What do you mean, it's 'something you always meant to do'? Why the hell didn't you tell me that when you signed on?"

Morgan's hand flew to her mouth. "Seth," she whispered aloud. Then she straightened, trying to compose herself. Good, she thought. He's leaving. I'm glad. Now Adam and I can continue our lives without interruptions. She started up the stairs, but turned quickly when the study door opened.

Gordon was frowning at Boyd. The tall foreman was putting a roll of bills into his shirt pocket. "And I don't want to see any of you again," Gordon shouted at Boyd's retreating back.

"Gordon, what's wrong?"

"Gold fever! My foreman and three of my best men are leaving in the morning. They wanted this month's wages." He threw up his hands. "I sometimes wonder if it's worth it. You can never get any help."

Morgan put her hand on his arm. "It's not the end of the world. You'll find someone else."

"Sure I will, but then this damned gold fever will hit them and *they* will leave. Wait!"

"What is it?"

"I have an idea. I'll be back in time for dinner."

He ran from the house.

Morgan was just getting Adam ready for bed when Gordon burst in. "I just hired Dave as my foreman."

"Dave?"

"You haven't forgotten Dave already, have you?"

"No, of course not. I just wonder if it's wise to hire someone you hardly know. After all, he's been here less than a week."

"Well, I've watched him and he works as hard as any two men. And Adam likes him, don't you, boy?" The child went to Gordon, and Gordon carried him to his bed and covered him lightly. He blew out the light and he and Morgan left the room.

"I've invited Dave to supper tonight. We have a lot of things to discuss. That is — if you don't mind?"

"Why should I mind what Mr. Blake does or does not do? He is of no concern to me."

Gordon paused at the top of the staircase and looked at Morgan. She was especially beautiful in the half-light in the hall. He kissed her cheek and then his arms went around her. Lightly, his lips touched hers.

Morgan wanted to feel the blood pounding in her head as it had when Seth kissed her, but there was no such feeling. Gordon broke from her abruptly.

"Dave, I didn't hear you come in."

Morgan turned to see Seth at the foot of the stairs, his brow creased. She patted her hair and adjusted her dress.

"Good evening, Mrs. Colter. I hope you are feeling well."

"Very well, Mr. Blake." She turned loving eyes up to Gordon. "Very well indeed."

Gordon led her down the stairs. He and Seth began to talk of the ranch. Martin held Morgan's chair for her. She tried to listen to the conversation, but she knew little about the work done on the ranch. She was acutely aware of Seth's presence, however, and kept her eyes averted.

She didn't see Seth's eyes on her, or note the way Gordon broke off talking to follow the larger man's glance. Morgan sat quietly, pushing her flan about in the bowl. She had eaten very little.

"Morgan?"

Gordon's voice caused her to start. She looked up into Seth's smiling eyes. "I'm afraid we're being rude. Why don't we have coffee in the courtyard?"

"What about your business?"

"It can wait. Dave and I will have plenty of time to discuss it later. Right now I'd rather spend my time with a beautiful woman. Don't you agree, Dave?"

"I'm afraid I agree more than I'd like to admit."

"Martin," Gordon turned to the butler, "we'd like coffee in the courtyard."

"May I, Mrs. Colter?"

Morgan looked warily at Seth's proffered arm. She chided herself for being so silly.

"Of course." His arm was larger, harder than she remembered. His body was so incredibly warm. Images of the times she had been cold and had snuggled against him for warmth danced in her mind. She took slow, even breaths, trying to calm her frantically beating heart.

"You two go ahead. I want to get a couple

of cigars."

The courtyard was still and quiet, with only a cricket's sounds. She removed her hand from his arm.

"Are you happy here, Morgan?" His voice was gentle. It was the first time he'd called her that.

"Yes, I am." She hesitated. There was no anger now. "Why are you here, Seth? Why couldn't you leave me alone?"

The moonlight played on Seth's hair, turning it silver. They held one another's gaze. Neither of them heard Gordon's footsteps.

"I want you. It's that simple. I decided I couldn't live without you, no matter what I thought you had done."

"What I had done! I have done *nothing* wrong."

"I know that — now. I met your friend Jessy and she told me everything. I had the whole story wrong."

Morgan tried to control the anger she felt surging through her. "Let me see if I understand you correctly. As soon as you discovered that I wasn't the . . . what you thought I was, you decided you'd take me back?"

"No, Morgan. That's not what I said. I decided a long time *before* I met Jessy that I wanted you and needed you, even if I had to buy you."

"Buy me! Why, you insufferable . . ." She stopped as Gordon noisily entered the courtyard.

"It took me longer than I thought it would." He quickly took in Morgan's stormy face and Seth's helplessness and bewilderment.

"I'm rather tired tonight." Her voice was curt. "Goodnight, Gordon. Goodnight." She did not look at Seth, but merely inclined her head in his direction.

The two men watched her leave. "Well, Dave, shall we go to my study and get down to business?"

Morgan tore her dress from her body and collapsed on the bed, nude. "Of all the despicable, insufferable —" She was at a loss for words. "He'll take me back! After all I've been through. After all the pain he's caused me, he decides he'll come back and forget everything. How generous."

This has all happened because I tried to save his life! I should have laughed at Joaquín and told him to go ahead. How could I ever have loved such a man?

She grabbed a vase from the table by the bed and hurled it at the bedroom door. It made a loud crash, mollifying her just a bit. "Damn *all* men except my son! *My* son, and no one else's!"

Below, in the study, both Seth and Gordon looked toward the ceiling as they heard the crash. Neither made any comment.

It was after midnight when they concluded their business. As Gordon walked past Morgan's room, he saw there was no light coming under the door. Everything was quiet. He went to his own room and removed his coat, vest, and cravat. He loosened his shirt and lit a cigar.

Gordon needed to think. He knew that Seth Colter and Dave Blake were the same person. It should have been a bigger surprise than it was. He realized in retrospect that everything had pointed to this: the way Morgan had reacted to "Dave" on the night of the party; her nervousness since then; and the way she had started flirting with him — but only when Seth was near.

Right now she fought Seth, but Gordon knew it would be only a matter of time before she admitted her passion for him.

What about his own love for Morgan? There were still times when just the sight of her made the blood in his temples throb. But that was beginning to be less painful. In fact, the last time he'd been in Albuquerque, he had been interested in some of the young women he'd seen there. Could he learn to love elsewhere? Could he get over his love for Morgan? Gordon thought he could.

Right now, he needed to do something to help his little cousin. Seth had done a terrible thing to her, not believing in her. But it was not really unforgivable.

What they needed now was to be together more, to be around one another constantly. Then their bodies would overrule their stubborn minds.

He could be the instrument for their getting together again. Tomorrow, he would begin.

As he fell asleep, he sighed and wished he had been reared in the simpler society of his mother's people. If Seth wanted Morgan, he'd just present her father with more horses than anyone else did. There wouldn't be any discussion about dishonesty, or forgiving — just simple bartering. Tomorrow he would move Seth into the house. There was a connecting door between her bedroom and the one next to it. He imagined it would be easy to fix the lock.

Seth was also just falling asleep. He had spent an hour cursing himself for his clumsiness. Everything he'd said to her had come out wrong. From now on, he thought, I won't let her bait me. I won't try to explain my reasons for coming back. I'll talk only about the present.

He'd tell her that he loved her, that he wanted her, over and over again. But there would be no more explanations. His resolutions made, Seth slept.

CHAPTER TWENTY-ONE

Breakfast had begun before Morgan entered the room.

"I'd like to take Adam with me today, if you don't mind," said Gordon. "Adam has taken such a liking to Dave. It's strange how alike they are. When Adam first saw Dave, he went right to him. You'd expect a boy to react that way only to his own father. And the way Dave protects the boy! I sometimes think he'd lay down his life for Adam."

"All right! I've heard enough about the great Dave Blake. Could we please talk about something else for a change?"

"Why, of course." Morgan didn't see Gordon's suppressed smile. "Remember your father's lawyer, the one you wrote to, in Albuquerque?"

"Yes."

"Well, Mr. Bradley and I have been corresponding lately, and I checked with him about a divorce."

Morgan's head came up abruptly. "Divorce?"

"Yes. You remember we discussed it. Mr. Bradley says you'll need to find your husband before the action can be carried out."

Morgan jumped up from the table. "But he left me alone! He didn't even know about Adam. I should think that would be sufficient reason for a divorce!"

"Ah, yes . . . Adam is another problem. Before he was born, a divorce would have been a lot simpler. Now, of course, there is the possibility that the courts would award Adam to his father."

Her mind went blank. She sat down again. "What do you mean?" Her voice was harsh.

"Well, I briefly told Mr. Bradley about your troubles in San Francisco. I assured him that you were totally innocent, but he said that no matter what the truth of the matter was, your stay at Madame Nicole's would look very bad on paper. And later, you lived with an unmarried man — Theron. It all looks bad."

"But none of that was my fault!"

"That wouldn't really matter. Seth's lawyer could use those facts to tarnish your character."

Morgan sat quietly, her hands folded in

her lap. She couldn't even imagine losing Adam.

"There is a way."

"How?"

"If we found Seth and persuaded him to waive all rights to his son."

Morgan felt helpless, defeated. "He'd never do that," she whispered.

"How do you know? We'd have to find him and ask him."

She stood up. "Please excuse me, Gordon, I'm not very hungry this morning." How do I know? I know because Seth loves his son very much and he would never give him up. Never.

Gordon smiled. He really shouldn't have lied that way. Not lied, really . . . but bent the truth. Mr. Bradley had said all those things, but had added that there were ways of getting around the situation. Gordon had simply neglected to mention them to Morgan. It was for her own good, though. Someone had to stop her from ruining her life.

"Well, Adam, shall we go ride a horse?"

Adam grinned, showing little white teeth. "Ride horse."

"Very good. A few more days and you'll be able to argue with your mother."

Morgan spent the morning helping Roselle in the kitchen. After lunch, she went to Gordon's study to work on the household accounts. She tried a hundred times to make the horizontal row of numbers match the vertical row.

"Mama."

She looked up to see Adam running to her, arms outstretched. She was glad for the excuse to leave the hated numbers. "What happened to the pink-and-white cherub who left here this morning? I think this boy must have lived all his life with coyotes. Do you have a kiss for your mama?"

Morgan looked up to see Seth's large form smiling down on them. "I brought him back. He needs a nap in the afternoon. It's too tiring for him to ride in the sun all day."

She began to inform him that she was perfectly capable of caring for her own son, but choked back the angry words. "That's very thoughtful of you." She looked down at Adam's head. He was sitting in her lap, his back to her. He was perfectly still, a sure sign that he was tired. She shifted him to one side in preparation for lifting him.

In one stride, Seth was across the few feet

separating them. He took Adam in his arms. His hand brushed her breast. It was as if a torch had touched her. Seth looked into her eyes, but she turned away quickly, hiding her reaction.

"If you'll show me where his room is, I'll put him in bed for you."

"I'll . . ." She saw in his eyes that he'd have his way. "Follow me."

"With pleasure." His eyes were on the sway of her skirts as they went upstairs. She felt the blood rush to her cheeks again.

"Just put him here on the cot. I need to undress him before I put him in bed."

Seth carefully deposited the sleepy Adam on the cot, and began unbuttoning his shirt.

Morgan started to intercede, but he brushed her aside. "I want to. I don't get to spend much time with him, and I want to, whenever I can."

Morgan stood back and watched as Seth awkwardly removed Adam's shirt. It was funny to see the rugged little body treated as if it were eggshells. Adam, for some reason of his own, decided not to bend his arm. Seth worked for several minutes with no result. Adam's eyes were half closed, but she knew he was very much awake and enjoying his father's increasing frustration.

A giggle finally escaped her.

Seth whirled on her. "What's so funny?" he demanded.

"You. You act like he's a piece of hand-blown crystal. I assure you he is very strong. I could show you bruises he's made on me —" She stopped because Seth's eyes were twinkling.

"I'd like that."

"Like what?"

"To see your bruises."

She looked away and stepped in front of Seth to tend her son. Adam's eyes opened wide. "Yes, you little imp, you know I won't put up with your nonsense. Now let's get out of these clothes."

She began to undress Adam quickly, all too aware that Seth had not moved from his place behind her. She could feel his breath on her neck as he leaned nearer to watch.

"Is that how it's done?" His voice was low and very close.

She turned to answer him. His face was only inches from hers. His eyes were slightly hooded, the lips parted and sensual. Her breathing became more shallow as she saw the strong neck and the blond hair that curled above his open shirt. She knew the look well. She had often fallen into his arms when he had looked at her like that.

"I remember a time when you undressed

a larger man."

With all her strength, she turned back to her son. She did not respond to the thigh that pressed against hers. She turned away from Seth and bent to pick up Adam. Seth moved in front of her and easily picked him up, put him into the bed, covered him, and kissed his forehead. He stared down at Adam for a minute.

"He's a good-looking boy, isn't he?"

She could swear Seth puffed his chest out. She looked at him in disgust. Her voice was cutting. "Yes. All the Traherns are handsome people."

Seth's eyes teased. "I know one little grandaughter who's a beauty."

She glanced away.

Seth looked around the room for the first time, walking to a group of drawings on the wall. He turned startled eyes back to Morgan. "This is you, isn't it?"

"Yes."

"But how did they get here? I thought you left New Mexico when you were a baby."

Morgan explained briefly about the agent her father had hired, and why he had written that preposterous will.

Seth threw his head back and laughed. Adam turned over in his bed but did not waken. Morgan opened the door and they both went into the hall.

"Would you mind telling me why my story is so amusing?" Her voice was hostile.

"Because I thought that will of your father's was one of the meanest things I'd ever encountered. But he was a sly one. He knew all along about that crazy mother of yours and the way she'd raised you."

"My mother was not crazy!"

"I shouldn't have put it that way. I'm sorry."

"I've found that a lot of things my mother taught me were perfectly true."

"Such as?"

"Men! Men are not to be trusted. They use women. Women are better off without them."

She didn't see Seth move, but all at once, she was in his arms. Before she could think, his lips found hers, quietly at first and then searchingly. Her arms went around his strong, hard body, pulling him closer. Her long-withheld passions came to the surface, and she felt she was falling.

Her body acted by itself, pressing her softness against his muscular thighs and hips. Her mouth opened under his and she returned his thrust with an eagerness of her own. Her lips moved with his. His lips sought her neck, traveling down the tendons with little nibbling bites, causing chills along the curve of her spine and on her legs. "I love you, Morgan. I've always loved you."

The words pierced her brain, recalling a time when she had said those words to him. She remembered his sneer. She couldn't let it happen again. She wasn't going to fall in love with him again and be hurt like that. He was not trustworthy. It might happen again.

"No," she whimpered. "No."

Somewhere in the back of his mind, Seth heard her protest. He loved her. He could not hurt her, not again. She wasn't ready yet. He'd gone too fast. He must leave, get away from her, because he wouldn't be able to contain himself much longer.

He would wait. There'd be another time, a time when she'd welcome him. He held her at arm's length. Her eyes held passion and rage. He smiled down at her and tenderly kissed her forehead. Her breath was soft and warm, still coming in gasps.

He turned and ran lightly down the stairs. Holding his hat in his hand, he stopped in the doorway and looked back up at her. He grinned at her. "I'm glad you still remember me."

Morgan stood for a long time, staring at the closed door. Remember him! She wanted to follow him and tell him what a selfish oaf he was, and how conceited. To think his kiss meant anything to her!

She went shakily downstairs to the study to finish balancing the accounts. She sat at the thick pine desk and began adding figures. But after a few minutes she turned and gazed out the window, unseeing. She stayed that way for a long time.

Morgan looked at the clock and realized the entire afternoon had passed. It was nearly time for dinner. Hearing Adam's squeal from the kitchen, she went to investigate.

Adam sat on a stool at the big work table in the center of the kitchen, shaping pieces of gingerbread.

"Those are the ugliest people I have ever seen. Why do some of them have four eyes?"

"I believe, Mrs. Colter, that some of those eyes are supposed to be ears."

Morgan tweaked Adam's ear. "Ears don't grow beside your nose."

Adam laughed and pushed her hand away. "Ears." He put a piece of raw dough in his mouth.

Morgan left the kitchen and went upstairs to change for dinner. Since Adam's nap had been so late, she decided, he could eat with Gordon and her tonight.

When Morgan entered the dining room some time later, the first thing she saw was Seth's broad back. He was impeccably dressed in the suit he had worn the night of the party. Morgan felt her anger rise again. She would have to tell Gordon to stop inviting him to dinner so often.

"Oh, Morgan, I hope you don't mind my inviting Dave to dinner tonight. I'm finding I can learn a lot about ranching from him."

She had no time to construct an answer before Martin entered, holding Adam's hand. Adam immediately ran to Seth, his arms outstretched.

"How are you, Adam? I haven't seen you in hours. Did you have a good nap?"

Adam smiled at his father and pointed to the table. "Eat."

"This boy certainly knows what he wants." Seth put Adam on a stool, next to what was fast becoming his own chair. The two sat directly across from Morgan.

"Might I say, Mrs. Colter, that you look especially lovely tonight? Red becomes you."

"Thank you," she said tonelessly. She just wouldn't look at him. She had a brief vision of the beautiful red dress she wore — wore for Seth — at Joaquín's party. It had disappeared on that horrible night, along with all her dreams.

Morgan stared at her plate as Seth and Gordon talked about the ranch. It seemed even Adam had deserted her. Of course, a mere mother always took second place to food. It infuriated her that Seth cared for the boy so easily. Adam's plate was never empty, and Seth saw to his needs as if he'd been doing this for years. Adam's placid acceptance of his father also made her angry. She was being betrayed by the person she loved most in the world.

Morgan was startled when Seth pushed his chair back. "If you'll excuse me, I think I'll put my . . . partner to bed." His smile was innocent, but she knew what he had wanted to say.

When they were gone, Gordon turned to her. "I'm glad he's gone, because I want to talk to you about something."

She opened her mouth to say that she was glad he was gone for any reason, but she closed it again.

"I know there'll be no problem, but I did want to discuss it with you first. For the good of the ranch, I'd like Dave to move into the house."

"What?"

"You know that trip I've been planning to New York will be soon. I don't like to leave you and Adam here alone. I'd like to have a man here in the house to protect you."

"Protect me! Has it ever occurred to you that maybe I need protection *from* Mr. Blake?"

Gordon was instantly concerned. "Has he ever mistreated you?"

"No, he hasn't . . ."

"Good. I thought I knew Dave better than that. Adam, of course, adores him. I just can't get over the way the child has taken to him, as if . . ."

"I've heard this before. Why do you think it is necessary for Mr. Blake to move into the house?"

"Morgan, I don't like to bear the entire responsibility for running this ranch. I'm afraid to leave, even to go to Albuquerque. Just when I think I can relax, something happens, like Boyd and the other men quitting to go to the gold fields."

"What makes you think Mr. Blake won't run off somewhere, too?"

"For one thing, he's older, more settled than the other men. And if I pay him more and offer him a room in the house, those would be incentives to stay. Dave's different. He shouldn't be treated like just another hired hand."

"So you plan to allow him into the house."

"He deserves it. Look at the way he cares

for Adam. I wouldn't trust Adam with any of the other men. They're likely to put him down somewhere and forget him. Not Dave."

"Must I be plagued day and night with sermons on this man's virtues? I'm sure if we knew all there is to know about Mr. Blake, we'd know things of which he isn't proud."

"I'm sure there are. But no one's perfect. Then you really have no specific objection to Dave moving to the house? The good really does seem to outweigh the bad."

Seth returned. "Dave, I've just talked to Morgan about your moving into the house, and she would be happy to have you."

They had already discussed it! Her opinion meant nothing. Gordon ignored the look she shot him.

"I thank you very much for the invitation, Mrs. Colter. I hope I prove to be of assistance to you and your son."

Gordon forestalled her reply. "I've taken the liberty of having Carol prepare your room." Gordon again ignored the look Morgan flashed at him. "Come upstairs and I'll show it to you. It was Morgan's father's room."

Morgan didn't follow them. She was furious with Gordon for planning all this without her consent. It wouldn't be easy to stay away from Seth when she saw him every morning at breakfast.

Her *father's* room? Hadn't Gordon said that? Morgan nearly toppled the dining chair in her hurry to get upstairs. Her father's room was next to hers, and there was a connecting door between them!

They were in the room and Morgan stared at the door that led to her room. She tried to catch Gordon's eye, but failed.

"If you'll excuse me, Mrs. Colter, I'll get my gear from the bunkhouse."

She held her tongue until she heard the downstairs door close. "He can't have this room! It's right next to mine!"

"Morgan, have you seen the other bedrooms in this house? The housekeeper your father and mine had when this house was built decorated every bedroom for women, except three — the one Adam has, my room, and this one. I can't see Dave with a pink coverlet and chintz curtains."

"We'll redecorate, we'll . . ."

"Don't be silly, Morgan. The door locks from both sides." He walked to the door and demonstrated that it was firmly locked. "It's as if there were no door."

"It's not the same at all," she murmured.

"Morgan, I know it was a shock, seeing

Dave for the first time. But his resemblance to someone you dislike is not his fault. The way you treat him is not fair. He's a very warm person when you get to know him . . . Well, it's been a long day." Gordon yawned ostentatiously. "I think I'll go to bed. I'm sure Dave can find his own room."

"Yes, I'm sure he can."

Gordon did not fail to note the sarcastic tone in her voice.

Locked in her own room, she removed her gown and put it away carefully. She stepped into one of her favorite nightgowns and sat before the mirror to unpin and brush her hair. She stopped in midmotion when she heard Seth enter the room next door. She listened. Drawers opened and closed. The wardrobe door clicked. She heard his boots drop to the floor.

It's as if he's in this room, she thought. She looked toward the connecting door. There was silence, and then she saw the light under his door go out. She went to her own bed, blew out the lamp, and snuggled under the covers. She was feeling that peaceful relaxation just before sleep comes, when the words carried through the door to her. "Goodnight, *mi querida.*" Seth's voice was a caress. The familiar endearment relaxed her even more and she fell asleep easily.

Seth stared at the room. He was glad to be out of the bunkhouse. Every time one of those men had made a crack about Morgan, he had had a difficult time controlling himself. Now there was only one thin door separating her from him. He was calm for the first time in weeks. He hadn't liked the idea of her being alone in this house, alone with Gordon. Even if there didn't seem to be a romantic love between them, she was his. He meant to keep her that way.

He laughed at himself. Now, Colter, that's what caused all your trouble before — your possessive jealousy. This time he wasn't going to ruin things. After the long kiss this afternoon, he knew she still felt something for him. It wouldn't be long before that little door would open. He drifted off to sleep, confident.

Adam was awake especially early the next morning. He tumbled out of his bed, opened his door, and sleepily made his way to his mother's room, just as he always did. Seth heard the stumbling steps and hastily donned his pants and intercepted Adam before he could pound on Morgan's door.

Adam opened his eyes in surprise when

Seth swept him up in his arms. His father put his finger to his lips and Adam understood. The little boy snuggled against the strong chest and closed his eyes. When Seth deposited his son in the big bed, Adam immediately turned on his stomach and went back to sleep. Seth removed his pants and climbed back into bed, leaving the hall door open. Soon both father and son were asleep.

When Morgan woke, she had a feeling something was wrong. She opened her eyes, frowning. The sun was up and there was a long ray of sunlight seeping in under the curtains. It was later than usual. She was so used to her son's waking her up and then climbing into her bed and going back to sleep that she had learned to sleep through the disturbance. She turned to Adam. He wasn't there!

Disregarding her robe, she ran from her room. The door to Adam's room was open, but he wasn't in the room. Gordon's door was closed. She was alarmed. He couldn't disappear, not her little Adam. Tears blurred her eyes. She looked down the stairs. He could have fallen down them in his long nightshirt. She must calm herself. Maybe Roselle or Martin had taken him to the kitchen. She listened, but there were no sounds downstairs. Her hand flew to her mouth. Then she saw the bedroom door next to her own standing slightly open.

She pushed the door open, brushing away the tears in relief as she saw the little curly head just above the covers. She offered a silent prayer of thanks. She'd been so silly. She should have known that Seth's presence would upset everyone's life. She shut her eyes in exhaustion.

Seth opened his eyes to see Morgan standing near him. He might move his hand and clasp her waist, but he lay still. Her eyes were closed and she was breathing deeply, her breasts thrusting forward under the thin gown. The gown fit her perfectly, hugging her body closely to the waist and then flaring out softly in a bell shape. It was a deep, rich blue with long, tight sleeves that curved out at the wrist. The neckline covered her collarbone and then plunged deeply, almost to the waist, edged by cream-colored lace. Her hair was rumpled and fell about her to the waist. Never had he seen her more desirable. He caught her hand in his and her eyes flew open.

"I —" she began.

"You don't need an excuse to be here." She tried to pull her hand away, but he held it easily, caressing the fingertips.

"I came to find my son. He usually comes

to my room. When he didn't, I was worried."

Seth's eyes were gentle. He pulled her hand to his mouth. He kissed the fingertips, raking the sensitive tips across his teeth. Her scalp tightened.

"Stop it!" His grasp on her hand was firm.

"I am limiting myself to only your fingertips. I like that blue thing, especially the lace."

Her hand covered the lace which played hide-and-seek with the soft curve of her breasts. She looked straight at him, one eyebrow arched, challenging. "Theron bought me this gown. He bought me many beautiful things."

"Theron," Seth murmured. "Nice man. Not your type, though. Lovely house." He was concentrating on his pleasant task. His teeth made little bites in the palm of her hand.

"Seth, will you stop that!"

"I don't plan to. I may stay here all day and make love to your hand. You used to love it."

"When did you meet Theron?" She had to think of something else or her whole body might start shivering.

"When I asked him where you were. You have the sweetest little veins in your wrist."

He nibbled at them.

"Seth! Theron told you where I was? Why would he do that?" She made one supreme effort and succeeded in jerking her hand from Seth's grasp. She took a few deep breaths to calm herself.

Seth gave a disappointed sigh and sat up in the bed. The quilts fell away to his waist, exposing his massive chest. The movement caused Adam to stir. He sat up and rubbed his eyes.

"Morgan, sit down, please, and I'll tell you about Theron." He nodded toward Adam, quietly staring from one parent to the other.

She sat carefully on the edge of the bed.

"I told Theron what a fool I'd been. He agreed. But I told him how much I loved you and that I wanted a chance to win you back."

"Oh, yes, you loved me — *after* you found out I was pure."

Adam watched his mother. He didn't like her tone of voice and he began to frown, her agitation scaring him.

"That's not really true, love." Seth's voice was calm. "I admitted to myself a long time before I met Jessy that I loved you." He continued before she could protest, "I would have come to you then, begged you to let me live with you. But I didn't think you'd want me, poor as I was, not after the way you were accustomed to living, with Theron. Did I mention that I am a rich man now?"

Her look was steely. "Twenty-five thousand dollars should make you quite comfortable."

Seth was puzzled. "Twenty-five . . . ? Oh, the money you offered me to marry you. I told you that never meant anything to me."

"How am I to know what to believe? Now you tell me you always loved me, but I remember some other things you said to me, such as accusing me of selling my body. You didn't seem to love me then. Tell me this: When am I to believe you, and when am I not?"

Seth didn't lose his slow, even smile. "I deserve your abuse. I deserve everything you have to say about me. I was a fool. I was hurt and jealous and I struck out at you.

"I want to make it up to you, Morgan. I love you and I plan to stay near you until you love me again, even if it takes years."

"You seem confident that everything will work just as you plan. What if I told you that I loved someone else and that I couldn't love you?" She looked toward the bedroom door.

Seth's smile broadened. "I've seen Gordon kiss you, and I've kissed you. If you love him and hate me, then I prefer your hatred. It has more fire."

"You — !" She struck him on the chest with her fist, but it was the same as striking an adobe wall, for all the damage it did.

Seth enclosed her fist in one of his, then encircled the other wrist with strong fingers. He pulled her to him, crushing her helpless arms between them. He entangled his hand in her hair, cradling the back of her head. He touched his lips to hers, sweetly, and then with a demanding eagerness. He forced her mouth open. Morgan responded fully, meeting his demands with more of her own.

Adam had never seen his mother kissed before, and he wasn't sure her moans didn't mean Seth was hurting her. He hit Seth's shoulder with his fists. "Mama. Mama."

Morgan heard her son and began to return to reality, forcing herself away from Seth.

Seth extended his now-empty arms to his son, to reassure him. "I don't know whether he's trying to protect you or me."

"You?"

"A little fire goddess like his mother could easily destroy a mere mortal like me."

She raised her hand to him again, but his

teasing smile reminded her of what had just happened.

Angrily, she lifted Adam into her arms. "You're going to have a long wait if you think I'll ever fall in love with you. I've made all my mistakes already."

She heard Seth's laughter behind her.

At breakfast, Seth ignored Morgan. Although she had planned to ignore him also, she found it infuriating that he should act as if she weren't even in the same room.

After Seth and Gordon left, Adam played in the courtyard with his wooden ranch set. Morgan needed to finish her ledgers and promised herself that she would not even think of Seth. But she looked up sharply each time someone passed the open study door.

At lunch, Adam proudly showed his mother his gingerbread monsters, explaining them in a mixture of gibberish and words. He went back outside for a while before his nap.

Morgan went upstairs to make sure the rooms had been cleaned properly. She hesitated at Seth's room, but then entered. His things were always neat, more so than hers ever were. She opened a drawer. He had too few shirts, and some of them needed mending. Angrily, she slammed the drawer shut. What was she doing? He was not her responsibility any longer. Let him care for his own shirts!

She ran into Carol, an armload of clean linen nearly falling from her arms. "Is anything wrong, Mrs. Colter?"

"No!" She fairly shouted at the girl. Morgan regretted it immediately, but Carol had already scurried away.

"Now he's making me yell at the servants," she mumbled as she hurried to her own room. Hastily, she donned her riding habit.

In the kitchen, she asked Roselle if she'd put Adam to bed for his nap, and she went outside to ride her horse. She started for her favorite place by the river, but she knew Seth went there, and she didn't want to see him. She remembered a pond that Gordon had shown her on the first day they'd toured the ranch together. It was an especially hot day and the sun was merciless. She loosened the high neck of the habit. The mare felt the heat, too.

The pond was a wider place in the river, forming a little pool, surrounded by tall cottonwoods. Gordon had said there would be cattails later in the fall. She dismounted, leading the mare to the trees. It would be good to splash her face with water.

She was startled by the sound of several horses beyond her, near the pond. Always cautious in the untamed New Mexico wilderness, she tied her horse and went to investigate before blundering into trouble. As she rounded a tree, she saw Seth leading several mustangs to water. As the dusty horses drank, Seth dismounted and walked to the edge of the water, letting his own horse drink.

Could she go nowhere without seeing him? She stood very still, knowing that any movement would cause him to turn and see her.

Seth removed his hat and wiped the sweat from his brow. Then he looked around. Morgan held her breath. She was thankful she'd worn her dark green riding habit.

Seth did not really see the place where Morgan stood, half hidden in the dense underbrush. Quickly, he removed his clothes and stepped into the water. He splashed himself, enjoying the coolness. Morgan looked on in fascination at the magnificent body she had once known so well, the powerful arms and shoulders, the muscles that stood out in his thighs.

Seth was used to the dangers of New Mexico, where a second's heedlessness could cause one's death. Over the years he had developed a second sense concerning these hazards. He stood still. He knew someone was watching him. He pivoted on one foot and faced Morgan, who gasped. Their eyes locked and held.

"Care to join me?"

She didn't answer, but whirled on her heel and returned to her waiting horse. She returned to her favorite spot and allowed the horse to drink before returning to the house. She tried not to think of Seth.

At dinner, the sight of Seth caused the blood to rush to her face. She refused even to glance his way during dinner. As they walked to the courtyard, Seth whispered, "Did you enjoy your bath as much as you enjoyed mine?" Blushes covered her body, and she was glad for the darkness.

CHAPTER TWENTY-TWO

It had been a little over two weeks since Seth had come to the Three Crowns. Since the time Morgan had seen him in the pool, she had avoided him. She saw him even less now than she had when he'd lived in the bunkhouse. He took his responsibilities as foreman very seriously and often missed dinner to straighten out some problem on the ranch. Even when Morgan came down to breakfast, she found he had already been at work for hours. What free time he did manage, he spent with Adam. Morgan sometimes felt Seth paid more attention to Roselle than he did to her. She was, of course, glad of that.

It was on one of the rare mornings when the three of them breakfasted together that Gordon made his announcement. "My letter finally came. I'll be leaving for New York."

"What?" She dropped her spoon.

"Morgan, I've told you about this trip for months, so don't look so surprised."

"Adam and I will go with you."

"Sit down. You are not going with me. It will be a hurried trip and Adam is too young to have to travel for days on a stagecoach and then on a train. I won't hear of it. It's too dangerous."

Seth turned to Gordon. "Is it ranch business that takes you to New York?"

"Morgan's father once heard about some cattle bred in the Scottish Highlands. He thought they might adjust to New Mexico, so he started working on getting them here. After several years, they'll soon arrive in this country. I figure if I'm not there to meet the ship when it docks, they'll sell my cattle to someone else."

"When are you leaving?" Morgan's voice was soft.

"Right after breakfast."

"Today! You'll be leaving *today?*"

Gordon stared at her a moment. "Yes. The letter took a long time coming and now I'll barely make it there in time for the ship. Martin is packing for me now."

After breakfast, Morgan tried again to persuade him to let Adam and her go with him.

"Don't worry. I'll be back shortly, and

Dave is here to take care of Adam and you."

"Adam, yes — but not me."

Gordon looked weary. "If I didn't trust Dave as much as I do, I wouldn't leave him here alone with you. When you get over your hostility, you'll trust him, too. I have to leave now or I'll never make the stage. Kiss me goodbye?"

"Gladly." She happily slid into Gordon's arms and lifted her lips for his kiss. Gordon was the man she wanted to love.

With great effort, he resisted her lips and placed a chaste kiss on her forehead. "Now, get Adam so I can say goodbye."

Morgan held her son and they both waved to Gordon. When she turned back to the house, it seemed empty already. Adam squirmed out of her arms. He ran to the kitchen and she followed him. Tonight she would be alone with Seth. Without Gordon's presence, he could talk to her about anything. She began planning the night's meal, remembering Seth's favorite dishes without realizing she was doing so.

She worked all day on the meal, glad to be too busy to think. Roselle put Adam to bed for his nap. Morgan rested for a while when the house was quiet. She worked again in the kitchen until it was time to bathe and dress for dinner. Roselle took charge of Adam.

From the back of the wardrobe, she took a dress that she had rarely ever worn before. It was simply cut, a deep golden yellow, embroidered with tiny sienna rosebuds around the neckline. The neckline was the reason she seldom wore the dress. It fell across her shoulders and the top of her breasts, stopping just above the rosy peaks. When she stood in front of the mirror, she remembered the last time she'd worn the dress. Charley Farrell had gaped at the enticing sight and she had been embarrassed at the open-mouthed stare he'd worn all evening.

She briefly asked herself why she was wearing this now when she and Seth were to be alone. She'd never worn it for Gordon. She told herself that she was wearing this only because she hadn't worn it in such a long time. She dabbed perfume on her wrists, behind her ears, and in the deep shadow between her breasts.

Carol came to tidy the room. "You look especially lovely, Mrs. Colter," the girl remarked shyly. "Mr. Blake will be very pleased."

"Mr. Blake — !" She cut short her remark.

"Will there be anything else tonight, ma'am?"

"No, Carol. You may go home. Be sure and say hello to your parents for me, and take them some gingerbread."

"Thank you, ma'am." She turned to leave, but saw Seth in the open doorway. He put his finger to his lips, conspiratorily. Carol did like Mr. Blake so much. He was always teasing — like Adam, except grown up. She left and closed the door behind her.

Morgan, at the mirror, heard footsteps behind her. "I don't need anything else —" She stopped when she felt his lips on the back of her neck, sending little shivers throughout her body. She closed her eyes, but opened them quickly when he moved away.

She whirled toward him. "What are you doing here?"

Seth smiled lazily at her and stretched out on her bed, his big, handsome figure nearly dwarfing the lacy, crochet-covered bed. "I live here, too, remember?"

"I just hope *you* remember that this is not your room. And may I remind you that this is my ranch, not yours."

"*Mi querida,* stop fighting me. I am looking forward to dinner. Roselle says you spent all day cooking, that you prepared a very special meal." His eyes were teasing.

"I did not! I like to cook and today I

wanted to, so I just made a few things." She turned her face away, took a deep breath, and turned back. "Kindly get off my bed and out of my room."

He moved his hips slightly, as if testing the bed. "Do you sleep well on it, or do you find it too large for one person?"

"Seth Colter! Get out of here!" She started toward him. Seth opened his arms to her and she backed away.

He sat up on the bed, feet over the side. "That another dress Theron bought for you?"

Morgan saw a slight frown crease his brow, and she felt momentarily triumphant. "Yes. Do you like it?" She bent over just slightly so her breasts swelled even more precariously over the top. "It's strange that you are just now noticing this dress. Most men notice it immediately."

The little imp is trying to make me jealous, Seth thought. He smiled at her. His eyes raked her body, devouring her. "When I look at you, my little wife, I see you as I always remember you — wearing nothing but your hair ribbon. So it takes me longer to notice your clothes."

"You —"

"If you try to throw something, I will have to restrain you." He held out his arm. "Let's go to dinner."

Seth sat across from Morgan. She refused to speak to him. They were into the second course, and Martin had left the room.

"Martin will know something is wrong if you keep your silence. He'll think we've had a lovers' quarrel." He raised his voice. "Tell, me, Mrs. Colter, about your travels in San Francisco."

She smiled up at him. "I met some very interesting people, some gentlemen." She emphasized the title.

Seth was serious. "Do you remember a Charley Farrell?"

"That's funny. I thought of Charley just tonight. Mr. Farrell is not a man one should think of too often. Theron and I did a lot of work for his wife. A pleasant woman, but the most atrocious taste imaginable."

"What about Farrell? Did you know him?"

"More than I wanted to, I'm afraid. Theron rescued me several times from his greedy little hands. Finally he told Mr. Farrell that if he didn't stop his attentions, we would not return. I think Theron also threatened to tell his wife. Charley was deathly afraid of her." She sipped her wine. "Where did you meet him?"

Seth looked down at his plate. "Just over a

beer once. I didn't really know him."

Morgan didn't understand Seth's sudden seriousness. If anyone should not be taken seriously, it was Charley Farrell.

Martin removed the last of the dishes.

"That was a feast," said Seth. "It seemed I couldn't get enough of everything."

"Well, if anyone could, you did. I don't believe I've ever seen anyone eat as much as you did."

He grinned at her. "I'm a growing boy. I need my strength."

"Martin, we'll have coffee in the courtyard — if that's all right with you, Mr. Blake."

They went outside and stood silent, listening to the New Mexico night sounds. There were coyotes near, howling. Seth walked to the little tiled pool. "It's nice to be here with you, Morgan. If I didn't know better, I'd think Gordon planned going away."

Morgan hid her face. The thought had crossed her mind, too.

"Remember the days we spent in the canyon, below the Indian ruin?"

"No."

He turned startled eyes toward her and then laughed. "Why don't you come over here and let me kiss you?"

"Stop it, Seth, or I'll go inside. All of that is over. We're just . . . acquaintances now."

"Good! Now that we're acquaintances, we can become friends. And then we can become lovers."

"Seth, you are impossible!"

"I hope you mean it's impossible for us not to love one another. Did you ever ask yourself why you asked *me* to marry you, and not one of the other men at the Ferguson ball?"

"I heard you had a ranch in New Mexico." She could hardly tell him she had liked his muscular thighs! She laughed.

Seth cocked his head and looked at her strangely. "Well, little one" — he walked toward her — "I think I'll go to bed." He put his hands on her shoulders and she drew back. He pulled her to him, their bodies close but not touching. Then he kissed her, lightly, on the cheek. "Goodnight, my wife." He released her and was gone.

She stood staring at the place where he had been. He had no manners! He should have walked her to her own bedroom instead of leaving her standing alone in a darkened garden. Angrily, she mounted the stairs. His door was closed and all was quiet in the big house. She pulled the pins from her hair and hastily removed her dress, carelessly tossing it over the back of a chair. She pulled a nightgown from the drawer, a thin muslin gown, almost transparent. In bed she tossed and turned, not even understanding the reason for her restlessness.

Seth smiled as he heard her movements. Oh, yes, sweet . . . you do remember the time in the canyon.

It wasn't long after Morgan fell asleep that she began to dream. She was back with Jacques and he had one hand on her hair, a knife at her throat. The Indians were watching. Then she saw Seth, heard his voice, calm and patient. "I'm here, sweetheart. There's no need to worry, *mi querida.*"

She woke up slowly, fighting the horror of the dream. Seth held her in his lap. Her arms encircled his neck and held him tightly to her. He spoke softly, using sweet words while caressing the back of her head. She cried softly.

"Do you want to tell me, little one?"

The story came pouring out in a torrent. She told him about Jacques, about the dream. Then she told of Joaquín's treachery, of the search that night for Seth, and then about the note. She told about Madame Nicole and how, on the night of the sale, she had seen Seth in the mirror and heard a music box. She didn't see the color drain from his face as he remembered the night before Christmas when he had smashed the little box.

Morgan sobbed out the story of her humiliation on the night of the auction. She told about her fondness for Theron. She told of that night when she had been so glad to see Seth, of how she'd prayed that he hadn't died, even though she had thought it was a hopeless prayer. There were tears in Seth's eyes. "I'm sorry, sweet one. I'm here, now, and I won't leave you again."

She was like a child. He cradled and rocked her. She needed his tenderness. And she desperately needed the release the tears brought. Gradually, her breathing quieted and he knew she was asleep. Gently, he put her in bed and pulled the quilt about her. She made a small sucking sound, like Adam. He kissed her cheek and the tears that remained in her eyelashes.

Reluctantly, he went to the door between their rooms. It was locked. Puzzled, he left the room through the door to the hallway. Out of curiosity, he tried the door again from his side. It opened.

Gordon, he thought. Somehow Gordon had found out about them and had arranged that they be alone together in the house. Of course, it wouldn't have been difficult to discover the truth, what with Mor-

gan constantly shouting, "Seth Colter! You
— !" It was music to his ears. If he guessed
correctly, Gordon planned to stay away until
he received word that Morgan and Seth
were together again.

Adam had just raised his fist to bang on his
mother's door when a big hand turned the
unreachable knob. He looked up to see his
father, his finger to his lips. Adam quietly
followed Seth into the room, stopping to
look down on the sleeping woman.

Seth planted a soft kiss on the little pulse
point below Morgan's ear. She smiled in
her sleep. Adam grinned up at his father
and decided to imitate him. The boy's
mouth missed the mark, falling loudly and
succulently on his mother's ear. Instantly,
Morgan's eyes opened and her hand flew to
her ear.

Adam and his father laughed together in
conspiracy. "The two of you! I can't even
sleep peacefully!" She had to laugh. They
were so much alike. "At least you should
behave better than your son. He has the
excuse of extreme youth."

Seth's grin broadened and Morgan could
swear his chest puffed out at least another
two inches.

"Why are you strutting about this morning?"

"That's the first time you've ever admitted that he's mine."

She frowned. "Of course, he's yours. Just look at him. I don't guess two people could look more alike."

Seth looked at his son adoringly. "I know, but I like to hear you say it anyway."

"You're worse than Lupita's roosters. He *has* to be yours. You're the only man I ever —" She hadn't meant to say that. He had no right to know.

Seth sat down heavily beside her. "I'm the only man who's ever made love to you?"

She looked away, absently watching Adam, who was pulling the lace trim from a pillowcase. "Yes," she whispered.

He grabbed her shoulders, pulled her to him, and kissed her loudly and heartily on the mouth. "I know it shouldn't matter, and I love you no matter what, but that makes me very happy. Son, before you destroy your mother's bed linens, how about a piggyback ride downstairs?" Adam climbed on his father's back and they stopped in the doorway. "Why don't you stay there? I'll give Adam to Roselle and I'll come back and join you."

Morgan rubbed her mouth, then her ear.

"I already have had two bruising kisses this morning. I certainly don't need any more."

"Maybe on second thought, I'll just push Adam out the door. He can yell all he wants — we'll never hear him." He closed the door quickly, as the pillow hit the door. Adam kicked his father in the ribs, laughing with gusto. He liked this man because exciting things always happened around him, like his mother throwing a pillow at them. She never did those things around other grown-ups. "Horse. Horse," he screamed.

At breakfast, Seth suggested that Morgan bring Adam to the river for a picnic lunch. He'd try to get away to join them.

"Well, it may be difficult. I have a lot to do." He was taking too much for granted.

"What is so urgent?"

He sounded as if she spent her days lounging in bed. Her voice was hostile. "This is September, so I have a lot of food to put up for the winter. And there's the household accounts, and . . ."

Seth looked down, contrite. "I just thought Adam might need a change of pace today."

Morgan turned away. "If I can get away, maybe we can go."

"Good!" She knew his pain had been an act. He kissed her cheek. "Have a good day, wife."

"Stop calling me that. Someone may hear."

He smiled at her. "I hope so, wife."

"Wife." Adam imitated his father.

"Oh, no. You're going to have the strangest vocabulary when Gordon returns."

"Gord?" Adam questioned.

They laughed together at their son.

Adam spent the morning playing with his ranch. The men of the ranch had spent some of their evenings carving new pieces. Now it was too big to carry inside at night. Seth had built a canopy over it, to protect it from the rain.

Morgan paid special attention to the cleaning of Seth's room and then spent two hours working with Roselle on a delicious picnic lunch.

When everything was ready, she and Adam went to their special place near the river. Seth was not there, so she spread the quilt and sat down with Adam. She recited nursery rhymes to him, illustrating them on the slate board she often packed.

"How're my wife and son?" He looked at Morgan innocently when she frowned at him. He was becoming far too possessive. Morgan immediately opened the picnic basket.

"*Brioches!* Morgan, you don't know how

often I used to think about these little rolls. In California, I ate some of the worst food imaginable. Jessy cooked for me for a while. I don't know how I survived it. Jessy would take a skillet and throw in some eggs with a generous helping of eggshells." He demonstrated with hand gestures. "When some of the eggs were still mostly raw and some were so hard you couldn't tell them from the skillet, she'd serve them to you. Now don't ask me by what magic Jessy was able to use one skillet and get the eggs to come out at opposite degrees of doneness. I was always too smart to ask."

Morgan was laughing helplessly.

"Wait, I haven't told you about the biscuits. They were so chewy that you put your fingers between your teeth, like this, and stretched them as long as your arm could reach. Now, explain that. No one dared ask about those biscuits. They were such a marvel that we rather looked forward to them."

Morgan held her stomach as she laughed. She could just imagine Jessy making biscuits like that. She'd had a taste or two of Jessy's cooking. She'd love to send a recipe for those biscuits to Jean-Paul.

As Morgan laughed, Adam held his slate to his father and said, "Horse."

Seth wrote on the slate: *Seth loves Morgan with all his heart.* He handed the slate to her. She looked into his eyes and saw that what he wrote was true. She wiped the laughter tears from her eyes, erased the slate, and drew Adam's horse.

"I have to get back to work now. Kiss me goodbye? On the cheek?"

She laughed at him for playing the same tricks as Adam did when he wanted something. "All right, I'll kiss your cheek." She stood up and leaned toward him, and as they both knew they would, they clung to one another. When their lips met, there was no resistance from Morgan.

"You won't forget me?" He smiled down into her half-closed eyes. He turned to Adam. "A hug for your daddy, son?" Adam ran to his father's arms and Seth tossed the boy into the air and then rubbed the stubble of his whiskers in Adam's neck. The child screamed with delight. Seth left them both, waving.

When they returned to the house, Adam took his nap and Morgan undressed and lay on her bed. When had she realized she still loved Seth? Maybe when she'd seen the slate and knew he could be trusted completely. Yes, this time he could be believed and trusted.

What about what he had done, that horrible night in San Francisco? Somehow, the memory wasn't so clear anymore. Now there were memories of Seth playing with Adam, Seth comforting her after a bad dream. She didn't know if he had changed, if maybe some little thing might still set him into a jealous rage. She didn't care.

She would let the future take care of itself. She had him near her, and that's where she wanted him to stay. If he wanted her, then she was his.

Dinner was pleasant and Morgan relaxed and enjoyed the freedom that admitting her love for Seth had bestowed on her.

Afterward, they drank *café au lait* in the courtyard. Seth sat on a stone bench and put his arm across the back. Morgan watched him closely, hoping he'd ask her to join him. It seemed that for weeks she had fought his aggression, and now he left her alone! He finally patted the seat beside him and looked at her questioningly. She tried to keep calm, to walk toward him sedately and not run into his arms.

They sat quietly together. Morgan realized she felt safe, at home here beside Seth. She had never felt that way in San Francisco or even on the Colter ranch. For some reason she thought of Jake, of the way he had been so angry with her for always eating. She laughed.

"Share it with me?"

"What?"

"What were you thinking about that made you laugh?"

"Jake and the way he used to get so mad at me."

"Why would Jake ever get mad at you? I wrote them all when I came here, so they'd know I was still alive. I'm afraid I didn't tell anyone where I was when I was in California. But tell me, what made Jake mad? Maybe that you'd even speak to me after the way I acted at Montoya's party? I guess he knew we'd . . . ah . . . spoken." His eyes twinkled.

"That was part of the problem. You see, when I was carrying Adam, I ate."

"I don't understand. How could Jake be upset about that?"

"When I say I ate, I mean I ate *constantly,* for six months. I ate anything Lupita cooked."

Seth laughed softly. "I've been doing that for years."

"That's what I mean. I ate as much as you and it made me the same size as you."

Seth smiled in disbelief.

"You remember how Lupita's cottons always swallowed me? By the time Adam was born, they barely stretched across my body."

"But Lupita's twice as big as you are! I would have liked to see that. I'll bet you looked like a little barrel." He smiled down at her. "You seem to have lost all that weight."

Morgan's heart beat faster as she looked up into his eyes. He'd kiss her now, and she wanted him to.

"I think it's time to go to bed."

She took his arm, feeling the muscles under the smooth fabric. Her heart was pounding and her ears rang. He stopped with her outside her bedroom door and leaned down, his lips very close to hers. She closed her eyes and then opened them instantly when she felt his kiss on her cheek. She frowned.

"Goodnight, *mi querida*." He was gone, into his own bedroom, the door closed.

She undressed angrily and flounced about the room before finally going to sleep.

Seth had misinterpreted her frown. He decided to go slower with her. She probably still needed time to learn to trust him.

CHAPTER TWENTY-THREE

When Morgan woke, the house was quiet. As she stretched her arm across the bed, she looked up in alarm, then lay down again, quietly. Adam was with his father again. She turned over on her back and then yawned, stretching luxuriously. It was good to admit she loved Seth. For the first time in a long while, she was at peace. Who knew what could happen now?

She tossed the covers aside and bounded out of bed. She looked at herself critically in the mirror. She brushed her hair just slightly, pulling a few curls close to her face. She nodded at her reflection, then giggled. "Why, Morgan Colter, you are becoming positively vain."

In the hall, she saw that both Adam's and Seth's doors were closed. She took a deep breath to calm her shaking body. What if he didn't want her anymore? He could have decided that she wasn't worth all the effort.

As she lifted her shaking hand to knock lightly on the door, she reminded herself of all the times Seth had chided her for her lack of self-confidence. She could ride a horse and she could cook, but it still always startled her when men stared at her.

There was no answer from within, so she silently opened the door and tiptoed to Seth's bedside. He had thrown the sheet back from his body, exposing his full, broad chest. Lightly, she touched the hair at his temples. His eyes flew open and she stared into them, losing herself in the depth of feeling she saw there. Without a word between them, he held out his arms and she went to him.

For a moment they just held one another. Morgan felt she'd come home: the arms were safe. Here at last was peace. Her restful state of mind left her as Seth began kissing her hair, her eyes, nibbling on her ears. She had had enough quiet.

"I love you so much." His soft breath made chills on her legs and down her spine. "I've tried to be patient, but it's not easy. I want you. I need you. Can't you tell me you have a little feeling for me? I know I did a terrible thing, but can't you find forgiveness in your heart?"

There were too many questions to answer.

Her mind was leaving her, her body taking control. Seth's lips were on her, his body touching hers. She wanted to tear the gown from her body, wanted her flesh to touch his. "Yes," she murmured.

"Yes, what?" He was kissing her neck — not just kissing it, but making love to it as if it were the only part of her body.

"Yes, I forgive you."

He pulled her from him and held her at arm's length. "You forgive me?"

"Yes, I do. I may regret it, but it seems I do forgive you for all the horrible things you've done."

"Horrible! I'll show you who's horrible." He pulled her close beside him, and he began tickling her, and rubbing the morning stubble of his beard against her neck and cheek. She laughed hilariously, enjoying the familiar play of Seth's love. But something was wrong. A second sense told her there was reason for alarm. The warning grew louder and louder in her mind, screaming over her laughter, her joy at holding Seth in her arms once again. *Adam!* Where was Adam?

"Seth." She began to push him away. The alarm blocked out all passion. "Seth! Where's Adam?"

"He's probably still asleep," he whispered

into her ear. His hand was on her body, stroking the soft curve of her hip.

"No. Adam never sleeps late, at least not in his own room. I have to go see. Something's wrong."

Seth drew back and stared down into her face. He saw the concern, the fear. He started to tell her how silly she was, but he stopped. He'd have the rest of his life to talk about Adam. Right now she needed reassurance. "Well, go then. And then you can come back here. Better yet, I'll go with you and then I'll make sure you come back with me." He held her close to him as they went to Adam's room. "I don't plan to let you out of my room for at least two weeks. Adam can pound on the door for hours, but I need you more than he does. See," they stood in the child's doorway, "he looks like a little cherub."

Morgan frowned. Adam was too peaceful. Something was wrong. Every morning Carol had to remake Adam's bed from the sheets up because he tore everything off during the night. This morning the light quilt was still tucked in, not in its usual place on the floor. Quickly, she crossed the room and smoothed his hair from his forehead. His face was hot, very hot.

Her face drained of color and she turned

to Seth. Instantly, he was beside his son, his large hands holding the boy's head. His neck was swollen and his skin was almost burning. Adam whimpered at his father's touch. Seth's face held the same look as Morgan's. "I'll get the doctor." His voice was harsh, reflecting a depth of fear he'd never known before.

Minutes later, Morgan heard him running down the stairs, and then there were the sounds of a horse's hooves.

Morgan was numb. She dropped to her knees and took her son's little hand. It was so dry and so very, very hot. Adam had never been sick. He couldn't be sick. He was too little to bear pain. "Adam, sweetheart," she whispered as she held the listless little hand to her cheek.

Adam's eyelids fluttered. "Mama." His voice was rough, barely audible. He swallowed and his eyes screwed up tightly as he tried to stand the pain.

"I'm here, baby. Mama's right here and Daddy's gone for the doctor. When he gets here, he'll make you well. You'll feel better then. The doctor will make it all stop hurting."

"Mrs. Colter!" Roselle entered the room. "I heard Mr. Blake running down the stairs. Is everything all right?" She stopped when she saw Morgan's face. Never had she seen such bleakness, such despair. She looked at Adam, too quiet, his mother holding his hand. "Adam!" She touched his burning little forehead and her eyes drooped.

Once before, this had happened. She was reliving that time. Her little girl had been like Adam, and about his age, too. Sarah, her sweet, always-active little girl. One morning she'd found her in her bed, so quiet and so hot. In less than a week, she'd died. She'd never really gotten over Sarah, or the pain of washing and dressing that sweet little body for the final time. Please, dear God, don't let it all happen again.

"What can I do?" Morgan's eyes implored the older woman.

Roselle tried to control her rising hysteria. "Did Mr. Blake go for the doctor?"

"Seth. He's not Mr. Blake, he's Seth Colter, Adam's daddy." She stroked Adam's hand and arm.

"I thought so." Roselle had to calm herself and calm Morgan. She left the room and returned with a dress and underclothes. She lifted Morgan from her knees and began dressing her, as if she were a child. She kept up a steady stream of talk. "It's probably just one of those childhood things, the things children always get. I'm sure he'll be well in no time at all."

"Adam's never sick. He's never even had a bad cold."

"Well, then, it's time he had one." Roselle tried not to let the fear into her voice.

"He's so still. Why isn't he yelling, 'Eat, eat,' like he always does? Adam." She fell to her knees again. "Mommy will get you some chicken. Would you like some chicken? Or cookies? Would Mommy's baby like some cookies?"

Adam made a great effort to open his eyes. Morgan gasped at the pain she saw in them.

Roselle put her arm around the other woman's shoulders, forcefully lifting her. "Please, Mrs. Colter, sit here." She pulled a chair close to the bed. "Adam doesn't want to eat now. Just wait until the doctor comes. He'll know what to do." She started toward the door. "I'll send Carol up with some breakfast for you."

When Morgan was alone, she felt the full fear rising in her throat, threatening to choke her. For some reason, Roselle's statement that Adam didn't want to eat was more frightening than his extraordinary quiet or even his fever-ridden little body. Adam always ate. He was born hungry and his little life was controlled by food. His first word had been "Eat!" It had not been a quiet attempt at the word, but one day it had just exploded from his lips in a demand. She remembered how she and Jake, Lupita and Paul, had all laughed. Adam had ignored them. He had demanded food and he expected it to be served to him.

Adam didn't want to eat. The words repeated themselves over and over in her brain. His face was flushed, the fever making his cheeks a vivid red. That couldn't be Adam, she thought. Adam was always a blur of motion. He's playing a game, to make me bake him some cookies. Yes, that's what he wants. I'll bake him thousands of cookies, but I can't go to the kitchen now because I must be here when he opens his eyes.

She stroked his forehead. It was so dry. Adam was usually wet. He sweat all the time, just like his father. He played hard, running and laughing so much that perspiration often soaked his hair.

"When you get over your bad cold, Adam, Mommy will bake you some cookies, and some little cakes with lots of icing. We'll write 'Adam' on them and 'horse' and 'eat' . . . and we'll draw pictures."

Adam opened his eyes and stared at his mother in bewilderment. He didn't understand what was happening to him. In his whole life, the only pain he'd experienced was scraped knees and skinned elbows. When those things had happened, he'd gone to his mother and her kisses had made the hurt stop. Now his mother was here and the pain didn't go away. He didn't understand, not at all.

Morgan didn't know how long she sat there. She was vaguely aware of Roselle and Carol entering and leaving the room. A few times she heard someone telling her to eat. The lump was still in her throat and she knew she could swallow nothing. Didn't they understand that if her baby couldn't eat, then neither could she?

She heard voices outside the door and recognized Seth's. He'd have the doctor. She felt relief flood her body. "The doctor's here, baby. He'll make you well. He'll make the pain go away."

She ran to meet Seth. "Where's the doctor?"

"He's coming. Is he any better?"

"No, Seth. He's so hot. So hot, and he's so little."

Seth held his wife's hand. It was cold. They went together to Adam's bed. Seth's fears mounted. In the few hours since he'd been gone, Adam looked as if he'd shrunk.

His entire face was red, splattered with ghostly white splotches.

"This is Dr. Larson, Morgan, and this is Mrs. Colter."

"Our son, doctor! He's so little and he hurts. He's never been sick before."

Seth took her arm, quieting her. He noticed she'd said "our son." He was glad she was ready to admit their relationship because, in his haste, he had given the doctor his real name.

"I'll do what I can, Mrs. Colter."

The doctor, an older, corpulent man, pulled back the covers and began to examine Adam. As he pulled up Adam's nightshirt, Morgan gasped at the redness. Seth's grip on her arm tightened.

"I think this is the culprit." He turned Adam's leg to show a bump, large and inflamed, on the calf of his left leg. "It seems to be some kind of insect bite."

"Some kind? *What* kind? What kind of insect bite?!"

"That, Mrs. Colter, I don't know. I've seen a couple of these cases, but not many. A lot of people think it's some kind of tick bite, but no one knows for sure."

Morgan sighed. It didn't matter what the cause was, just the cure. "What do we do now? How do we make him well?"

"There's not much I know to do, really. If the boy's healthy, he'll fight it off. But if not, then you ought to prepare yourself."

She smiled at the doctor. Her hearing wasn't working at all. Through the mist, she heard Seth's voice.

"There's absolutely nothing we can do?"

"Try to get some liquids down him. And pray. That's all anyone can do. He'll probably have diarrhea soon, and he'll need to replenish the water he loses."

The fog was beginning to clear. What did he mean, "prepare yourself"? The doctor was leaving. She pulled away from Seth. "You can't leave! My baby is sick. He needs you! You have to help him."

The doctor's eyes were sad. He looked up at Seth as the big man took his wife's shoulders in his hands. At Seth's silent nod, he left the room. God! he thought, there were times when he hated his job.

Her voice was high, rising higher. "He can't do anything? My baby is sick and he can't do anything? He says to prepare myself."

Seth's fingers bit into her shoulders. "Listen to me. Adam is sick, very sick. He needs you. You can't indulge yourself in hysterics now. Do you hear me? Adam needs you."

"Yes." Her chin came up. "Adam needs me."

"Now the doctor said to try to get some liquids into him, and that's what we're going to do. Adam knows you best of all and he trusts you. You'll feed him."

"Feed him, yes."

"I'm going to the kitchen to tell Roselle, and when I come back, I want you in that chair and quiet. Adam needs his mother now, not some crazy woman tearing her hair. Do you understand?"

"Yes. Adam needs his mother."

Morgan sat obediently by Adam's bedside. Carol entered. "I'm sure he'll be all right, Mrs. Colter. My little brother has fevers all the time, but he always gets well."

Morgan tried to smile at the girl.

Seth returned carrying a steaming bowl of beef broth. "I'll hold him up while you feed him."

Adam's eyes hardly fluttered when Seth lifted him. Seth was shocked by the incredible heat emanating from the child's body. He felt so fragile in Seth's arms. He opened his eyes when the warm spoon touched his lips. He swallowed and then his eyes screwed together in pain as the liquid went down his throat. He moaned in agony. He turned away from the spoon his mother held and looked at her in question. Why did she want to cause him pain?

"It hurts him, Seth. He can't eat it."

"Try again." Adam kept his lips sealed, refusing more of the broth. Seth lowered him. "We'll try again later."

Carol came into the room carrying clean towels and a basin of warm water. She also held diapers. Seth stared at the diapers. Adam hadn't worn them in months.

His mother and father bathed the fevered child and changed his gown. Then they sat down to wait. There was nothing else to do.

The house was silent. No one made any loud noises. Morgan bathed her son's face continually. Roselle brought food, but neither parent touched it. They watched their son, locked together in one purpose.

"I feel so helpless, Seth, I just don't know what to do. Adam has always been such a sweet child. Everyone has always loved him. The only time he's ever selfish is when someone threatens his food. Now —" She wiped a tear from her eye. "— now he can't eat."

"Morgan!" Seth's voice held a warning. "I don't know what to do. If only there were something . . . someone . . ."

He dropped his head onto his hands, his elbows on his knees. "I never know what to do. I nearly died once, when Montoya shot me. Lupita said I had a fever for two weeks. She said . . ." He stopped and looked up at Morgan. "Lupita," he whispered. He stood up. "Lupita!" He shouted her name. "I'll go get her. Lupita will save my boy. I know she will. I'll get her."

Morgan ran to her husband. Here, at last, was hope. "Can you do it, Seth? Can you get her here soon? It took us two days to get from your ranch to here."

"I'll do it. Hell won't stop me. Lupita will save him, I know she can." He stared down at his wife. He kissed her mouth hard, quickly. "Take care of him. Get Roselle to hold him and you feed him. Ill be back as soon as possible — with Lupita." He pulled her to him and held her for a few seconds. "God knows Adam, and He'll take care of him. He won't let anything happen to our little boy." He released her and was gone. Within seconds, she heard the horse's hooves.

"Mrs. Colter, you really should eat You must keep up your strength."

"Could you get me some milk for Adam? Maybe that will coat his throat and hurt less."

Adam took very little of the milk, whimpering in pain when his mother tried to make him drink it. She gave in to his help-less pleas and set the glass aside. She moistened his lips with a few droplets of water. She bathed his body.

All night she sat by his bed, watching for any signs of change. There were none. In the morning, he began to moan and toss about on the bed. He began to sweat and the dreaded diarrhea started.

"Roselle, you'll have to help me. We need to get fluids into him, or he'll lose every-thing."

Together, they tried to force him to drink the liquids, but they did not succeed. Most of it spilled down his front.

Roselle watched her mistress as she changed Adam's gown. Her hair was a tangle of snarls, her dress was covered with stains from trying to feed Adam. There were bluish circles under her eyes.

They heard a horse outside the house and Morgan ran to see who it was. Her shoulders drooped when she saw Martin. Of course it couldn't be Seth. He hadn't had time to get back yet.

"Martin's been to the bunkhouse to tell the men about Adam, and that Seth will be gone for a few days."

Bunkhouse? Oh, yes, there was a ranch . . . but she cared nothing for it right now.

"Mama. Mama." Adam's head turned on the pillow. He was asleep, or seemed to be.

"I'm here, baby. Mama's here." His little palm was wet though she had just washed him.

Hours later, Roselle brought tea for Morgan. Adam's body was hot again and he made feeble attempts to kick off the light quilt, but he had no strength. She tried again and again to feed him.

Roselle handed Morgan the cup and saucer and, automatically, she took it. The porcelain dishes rattled against one another as she held them in her shaking hands. She sipped the tea, finding it an effort to do so. Her whole body seemed to be trembling.

"You have to get some rest, now. Stretch out here and I'll stay with him while you sleep."

"Yes." She was weary, but when she lay on the cot, her body remained tense.

"Mama." She was at his side instantly. He was cold now, and even his teeth were chattering. Roselle ran for more blankets, and Morgan held her little son tightly in her arms. His body seemed to become more frail with each passing moment. She tried to get him to drink some hot milk, but his little throat was too sore.

In the late afternoon, Roselle got Morgan

to drink some hot broth, and again tried to persuade her to sleep on the cot. She had Martin carry a loveseat from downstairs into the room. Morgan sank onto it and leaned back into the corner. Adam was still, sleeping peacefully again.

Morgan didn't know when she fell asleep, but when she woke, there was a quilt over her and Roselle smiled at her from across Adam's bed. She was grateful to the woman and said so. The sleep gave her new energy. She renewed her vigilance, this time trying to coax apple juice into the little body.

Seth rode hard all the way to Albuquerque. At the livery stable, he gasped out his reason for hurry and soon there was a fresh horse saddled and ready to go. In the middle of the night, he galloped to a stop at a homestead between Albuquerque and Santa Fe. The owner of the adobe house understood about the hurry. He loaned Seth a horse and refused his offer of money.

"Your horse will be here when you return with the woman who will help your little boy. I will have another ready for her also. No, keep your money. Juan Ramón may need a friend someday. Then you can repay him."

Seth rode the horse harder than he had

ever driven an animal before. He reached his ranch in the late afternoon.

Lupita was standing in the middle of the chickens when she saw the lone rider coming toward them. Her first thought was for the horse. No one had a right to work a horse like that. She couldn't see his face, but she knew it was her Seth. Something had to be very wrong for him to treat an animal so cruelly.

She dropped the basket of chicken feed, picked up her skirts, and began running. Jake, in the barn, dropped a bale of hay at the sight of the overweight woman running. He shouted for Paul and ran after Lupita. He knew that only Seth could cause her to lose her usual calm.

Seth pulled the horse to a stop and dropped to his feet beside Lupita. He looked awful — sunken, dirty — and his eyes were crazy, burning. "Adam. A fever. Some kind of tick," he gasped out at her.

She needed no more explanation. "I'll get my medicines." She started running back to her little house, behind the main house. She passed Jake and started to give orders, but closed her mouth. The old man would be useless until he'd seen Seth.

Seth was running beside her, Jake following. "What's he like?"

"There's a high fever and a knot on his leg, swollen and red. The doctor said it was an insect bite, maybe a tick."

"Adam! This is Adam you're talkin' about? I knew the little girl shouldn'ta taken him away. Now he's sick." He watched Seth. He had known the big man since he was a little boy and he knew Adam must be very sick to cause the terror he saw now in Seth's face.

"Seth! It's good to see you!"

Seth absently shook Paul's hand. He watched impatiently for Lupita to come out of her house.

"Adam's sick," Jake whispered. "Seth's come to get Lupita."

Paul understood what was needed. "Jake, you get some food." At Jake's look of bewilderment, he added, "Dump some beans on Lupita's tortillas and get them ready to go. I'll get two horses saddled."

"Come with me." Jake motioned to Seth. "You and the little gal make up?"

"Yes. I guess so. I don't know. My head's groggy. I can't think. What's keeping Lupita?" He seemed to remember Jake and put his hand on his shoulder. "I'm just worried now. I'll come back when . . . when Adam's well and I'll visit with you then. I have missed you."

"I understand. Here's your *burritos*. They're not like Lupita's, but they'll fill you up." He wrapped them in a cloth and Seth stuffed them in the pocket of his vest.

Lupita was just leaving her house. She carried a large cloth bag. "I am ready."

Paul handed over the reins of the horses, and Seth helped Lupita mount. It had been a long time since she'd ridden a horse and already the muscles and tendons on the inside of her thighs hurt from the unaccustomed stretching.

"You take care of our boys, you hear, Lupita? And then you bring *all* of 'em back with you," Jake called after them. He turned to Paul. "It's goin' be a long time waitin' here and not knowin' what's happenin'." They turned back to their work, silent.

Lupita used all her strength to stay on the horse, but even so, they had to travel much more slowly than Seth had alone. Once Seth apologized for making her ride so hard. She dismissed his statement. "For Adam it is worth it." She tried to wipe some of the haggard, drawn look from his face. "I have seen this tick before — it is not so bad as you think. There are many medicines I can use." Seth's trust in her made her swallow hard. She prayed that her words were true.

They changed horses at the homestead.

Seth promised to return the extra horse, and he swore to himself that the poor farmer would have some new livestock as soon as he returned to his own ranch.

The moon of the second night was high when they reached the Three Crowns. Seth lifted Lupita from her horse, throwing the reins to Donaciano. The tired woman followed, stumbling, as he led her into the big house.

"They're here!" Morgan's voice was incredulous. She ran to meet them, throwing herself into Lupita's arms with such exuberance that she nearly knocked the plump woman down. "I knew you'd come. Please save my baby, Lupita, please. He's so little . . ."

Lupita pushed her firmly away and walked to Adam's bed. The child was dry and hot and his little cheeks, once so healthy, were sunken, as were his eyes.

"How long has he been like this?"

"I don't know. Nearly four days, I think. The time is all mixed up in my mind. What do we do first?"

Lupita was studying Morgan intently. "Heat water. I am going to make some tea."

"Tea! We don't need tea when my son is so sick." She was screeching.

"Seth!" Lupita turned to the weary man,

slumped by his son's bedside. "I can care for Adam, but I cannot care for both of them at once." She nodded her head toward Morgan, who watched Lupita with an unnatural light in her eyes. "Is there someone else who can help me?"

"Me. I'll help." Morgan stepped forward. "I'll do whatever you say, Lupita."

"You! Look at you. Another few minutes and I will have two patients."

"May I help?" Roselle stood at the door in her dressing gown.

Lupita appraised her. "Yes. I will need someone."

"I can't leave my baby. He needs me."

"He does not even know you are here. Seth, take your wife to the kitchen and feed her good. And you eat, too. Then wash her, put her in a clean nightgown, and then into bed. And you do the same for yourself."

"No, I can't . . ."

Lupita's eyes were as hard as diamonds. "You do everything I say or I will leave."

Morgan allowed Seth to lead her from the room.

Roselle watched them leave. "You wouldn't really leave?"

"Of course not." The answer was snapped back.

"I've tried to get her to eat, to sleep, but

she wouldn't."

"I have been caring for sick people and bringing babies into the world since I was just a girl, and I have learned that you do not ask tired mothers anything, you give orders. If they do not obey, you give them a reason why they must. Now, let us go to work. I need water to brew a tea."

"He won't drink anything."

Lupita arched an eyebrow at her. She didn't tolerate disobedience from her helpers, either.

Roselle left the room to get water.

Seth led Morgan to the big work table in the middle of the kitchen. He put bread and cheese, cold chicken, and milk in front of her.

"I can't eat, Seth, really I can't."

"Lupita's right. Neither of us is any use to Adam. We'd be in the way."

Roselle entered to get the hot water. Morgan stood up to follow her out. Seth unceremoniously pushed her back into her chair. "Eat!"

Morgan began to eat, at first lightly and then with gusto. She hadn't realized how hungry she was. "I guess I was hungry," she mumbled through a mouthful of bread and cheese. "He is going to be all right, isn't he?"

Seth held her hand, squeezing the fingers. "Now that Lupita's here, I think he will be. Finished?"

"Yes." Her body felt so heavy, worse than when she'd carried Adam. She must rouse herself, because she had to go back to Adam. She'd been away too long. She started wearily toward the door, her eyes blurring.

Seth grabbed her skirt to stop her.

"Adam might call for me." Her goal was the kitchen door — such an ordinary thing really, but now it seemed impossible.

Seth lifted her in his arms.

"I'm too heavy. You . . ."

"Heavy! You nit! You hardly weigh more than Adam. Now that I'm here, you are going to be taken care of. Right now I am going to put you to bed."

She leaned her head against Seth's shoulder. It felt good to depend on someone else for a change, and there was no one she'd rather trust than her Seth. She sighed. "Her Seth" once again.

He set her on her feet again in the bedroom. "Get out of that dress and tell me where you keep your nightgowns."

"Third drawer." Her hands were shaking

as she fumbled with the buttons. Seth was in front of her and pushed her hands away as he unfastened the row of little buttons. She watched his face and knew that he, too, was very tired. She touched his hair. It seemed that the more tired he was, the more gray there was in his hair. Right now he looked like an old man.

She stepped out of her dress and Seth began to unlace her corset. She let out a sigh as it fell to the floor. She thought she'd probably never get used to that tight, stiff thing binding her waist and rib cage. Seth removed her chemise and she stood nude under his gaze.

"Why do you wear that thing? You have red marks all down your body where it cut into you." His big hands rubbed at her sides, briskly.

She felt slightly uneasy under his touch. "My gown."

"First, a wash." He pulled her to the basin on the table and began washing her face and hands. She stood still, enjoying the way he scrubbed at her skin. He dried her and then slipped the clean, soft nightgown over her head. "I should be hanged for covering all this up." His hand lightly caressed her breast. "If I tried to take advantage of you now, it'd be like making love to a wet dishcloth." He smiled into Morgan's drooping eyes. "I think I'll wait. Let's go, little one."

Again he picked her up and carried her to the bed. She was practically asleep before he had tucked the covers about her. Seth started toward the door.

"Where are you going?" she murmured.

"To my room. Lupita seemed to think I need some sleep, too."

"Stay with me. I need you."

An incredible joy surged through him. "Yes, *mi querida,* I'll stay with you . . . for as long as you want."

Morgan immediately turned back onto her stomach and went to sleep. Seth took his time washing himself, and then he removed his clothes and climbed into the bed beside his wife. "Damn nightgown!" he murmured as he pulled her close. Their bodies fitted together with an old familiarity. Seth's breath became slow and even and he, too, slept.

Adam didn't know who held him or who forced the bad-tasting tea down his throat, but he knew the voice of command. It hurt terribly, but no matter how much he complained, the cup was always there again. His body hurt and ached so much, yet someone kept lifting him, turning him, and putting hot cloths on him. He didn't like this at all. He wanted to be outside. "Horse," he whispered, but the word didn't come to the surface.

Lupita forced several herb teas down Adam's throat, each laced with powdered rose hips. She and Roselle wrapped his little feverish body again and again in hot, steamy towels. Toward dawn, the fever began to lessen, and Lupita collapsed on the little sofa. She hadn't slept in nearly two days, and now that she knew there was nothing else she could do except wait, she fell asleep instantly. Roselle tiptoed from the room. No matter what happened now, there would be a need for food.

"Eat." The word didn't come out as loudly as he had planned. He tried again, but his mouth still didn't work. He looked at the big woman asleep beside his bed. Who was she? He was wet all over his body and he was hungry and thirsty. Where was his mother? He'd go to her room. She'd get him something to eat.

He started to move but his body didn't obey. It hurt, and his head hurt, too. "Mama," he whispered, and the tears began to flow. He felt so awful and there was no one with him except this woman that he didn't know.

Lupita opened her eyes to see Adam's face screwed up and tears rolling down his cheeks. Her tears followed, because she knew the danger was over.

"Ah, little one. You will be safe now." She immediately set about making the little boy comfortable. She changed his clothes and bed linens, talking to him soothingly all the while.

Adam decided he liked the woman. And he seemed to remember her voice from somewhere. But he was still hungry and he still wanted his mother. "Mama," he whispered again.

"Yes, I'll get your mama for you."

Lupita tried two doors before she found Morgan's room. She paused a moment to stare at the sight of Morgan and Seth curled together in the big bed. She was glad they were together again. There was no need to wake both of them. "Morgan." Seth stirred and rolled away from his sleeping wife. Lupita touched her shoulder. "Morgan, Adam is calling you."

"Adam?" she murmured sleepily, eyes still closed. Then suddenly they were wide open.

"The fever is broken. He will be well. I will go back now. You come when you can."

Morgan jumped from the bed and ran to

her wardrobe. She snatched a dressing gown and rapidly thrust her arms through the sleeves and tied it.

Adam whimpered slightly when he saw his mother. She held him close and he was comforted by her presence. He looked tired and he'd lost weight, but for the first time in a long while, his eyes were clear and focusing.

Seth came into the room, his eyes riveted on his son. He held the boy's hand and ruffled his hair. "I'm glad you're going to get well, son." Morgan saw the tears in his eyes. No matter how much she ever doubted Seth's love for her, his love for his little son was never in question.

Seth came to Morgan's side and took her in his arms. "I have to see to the ranch now. After four days without supervision, it's probably near bankruptcy. I'll try to get back for dinner, but if I can't, I'll send word." He kissed the tip of her nose. "I love you." He released her and left the room.

She stared after him for a second, but she couldn't worry about Seth now. Adam was still very sick and he needed her.

Morgan spent the entire day with Adam. She spoon-fed him, read to him, and drew pictures on his little slate. Lupita slept most of the day and Roselle stayed downstairs

601

except to bring food.

"Mrs. Colter, why don't you go for a ride?" said Roselle next afternoon. "Adam is asleep, and I'll be here if he wakens. You need some fresh air."

"I know, Roselle, I guess I should. But I'm afraid he'll wake up and need me. I'll get over the feeling, but I came so close to losing him that right now I'm almost afraid to close my eyes."

Roselle agreed. Had her little girl lived, she would have felt the same way about leaving her.

When Lupita entered the room, Morgan ran to her and hugged her. "It seems I'm always saying thank you for all the things you do for me."

"I did not save the boy for you . . . only maybe a little for you. If anything had happened to him, my Seth would not think so highly of me. I cannot have that." She grinned at Morgan. "Also, remember, Adam is one of my children."

Adam gave Lupita a tentative smile when he heard his name. The woman was becoming familiar to him very quickly.

Lupita caressed the hair by his temple. "Now you will grow as strong and as big as your daddy. I think I will go to the kitchen and see how this Roselle is feeding my children."

"Her cooking is a lot different from yours."

"Hmph! That is why the child was so sick. He needs more chili. I'll see what I can make for supper."

"Chili! That sounds marvelous. How about a green chili stew with potatoes and meat? The three of us could eat here, together."

Lupita smiled at her. "Yes. The three of us together. That is nice."

In a short time, the two of them were happily eating quantities of green chili stew and freshly made tortillas. Morgan fed Adam a beef broth flavored with green chili. He ate all of it, and drank some milk. Once he smiled at them, the first time Morgan had seen his dimples in a long time. There was a milk mustache on his upper lip, and he said, "Eat."

The women had laughed together. "Now I know for sure that he's going to be all right," Morgan declared.

"Food has to be interesting, or it is not good to eat. He would not eat before because the food had no taste."

Adam put out a hand toward his mother's tortilla and she broke off a piece for him.

Martin came into the room. "Mr. Colter

said to tell his wife" — his eyes twinkled — "that the ranch is falling apart. He'll be very late tonight, since he needs to put it together again."

Morgan laughed. "Thank you, Martin. Who brought the message?"

"A young hand called Tim."

"Well, take him to the kitchen and give him some green chili stew and tortillas. There's enough, Lupita?"

"What you think — I cook only a little bit for the three of us?"

"And Martin, you and Roselle help yourselves."

"We already have. The smells from Lupita's cooking were irresistible."

"Oh, Lupita," she laughed when Martin was gone, "I spent an entire year training with a French cooking master, and none of my food ever gets the raves your food does."

Morgan turned back to Adam. She felt slightly guilty because she hadn't really thought about Seth all day. She was too concerned with Adam, always aware of how close she'd come to losing him. She put her hands on the small of her back and stretched.

"It is time for you to go to bed."

"I'll sleep in here, in case he wakes in the middle of the night and needs anything."

"No. You will go to your own room and sleep. I will stay in here. If he needs you, I will call you."

Morgan knew when she was attempting a losing battle. She was asleep as soon as she snuggled under the covers.

It was late when Seth got back to the house and he stopped outside Morgan's door, his hand on the knob. He smiled in anticipation because he knew they could not possibly sleep together in the same bed for the second night in a row without making love.

He looked down at himself. He was dirty and tired. And in the morning, Morgan would be running into Adam's room. No, it would have to wait. When he made love to his wife for the first time in years, he wanted time to caress her and touch every part of the body he'd once known so well. With a sigh, he turned to his own room.

Morgan awoke early. She still wasn't used to Adam not banging on her bedroom door. She threw on a dressing gown and went to her son's room. Immediately she knew something was wrong. The room was a mess. There were towels on the floor, a tea kettle beside the bed. Both Adam and Lupita were asleep. She sat down heavily in a chair. It came back to her with renewed force that she had come very close to losing her son. Last night, while she slept, she had almost lost him again. If Lupita hadn't been with him . . .

Morgan turned and saw Lupita's eyes open. "What happened?" Her voice reflected her despair.

"Nothing happened. He was restless so I made him tea."

"What about the towels?"

"I had them ready in case the fever returned, but it did not."

"He had a relapse, didn't he?"

"Morgan, no! I was just being cautious, but he needed no more treatments."

"Why didn't you call me?"

"You weren't needed. Nothing happened. I —"

Seth entered the room and looked in puzzlement from one woman to the other. "Is something wrong?"

"Adam was ill again last night," said Morgan. "He isn't over it at all. He's still very sick."

Lupita threw her hands into the air, mumbled something under her breath in Spanish, and then turned to Seth. "Adam is all right. Last night he was restless and I was afraid it was the sickness again, but it was not. Your son is getting well quickly and there is no more danger."

Morgan looked skeptical. "I'm just worried, that's all."

"Well, I believe Lupita." He kissed the woman's forehead. "Let's all go downstairs and eat breakfast. Carol is here and she can stay with Adam."

"I'd rather stay with him myself."

"Of course, you stay with Adam if you want. That way I'll have Lupita all to myself." He winked at the large woman. As he kissed his wife's cheek, Seth was vaguely aware that Morgan wasn't even looking at him. He frowned slightly when she turned away quickly.

Seth and Lupita sat at the breakfast table. "There really is nothing wrong, is there?"

"No, nothing. I am just an old mother hen and I wanted to be safe. I am sorry I did not clean up the mess before Morgan saw it. It is good to eat with you again, to see you again."

"Lupita, I can't thank you enough for what you've done for Morgan, and Adam, and for me. I knew you'd come when we needed you."

"Of course, I come. Is everything all right now, between you and the *señora?*"

"It's coming along. It isn't easy to forgive what I did to her."

"She must see how much you love her."

"No, I don't think she does. Sometimes I think she does. Maybe she doesn't trust me. I just try to wait and be patient."

"Wait! You do not need to wait. You should not wait. She is your wife. Take her."

Seth smiled indulgently. "It's not like that. I've lost rights . . ."

"Rights! She is a woman and you are a man. And besides, you love each other."

"I want Morgan to make up her own mind when she wants to come to me."

"She can't make up her own mind. I know Morgan very well. All her life she has had people tell her what to do. She has never had a chance to be her own self. At first, she spoke the words of her mother, and then she had an uncle to control her, and then she had you. Even in California, she was pushed and pulled by others."

For some reason, Seth felt a need to defend his wife. "She made up her own mind when she asked me to marry her. That took courage."

"Yes, I know all about that. Even then she bought someone to control her. I am sure she sensed that you were a strong man. Another woman might have told her problem to everyone. Then she would have had her choice of many men. But Morgan has always been too sheltered to make choices."

Seth sipped his coffee. Lupita was right.

"Now she needs someone to help her." She nodded her head toward the stairs. "She loves that little boy. But if someone does not help her, she will let him rule her life. She is a little girl herself."

Seth sat silently for a moment. He had always been too involved with Morgan to look at her clearly, like Lupita did. Seth had always blamed Morgan's mother, but he'd never realized that he filled the same place Mrs. Wakefield once had.

"I thought I might go home tomorrow."

"So soon?"

"Yes. The boy is fine. He does not need me, but Jake and Paul do."

"Lupita, I wish you'd stay. It's been a long time since I've seen you, and you know what you've always meant to me."

"I must go home. Soon, I hope the three of you will come home, too."

"Yes," Seth grinned. "I'd like that. It would be nice to be on my own place again. I hope we will go. Maybe when Gordon gets back, I can leave. I'll bring my wife and son with me. Morgan hasn't really . . . accepted me as a husband, yet."

"Accepted! These modern men! In my day, women did not choose their husbands;

their parents told them who their husbands would be. That is what should have happened here."

"What if Morgan had gotten Jake instead of me? Then where would I be?"

She turned to snap at him and then saw his teasing eyes. "We are too long at this meal. We both have work to do. Let's get started."

Seth kissed her on the cheek as he left for a long day on the ranch.

Lupita again spent her day with Adam and Morgan, talking and quietly laughing together. Lupita didn't like the worried look Morgan's eyes always held when she looked at her little son. The older woman could not convince her that he was out of danger.

At dinner, Morgan again refused to leave Adam. Seth saw the alarm and fear in her eyes and he agreed. He, too, was not completely satisfied that Adam was really well.

Seth and Lupita ate dinner alone and enjoyed talking about the Colter ranch. Seth was entertained by the stories of Morgan's pregnancy.

As Seth led Lupita to her room, they stopped to look in on Adam. Morgan lay curled up on the cot.

"No, don't wake her." Seth put a restraining hand on Lupita's arm. "Let her sleep."

"She should sleep in her own bed. There is no need for her to stay in here all night. Her son is fine."

"Let her stay. She needs the reassurance that he's well. When she wakes, she'll see him. Then she won't worry."

"Someday you will remember my words."

"Lupita, did I ever tell you how pretty you are when your eyes flash like that?"

"You!" She couldn't stop her giggle. How easy it was for this big handsome man to reduce her to an eighteen-year-old *señorita!*

Lupita fell asleep quickly, but Seth tossed about in his big empty bed for a long time.

The sun was barely up when Seth awoke. He pulled on some pants and padded towards Adam's room. Morgan was asleep, one arm hanging off the side of the cot. He kissed her mouth. Her eyes fluttered open. Seeing Seth so close to her, she put her arms up to him, pulling him closer. As his lips fastened onto hers, she heard Adam's plaintive voice: "Mama. Mama."

Instantly, she was wide awake. She rolled quickly away from Seth to the other side of the cot and went to comfort her son.

Seth laughed. "I never thought my own son would become my enemy."

Morgan's face was serious. "He's still a

611

very sick child. He needs me."

Seth turned away. "I need you, too," he whispered. He looked back, chiding himself for his selfishness. "I'm going to take Lupita home. It'll be a slower trip than before, so I'll probably be gone for at least a week."

Morgan was hardly listening. "You want something to eat, Adam? Lupita made some apple juice for you."

"Morgan, did you hear what I said?"

"Something about a week?"

"I'm going to be gone a week, to take Lupita back to the ranch."

"Yes. Well, don't leave before I say goodbye to Lupita. I owe her a great deal." She turned back to Adam.

Seth left the room angrily. *Just when I thought things were going well, she doesn't even seem to know I'm alive. I liked it better when my presence made her throw things.*

Morgan ate breakfast with Adam while Lupita and Seth ate downstairs. Seth avoided all discussions about Morgan. One of the hands hitched a wagon while Lupita said her goodbyes. Morgan wanted the older woman to stay in case Adam's fever returned, but this time Lupita didn't even argue with her. She shrugged. *Let the young ones solve their own problems,* she thought.

"I am glad I do not have to ride a horse again." She frowned, as though in pain.

"After two days on this thing, you'll wish you had a soft saddle to sit on."

They traveled for two days in the springless wagon, over hole-riddled roads. When they reached the ranch, at sunset on the second day, they were hot and dirty and tired.

Jake and Paul ran to meet them. Seth picked up the little man and whirled him around. His grip nearly crushed Jake's frail body. "Just as skinny as he always was. When's he gonna get some muscles? He looks like a girl."

Paul shook the big man's hand. "I reckon the boy's all right."

Seth beamed. "Thanks to Lupita here." He put his arm around her ample shoulders.

Embarrassed, Lupita pushed his hand away. "You be careful or you might hurt yourself, trying to get your arms around me."

"Hurt myself! Why, Lupita, you're no bigger than a tadpole."

She looked at him as if he were crazy.

Seth winked at Jake and then swooped Lupita into his arms and ran with her to the house.

Jake's chest puffed with pride. "That's my

boy," he declared.

They had a lot to talk about at dinner. Lupita didn't tell the entire story, but she said that Morgan and Seth were together again. Jake entertained them with more stories of Morgan's pregnancy. "We was scared to death she'd fall down an arroyo. The way she was built, she'd still be rollin'."

Seth shook his head. "I just can't imagine Morgan like that. Are you sure you aren't exaggerating, maybe just a little?"

"Well, let's just say that after the seventh month, she quit usin' the back door."

Seth frowned, not understanding.

"It was too small. She had to go in and out the big front door."

They all shared in the laughter.

Seth spent two days on the Colter ranch. Jake and Paul ran the place competently, and he could find no fault with any aspect of their management. Seth told them of the more complex problems of running the Three Crowns. "You could put the Colter ranch in the house, maybe just in the dining room."

"The little girl's sure gonna hate givin' all that up, ain't she? All them servants and all?"

Seth didn't want to discuss with anyone — even himself — the possibility that Morgan might not want to return with him. She and Adam had been happy at the Three Crowns without him, and she might want to stay there. If that's where she wanted to stay, then he'd stay with her. He needed to be near her, and his son.

On the morning of the third day, he hitched the wagon and prepared to leave. Lupita packed an old Indian basket with food for him to eat along the way, and several boxes more to take to Juan Ramón. Seth tied a milk cow to the back of the wagon, a gift to the farmer who had helped when Adam was ill.

After goodbyes, the three watched him go. "I don't understand all this to-in' and fro-in'. Why don't the three of them come back here and live, where they belong?" There was no answer for Jake.

Seth stopped in Santa Fe and bought Adam a little metal toy train from one of the passengers on a wagon train. People were still streaming out to California.

He decided to buy some fabric for Morgan, and as soon as he walked into the store, he saw Marilyn Wilson.

"Seth! How are you?" she purred. "It's been so long since I've seen you." She possessively took his arm and rubbed her overly ripe breast against it.

"Hello, Marilyn."

She missed the coldness in his voice. "You're just as handsome as always. I heard you were in California. I imagine that's real excitin'."

He looked her up and down. Her dress was a gaudy taffeta of red and green stripes. Her hair wasn't too clean. "You would probably like the gold fields."

Again, she missed his tone. She was encouraged by his looking at her body. "I guess you knew about my shop. My daddy bought it for me."

"No, I didn't know." He could hardly look at her without remembering the lies she'd told the night of Montoya's party. If I had known, he thought, I would not have come in here.

"But your . . . Mrs. Colter" — she spat out the words — "was here."

"Was she? She never mentioned it to me."

"Oh? Well maybe she also forgot to tell you about the man she was with. Very good-looking. And the little boy — he seemed to resemble the man. She was probably just taking care of him, although she did say he was her son."

Seth laughed at himself. How could he ever have believed this woman's lies? "Gordon is a friend of ours and Adam is my son."

"Well, Seth, love," she had her hands on his arm, "if that's what you think. Of course, Joaquín left town about the same time as your wife, and I've always wondered —"

"Good day, Marilyn." He left the store. He felt dirty for ever having touched the woman.

After Seth left, Morgan began to spend all her time with Adam. She fed every meal to him, allowing no one else to feed him. At night, she awoke frightened and was frantic until she was sure Adam was all right. During the day she'd sit for hours, just staring at him while he slept, holding his hand.

Roselle constantly tried to get her to go outside. She was pale and had lost weight. After the first few days, she wouldn't allow Carol to clean Adam's room; she wanted to do it herself. She didn't go to the kitchen to cook any longer, but gave Roselle instructions about what to prepare. Adam had lost his appetite, and Morgan needed to coax and plead with him at every meal.

Seth was surprised to find the front door locked during the day. When Martin opened it, Seth thought the man looked older, and sad.

"It's good to have you back, Mr. Colter."

"It's good to be back. Could you have Donaciano carry a bath to my room? Is Morgan out riding?"

"No, sir, she's with Master Adam."

Seth raised his eyebrows. 'Master' Adam? He bounded up the stairs, three at a time.

He stopped at the door and stared at the sight that greeted him. The room was airless, dark, and smelled bad. Morgan, her hair pulled once again into a tight little knot, was coaxing Adam to eat. "Please, sweetheart, eat something. For Mommy."

"No!" Adam yelled the word at her and pushed the cup away, nearly upsetting it.

"Morgan?" Seth's voice was a whisper. She turned. He gasped at the sight of her. She had on the same dress she'd been wearing when he left, and there were food stains all over it. But her face was what frightened him: her eyelids were drooping, and the bluish circles under her eyes were now almost purple. Her skin was pale. She had an expression of great weariness.

"When did you get back?" Her voice was hoarse.

"Just now. What's going on here?"

"I'm trying to help Adam get well."

"Trying to — !" He tried to control his rising anger as he went to the window and threw back the curtains. The sunlight revealed the room to be even dirtier than it had first appeared.

Morgan followed him to the window and closed the curtain. "No. You mustn't. It hurts Adam's eyes."

Seth grabbed her shoulders. "Morgan, how much sleep have you been getting?"

She looked away. "Enough."

He pulled her chin up so she met his eyes. "Answer me."

"Adam needs me sometimes in the middle of the night. Aren't you going to greet your son?" She turned away and smiled at Adam.

For the first time, Seth looked at his son. Except for having lost a little of his tan, he looked healthy. Seth smiled at his son. Adam turned away and picked up a spoon by his bed and began to bang on a little metal tray. "Mama!" he demanded.

Morgan looked at Seth in explanation. "That's for when he wants me."

"What happened to his learning to talk?"

"He'll learn to talk. Right now, he just needs time to recover."

"Morgan, he should be outside. In the sunshine."

"No! I told you sunshine hurts his eyes."

"Well, it never did before." He stepped nearer Adam. "You want to go with me on a horse?"

Adam looked up at his father with a bored expression and then turned to his mother and began to whine, "Mommy."

Morgan lifted the covers and put her hand underneath.

"What are you doing?"

"Checking his diaper."

"But he hasn't worn a diaper in a long time — just the few days he was sick."

"But he's still weak, Seth, very weak."

Adam threw Seth a look of hostility and continued his whining.

"I think you ought to leave now. Adam needs his rest."

He had been dismissed! He turned and left the room before rage began to control his thinking. He stormed into the kitchen where Roselle and Martin were drinking coffee together. "What the hell's going on here? I leave for one week and what do I come back to? A shell of a wife in a filthy dress who hasn't slept in a week, and a son who whines and demands! What happened to the little boy I left here, the one who smiled and laughed? Do you know what she was doing when I walked in? *Begging* him to eat! My little son, whose whole life is controlled by food! She's up there pleading with him to eat.

"He's finally learned to say no, and from

what I heard, he says it quite often. And that goodamn spoon on a tray —"

"Mr. Colter, we know. We've been watching it all happen."

"Well, something has to be done about it. Maybe I'll be able to reason with her at dinner."

"Then you'll be dining downstairs?"

"Of course, we will. Where else would we eat?"

"Mrs. Colter no longer uses the dining room. She takes all her meals in the nursery with Master Adam."

"When did you start all this *Master* Adam?"

"Mrs. Colter thought it was more fitting to the young sir."

"Young . . . !" He spun around and left the room. He doubted he'd ever been angrier in his life. He had to calm himself. After a bath and a shave, maybe he would feel like reasoning with her.

When he'd finished, he was still angry, but he realized that some of this was his fault. Lupita was right. Morgan needed someone to control her life.

She was sitting beside the bed, reading to the little boy. Adam was frowning, so unlike his old dimpled self.

"Morgan, are you ready to go down to

dinner?"

"I'll stay here. Adam may need me."

He lifted her under her arms. The dress was wet. "How long has it been since you've had a bath?"

"I don't know. I guess I've been too busy lately."

He pulled her to him, his arms around her. "I don't care. I still love you. Come eat dinner with me and then I shall personally give you a bath."

Behind them, Adam made a whining, petulant noise.

Morgan tried to pull from Seth's grasp. He held her, but she looked at him with fierce eyes. "Let me go!" she snarled at him. Surprised, he dropped his hands. She went to her son's side, feeling his forehead. She sighed in relief.

"Morgan, he's not sick any longer. He's perfectly healthy. All he needs is to get up and run, maybe ride a horse."

Morgan faced him, hands on hips, her face shrewish. "Ride a horse! The doctor said his illness was caused by some insect bite. He probably got it *while* riding a horse. Now, if you want to stay here, be quiet. I have a sick child to care for, and he needs my attention."

Seth could swear he saw a look of triumph

in Adam's eyes. He left the room, closing the door behind him.

Dinner was a lonely meal. Seth stared at his plate. He'd sworn to wait for her even if it took years, but he couldn't stand by and let her ruin her life and their son's as well. What was he going to do?

He especially didn't like what she was doing to his son. The little boy he'd grown to love and the whining tyrant upstairs were two entirely different people.

Colter, he thought, you've stood back too long. There's only so much a man can take before he has to assert himself.

Upstairs, he decided not to go to the nursery again. He wanted to see no more of what he'd seen today. He lay awake a long time, thinking. It wasn't an easy plan he came up with, but it was a necessary one.

In the morning, he went back to the nursery. Morgan was asleep. She looked worse than he remembered. He kissed her cheek and she jumped, awake instantly.

"Did you sleep well?"

"Adam had a restless night."

"Poor boy. How is he feeling this morning?"

"I think he's better, but I'm never sure. It's such a chore to get him to eat now. Roselle is making crullers today, and I hope I can coax him to eat at least one."

Seth smiled at her. "Would you like to join me for breakfast?"

"No, I ought to stay with Adam. He might need something."

"You're right, dear, he may need something."

Morgan returned his smile. She was grateful for his understanding.

He kissed her cheek again. "I may be late tonight. I'm sure there are a lot of things to do on the ranch." He watched as Morgan wiped Adam's brow. The older man squinted his eyes in threat to his son and he could have sworn he saw the hint of a dimple. In the hallway, he chuckled to himself. At least his son wasn't ignorant. Adam was playing a good thing for all it was worth. The problem was Morgan.

Seth spent the day organizing men, assigning work crews, and arranging plans. When he got to the house, everything was dark and everyone was in bed. Roselle got up when she heard Seth in the kitchen.

"Mr. Colter, I've kept food warm for you."

"Roselle, I hate to do this to you. I know it's late, but could you wake Martin? I have something rather important to discuss with you."

It was very late when the three of them

finally got to bed. As Seth sank into the soft mattress, he smiled. He felt better than he had in a long time. Everything was ready. He did not look forward to this. He hated himself, but it had to be done.

CHAPTER TWENTY-FOUR

When Morgan awoke on the cot, Adam was still sleeping. She was tired, but the minor aches she felt were worth it if Adam was well again. She couldn't forget those horrible days when he'd been so ill, so near death. She'd gladly give up part of her life to keep him well, to protect him from further illness. It was her fault that Adam had been so sick. If she had not given him so much freedom, he would never have been so ill.

Something was wrong in the house — it was too quiet. People were usually stirring by now. Roselle could be heard in the kitchen, and Carol always brought breakfast upstairs for the two of them. Adam opened his eyes and moaned. She flew to his side. Always, in those first few seconds, she fought a rising panic.

"Are you hungry, baby? Eat?" She pantomimed the last word.

Adam nodded curtly, his lower lip extended in a pout.

"Carol is late this morning." She went to the door and looked out. The hall was empty. "I can't imagine where everyone is." She called for Roselle and Carol but there was no answer. "Adam, sweet, mommy must leave you for just a few seconds. You rest and I'll be right back."

She opened the bedroom doors next to Adam's room. The rooms were all empty. She stopped at the top of the stairs and called again. There was still no answer. She ran back to Adam's room. "Mommy has to go downstairs. She'll be back very soon." She kissed his forehead. Where was everyone? How could they desert her and a very sick little boy? There was also fear. It started at the nape of her neck and moved down her spine.

The dining room was empty. She knew Seth always ate breakfast downstairs. The kitchen was empty, with the stove cold and nothing on the big work table. The fear inside her began to spread. Something must have caused their disappearance.

She tried to calm herself. There had to be a simple explanation for all this. At the same time, she wanted to run back upstairs and protect Adam.

The kitchen door was open and she walked outside. The sunshine hurt her eyes. She had not left Adam's room for nearly two weeks, and she squinted against the glare. The barn door stood open and she hurried toward it. Her legs were weak from disuse. It was dark and cool in the barn. She saw no one. She heard a movement from an empty stall and breathed a sigh of relief. She had a vision of the time she'd caught Donaciano asleep in an empty stall. She'd certainly be glad to see the boy now!

She took two steps toward the stall, and then — blackness! She was suffocating! Something very heavy was on her body, covering her. She couldn't breathe. There were hands, many hands, pulling and twisting her. She began to fight, but there was no fighting the enormous weight of the thing that was cutting off her breath. She screamed, but even to her the sound was slight. Where was everyone? Was she truly alone with her attacker?

As she was moved a few feet, she tried to remain standing, but the long skirt tripped her and she fell to her knees. There were rough, cruel hands handling her. She felt them on her wrists and there was something else, too. It was a rope! If only she could breathe! She fought her unseen foe, struggling while gasping for air. But she couldn't even ascertain the direction in which her enemy stood.

The thing on her head, covering her entire body, weighed her down. Her neck was going to break under the weight of it. She began to breathe deeply. It was no use struggling. She tried again to scream.

She struggled to stand on her feet but fell forward onto her face. More hands tied a gag around her mouth. Another cloth was tied across her eyes. The enormous weight was lifted from her body. She breathed deeply of the cool air, glad to fill her lungs once again.

She could see nothing. Hands pulled her to her feet. Then she was thrown, roughly, and something hit her in the stomach. She was being carried upside down. She tried to push away with her tied hands, but met only with a wall. Something clasped her legs together in an iron grip.

Abruptly, she was stood upright, on her feet. She could see light through the blindfold, feel the sun on her body. She turned at the sound of a voice. Someone was near! Please help me, her mind cried. Please! My little boy needs me!

It was very much like the time she'd been taken by Cat Man, but that time she had been sure Seth would rescue her. This time she was not so sure he would, not after the way she'd been treating him. She was tossed astride a saddle and instinctively grabbed the pommel. Her attacker mounted behind her, and she kicked back sharply with her right heel. She heard his indrawn breath. She started to kick again, but an arm was fastened around her waist and, as she lifted her foot, it tightened, cutting off her breath. It relaxed when she lowered her foot.

They rode for a long time. She couldn't see. She concentrated on breathing slowly and deeply, and on balancing herself on the horse. She heard the horse's hooves occasionally splashing in water, as if they crossed several streams. Sometimes she felt her attacker's thigh muscles, pressed against hers, as he urged the horse uphill. She was weak from two weeks of little food and even less sleep.

She began to gather her senses. Maybe this madman who held her was just one of many. Maybe they'd already killed Roselle and Martin — and Seth! Would Seth be safe? She hadn't thought much of Seth lately, but now she was very concerned about him. How could she have ignored him so much lately?

Abruptly, she was taken off the horse. She

stood quietly, holding her balance. She heard footsteps behind her and then a door opened. Hands guided her through the door, up the one step over the threshold.

She listened. She sniffed the air and soon discovered burning logs. He began circling her. She heard his slow, easy footsteps.

His hands were on her shoulders, then on her head. She felt the tie that bound her hair being pulled away. The hands were spreading her hair, combing it with gentle fingers. She stepped away from him, but the grip on her shoulders tightened.

The hands were on her waist, encircling it, the thumbs in front as they moved upward to touch the undercurve of her breasts. She stood still, rigid. He touched her face, his palms on her cheeks.

He began unfastening the little buttons down the front of the soiled cotton dress. No! She shook her head. She made a noise in her throat. His hands worked slowly. She felt the bodice part and knew the corset and underlying chemise were exposed.

She felt a tugging, and something cold touched her shoulder. She jerked away, falling to her knees. She sat back, ready to kick her assailant. Her shoulder hurt and it was warm and damp. Blood! He'd cut her.

She stood very still. A cool cloth was

placed on her cut shoulder and the pain stopped. She felt a tug again on the shoulder of the dress, and it fell away on one side. She felt another tug and then a tearing sound. The dress had been removed from her body. She heard footsteps and then felt extra heat from the fire. He had burned the dress!

She felt sharp little jerks as the laces on her corset were cut. Then it, too, fell away. She breathed deeply when the constricting garment was gone. He tore off her chemise and threw both it and the corset on the fire.

Hands went to the back of her head and unfastened the blindfold. Everything was a blur and then her eyes began to focus . . .

"Hello, little wife. Oh, no, I plan to leave the gag on for a while. I have a great deal to say to you, and I don't want any interruptions."

She leaned forward to cover herself, her eyes pleading with him to allow her to shield herself.

"As you can see, I burned your clothes. I plan to keep you just like that for some time." He sat in a chair by the fireplace. "Come here, a little closer. I want to really enjoy you." He took her arm and she tried to jerk away, but he held fast.

"You're really angry, aren't you?"

She nodded vigorously, staring intently.

"I will explain. I am a very patient man, but I am not a martyr. I was willing to wait for you for years, as I've told you, but the way things were going at the Three Crowns would have tried the patience of a saint. How many women can say their husbands have made only one mistake? It was a big mistake, and I was rather ah . . . unpleasant . . . about it. And it did cause a great deal of misfortune for us both.

"Morgan, if you keep frowning at me with such ferocity, your entire forehead will be wrinkled in two days. I know I'm simplifying things, but I've stood by now for nearly a month and watched you 'leading your own life,' and I believe you are only making a mess of it."

She started to pull away from him, but he pulled her onto his lap, her head on his shoulder, legs across him. "I like this very much.

"I don't know if I can go on talking to you." His voice was husky as he stroked her thighs. "It was such a surprise when I first saw your body. And every time I've seen it since — too few times — I have marveled again at the perfection of it.

"Morgan, I love you so much." He ignored the loud noise of protest she made in her throat. "I thought everything was solved when Gordon left, but then Adam got sick and I had to leave to take Lupita home. When I returned, I knew something had to be done, and done quickly. You need someone to guide you, to care for you. I leave you alone for a week, and look what happens! You quit eating, bathing — you smell awful, you know — and you turn my nice, laughing little boy into a whining monster.

"Every time I have been away from you, terrible things have happened. I left the wagons on the way to New Mexico, and Cat Man took you. I was late to a party and, well . . . you know what happened then."

She turned her head away.

"I just couldn't do it anymore," he switched subjects abruptly.

She looked at him in question.

"I couldn't stand by and let you make a fool of yourself. You need me."

She jerked her head up, chin out.

"You're very good at pantomiming. You do need me, and these last few days prove it."

His voice was lower. "Would you like to know what I have planned for you? I plan to keep you here until you get over your anger. That may be a year or so. And then we'll wait until you admit that you love me.

Oh, you think that's impossible, but I assure you it's not. Meanwhile, while you're making up your mind about your feelings for me, I plan to drive you wild with passion."

Her eyes widened and her body stiffened.

"Not right now, though. First, I'm going to bathe you, feed you, and let you rest for a time. Maybe." He looked at her golden skin. "I should like to see you just as you are for a while, a long while. I hope you like it here because Roselle — yes, Roselle, and don't look as if she were a traitor, she nearly gave me away at the barn — Roselle packed enough food to last us a month. If that isn't enough time, I'll lock you in here and go get more. You, dearest" — he kissed her nose — "are my prisoner of love."

He rubbed the stubble of his whiskers on her stomach, and she laughed against her will.

"Do I perceive a softening? I'll remove the gag if you won't scream — not that anyone would hear you, but because it grates on my ears." He removed the cloth binding her mouth.

"Seth Colter! You are the most horrible —"

He closed her lips with a kiss, a sweet kiss. "You can't escape, so just relax." He

635

kissed her again, this time with more passion. His lips touched hers as he talked. "Morgan, sweet, did anyone . . . ever tell you . . . that . . . you . . . stink?"

"You!" She bit his shoulder hard.

He stared in puzzlement at the bright drop of blood gathering there and then laughed. "I guess that repays me for your shoulder. I wouldn't have cut you except you jumped like a jackrabbit."

"Seth, Adam needs me."

"That, love, is where you're wrong. Adam does not need you. At least for a while he doesn't. The way you were acting, I could imagine Adam thirty-two years old and still being diapered by his little old mother, who hadn't had a bath since he was two years old."

Morgan started to protest, but then a giggle escaped her. It was such a silly picture. "Was I that bad?"

"Another week and he'd have forgotten how to walk. He'd already forgotten how to talk."

"But why all this?" Her glance included the cabin and her still-tied hands.

"What would you have said if I'd said, 'Morgan, let's go spend a couple of weeks alone in a mountain cabin'?"

"Well, I would have —"

"You'd have found two hundred excuses why we couldn't go."

"But why the gag and tying my hands, and the tearing off of my clothes?"

"You had to be gagged or you would have screamed all the way here, and I didn't feel like fighting you all the way." He grinned at her, showing deep dimples. "Removing your clothes was my lustful idea. I guess I'm a pirate at heart, a kidnapper and ravisher of young girls." He tickled her with his beard.

"Seth" — she was laughing — "will you untie my hands now?"

"No."

"No?"

"Not until you've had a bath. You smell worse than the men in the bunkhouse."

"Seth!"

"I mean it. If a bear came in here right now, he'd think you were his mate."

"You!" She tried to raise a tied hand to strike him. "Why can't I have a romantic lover, like the ones in novels?"

"Which one of those characters do you want? The one who throws you to the ground and has his will of you, or the on-his-knees, hand-kissing type?"

"I don't . . ."

"Just tell me, my Guinevere. I am your Lancelot."

She giggled.

"Well, sir, the rules of chivalry definitely state that knights do not tell their ladies that they — stink."

"My sweet — ah, maybe sweet isn't the right word . . . My love — believe it or not, I do still love you — royal ladies do not stink. They take baths."

"Fair knight, will you lead this lady to her bathing chamber?"

Seth unceremoniously dumped Morgan from his lap. He strode to the door and opened it. "Your bathing chamber awaits."

"It's cold out there. Let's heat some water in here."

"I have a large bar of scented soap, and I plan to use the entire thing on your lovely body."

"That's all right. I have grown up now, and I can bathe all by himself."

His eyes raked her. "I can see that you have grown up, and that is precisely why I plan to bathe you. Now if you don't want to get raped, you better go outside where I can cool off."

She hesitated.

"Oh, no, you don't. If you don't bathe, I promise I won't rape you."

She scurried out into the cold mountain air, throwing him a look that made him catch his breath.

At the water's edge, she turned to him. "What about these?" She held up her tied hands.

He reached for his knife. "On second thought . . ." He sheathed the knife.

"Seth, they hurt."

His eyes relented for a second. "I don't believe you. Remember, you're my prisoner. Most husbands would have left the gag on."

"Seth."

"If you don't hurry and get your bath over, you'll freeze. Now I'm not sure how to do this. I'd hate to ruin a good pair of boots. Aha! I have the perfect solution." Quickly, he removed his clothes and boots, and Morgan had only a brief glimpse of his magnificent body before he pulled on her bound wrists. "Come, slave."

She gasped as the water touched her. "It's too cold."

"That's all right, you'll be warm soon." He began rubbing soap on her, mixing it with some fine sand he carried in a little bag. He scoured her vigorously, all over, until she thought her skin was going to come off. He didn't listen to her pleading. He rinsed her body, then soaped her again, gently this time. He stopped abruptly and began soaping himself.

"You aren't going to leave me soapy, are you?"

Without a word, he pulled her to him and held her, close. The soap on their bodies felt good. They rubbed together, their lips drawn to one another. Morgan's tied hands touched his manhood, and when she felt him shudder and heard his sharp intake of breath, she tightened her grasp. Their kisses became serious.

Seth stepped away from her to his clothes, and quickly cut the rope that bound her hands. He gently laid her down on the sweet grass near the stream.

He entered her with an urgency that Morgan more than met. The long-denied passions carried them to a violent wave.

After their first frantic passions were spent, they clung to one another, their hearts pounding in unison, their panting breaths drowning out all other sounds. Morgan felt a great release from tensions she hadn't even realized she carried.

Seth rolled from her. They lay side by side, not touching or speaking. Twilight gathered around them, and the stars were beginning to show.

"You know, when they find us here together, our bodies frozen, they're going to wonder what the hell that white slimy stuff is all over our bodies. Let's wash this off. And I'm starving. After I eat, I want to start all over again."

"You mean with the blindfold and the gag?" she teased. "What was that heavy thing you threw over me? I thought it was going to break my neck."

"Heavy thing?" He looked puzzled and then laughed. "That was a quilt!"

"It couldn't have been just a quilt. I thought I was dying of suffocation."

"You're going to die of the cold if we don't go inside." He pulled her into the stream and they rinsed quickly. Together, they washed Morgan's abundant hair.

Seth grabbed her hand and pulled her to the cabin. "One minute I can't get you to take a bath, and the next I can't get you out of the water." When they were inside, he pulled her close. "Did I ever tell you I love you?"

"Never."

"Not once?"

"Not a single time."

"Good, because I don't love you. I worship you. You're my . . . wife. Yes, my wife. Morgan," he said seriously, "do you feel anything for me?"

"Only a passing fancy." She saw the hurt look in his eyes. "Seth, I've loved you from the moment I saw you at Cynthia Ferguson's ball, and I guess I'll always love you, no matter what."

She watched as he walked toward the door. His naked body was bronze in the firelight. His broad back tapered to a slim waist and trim hips, all on those muscular legs that Morgan had first noticed.

"Where are you going?" she asked.

"To get my clothes, and chop some firewood. There's food in that cabinet."

"Food?"

"Of course. You do remember how to cook, don't you?"

She put her chin up. "I'm a valued prisoner. I do not do menial labor."

His eyes narrowed. "If that food isn't started by the time I get back, there'll be big trouble." His eyes caressed her body lingeringly. "I have a lot of work to do tonight, and if I know my 'business partner,' I'll need a lot of strength."

He left, shutting the door behind him.

Morgan leaned against the back of the chair and inhaled deeply of the evening air.

How very far she had come in just a little time. Her old dream, a solitary life in Trahern House, no longer meant anything at all. She needed no more dreams. She had all she could ever want . . . a home, her son, and her Seth.

She turned toward the cabinet. It was time to prepare the first of many meals.

ABOUT THE AUTHOR

Jude Deveraux is one of America's most beloved authors of historical romance. A resident of Santa Fe, New Mexico, she began writing in 1976 and to date is the author of twenty-two novels, of which there are more than twenty million copies in print.

The employees of Thorndike Press hope you have enjoyed this Large Print book. All our Thorndike, Wheeler, and Kennebec Large Print titles are designed for easy reading, and all our books are made to last. Other Thorndike Press Large Print books are available at your library, through selected bookstores, or directly from us.

For information about titles, please call:
  (800) 223-1244

or visit our Web site at:
  http://gale.cengage.com/thorndike

To share your comments, please write:
  Publisher
  Thorndike Press
  10 Water St., Suite 310
  Waterville, ME 04901